THE
Motor
Boys in
Ottawa

A NOVEL

Also by Hugh Hood

Novels:

White Figure, White Ground   1964
The Camera Always Lies   1967
A Game of Touch   1970
You Cant Get There from Here   1972

The New Age/Le nouveau siècle

I: *The Swing in the Garden*   1975
II: *A New Athens*   1977
III: *Reservoir Ravine*   1979
IV: *Black and White Keys*   1982
V: *The Scenic Art*   1984

Stories:

Flying a Red Kite   1962
Around the Mountain: Scenes from Montréal Life   1967
The Fruit Man, the Meat Man and the Manager   1971
Dark Glasses   1976
Selected Stories   1978
None Genuine Without This Signature   1980
August Nights   1985

Non-Fiction:

Strength Down Centre: The Jean Béliveau Story   1970
The Governor's Bridge is Closed   1973
Scoring: Seymour Segal's Art of Hockey   1979
Trusting the Tale   1983

HUGH HOOD

THE Motor Boys in Ottawa

A NOVEL

Stoddart

First published in 1986 by
Stoddart Publishing Co. Limited
34 Lesmill Road, Toronto, Canada
M3B 2T6

The author gratefully acknowledges the invaluable assistance of the
Canada Council and the Ontario Arts Council in the completion
of this work.

Canadian Cataloguing in Publication Data

Hood, Hugh, 1928-
 Motor boys in Ottawa

(The New age = Le nouveau siècle; pt. 6)
ISBN 0-7737-5080-0

I. Title. II. Series: Hood, Hugh, 1928-   The new age; pt. 6.

PS8515.049M67 1986   C813'.54   C86-093795-X
PR9199.3.H66M67 1986

Cover design by Brant Cowie/Artplus Ltd.

Printed and bound in Canada

For the king and queen of
Silver Lake, Pa.,
Kate and Alex Hood,
with love from
the original
why-worry boy

Although it was already past nine-thirty, Frank, Dick, and Chub managed to find a tony restaurant still open, and soon were seated before a swell feed . . .

The Motor Boys. Ca. 1911.

I

1

Twenty-five years removed from childhood in the Führer's Germany, nowadays the young lion of Montréal investment banking, Henry Golmsdorfer rarely had much to say, even to his new young wife, Esther. Perpetually recollected anxiety and distress kept him taciturn, morose. Perhaps he spoke more freely to his father-in-law than to his wife. Now he said, "No one in his right mind goes into the business of manufacturing automobiles today, not on this continent. No miracle of Wölfsburg of us."

He imagined the stripped, insect-like people's cars that had circulated briefly around the inner Alster in his infancy, before the family fled to England. "We would have to have Ferdinand Porsche at our disposal," he stammered, offering a joke, "not even a Kaiser could succeed in such an undertaking."

"You mean Henry J. Kaiser?"

"All the other Kaisers are dead."

"You're a gloomy cuss, Henry," said George Robinson, "and you shouldn't get into the habit of predicting disaster. Not one cent of Robinson money will ever go into final automobile assembly and sales. At the same time, mind you, there used to be a Canadian car assembled right here in Stoverville, long before you were born. Almost the last of the Canadian cars. Of course they never completed more than a few hundred vehicles; they used to bring in engines from Toledo on the lake boats. I don't suppose they ever paid any duty on them. I wonder how they got away with it."

"It was a cottage industry," said Golmsdorfer tersely. "Nobody paid any heed to them. I have seen the assembly sheds. Weren't they down beside the coal docks and the railway siding?"

"Exactly. We own all that property now, and the coal company too."

"An unsound investment. Nobody will ever use coal again."

"I'll grant you that, but river-front land will always be a solid proposition in Stoverville. We might develop an apartment-block complex there one day. Come and take a stroll with me."

They wandered idly along the winding descending paths towards the river, emerging suddenly from the shadow of Robinson Court into obscurely misty November light. Golmsdorfer shivered.

"In Montréal there is no question of approaching the river. One never sees it," he said.

"You're going to love living in Stoverville," said George Robinson. "I'm depending on you, Henry. We expect great things from you, now that Gus has made himself unavailable. Just cast your eyes along there to the west where the shoreline curves in, past the Maclean place with the two-storey boat-house. It's a shame the way they're letting that property go downhill. And then there's the Codringtons' garden and a few more houses along King William Street, and after that it all belongs to us, down to the water and right into the middle of town. We used to ship from that warehouse, do you see?"

"Where was the automotive factory?"

"Between our warehouses and the wharves. It's all falling to pieces now, the building. I don't think there's an unbroken window in the place. Tucker!" Robinson slapped his thigh.

"Tucker?"

"The last lunatic who thought he was going to get into the car business, Preston Tucker. I remember seeing one of his cars at the Motor Show in Toronto. I believe he made three of them in all; the one I saw had no engine. It had to be wheeled into position on the stand. It was a slick-looking little buggy but it wouldn't go."

"That man was a thief," said Henry.

"I actually knew somebody who put money in the

Tucker," said George Robinson, laughing boisterously. "She lost every nickel." He appeared to regard the unfortunate investment as a colossal joke. "Learn from the misfortunes of others, Henry," he said, "the investor's maxim. Preston Tucker. I haven't thought of him for years. I wonder where he is now."

"In jail or in Argentina."

"Possibly both. I'll tell you what, though, when the tariff structure is modified—and it will be—there'll be plenty of money to be made in the automotive industry in this country. Isn't that bound to be the conclusion of the Royal Commission?"

"Oh the tariff, the tariff," said Golmsdorfer pettishly. He turned away from the chilling riverside and began to walk briskly back towards shelter. "Scratch a Canadian and he starts to talk about the tariff. It isn't by eliminating duties that one makes money in North America. It's by a wise, legal avoidance of them."

"Spoken like a dyed-in-the-wool Conservative," said George Robinson, the sitting Liberal member for Stoverville/Smith's Falls.

"It was a Conservative administration that created the Bladen Commission."

"Darn right. And it was the same administration that tried to dictate the commission's findings."

"Now George, that simply isn't true. The commissioner was as impartial as he could possibly have been under the circumstances."

"Are you going to tell me what's in his report? And how did you happen to accompany him on his excursions anyway?"

"I only went on one or two. It happened that the family chose me to attend the Ottawa hearings and make representations on behalf of the Montréal investment community. I considered the commissioner the soul of fairness. Some proponent of the tariff barrier would come in, and the commissioner would warn him that on his principles, in a year or two, he'd own one hundred per cent of a dying industry. And then some doctrinaire continentalist would speak up, taking a tough line. What do jobs matter? Costs are

what matter! And he'd be told that Canadian jobs will always
have to be protected. Once or twice I burst out laughing
during the hearings. I think it was my laughing at his jokes
that persuaded the commissioner to take me along. He said
he always liked to listen to what investors had to say, particularly young ones."

"What's he going to recommend?"

"Further extrapolation from the value-added concept;
some revision of excise duties; redefinition of the content
requirements with reference to assembly and the marketing
of parts."

"Ahhh," sighed Robinson, his ears visibly pricking.

Golmsdorfer giggled. "You're an old terror."

"Not so old that I can't smell a deal, Henry. What was the
most interesting thing that you saw in your travels with the
commissioner?"

"It was near Detroit. They're a law unto themselves in
Detroit, you understand. What they don't want to tell you,
you don't get to hear. They don't observe Canadian company
law; their subsidiaries aren't Canadian corporations, except
for Ford. And even Ford wraps up its annual report in a lot of
mumbo-jumbo about Indian and Australian operations. No.
You hear what they want you to hear, and that's that. The
commissioner was obsessed with automatic transmissions,
nobody knows why. It was his thing. He kept after the Big
Five executives to open up their transmission plants to him,
for examination and report. Ford offered to fly us to some
little town in Indiana where they had a transmission-
assembly plant, but the commissioner insisted on hanging
around Detroit and nosing things out for himself. Finally
they relented. They took us to the Dearborn shops. They
were very reluctant."

"Why was that?"

"It was an enormous mausoleum, a temple of lost
illusions. It reminded me of some of the buildings that Speer
designed for Hitler. Huge, without human scale." Golmsdorfer lapsed into a curious, sulky silence, which his father-
in-law was already able to recognize as almost impenetrable.
Esther put her head out of one of the terrace doors.

"Did you see Angela on your walk? Mother wants her."

"I haven't seen Angela for a week," said George Robinson impatiently. "I don't believe she's in Stoverville at all. You ladies should take better care of that child." He stood aside and courteously allowed Henry to precede him into the house. They found themselves in a commodious games room. Henry picked up a Ping-Pong paddle and swung it irresolutely; he seemed to brighten up.

"We have not been approached by your sister," he said to Esther. He whacked his palm with the paddle, staring earnestly at his young wife. "Would you care for a game?"

"Not just at this moment, Henry," said Esther. "I suppose I'll have to go and find her; the child is incorrigible."

Golmsdorfer watched as Esther left the games room through the French windows. She disappeared around the west end of the terrace. "It was like some Pharaonic tomb, of a decadent dynasty, unnecessarily elaborate. Where they let us in there were enormous sliding doors, large enough to receive vans of any imaginable size. I remember the thunder they made when they were raised. I believe the Ford officials were attempting to cow us, overawe us, and they succeeded. Even the commissioner seemed taken aback, for the space inside stretched away into a vast distance. There were enormous windows, criss-crossed with the divisions of the panes, which threw barred shadows on the gangways between the conveyor lines. It was dead silent."

"What had they been making?"

"Automatic transmissions. Ford-O-Matics with specially modified mountings."

"Were they on holiday? Was it a Sunday?"

"You don't understand. That plant had been completely retooled three years before; everything in it was virtually new and unused. The building *smelled* new, but it was shrouded in half-light, half darkness, and all along these rows and rows of conveyor lines were big irregular shapes under white cotton sheeting, dust-covers. They looked like parts of elephants. It made you think of the fabulous elephants' graveyard."

"What was under the sheets?"

"Automatic transmissions for Edsels."

"Well I'll be damned."

"They had brought us to the place where marketing executives go to die."

"For Edsels," said George Robinson in muffled tones.

"So you do see, George, nobody is big enough to tackle the automobile industry alone, not even Ford. Certainly not Robinson Pharmaceuticals."

"But Henry," said Robinson, "Henry, consider this: they paid their suppliers, didn't they? Being Ford, they'd have had to pay off the subcontractors."

His wife came into the games room at this moment, an otherwise characterless woman much devoted to her children, Gus, Esther, Angela. "Hasn't anybody seen her?" she demanded.

Golmsdorfer and Robinson exchanged looks of complicity.

2

The next year was an election year. They all seemed to be election years in those days, and for a while most of them were, 1962, 1963, 1965, 1968. In 1962 George Robinson had to give at least some of his attention to the question of re-election in a campaign which, it seemed, might almost dictate the retirement from public life of John George Diefenbaker. The election was duly fought: nobody won it. The Progressive Conservatives won a hundred and sixteen seats, the Liberals won ninety-nine, and the fate of the government was therefore in the hands of the third and fourth parties, a state of affairs that could not long endure. Mr. Diefenbaker continued in office, but every political observer realized that some realignment of political forces must come soon. In an election that seemed to indicate a shifting of public opinion towards the Liberal party, George Robinson suffered the shock of a reduced majority, a relatively narrow victory, and some serious questioning of his actions in the pages of the Stoverville *Intelligencer*, intimations that his grip on the affections of the electors of Stoverville/Smith's Falls might be loosening. He had gained no prospect of a long term of power. Another election could hardly be deferred. George Robinson was now a lonely man, since the peculiar career choice of his only son, Gustave.

Late in the summer of 1962, he and the son-in-law for whom he had now conceived a solid attachment—if not specifically affection—took a little trip to western Ontario in a large, hired, chauffeur-driven Buick, a quiet, comfortable car. They wanted to examine for themselves the route of the spanking-new main street of the province, Highway 401, from Toronto to Detroit. They left Toronto early on a

Monday morning and proceeded at a moderate speed towards
the rise of the Niagara Escarpment just north of Hamilton,
thenceforward to the Guelph region, continuing past
Preston and Galt on one side of the road, and the twin cities of
Kitchener and Waterloo on the other, a totally different
collection of landscapes from what they were accustomed to
observe around Stoverville and the banks of the St. Lawrence.
At noon they arrived in the Woodstock area, where they left
the highway and drove into town in search of luncheon.

"We'll try the hotel first," said George Robinson to his
driver. "We should be able to get something to eat there. We
have something to look into after lunch, so you may as well
put the car in a parking lot for an hour or two. Suppose we
meet you back at the lot about two-fifteen? Here." He
handed the chauffeur three dollars. "You'd better get yourself
a sandwich."

They split up in front of the hotel. At the desk Robinson
arranged for three rooms for the night, then conducted his
son-in-law along a dark corridor, past a cheerful room in
which the Kinsmen were assembled, to the deserted dining-
room.

"You can often get the best food in a small town in the
hotel dining-room," he declared innocently. Golmsdorfer
made no reply. They sat over an unexceptional light meal
for perhaps three-quarters of an hour, reviewing the opinions
of their board of directors.

"That's the best of a privately held company. You can
bring pressure as pressure is needed, without anyone being
the wiser," said George.

"You ought to see my uncle at his dire work," said
Golmsdorfer. "To my knowledge he has quite happily
ruined half-a-dozen cousins. But he never dares to menace my
father with his plots, I'm able to say. My father would destroy
him without exerting any special force of will."

"We are looking to your father at all times for his expertness in such matters, corporate structures, company law.
Finance."

"Of course he is on the spot in Montréal and can study the
movement of capital across borders. He has the best models in
view."

"I'll say he has; you name it, they get away with it, and never a congressional committee to raise questions. I often wonder how they manage it."

"They know every import-export trick in the book. And we will have to do the same, if we go ahead with your plans."

"No ifs about it. I've got a weak board of directors."

"You've already made your bid," said Golmsdorfer acutely."

"A sort of bid, not one that I couldn't revoke." Robinson rose to his feet as an ancient waitress approached them with a bill. She handed him the slip of paper, a meagre total inscribed at the bottom, two dollars and eighty-five cents for two, no tax. Below the total, on the neat white margin of the bill, appeared the legend "Art Printing Company, Toronto." "I'll get this," said George Robinson expansively, as the two men sauntered across the empty room. At the cashier's desk they paused to ask directions and were given explicit, though slightly confusing, indications of the location of the river.

"What is that?" asked George. "Is it the east branch of the Thames?"

"Well, yes," said the cashier dubiously, "some calls it the east branch, some calls it the south branch, most just calls it the river and never mind the name."

"Every little trickle in this district is called the Thames," said George as they left the room, "and when they come together in London you've got yourself quite an impressive landmark. It runs along beside the old highway for thirty or forty miles, over back of Thamesville. So do the railways."

"Thamesville?"

"Of course Thamesville; the town and the rail lines are there because the river is there, and naturally the old highway runs along the river valley."

Golmsdorfer said idly, "This province is full of rivers that would be world-renowned if they were in Europe. Here they're simply the little local waterway. I suppose that's some of the Thames down there?"

"That's it."

They were looking down a long, easy slope in the north end, towards two or three straggling red-brick industrial buildings. There was a cluster of traffic lights at hand, some major intersection, with a lot of Queen's Highway signs insecurely attached to crazily angled poles.

"That's the old highway, number two," said Robinson.

"Nine miles to Ingersoll. Are we going to Ingersoll?"

"No, and we aren't going to Thamesford either."

"I thought you said Thamesville."

"Pay more attention, Henry. Thamesville is another place entirely. We've just a few steps to go, you see? They had the old plant situated between the main highway and the river; they weren't so dumb. They could ship from here to Windsor or Ottawa by the most direct route."

"Not a very direct route, if you're referring to the highway we just crossed."

"No, it's a mess. Getting rid of Highway 2 is the most important public work ever accomplished in Ontario. I don't think anybody understands that yet. I'm sure Andrew Goderich doesn't."

"Don't get started on that," said Golmsdorfer.

"I'll dismiss him from my thoughts." They had come down from the intersection and were passing what appeared to be a piano factory. George Robinson said, "I wonder if they could have moved pianos and organs by barge, along the river, and harrows and reapers too. I wonder if there are any canals hereabouts. They've got both railways, CPR and CN. The Canadian National is the old Grand Trunk line. You could ship anywhere from here, to Ottawa through Peterborough on CP, and through to Detroit, Chicago, and the whole middle west on the Grand Trunk trackage. And if you happened to be shipping small objects such as door handles, they could go via truck transport along the highway. What a location!"

"You've bought this?"

"This comes as part of the total package. It's an important first step, Henry. I've been wanting you to look it over."

They stood contemplating one of the brick industrial buildings that lay along the river bank close to the highway and the rail lines. The building possessed a certain architectural distinction: wide high windows framed by elegantly lain brick with many ornamental courses, projecting headers, pilasters, some yellow brick let into the quoins in strict patterning now weathered and almost invisible. Along one blank wall, which faced east overlooking a spacious parking lot, just below the roof line appeared the large block letters of a sign painted in black and white. Its message was now flaked and eroded, in places unreadable where rainfall had eroded the brick surface. Henry Golmsdorfer squinted against the afternoon sunshine as he tried to pick out the lettering.

AUTOMOTIVE LOCK AND LATCH, WOODSTOCK, ONTARIO

"It's a start," said his father-in-law, trying hard to keep exultation out of his tone.

"Where are the loading platforms?"

"Around back by the river. I know they're badly located but there's nothing going on up here anymore. We're getting the building as part of the deal. Later we might donate it to the city for a war memorial or a park. I just wanted you to see it. It wasn't a bad little plant by any means, nothing special to look at, but they made every door handle, latch, ignition switch, trunk lock, hood latch, and glove-compartment lock that went into a Canadian car over the last fifty years."

"A small market," said Golmsdorfer gloomily.

"But a hundred per cent of it."

"There is that, of course. How did they bring in their steel, nickel, and aluminum?"

"By rail from Hamilton and Québec, nickel from Inco. Easy distances and assured supplies. I know it doesn't look like much."

"George, it doesn't matter what the installation looks like if it's dry and secure. I can see what we've got here. Maybe we should go and look at the new building."

"Ah yes, well it's right the other side of town, down past the 401. We'd better find our car. He must be up in the parking lot by the hotel."

At 3:00 PM the little expedition stood on the graceful lawns studded with beds of geraniums in front of the new plant on Highway 59, just about three hundred yards south of the 401 overpass and the eastbound entry ramp. The westbound ramp lay on the other side of the overpass and the traffic on the 401 buzzed incessantly back and forth night and day, never silent, never still, the big twenty-four wheelers rolling across the northeast like ocean freighters in convoy by their thousands, lit up at night like Christmas trees in front of supermarkets. Staring at the fresh bright buff-coloured brick of the new plant, George and Henry enjoyed the sound of the transport trucks as if it were the murmur of blood rushing through their own unclotted arteries.

"This plant has been in operation for three years. They picked the location, acquired the land, and drew the plans as soon as they were sure of the route of the 401. Pretty smart bimbos, Henry."

"A controlling interest, you say?"

"A wholly owned subsidiary of Robinson Pharmaceuticals." You could hear deep satisfaction in George Robinson's voice as he brought out the words. "We're moving up, Henry, moving into the big time. *Diversifying.*"

"There is such a thing as diversification for its own sake, I guess," said Golmsdorfer.

"Don't mock me, Henry, I've given this takeover a lot of thought and I think we'd better go ahead with it. Look at the location. Connections with Interstate 75 in a couple of hours, or you can go down through Delhi and along Highway 6 into the Buffalo region and the throughway. Or straight along the 401 to Oshawa or Windsor. We'll be shipping mostly to the US."

"You seem very sure of that."

"If you were a member of inner party circles, Henry, you'd understand what's happening. There's a growing interest among Liberals in continentalism."

"I thought the Liberals had always been free-traders."

"Only when it suits us, my boy. We can expect to be shipping assembly kits to Indiana, Michigan, and mostly, I hear, to Ohio. We'll be locked into a totally computerized parts inventory, with free entry to the States, and a certain amount of protection for our Canadian market because of the content and value-added requirements."

A great light began to dawn in Golmsdorfer's face. "Why sure," he said, "of course, you might be able to have it both ways. You might even disguise yourself as a Canadian subsidiary of a US corporation."

"Henry," said George Robinson, "we've got to walk before we can run."

They beckoned to their chauffeur, and were driven back to the hotel uptown, where they placed a series of phone calls, then settled down to await replies.

Next morning saw them bound for Detroit. They passed Tuesday afternoon and most of Wednesday there, in very private conferences. On Thursday they swung down through Toledo and Akron to inspect major plant locations during appointments set up for them from Detroit. At the end of the week they followed the Erie shore back into New York State and continued along the throughway as far as Syracuse; then they turned back north, arriving in Stoverville late that day. There they dismissed their chauffeur with thanks and a modest gratuity.

They had completed a circuit of Lake Ontario and Lake Erie that traversed the most concentrated and multiform industrial empire in existence at that date, all of it describable, controllable, recoverable by emergent data-processing and computer systems and information-storage resources.

"If we became a legal corporation in Delaware or New Jersey," said Golmsdorfer to Robinson, "we might be able to profit from the tariff regulations coming and going."

3

Cutting across Soho Square one bright afternoon in 1963, Tony overtook Linnet Olcott headed in the same direction. He steered her onto Carlisle Street and cannily pointed out his publisher's former offices as they passed in front of them.

"I used to pack books in there," he said, neglecting to mention that he had done it for amusement. He had a vague, quite mistaken notion that Linnet came from a working-class background. She had surfaced first at the Nottingham Playhouse; he supposed that she had her origins in the industrial midlands. This was quite wrong; she was the youngest child and only daughter of a crowded parsonage down in the West Country near Crewkerne, who had early shown a great gift for acquiring new accents with lightning speed. She could convincingly represent in her speech a wide variety of regional vocal idiosyncrasies, with total conviction. Tony found this an immensely endearing gift. He was always begging Linnet to do this or that accent to amuse him. Lately she had seemed to be picking up his own variety of Canadian English and had taken great delight in tracing Adam Sinclair's passage through successive forms of actors' speech. A difficulty with Linnet was that you could never tell what her own voice sounded like. At home in South Perrott on the Somerset-Dorset border, she spoke in a very quiet, very nineteen-thirties-daughter-of-the-vicarage accent, which she had never used onstage.

"Ooooohhhhh," she squealed cheerfully, in response to Tony's "I was a poor book-packer" declaration. She knew perfectly well what his origins were, and did not intend to allow him to impersonate a child of the streets. She used her Charmian Windrush voice when she said "Ooooohhhhh."

"Say that again," demanded Tony, choking with pleased laughter.

"Ooooohhhhh," said Linnet in her Charmian tones, "naughty."

She was carrying a long-playing record under her arm, and was clad in a very suavely tailored dark grey flannel skirt, sheer nylons and tiny pumps. She wore a crisply starched, open at the neck, white sport shirt with exaggerated collar points folded down over the lapels of what seemed to be some sort of cricketer's blazer. The blazer was tailored in a soft lightweight linen and dyed in inch-wide stripes in the colours of no eleven that ever played an innings at Lords: stripes of exquisite apple green, a pale, almost vermilion red, and nubbled virginal white. Nothing wrinkles as sexily as linen. Linnet looked straight out of some legendary Wodehouse summer. Tony's head filled at once with visions of Wodehouse adaptations, all starring Linnet as Jill or Sally or Kay or some other of those fresh sweet gallant girls. She looked like a wonderful candy cane.

"Me dad got 'imself elected to the 'ouse agyne, only yestiddy," he offered in a strangled mishmash of vowels.

Linnet giggled. "You wouldn't say it that way," she said, repeating his words in the purest scouse. Her fine golden hair rose and fell at her temples and over her forehead in the faint breeze. She strode along beside him, an emblem of good health, good looks, talent. "I know about your father," she said. "He was mentioned in the *Guardian* round-up on the Canadian election. He's not in the government party though, is he?"

"Blinkin' roight. They're all terrified of him," said Tony rather abstractedly. He couldn't take his eyes off her. Now they turned down Dean Street, just strolling along. "I'm going to write a couple of *Bed Sitters* scripts for this season, and I'd be glad to have your ideas. Your character really is the audience's favourite."

"Yes, I think so," said Linnet, appearing to give the matter a droll semi-professional consideration. She smiled dazzlingly. "How is the play coming?"

"*Cross Now?*"

"Is that what you're calling it?"

"What do you think of that for a title?"

"Smashing. It must be about a street accident." She paused. "No pun intended," she added.

"No, you're quite right; it is about a street accident. How did you make that out?"

"It's what the lights say at the traffic crossings, isn't it?"

"Bang on. And you think that people will catch the reference?"

"I should say undoubtedly."

"What a good audience you are, Linnet. You might be a great help to me, if you liked."

"*If* I liked? Of course I'd like."

"We go in here, don't we?" asked Tony, looking dubiously at a doorway between two questionable shops. They had come about three hundred yards down Dean Street. "It doesn't look like much."

"It is though," said Linnet. She shifted the record she was carrying into her left hand, caught the door handle with her right, and flung it wide. "After you," she said with great courtesy.

"I've never gone through a door before a lady in my entire life. I wouldn't know how to do it," said Tony.

"You may come to it yet," said Linnet. She allowed him to follow her up the stairs and into the Granada offices, where a major production meeting was about to start. Miss Bellows showed them into a conference room, asked them if they wanted tea, and upon receiving a polite negative, withdrew. Linnet and Tony were sharp on time. Punctuality was a common trait, which drew them together. The others drifted in at odd moments over the next quarter of an hour, and around two-thirty the meeting got underway, perhaps a little later than was convenient for most of those present. Last to appear was Lesley Henderson, the top production executive. He carried a bundle of scripts old and new under one arm, and was followed into the room by Martha Bellows, who distributed copies of production notes and various memoranda to all participants.

"Aren't Sadie and Adam going to be here?" asked Tony.

"Now Tony," said Henderson, "now Tony, we've been through all this. I've explained it all before. There is no question of concealing anything whatsoever from either Sadie or Adam. We're all above subterfuge here, I believe."

"Oh damn subterfuge," said Felix Goad, one of the writers, "damn anything in the least underhanded."

"Quite!" said Henderson. "Then would you explain our position to Mr. Goderich, my dear Goad?"

"Of course. I should enjoy that above all things," said Felix, who was also one of the two originators of the series idea, and a young man who looked forward with confidence to becoming immensely rich from his share of the sale to America. In April 1963 nothing could possibly discompose Felix Goad; he was simply too pleased with life and with his own destiny to feel menaced or threatened by the scruples of even the most promising playwright or actress. He squinted hard at Tony and Linnet and said, "It's simply that Sadie will have to be written out of the show, and that means Adam as well. *You* know all about that, Tony. We've been through it all. Sadie's going to sign for the CBS series."

"Is that certain?"

"It's as certain as anything ever is in this business."

"It's perfectly certain, Tony," said Linnet, tugging at his sleeve. "Sadie knows how to look after herself."

"Is that for sure, Linny?"

A very pleased smile crossed Linnet's face. "I have my methods, Mr. Goderich," she declared. "You may place perfect confidence in what I tell you. Sadie will sign a long-term contract with CBS next week, to appear in thirty-nine episodes of the new show. I have this upon unimpeachable authority."

The others at the meeting knew better than to cross-question her.

Henderson said, "Trust our little birdie. She knows."

"So what it is, you see, Tony," said Felix Goad, "is the question of devising a whole new direction for *Bed Sitters*. We have to write Mavis and Monty out of the next scripts. We have to develop Charmian's part—which won't be in the least difficult, I do assure you. We shall have to reintroduce the character of Herbert and we have to find a new girl for him. We should try to give the show more appeal to younger folk. How old would you say Charmian is?"

"I think of her as not quite twenty," said Tony.

"What do you think, Linnet?" said Henderson.

"I could make her eighteen," said Linnet. "I don't think we've ever said definitely, have we? I should say that the Ronnie character is a tiny bit older. Here." She unwrapped the record she'd brought to the meeting. "I want you to listen to this. It's precisely the sort of sound-track we ought to be dealing with."

"Not now please, Linnet," said Henderson.

"Miss Bellows," said Linnet persuasively, "would you have them put this on the sound system for us? Ask them to play the tracks I've indicated on the sleeve."

Miss Bellows left the room hurriedly and in a few seconds a rock recording came over the speakers, enormously amplified, lead, rhythm, bass, and drums and four voices chanting, "Roll over, Beethoven, roll over, Beethoven, roll over, Beethoven." The music was beyond anything exciting. When the track came to an end the people in the meeting were thoughtfully silent. A second number began, more driving than the first, something about long tall Sally. The third and final selection in this impromptu program was more or less the signature tune of a decade, "She loves you, yeah, yeah, yeah."

All the people in the room sat back stunned.

"That's the sort of sound-track we'll be needing. That's the sound of the nineteen-sixties," said Linnet. "If I'm going to play Charmian Windrush at eighteen, that's the music I want behind me."

"It really does something to you," said Felix Goad, no fool.

Tony was silent. He stared at Linnet in her candy-cane blazer, the huge excitement of the music still vibrating in his ears. "She loves you," he thought, "yeah, yeah, yeah."

4

At precisely the same moment—just on ten o'clock in the morning on a rainy day in Stoverville—George Robinson sat in his sparsely peopled committee rooms and questioned himself and everybody else about his election defeat of the previous day. These rooms, by tradition located in a vacant store-front in the Royal Edward, facing King William Street, echoed with emptiness and the occasional election worker's voice, most often inquiring about payments due. Crumpled balls of paper lay all over the floor; posters of the defeated candidate hung lopsidedly in place on otherwise bare and cracked plaster tinted in that yellowish-greenish tone favoured by law offices in our smaller cities. Notable by his absence was Henry Golmsdorfer, whose entire mental poise and set forbade all party activity, indeed most activity of a public nature. He functioned best—if at all—in modest retirement. His wife, Esther, sometimes complained to her father or sister that Henry insisted on making clandestine appointments to see her that could have been proposed perfectly openly. At the same time, Esther found this flavour of the secret and illicit distinctly a stimulus to her imagination.

"I don't know at all where he is," she said to her disappointed papa this morning. "He did admit that he'd be in to dinner."

"Where is there to go in Stoverville?" said George Robinson. "I did think Henry might find time to stand up beside me today of all days. I know I've lost elections before but I've usually won. I won the last three times in a row when the Conservatives got in. Now that my own party is in, I'm out, and it seems like there'll be no place at the victory celebrations for me. It's hard. This may be my last campaign."

Esther placed little confidence in this declaration. "You don't really think so, Father," she said.

"A union lawyer from Smith's Falls," exclaimed Mr. Robinson, "of all things. I could understand it if they'd parachuted some heavyweight into the riding to try to cut me down. I'm the only Liberal who's ever been able to hold on to Stoverville/Smith's Falls. I could see them fighting this election on the language issue or on the tariff. But unemployment in Smith's Falls? There's always unemployment in Smith's Falls. There's unemployment in any railway town, depending on the traffic. Railroading is finished in eastern Ontario. You'd think the citizens would understand that when they look around and see the new highways. I tell you, Esther, it was the Department of Transport that lost this election for me, when they cut back the freight service from Ottawa through Smith's Falls to Peterborough and Stoverville. And this fellow Horseball, or whatever he calls himself. . . ."

"Horsbaugh, Daddy."

"Horsbaugh then. Philip Horsbaugh, a former Liberal, a dues-paying member of our riding association, switches to the Conservatives eighteen months before this election because he can smell a local issue. Worms his way into the confidence of two union locals, and the result is, I'm out of office while my party is in. It's hard. Hard."

Various canvassers and agents now advanced to shake the defeated candidate's hand; some desultory conversation ensued. Outside a hard cold rain whirled down King William Street, and on the other side of the street crowds of people passed in and out the doors of the local PC headquarters. You could make out the form of the newly elected member through the plate-glass windows, shaking hands with some, exchanging hugs with others. To the Robinson partisans it was a dismal sight.

"I'll steal a march on that awful man," said Robinson *père*, in an agony of jealousy.

"Don't upset yourself," said Esther.

"Dief the Chief," said her father, grinding his dentures horribly.

"He's out of power too," said Esther, offering what consolation she could.

"Don't I know it?" said her father. "The old fart. 'I'll lie me doon and bleed awhiles. And then I'll rise and fight again.' Here, Tompkins," he called to a hovering journalist, Mallory Tompkins of the Stoverville *Intelligencer,* "I've got a scoop for you."

Tompkins winced.

George Robinson repeated the lines of the ballad to him laboriously. "And then I'll rise and fight again." His Scots accent was absurd.

"I'm afraid I can't use that, Mr. Robinson. Dief quoted those lines on the late news last night. Have you any further comments on the election? After all, Mr. Pearson almost got his majority. A hundred and twenty-nine to ninety-five. Do you think he and Mr. Gordon will have to compromise themselves to retain the support of the Socialists? "There was a bright gleam of malice in Tompkins' bifocals as he launched this shaft. He was as aware as anybody how much Mr. Robinson detested the opening to the left in his party.

"I can find common ground with Mr. Gordon," said George Robinson uncomfortably.

"You know that they're saying in Ottawa that the party deliberately dumped you this time?" Here was bitter medicine indeed.

"Who dares say such a thing?"

"Bill Wilson for one, commenting on the results last night. He says that you were one of the older element in the party that was considered expendable."

"Oh he does, does he? Now mind you, Mallory, I've got nothing to say specifically against Bill Wilson. I consider Bill Wilson one of the ablest journalists on the Hill, somewhat like yourself, and I don't know where he'd get any such notion. Esther, my dear, would you trot into the lobby and see if the Montréal papers are in yet? We want the *Star.* Just see to that, would you?"

In a moment or two Esther came back into the echoing room with two copies of that day's noon edition of the *Star.* George Robinson took one, and passed the other to the man from the *Intelligencer.* Together they scanned the op-ed page.

"Oh dear, oh dear, that's very strong language," said
Mallory Tompkins. Faced with the indignation of the old
war-horse, he felt slightly abashed.

"Get the party moving, trim the dead wood. Sixty days of
decision indeed! Well, we'll see about that. You haven't heard
the last of George Robinson, let me tell you." He seemed to
swell visibly as they looked at him. The telephone rang as he
inhaled a huge breath and his face reddened. Esther took the
call, then handed the phone to her father. She shook her head
warningly once or twice. "It's Auntie May-Beth."

Undeterred, George accepted the call. "Is that you, May-
Beth? Well, my dear, I'm surviving, yes, surviving. I'm disappointed of course, I feel a bit betrayed by some of my
constituents in the up-county polls. It was close, May-Beth,
a few dozen votes one way or the other. No. No, I'm planning
a long vacation in the Bahamas. I need the rest. Most of the
summer, I believe. I'll see you when I return . . . yes, I miss
him too. I know Earl was never identified as a party man, but
I like to think that he'd have stood by me in defeat. That's
right, dear, thank you for calling." He hung up the receiver
and turned to the others in some bewilderment. "May-Beth
Codrington says she'll have something to show me when I
come back from vacation. Compensation for betrayal, she
says. Of course she's quite mad."

5

"Montréal?"

"Yes."

"Montréal?"

"That's what I said."

"Well yes, I see that, but I mean, why Montréal? We don't have any connections there. I don't know anybody who went to McGill. Of course there's Maura, and I believe little Angela Robinson goes there for weekends, goodness knows why. But I'd have to think twice, or more than twice, to recover the names of any known Montréalers. Aila Strathdrummond. Haven't seen or heard of her for years. There's that very mysterious man who married Esther. Gumberger or some such name."

"Golmsdorfer," said Edie tightly.

"A very distressed person, in my opinion, never says boo, barely acknowledges greetings on the street. A poor colour. If he's your typical Montréaler give me the streets of good old Stoverville any day. And as far as that goes, if we're thinking of moving, what's wrong with Toronto?"

"I should have thought that was obvious."

"It isn't obvious to me; we have lots of friends in Toronto. My mother lives there and my father is there when the House isn't sitting, and on most weekends when it is. Good schools. I don't quite understand what you want. I could go for something in the nature of a *pied à terre,* a small apartment that we could use on weekends, but as for uprooting ourselves and moving the children into a totally new environment . . . I just can't see it. Anthony ought to be in a good nursery school and Andrea will be ready in a year or so. Do you want them to begin life in a French-language school? Not but what that

might be a pretty good idea at that, because it looks to me as
though a knowledge of both languages is going to be
obligatory for anybody in a responsible position in Canada
over the next little while. I understand there's already a lot of
unrest in Québec about language rights and the constitution
and all that . . ."

"Oh stop maundering on like that. You make me feel quite
dizzy when you do it. Like a dripping tap that I can't turn off.
Surely you can see why it might be a good idea for us to get a
place in Montréal."

"You'll have to spell that out for me."

"You're right about the schools for one thing. It would be
a blessing for the children to attend French-language nursery
schools. They'd have a grounding in the language that they'd
never forget."

"I've never heard you express the slightest interest in this
before. You must have been talking to the little Robinson
girl."

"The Robinsons are King Charles's head to you, Matt. You
intrude them into every conversation, every train of thought.
What the hell has George Robinson ever done to you?"

"Nothing that I know of. I was thinking more of the girls.
At the same time, your mother had George Robinson over to
tea yesterday afternoon. They were closeted in her studio for
more than two hours."

"It's her house, after all."

"Now Edie, it is and it isn't, as you very well know. She
enjoys having us here. I can see that we might have been
smarter to stay in Toronto after your father died instead of
buying a cottage near Stoverville and spending most of our
time here. But it's working out."

"I feel that it's hurting my development," said Edie. "I
ought to be in Toronto or Montréal to show my work."

"You'll get a Toronto gallery."

"Oh you don't understand at all. You haven't the slightest
idea what it's like, trying to make it as a painter. You think it
ought to be worked through the old family network, through
your father or my mother or their friends. It isn't a bit like
that. It's the impression your work makes on its own, and it's
your continual presence on the scene. You have to be on the

scene, visible. I can't keep moving back and forth between a small apartment in Toronto and my mother's house in Stoverville. I've got to be out in front pushing, and I'm getting on, Matt. I'm thirty years old and there are hundreds of art-school graduates coming up behind me every year, and only so many galleries and museums and design assignments. I can't go back to working in the theatre; that would be a retreat into the past, which is what you like, but it isn't what I like."

"I don't know what you mean."

"Poor Matt, now I've hurt his feelings. What about *Stone Dwellings of Loyalist Country* and the preservation of our colonial heritage?"

"That's not the biggest thing in my life. You're the biggest thing in my life, and the children and the new baby."

"Handsomely spoken."

"Handsomely meant," I said. "And then there's our book together, don't forget that."

"I haven't forgotten, though, mind you, architectural painting isn't my long suit."

"Nonsense," I said dismissively. "There's no competition. Nobody in this country has bothered to look at the buildings hard enough to paint them. There's one fellow in Toronto who does the back yards in the Annex, what's his name? Is it Albert Frank?"

"Matthew, will you listen to me? Stop putting out these smoke-screens. I hate it when you start that. Now listen, we've gravitated to spending most of our time in Stoverville because, while I love your mother and father, I don't want to live in their pockets."

"For God's sake, we never see them. My father's in Ottawa when he isn't in Germany or Israel. Tony's in Britain getting rich. Amanda Louise has been in New York for ages."

"Don't bring all that stuff up, Matt. That's yesterday's news."

"But my point is, we never have to see them. We saw my mother once a month in Toronto. We had her to dinner in our apartment once a month maximum, so she could see the children. She baby-sat for us about three times. You can't call that living in each others' pockets. That's simply untrue."

"Toronto is their town; it's as simple as that."

"Toronto is two million people's town, and that's where you need to place your work. Montréal's a backwater compared to Toronto."

"How would you know, Matt? Just how would you know?"

"All right," I said, "I'm willing to be perfectly reasonable about this. We'll hire a sitter for a weekend some time this fall. We'll go down to Montréal for a long weekend; we'll take our time. Get the feel of the place. You're perfectly right, every Canadian should have a close knowledge of Québec. We'll polish up our high-school French."

"Oh God," said Edie.

"Now what have I said?"

"Nothing darling, not a damn thing. Let's do it. Maura has contacts in some of the galleries, or so she claims, and Sallee goes there on buying trips all the time. I really think we should do this."

"Whatever you say," I said indulgently, suspecting that I'd scotched her outburst.

So we did it, later in the fall. We didn't just take a weekend, we took the whole inside of a week. We got a round-the-clock baby-sitter who charged us the earth. In the end we paid her a hundred and fifty dollars plus her room and board, and we were only away five days. I don't think Mrs. Codrington had to come downstairs once the whole time we were away. Edie and I took the train to Montréal and stayed in a small suite in the Windsor Hotel, just across Dominion Square from Central Station.

We didn't take our car because we were both scared to drive in Montréal, or even inside the Québec border. My God, those Québec drivers. Montréal and its approaches were all dug up and surrounded by detours and new construction, and highway re-routings. Everybody in the city was beginning to realize that they were committed to hosting a world's fair in less than four years, and unless the roadways and the rail links were cobbled into some semblance of order nobody would be able to get there. The superhighway link with the 401 was just going through in those days. If you tried to drive in from Stoverville or Cornwall you ran into one piece of construction after another. So we went by train, an easy two-hour trip. We'd been making notes of properties offered in the want ads in the Montréal *Star* for several days, so we had a file of half a dozen houses in districts that we knew about and liked, Westmount, the Town of Mount Royal. We couldn't use a house in a distant suburb. Neither of us knew Montréal at all well, but we found that we could get quite a line on prices, and on what was being offered in different parts of town, from a careful review of the want ads. A few days before we took the train I sent letters to a couple of realtors to let them know about places we'd like to inspect. When we got into the hotel on Monday, I rang up various offices and prepared a list of appointments. We arranged to go over four places that week, one a day Tuesday through Friday. We spent the rest of each day having fun.

I can see that this all sounds deadly dull, over-organized, leaving nothing to accident or serendipity. I know I'm that sort of man. Lots of times I wish I wasn't! On the other hand it's possible to leave too much to chance. I've always erred on the side of prudence. As things turned out that week, maybe I was right to take this line. It's really impossible to say. Sometimes Edie would smile at my best-laid plans in a way that made me very uneasy. I know that most of the time she treated me as a bit of a fuddy-duddy, but my God, we'd spent a decade together by that time. We'd had three children, little old John Sleaford Goderich having arrived four months previously, in July 1963. It looked as though we would eventually settle on a permanent place to live in our own home, either in Toronto or Montréal, but in either case not too far from Stoverville. I could see why Edie didn't want to live in the same house as her mother. I understand all that, I really do. And surely it was all right to leave John with a competent baby-sitter for a week. He was in perfect health. You can't let your children make you their prisoners. Family life, a blessing and a curse. We'd had ten years of it.

I'm going to have to do something about my impulses, but I don't know what.

Anyway we looked over four houses. The first one was way over towards the east end, on Querbes Avenue, a pretty, red-brick, detached cottage, with front and side verandas, which I

liked very much until I spotted the signs of water damage in
the upstairs ceilings. A new roof at least, and probably dozens
of other repairs to be done over the first year. I shoved my
pocket-knife in between a few courses of brick, and the
mortar was sand. We passed.

On Wednesday and Thursday we inspected two small
houses in Westmount, one of them near the Westmount
Library, on Strathcona Avenue, with only three bedrooms, a
bit too small for what we had in mind, and the other up the
hill on Victoria Avenue near the Villa Maria property. I liked
this house a lot. The hillside location gave you a long view of
the lower part of the city. In the fall, with the trees bare, you
could see the river and the south shore, and even the hills near
the US border. If it hadn't been for something the agent let
drop, we might very well have closed a deal.

He said, "You don't want to be frightened off by newspaper hysteria."

"Frightened off what? How frightened off?" we said
together.

He seemed to want to retrieve a slip. "I guess you haven't
been following the Québec news too closely."

"We haven't been following it at all. What are you talking
about?"

"It was nothing really."

"If it wasn't anything, you can tell us all about it." Edie
nodded and took hold of my hand.

"It was only a few little bombs."

"What the hell are you saying? Bombs?"

"Only one or two."

"Were they near here?"

"No no no, way over in Outremont on Bates Road."

I said, "I think that's close enough."

"Fucking right!" said Edie succinctly. We both eyed her
uneasily.

On the Friday morning we went along to an appointment
with a realtor at a house on Côte Ste.-Antoine Road on the
border of Westmount and Nôtre-Dame-de-Grace, a weird
property, a large house divided into two distinct dwellings.
Two full-sized houses in the same shell. There was a complete suite of offices on the left side of the building, formerly

a doctor's waiting room, consulting room, examination room and lavatory. There was even one of those physician's balancing scales still standing in the examination room. Now I knew that Edie had coveted an accurate scales for years; this was the sort of detail that sometimes swings a sale. She could have lived, almost isolated, in the east side of the house, while the children and I rubbed along in the larger half. Something of the kind seemed to be on her mind. We left the building about one-thirty, telling the realtor that we'd be in touch with him before we left the city, probably the next morning, a Saturday. We'd phoned for a cab, and in a few minutes it appeared, with a monolingual French driver at the wheel. We got in, gave the address of the hotel, and sat back. The radio was playing on one of the French stations and in a moment I heard a news bulletin, something about *le président des Etats-Unis assassiné à Dallas.* I thought it must be a radio play in French. It couldn't be real. But I said, *"Excusez,"* to the driver and twisted the tuner of the radio until I found an English-language station, I think it must have been the CBC. President Kennedy assassinated in Dallas.

Edie was sitting in the back seat. I twisted around to look at her. That was the first time that I ever saw my wife look really frightened. I said, "Honey, I don't feel that we're really ready to make a big decision at this time. Everything is just too much up in the air."

We took the train to Stoverville the same afternoon. We never even remembered to call the realtor back.

6

"So you don't go over to the Château any more?" asked Charlie Pope, laughing.

"The last time I went there," said Andrew, "it resulted in seven years of exile, like something in a fairy tale. Something you'd use to frighten children with." He paused in his speech to catch the eye of their waitress, who stood beside the long serving counter towards the back of the restaurant. He was well known to her. He saw her rescue his side order of sausages from a competing waitress; there was a brief discussion between the young women.

Charlie Pope followed his glance. "Where do they find their Miss Murrays?" he demanded. This was a rhetorical question. "They run to type."

"Quite a lot of them are immigrants nowadays. In the old days they were usually the daughters of working-class English Canadians. 'Miss Murray.' I haven't seen a billboard advertising Miss Murray in years."

"The great triumph of Murray's is the strict portion control," said Charlie, "that and the unmixedly Canadian middle-class atmosphere."

"And for this we must be thankful," said Andrew. "There is hardly another Canadian institution so expressive of the quality of our lives . . . certainly not in eastern Canada."

"How many are there?"

"It's never been a very extensive chain. A very few in Montréal, perhaps five. This one—of very recent date—in the Lord Elgin. How many in Toronto? I can think offhand of three, the ones near the Royal York, the Park Plaza, and St. Clair and Yonge. There might be one in Hamilton."

Elsa brought the side order of sausages, which emitted a most tempting smell. Charlie Pope eyed them as the waitress stood by, perhaps expecting him to place an additional order. There was a brief silence.

"Would the Undersecretary care for anything else? Some sausages?"

Pope gave her a startled look.

"Elsa is a journalism student at Carleton," said Andrew proudly, "and more than that, the soul of diplomacy."

"Yes, I'll have some sausages too," said Charlie Pope, "and, do you know, I'd like some maple syrup to put on them. Thank you, Elsa."

"You know the thing in *The Gondoliers,* if it's *The Gondoliers* I mean," said Andrew. "'If everybody's somebody, then nobody is anybody.'"

"Yes."

"If everybody has his breakfast in the coffee shop, or the breakfast room or whatever they call it, downstairs in the Château, then nobody who goes there is anybody. Result? Murray's in the Lord Elgin is packed at breakfast time with very secretive people in quiet grey suits. No, don't turn around. Keep on facing the serving counter. It's precisely who you think it is. You would be surprised at the people who come and go in the Lord Elgin Hotel. I live here, you know."

"No, I didn't know that."

"Charlie, you'd better look into the operation of your security services. I keep two rooms in the Lord Elgin, and have done so for over a decade, since I was first elected to the House. On the eighth floor. I've got a pleasant bedroom and bath and a sitting-room, or writing room—there's a writing desk and some bookshelves and a conference table, nothing elaborate—all on a monthly tenancy arrangement. I pay for it myself, of course, and the revenue people allow a partial deduction for it. I'm very well known around the hotel. There's a small degree of inoffensive surveillance. Elsa, for example, knows perfectly well who you are; she probably knows why you came here for breakfast today. It certainly hasn't anything to do with our friend in the neat grey suit.

That would be matter for another department altogether. When you've gone I'll have to check with Elsa to find what you wanted to discuss."

For a few moments the two old friends busied themselves with breakfast. Charlie offered Andrew the pitcher of maple syrup.

"I don't think that would sit too well beside fried eggs."

"Oh go on, try it on that penultimate sausage."

"Why not, after all? It's necessary to take certain risks in life, if we are to realize the Holy Land in Manitoba and Québec."

Pope shook his head mournfully. "Nobody who was present on that occasion will ever allow me to forget that."

"Quite right," said Andrew, "though it's a sad thing to begin one's public life with one's most memorable utterance. You're in somebody's book of Canadian quotations with that statement, you know."

"I didn't know that."

"The things you don't know, after forty years in diplomacy. It must be quite forty years now. You're approaching retirement age, Charlie."

"I'm a year older than you are, I'll be sixty-five in two months."

"A child of the nineteenth century."

"Yes, and there are fewer and fewer of us who are still effective in public life. I just make it, of course, November 1899."

"Will you take retirement on schedule?"

"Perhaps not. There are certain matters that I've been asked to follow through to their natural conclusion. They date back a long way."

"Only to 1949, 1950, 1953. That's not so long, fifteen years at most."

Pope opened his eyes very wide at this. "Damn you anyway," he said, "who's been talking?"

"Nobody's said a word, Charlie, certainly not to an obscure back-bencher from a third-party constituency. I'm only an innocent with an amateur interest in China."

"The only people in Ottawa who know more than you about China are Ronning and Menzies."

Andrew gave no indication of his reaction to this remark.

"It's true, Andrew, and you know it!"

"I've got a son-in-law in New York who works for the Luce publications. You might remember my daughter, Amanda Louise?"

"I certainly do, a most charming young woman, like her mother."

"Two of the most agreeable people known to me," said Andrew reflectively, "but that's beside the point. Amanda Louise married a chap called Tommy Underwood who writes—if any single person could be said to write—for *Time*. He's an old, or rather a middle-aged, China hand."

"So?"

"He's very close to Luce, who is himself, of course, a really old China hand, though perhaps of somewhat questionable opinions."

"Uh-huh."

"Well in one way and another I have access to material from the mainland that would not be available to most members of Congress, say, or to most private MPs."

"I know that."

"I know that you know it. Who told you where to look for me this morning?"

"Your Miss Keogh. I rang your office yesterday."

"I see. And you don't really want to talk about China at all, do you? You're not a member of the government, Charlie, you're not a political animal. You're the undersecretary."

"Andrew, we have to have a majority government soon. There's bound to be another election next year."

"You can't say such things to me, Charlie. You're a public servant and I'm that wicked thing, an MP."

"But surely I can speak to you informally in Murray's Restaurant in the Lord Elgin Hotel at breakfast on a clear September morn. You talk as if we were characters in a spy novel."

"We've both *been* characters in a spy novel, to our cost. Look at you, you're on the brink of retirement and I'm treading on your heels."

"Ah, but that's the point. We won't be allowed to fade away gracefully."

"One indiscretion after another," murmured Andrew. "Shocking."

"But I can trust you."

"And they won't let you retire?"

"No. I have to stay on until after the next election, to make policy for the new wave."

"You'll be permitted to do that?"

"Absolutely, old chum. I'm essential to the workings of good government."

"Sure you are, Charlie. Now why don't you stop the manoeuvring and tell me what you're worried about. It isn't China, and it isn't your pending retirement, and it certainly isn't my problems with the voters and the next election."

"It's all those things and more. Nothing ever comes across my desk in isolation, Andrew. Everything seems to intertwine with everything else."

"That's a specific consequence of age."

"Never mind about age!"

"One does think about it all the same. Quite a good friend of mine was found dead last week—or was it the week before? No warning. My son's mother-in-law. Just sitting there quietly with her face to the sun. It makes you wonder."

"How old would she have been?"

"Round about our age, Charlie, maybe a bit younger. I think she was sixty-one or two. My son was very distressed. He kept asking me about my own state of health."

"What answers did you provide?"

"Mixed answers."

"Just what I'd have done. I'm afraid to tell anybody anything. Oh, but I can tell you a few things that will interest you. Not exactly external affairs, and not exactly not external affairs, if you follow me."

"Why," said Andrew, "you might almost be talking about the automotive industry."

"So I might."

"And how are matters proceeding?"

"There ought to be something on the table right after Christmas. Say by mid-January. But naturally it won't come from us."

"It will come from Bud Drury."

"Yes."

"It won't work, you know. In trade and in politics you can never have everything your own way. In Canada you're either a free-trader or a protectionist. You can't be both and you can't be neither."

"You might be one thing in one area, and the reverse in some other."

"That's what the British would like to be, vis-a-vis the EEC," said Andrew, "and that's why they'll never be able to participate in it to their entire satisfaction."

"You think they'll join eventually?"

"They'll join, all right. It may take another decade to persuade them, but in the end they'll have to test the waters, and they'll find the waters much too warm and the currents too swift."

"In the long run, we're all dead," said Charlie Pope.

"That we are," said Andrew.

7

"It was right after I was defeated at the polls, when I was licking my wounds and beginning to cherish my resentments, that she called me the first time. I was most grateful, I can tell you, to receive some expression of sympathy and fellow-feeling from a member of my generation, though I'm not sure May-Beth was quite as old as me. Some days I feel as old as God, and a few months in the sun on the beaches of Lyford Cay have not been sufficient to banish the sense of impending breakup." George Robinson smote his breast energetically. "They fly from me that sometime did me seek. Nobody feels his human loneliness more than the elected official temporarily out of office. That is why I have chosen to divide my life into two connected parts or streams, that of the dedicated public servant and that of the animator of business, investment, industry, and employment. For employment must follow investment and industry. There can be no security for the working man without the enterprise of the property holder, what we call free enterprise or capital risk-taking."

The seven silent persons seated in an irregular row in the deserted storefront began to shift about and scrape their feet on the splintered and gritty floor. It was past nine-thirty; all Stoverville had found some evening task or entertainment more or less appropriate to age and circumstance, the young, one hopes, in one another's arms, the old in bed asleep, or moving restlessly in pain. Only George Robinson and the seven committee members remained downtown. They had drawn the drapes along their rods so that the show windows in the vacant store were decently masked. Light from two desk lamps and a single overhead globe was filtered by the drapes, allowing only a soft green glow to show itself to rare passers-by. The appeals for electoral support had been taken down months before. Perhaps most citizens recalled only imperfectly if at all that these premises did not go entirely vacant during the intervals between general elections, but remained the headquarters of the Stoverville/Smith's Falls Liberal Party Riding Association. Few of us who do not concern ourselves professionally with electoral politics call regularly to mind the affairs of the little cadre of party members whose task it is to preserve the party structure: the mailing lists, the street maps, the names of the most willing workers, the next most willing workers, and those who can only with difficulty be persuaded to come out and canvass, among the folk who have from time to time actually contributed money to the organization. How many people understand how a political party in Canada supports itself in being during those long months when nothing seems to be happening politically outside of Ottawa? The Stoverville/ Smith's Falls Liberals possessed considerable funds, as well as two or three eager potential candidates to whom they might give their voice as standard-bearer in any forthcoming election, including the former member whose readiness to return to the hustings was counterpoised by the suspicions of four of the seven party members in the room that he had outlived his usefulness.

So it was that this extremely rich man, for long the elected representative of the riding, was obliged to make a formal appearance on this late November night, had to show himself full of restored energy, plans, fresh electoral strategies, had to cajole and manoeuvre and in the end persuade the seven to allow him to run once more. He didn't enjoy doing this. There wasn't one of the seven whom he would readily invite into his home for mere social discourse. One was the principal of the high school; one was a medical doctor; two were retail traders; another was a newspaper publisher. The two women who were members of the committee were widows who lived on the income from their investments. A mixed group, and in this situation a powerful one. The two women were unconditionally prepared to support George Robinson's renomination quite ardently. But despite their

solid commitment to his cause, George Robinson seemed to
have little time to spare for these diligent women; he never
courted them or gave them much encouragement in the
committee rooms. And yet there was a trace of courtliness
about him, an attraction for women that overwent his
distinct limp, his empurpled facial veins, his occasional
resemblance to an angry turkey. He had an undeniable air,
and it was clear at this meeting that he could rely on the
support of two of the seven members of the nominations
committee in his bid to go with his pitcher to the well yet
once more.

Perhaps his support stopped there. Plenty of the people in
the riding were fed up with the old Stoverville families and
their unchallenged sway over local affairs. In the back townships enthusiasm for Robinson, at no time a powerful tide,
seemed these days at a low ebb. He had to gain commitments
from at least two more of the committee sometime over the
next couple of months, before the between-elections canvass
for new members and contributions to the support of the
party organization was completed. It is during this period of
low water and voter apathy between elections that the
professional politician shows his mettle, that midwinter
season when nobody comes to meetings and people are
deadly tired of the political contest, wanting only to be left
to themselves. Probably the comparison with winter growth,
under soil frozen solid, of infinitesimal forgotten seeds
suggests itself improperly. The courtship of the will of the
people is nothing like a biological process. Yet in that time—
at a point of no return—when an election is eighteen months
in the past and another election is just beginning to rise over
the horizon, a stirring and quickening undeniably moves in
the prospective candidate's heart. This is a strongly physical
feeling, one that George Robinson relished; it made him
understand that he was still alive, still almost young. He felt
blood coursing into his toes. Now he cast around in his
imagination for some baited hook with which to draw the
five obdurate men to his side, doctor, editor, two retailers
(books, menswear), schoolmaster. Which of them would
readily vote with the girls? Not the doctor, whose attitude
towards all women was one of condescension. The editor?

The book man? Womanish occupations, thought George. I'll aim my pitch at them.

"Just before May-Beth Codrington passed on," he said slowly, feeling his way, "sometime in the middle of August, it was, she invited me to the house." He paused for effect. It was widely known in town that Mrs. Codrington never, never invited anybody to the house.

"She had something she wanted to show me," went on the would-be candidate. "Something that she'd been working on for over a year, a painting of our good friend Philip Horsbaugh. She'd mentioned it to me off and on for most of the year after the last election. Something about Phil Horsbaugh had stuck in her craw. Now you and I know, my friends, that what May-Beth thought threw a good deal of weight in this locality. Well sir, I wish that you could have seen this painting. I wish I had it here with me now. You never saw such a damning indictment of a political figure in your life. For she'd painted him as a Biblical character. I leave you to guess which one."

"Judas!" exclaimed the bookstore owner, the doctor and both the widows, all together in one breath.

"Damn right!" said Uncle George. "And I tell you, if we can exhibit that picture in some way or use it in publicity we'll win the riding hands down. I tell you, ladies and gentlemen, next time we'll get our majority and *down with Horsbaugh!*"

If there'd been anybody across the street at PC headquarters they'd have been shaken by the vigour of the shouted response. *"Down with Horsbaugh!"*

II

8

The shining white paper smelled inky and hot as though it had just passed through some reproductive process accomplished at infernally high temperatures. The smell was metallic, and if inhaled left a slight burning sensation in the nostrils.

"Ammonia?" asked Henry Golmsdorfer.

"I think that's the bleaching agent in the paper, some sulphite or other. I used to know. Mallory Tompkins would know. It's paper of the very highest quality." George Robinson, who had this very minute arrived from Ottawa, his majestic automobile still standing under the *porte-cochère* with its doors wide open, passed his palms over the glistening surface of the release. His hands remained perfectly clean. "Clean hands, clean heart," he said offhandedly, staring at the tip of his left thumb. Henry relieved him of the burden of freshly mimeographed documentation; this was in an age immediately prior to the widespread employment of xerography.

NEWS RELEASE

DEPARTMENT OF INDUSTRY
OTTAWA, CANADA.

Not for release before Friday,
January 15, 1965—6:00 PM, EST.

AUTOMOTIVE PROGRAM OUTLINE

OTTAWA, January 15, 1965: The Honourable C.M. Drury, Minister of Industry, released the following statement in Ottawa today.

"A new far-reaching program for the Canadian automotive industry is being introduced to take effect Monday. This program is designed to achieve a substantial expansion in production and employment and promote improved competitive efficiency in this important sector of Canadian manufacturing."

"I think we'd better go inside," said George, shivering in the mid-January chill. Sheets of paper flapped and clapped together in a sequence of tiny sharp reports. It became harder and harder to hold on to the dozen stapled-together handouts he had brought post-haste from the capital, where he retained an office while awaiting electoral resurrection. "They'll get away from us in a minute."

They trotted towards the front doors of Robinson Court, which stood slightly ajar to receive them, a very unusual circumstance, some sort of gesture in the direction of Janus, god of the new year, whose name Henry now invoked. "The original Mr. Facing-both-ways," he said, leading the way in from the cold.

"Who? Me?"

"Not you, George, Janus, the god of open-and-shut cases. He is traditionally pictured as facing backwards and forwards simultaneously. The doors of the temple of Janus were cast open in time of war, closed at the return of peace." Golmsdorfer gazed anxiously at the front doors of the house, still standing open admitting chill.

"Shut up, Henry, for God's sake. We're not going to war with anybody."

"We're embarking on a long and vigorous campaign, sir," said Henry. "And we may as well admit it from the start." He looked over the press releases searchingly. "God, how disingenuous governments are! I note that the release is timed for late Friday afternoon. They always do this; it's such a child's stratagem. Who do they imagine they're deceiving?"

"Ah, but don't you see, Henry," said his father-in-law, "it makes the Friday-night TV news and the Saturday-morning edition of the *Globe and Mail,* and the opposition can't say a word against it officially until Monday, by which time it's a *fait accompli.*"

"I think it's too smart by half, George. I think it's what's called outsmarting yourselves. It's simply not a clever policy."

"But Henry, when you've read it you'll see. It can't help but be a big winner for us. It's going to be immensely popular across the country."

"I don't see that it does much for Newfoundland nor for Alberta. There are no jobs in the automotive industry in those provinces."

"What's good for the automotive industry is good for Canada," said George, parodying a well-known utterance. "And good — very good — for you and me. I tell you, Henry, we're made for life."

"We were made before this."

"Oh we were not! We were simply rich, but this is different, my lad, this is a totally different plateau. We'll be playing in the biggest league of all. We'll go international."

He paused for a moment, then, struck with inspiration, he made the first recorded use of a neologism of capital importance to contemporary history. "We'll go multinational," said George Robinson. "I've already coined our new name. We're no longer Robinson Pharmaceuticals. We're calling ourselves RobPharm."

Golmsdorfer paid him no mind; instead he browsed through the text of the release, picking out the most tendentious passages and rolling them around in a sinister fashion on his palate and between his pursed lips. He seemed to consider the whole undertaking deeply deceptive:

> The central feature of the plan is a mutually beneficial Agreement between Canada and the United States for the removal of tariffs and other impediments to trade between the two countries in motor vehicles and original equipment parts. This agreement is being signed tomorrow by the Right Honourable L.B. Pearson, Prime Minister of Canada, and L.B. Johnson, President of the United States. . . .

Henry murmured, "I notice that the writer doesn't ascribe any particular degree or kind of honour to L.B. Johnson."

"Doubtless for excellent reasons," said George Robinson.

"I haven't met President Johnson, but I understand that honour isn't in his line."

"Yet a little further," said his companion.

> . . . will seek Congressional authority during the Congressional session which has just commenced to enact duty-free treatment for imports of vehicles and original equipment parts produced in Canada and to make such duty-free treatment retroactive.

"You see?" said George. "I might have written the thing myself."

"Retroactive? When will this agreement become law?"

"That's impossible to say. They'll sign it tomorrow in Johnson City, Texas, if you can imagine. Lester Pearson and Paul Martin in Johnson City, Texas, in mid-January. Hah hah hah! Sooner them than me. Anyway, the president will message Congress about it later in the year, and it should be at the stage of Congressional approval in the fall. But as you so acutely point out, it's retroactive. Now we can move."

"RobPharm," said Golmsdorfer, trying it out, "Rob-Pharm. I like it. It has a poetic ring."

"Damn right. Now look here, Henry, the first thing we've got to do is to perfect our control over all information. Inventory. Finance. Purchasing. Billing. Orders. Accounts receivable. The whole mess, all controlled from in here. I want computers, Henry. I want memory, and I want it miniaturized, so that the whole operation can be kept in our house. There's enough spare room in Robinson Court to house an entire computer centre, so that's what we're going to do, and we'll be the only ones to have access to it, just the two of us. Esther wouldn't understand any of it."

"And your own good wife?"

"A non-starter, Henry. Need I say more?"

Golmsdorfer remembered his own early conversations with Mrs. Robinson, including a famous one in which she had cross-questioned him idly for an hour about Québec provincial affairs, with every appearance of polite interest, then confessed that she knew no word of the French tongue. He recalled very distinctly the glum look of disavowal and rejection that had settled on her daughter Angela's adolescent

visage at that point. Mrs. Robinson might be a non-starter
and so might be her son Gus, or his own wife, Esther, but the
younger girl, Angela, now twenty or thereabouts, seemed
likely to demonstrate qualities of character the reverse of
those shown by mother, sister, or brother. (And where was
Gus now?) Angela's mastery of a somewhat academic spoken
French was already formidable. Nobody could form a just
estimate of what extravagances might follow.

"You wouldn't want Angela mixed up in your computer
centre?"

"Are you mad?"

"No. I'm simply establishing lines of definition. This isn't
the time to get all the way into a memory bank, George.
There isn't yet the volume of information to be processed. In
a year or two, perhaps, especially if we continue with other
acquisitions."

"Stock control for Automotive Lock and Latch?" George
suggested wistfully.

"All that will come in time, I promise you. I think the
music room might be the appropriate setting for the installations."

"Philippa isn't going to like that." Philippa was Mrs.
George Robinson, mother of Gus and Esther and Angela, the
person who had first spoken of Henry Golmsdorfer as "an
elegant bond salesman," a description he had at first deeply
resented. Later, as he grew richer, he came almost to cherish
it. He said, "A computer centre needs heavy underpinnings. If the beams will support a grand piano, a harp and
a small orchestra, they'll certainly take the weight of your
equipment. We'll need special telephone lines, you see,
and auxiliary generators in case of power failures. I think
we'll have to hatch our plans with care. The head office is
supposed to be in Commerce Court, after all."

"A sop to the family, Henry," said George Robinson
airily. "We'll form our true headquarters here in the music
room. Philippa will have nothing to say against it."

"I should hope not, for her own peace of mind."

George Robinson's attention, invariably fluid and hard to
contain, now passed to other matters. He turned to the
scrutiny of other press hand-outs annexed to the historic

event that was to take place the following day in Johnson City, Texas.

"Listen to this," he said in a few moments, getting his tongue with some difficulty around the clotted syntax of Article II, Section (b.)

> The Government of the United States, during the session of the United States Congress commencing on January 4, 1965, shall seek enactment of legislation authorizing duty-free treatment of imports of the products of Canada described in Annex B. In seeking such legislation, the Government of the United States shall also seek authority permitting the implementation of such duty-free treatment retroactively to the earliest date administratively possible following the date upon which the Government of Canada has accorded duty-free treatment. Promptly after the entry into force of such legislation, the Government of the United States shall accord duty-free treatment to the products of Canada described in Annex B.

"Oh how I love that old Annex B," said Golmsdorfer, smiling widely.

"Deep waters, Henry, deep waters."

"That's where the big fish swim," exclaimed the elegant bond salesman.

9

The principal, the publisher, the physician, all recently brought onside by economic developments, the two retailers, Robinson supporters from the beginning (books, menswear), and the two ladies of independent means about whose affiliations there had never been any question — the magnificent seven — sat in a row on a dais at the east end of the mezzanine ballroom, the beautiful Crystal Room, of the Royal Edward Hotel, Stoverville, their faces illuminated, then shadowed, then creased with streaks of changing colour as a lad from the high school rotated filters over a baby spot on the balcony at the other end of the ballroom. Many other lights flashed on and off, and an enormous bulletin board glittered and radiated colour from its enamelled surface, upon which a large-scale rendering of the Pearson flag shone and gave off bright reflections. Three red maple leaves on a white ground in the centre of the design, two broad bands of genial blue to either side, a pleasing composition, perhaps more pleasing aesthetically than the simpler layout officially adopted two weeks afterwards and eventually globally familiar as a patch on the hip-pockets of travellers' jeans. The Pearson proposal, not perhaps the most tactful emblem of Liberal aspiration that one could have chosen at a nominating convention early in 1965, was nevertheless tasteful, well-composed, accurately symbolic, memorable, also and most important the fruit of the labours of a Stoverville native, hence highly acceptable to paid-up voting members of the Stoverville/Smith's Falls Liberal Party Riding Association as a banner under which they might join hands and face the future of Canadian society with high hearts and keen hopes. There were decorations composed of crèpe-paper reproduc-

tions of Mr. Pearson's proposed flag hanging in the deep well
of the ceiling, criss-crossing under the fancy plaster mould-
ings of cupidons and Venuses, dolphins and Tritons. This
ceiling, for a long time the most gorgeous interior design in
any public room in Stoverville, showed to magnificent effect
above and behind the birthday-cake colours of the pendant
streamers, which slowly turned over and over and presented
first one side, then another, of their interwoven surfaces, to
the lifted eyes of the milling gang on the polished floor.
There was a sound system with several clusters of loud-
speakers in energetic operation:

> Up, up, and awayayayay
> In my beautiful, my beautiful balloon.

People struggled through knots of would-be dancers,
picking out friends and associates or political enemies,
always spoken of or characterized mentally as hatchet men, or
less injuriously as henchmen. The room was full of henchmen; hatchet men were less in evidence. Perhaps most of
them were hanging around George Robinson's campaign
headquarters and hospitality rooms, a fifth-floor corner suite,
the largest in the building, to which all doors stood widely
open tonight, in a Janus-minded gesture towards departure
on new campaigns. Nobody meant the open doors as an
obliquely poetic suggestion of the strict parallel between
electoral and military campaigns, but the metaphor was
available for the reflective. Strategy, tactics, choice of terrain,
troops, commanders, non-commissioned officers, logistics
and supply, all elements of both political and military
manoeuvre. This may be why retired general officers like
Grant, MacArthur, Eisenhower, de Gaulle, or serving
campaigners such as McClelland or the first Napoléon, so
often feel impelled to draw the implications of the parallel. If
political action so closely resembles military action, they
reason, why shouldn't they have a crack at it? The reverse
process is fortunately less often acted out. Few political
agents, in the English-speaking countries at any rate, have
been ready to transform themselves into naval or military
captains. Hardly an instance suggests itself. George Robinson

never fancied himself as a great field commander. His vision of himself as a leader was neither political nor military, but that of a qualified third kind of leader, what used to be called (without anybody laughing) in the nineteen-twenties a captain of industry, a substantive to which nobody's imagination ever rose after the year 1945, unless that of Robinson himself.

Now, while they waited for the results of the vote to be announced, the members of the riding association strove to envisage this high destiny for their candidate, captain of industry, captain of politics. They were unable to sustain the flight. They could imagine Mr. Robinson as their local member, proprietor of the largest manufacturing concern in the city, master of Robinson Court with a retiring wife, a clergyman (can you beat it?) for a son, and two dozy daughters, somebody who satisfied their conceptions of themselves in being the rich man whom they met along King William Street and addressed by name. They would give their voices to familiarity. A young man and a young woman had also sought the nomination. Either of them — particularly the young woman — would have made a more energetic and able Parliamentarian than George, who never raised his voice in the House, or very seldom, and then on matters of the most humdrum kind, tariffs, duties, excise. But these alternatives, one from Smith's Falls, one from Athens, lacked that old-shoe quality that George Robinson possessed in excess. A surprising thing about the old standard-bearer was his striking and instantly identifiable image on television. Nobody in the world looked like him but him, and he looked like some man whom you might have seen from time to time in a television series, cast as uncle to a widower with three young kids, or as protector of a blonde young woman much in need of protection, a Bill Demarest type, alternatively an ageing Louis Calhern. He seemed real in photographs and on the TV screen, at least as real as in real life, sometimes more.

Now if anybody had told the young man or young woman who had contested the nomination that George Robinson looked and performed better on TV than they did, they

would have hooted with self-assured mirth at the assertion.
Born in 1902, he seemed immeasurably ancient to them,
ready to be turned out to graze.

"That old buffer? He doesn't know enough to clip his nose
hairs."

Anne Woolsey, the young woman lawyer from Athens,
never said this out loud about her opponent; she had far too
much good sense ever to make public an unkind judgement
of taste such as this. But she thought it privately and was now
and then on the point of saying it to her counsellors. Hugh
Harness, the other candidate for the nomination, a law
partner of the sitting Conservative member, Phil Horsbaugh,
formed no judgements of this kind, or if he did nothing is
known about them. He just went ahead and entered the race,
thinking that an attempt to undercut and undermine his law
partner would prove palatable to the riding's Liberals. After
all, such cases are frequent, even regular, in Canadian
politics, where sometimes all three members of a law partner-
ship such as Lang, Michener and Jolliffe, of Toronto, may
lead long public lives as exponents of the doctrines of three
different parties. Say what you like, there is an element of
betrayal, or at least failure of confidence and trust among
partners, where such arrangements are acceptable. When
Hugh Harness asked the Liberals of the riding to choose him
as their leader, he was in effect proclaiming that nobody cares
about ideology in eastern Ontario, that party differences are
trivial, that he just wanted a shot at a job, the same as Phil
Horsbaugh, and why should he not have his chance? Anne
Woolsey and Hugh Harness entered the lists cheerfully and
confidently against Uncle George, figuring, each in his or her
way, that the old buffer-bugger was long past his climacteric,
that it was time he was left at grass. In this they were mistaken, and they found it out long before that agreeable
evening riot of sensation in the beautiful Crystal Room of the
Royal Edward, the nomination meeting of late April. Almost
as soon as they announced for the nomination, each young
candidate made approaches to the members of the nominating committee, discovering at once that four of them had
made up their minds already, though they wouldn't say so,
nor would they give any indication of their preference —

though this made it clear that their preference was for Robinson.

"What are those two old hens doing on the committee?" demanded Anne Woolsey of her friends and backers, speaking of the two widow ladies who lived on their rents and admired George Robinson's figure. "How do they manage to perpetuate themselves in place?"

"Well Anne, you see, they've always given money and stuffed envelopes and canvassed. I think they do it for fun."

Anne knew that neither of these ladies would consider for a moment giving her voice to a young woman, which meant that she had to secure four votes out of five to swing the committee behind her. The committee did not exactly determine the election. Paid-up participating members of the association all voted. But they voted pretty much the way the nominating committee urged them to vote, as historical precedent amply showed. A decade later, Anne Woolsey might have used the tactic often deployed in the nineteen-seventies and eighties of flooding the membership list with new people committed to her support. But this stratagem was not acceptable in Stoverville/Smith's Falls in 1965, and therefore Anne Woolsey and Hugh Harness failed to find support among the members of the nominating committee and the association at large, and their names disappear from the pages of history, even as footnotes.

Long after, Anne Woolsey was to find immense satisfaction and even joy in the pursuit of community social service in the Athens neighbourhood, but she never got elected to anything. Harness moved to Belleville, and that is the last anybody heard of him.

Now at last the votes had been counted, the spoiled ballots identified, the count verified and rechecked, and checked again under the watchful eyes of supporters of two of the candidates. George Robinson had not supplied a scrutineer on his own behalf, for some private reason. At ten twenty-five the results were brought to the dais and the chairman of the committee begged through the microphone for everybody's attention.

"I have the results of the balloting here, ladies and gentle-men, if I can have your attention please . . . please! Your

attention please! I've got the results right here, folks. Could
somebody turn the Victrola off, please, there'll be lots of time
for music after. All right everybody, here are the results. Of
five hundred and twenty-eight registered voting members of
the association, that's *five* hundred and twenty-eight, almost
five hundred were present and cast their ballots. I think we
can congratulate ourselves on such a turn-out. There were
four hundred and eighty-three votes cast, and of these sixteen
were spoiled in some way or other. Sixteen."

"What was wrong with them?" came a loud voice from the
back of the crowd. Cheers, whistles, boos, and another voice
grumbling, "They were all Harness votes." Cries of, "No,
no!"

"Some were torn, some were defaced, on some the marks
were not clear. The scrutineers have agreed to reject all
sixteen."

"Get on with it!" "Let's have the results!"

"And of the four hundred and sixty-seven correct votes
cast, the tally is as follows: Harness, Smith's Falls, thirty-
nine."

Groans, boos, dissent, a good deal of laughter.

"Woolsey, Athens —" a protracted silence while the
committee chairman shuffled loose papers in his hands,
which shook visibly. "Woolsey, Athens, one hundred . . ."
Shouts and cheers from the audience, which could do simple
arithmetic perfectly well.

". . . one hundred and eleven votes."

"We want George. We want George. We want George.
Rob-in-son. Rob-in-son. He's the one. He's the one. Rob-in-
son. He's the one."

"Robinson, Stoverville. THREE HUNDRED AND
SEVENTEEN. And the winner is . . . GEORGE ROBIN-
SON, ladies and gentlemen, GEORGE ROBINSON. Where
is he? George? George? Come on out here, George. Would
somebody look and see if he's behind the curtain? Come on
up here, Anne, come on up, Hughie. Where's the man from
the *Intelligencer?* Somebody get George!"

They had to fetch him from his suite upstairs, and when he
finally came onto the dais he was greeted just as if he had
never won the nomination before. George Robinson em-

braced his vanquished rivals, kissed Anne Woolsey on both
cheeks, a gesture she would have rebuffed ungraciously
under all circumstances but these. He shook Hugh Harness
by both hands, muttered something about closing ranks and
facing the future together, then seized the microphone and
didn't relinquish it for almost an hour. He told his hearers so
much more about the Automotive Production Trade
Agreement than they cared to know that he damn near
emptied the hall. ". . . our opponents wish to God they'd
introduced it, that's all I can say," he bellowed. "Let me tell
you, my friends and loyal supporters, they're going to wish
they'd never heard of the APTA. The Conservative party has
been for protectionism since day one of Canadian history.
They're for high prices and short production runs, but the
day is long past when the Canadian consumer is content to
pay thirty per cent more for his car."

Cheers. "You bet your boots." "Go get 'em, George."
Applause.

10

Three or four of the photographs were pretty awful, and two were eye-openers, smashing though in certain respects hard to read, vast areas of creamy flesh tones appearing in places where they could not ordinarily be expected to be, just below the middle of the frame.

"I'll say this for your brother," said Edie, suppressing a surge of nervous hilarity, "he's one lousy photographer."

"Mmmmmn. Mmmmmmnnnn. Hell of a subject though."

The coloured snapshots had tumbled out of the envelope as soon as I'd opened it, and the eccentricity of the photographic technique they demonstrated had led me to study them closely without bothering to see what else might be enclosed. The pictures were distracting, if you see what I mean. There were six, four of them full of sun-dogs and flashing criss-crossed beams of light. God knows what Tony thought he was doing when he took them. He must have been shooting straight into the sun. This made me think of the implied symbolism of such an action, aiming the eye of the camera into the unbearable flood. I considered this wording of the act for some moments, then rejected it as pompous, even for me. "The unbearable flood." It sounded like an academic work on structuralism, or some other such nauseous bolus. Tony wouldn't have been so wholly without humour as to imagine anything in those terms, but the banality of the words forced certain notions on you, once you'd thought of them. A poor poem in a small literary magazine:

> I turned the camera eye against
> the unbearable flood; blind,

staring, the small black box
with the sun inside
silvering out the nitrates into
likenesses of dark

I shook my head to clear it of these nasty fantasies and spread the snapshots fanwise on the table in front of me. Six. I handed Edie the two that pictured comprehensible images, and took a long hard look at the remaining four failures, wondering why Tony had bothered to include them in this mailing. Did they conceal some sort of secret, some erotic cue that I ought to be able to echo? What I saw in them was this: streaked rays of sunlight, a more or less round spot in the upper part of the frame, the sun; an unusual black and purple blob, not very big, in the middle of the pictures, and below some of the creamy tone. I knew what it was of course, from my examination of the successful pictures. Thigh. Turning lower down into leg. There was a lot of green colour around the edges of the frames. I had a desperate feeling that if I looked at these bad shots from some particular distance I would spot something that I couldn't see now. Could I perhaps be holding them upside down? Or could they have been taken very far away from something or very close to something? I moved the little rectangles close to my eyes and squinted, then held them at arm's length and closed first one eye and then the other. When I held them away from me and closed my good eye, the right one, I saw all at once that the pictures had something of the quality of a very good post-Impressionist canvas, perhaps a Vuillard. Then all at once I found the right distance and focus. They were simply pictures of a very young woman seen from about thirty feet, dancing or otherwise frolicking behind shrubs or bushes, apparently in some public park. They were "art" shots. This seemed pretentious and unlike my brother and I thought that some strange sickness must have overtaken him. This wasn't the Big T of my childhood.

"He's in love with her," said Edie drily, when I passed the bad shots over to her. This seemed a hasty judgement. "You know who this is, don't you?" she said, turning the full refulgence of her wifely gaze upon me. "This is Linnet

Olcott, that's who." She spoke with more of *amertume* than I could have predicted. I didn't know why the pictures moved her so; she passed the good ones back to me and I looked at them and my perplexity was in part resolved. What a girl!

"So *that's* Linnet Olcott," I said. In mid-1965 she was still an unknown in North America; none of her few films had penetrated the North American distribution system, and the British comedy programs made for extended run on television had not yet become the staple fare of the public broadcasting system. By this time everybody was familiar with the face and form of Sadie MacNamara, now an enormous international star. *Out by Midnight* had completed a season and a half on the network; most of the past season it had been the top show in the ratings. Sadie's Eton crop and gamine expression and her character of Bubbles McCoy were caviare to the general that year; we were up to our necks in reruns of *Out by Midnight.* But of its source program, the original English version, *Bed Sitters,* nobody on the North American side of the Atlantic knew anything. Linnet was therefore an unknown except as an occasional reference in Tony's letters. A stage actress, he would state approvingly, sometimes even a *writer.* She had helped him a great deal with *Cross Now,* and was fully entitled to a credit on the screen version. She was supernally intelligent and very lovely, but Sadie MacNamara she wasn't and would never be.

"There's a letter in the envelope," Edie pointed out, "are you going to sit around slavering over those skin shots or are you going to read it?"

"Slavering" seemed hard. I put the two sexy pictures down on the Codringtons' kitchen table and extracted the letter, a one-page screed, concise, even writerly.

> Windmill Street,
> Ascension Thursday, 1965.

> Dear Edie and Matt: a good day for a letter from a writer who imagines he's rising in the world — I suppose the danger of rising is rising too far, right out of the upper atmosphere. I wonder how far up Jesus went. Out of sight? After all, if you ascend in the body, there's a point where you begin to feel the

cold. It gets hard to breathe. Jesus was probably wearing the costume suitable for the spring weather of the Near East — certainly not a space suit. How far did He rise before changing His state, disappearing beyond the natural world? It's a nice question for the hard-boiled fundamentalist. I only mention it because I have a sense of getting up in the world.

How are the kids? How's my huge enormous nephew and namesake? Did he get the lead soldiers? Have I mentioned before that there's this terrific toy museum about two blocks from where I live? You've probably seen it in the movies or on TV. It was used as a set in a recent seg of "The Avengers." If you ever see the episode announced on TV, you ought to let Anthony Earl sit up late to watch it; you could tell him that's where all the toys come from. I've been getting things there for years. The subject of these photographs — of whom more in a moment — used to live upstairs over Pollock's Toy Museum, which is how I came to spend so much time there. You really ought to see it sometime. When are the two of you going to get over here, for God's sake? My friend of the snapshots — all right, Linnet Olcott and I — are working on a *Bed Sitters* script which takes place in Pollock's Toy Museum to great effect. Charmian and Ronnie go there to buy a rubber ducky for his nephew, but the rubber duck is so cute that Ronnie can't bear to part with it so he buys another and then another, and by the time we're seven minutes into the half-hour he's loaded down with so many rubber duckies that the two of them can't manage the weight. Visual possibilities there! So do you know who I'm talking about, Ronnie and Charmian, or maybe you haven't seen any of *Bed Sitters* yet? Probably only seen *Out by Midnight*. Sometimes Linnet looks a little pensive when she thinks about Sadie, but I tell her she can't really complain. *Bed Sitters* is into its fifth season, that's unheard-of over here, and Linnet is still only twenty-two or three. They're preparing the first shows for the 1965/66 season now. Linnet and Ronnie are the main characters now, and have been for years. I write a couple of scripts each season for them because of Linnet. We're both very keen on the toy-shop script, the place looks utterly marvellous in any kind of controlled lighting.

I'm sending on a few pictures to establish the Olcott connection, and no, Matt, I didn't make a mistake with the camera. The four that you can't make out are *supposed* to look like that. The two recognizable ones are for identification merely. They were taken in Lincoln's Inn Fields on an absolutely gorgeous afternoon. The building visible across the street behind Linnet is Sir John Soane's Museum, another weird-looking potential set for a TV show. Come over and see us soon and bring the niece and the nephews. Meanwhile, hang by your thumbs.

The signature was Tony's customary indecipherable squiggle.

"What's he talking about? 'Hang by your thumbs.'"

Edie had her eyes fastened on the pictures. She said, "I don't believe that woman is wearing anything below the waist."

I took them away from her. Linnet was shown seated on a park bench just at the edge of some grass. There was a roadway behind her, and across the road some terraced houses with broad front staircases. She was comfortably seated, almost lounging, and she was smiling widely with her head thrown back. Her throat was exquisite, creamy. She was very slender. And she really didn't seem to have very many clothes on. I studied the two pictures. As far as I could make out, she was wearing something like very very very short shorts, or the kind of skirt that a figure-skater wears over her tights. It was about the dimensions of a medium-sized Band-Aid.

"What kind of skirt is that?" I said to myself, half aloud.

Edie snorted scornfully. "It's the tiniest little itty-bitty-baby-girl skirt. That's a look I could fancy for myself."

"What would you wear underneath?"

"Dirty thing!"

"No, seriously."

"Certainly not panties, for they would show. I expect you might get away with some sort of tights in a sheer stretch fabric, like a kind of pantie and stocking knit together into one."

"Invent them, Edie, and you'll make us rich."

"I've got better things to do than that," she said with a grimace. "Why don't you put your mind to it? Panties are rather your thing, aren't they?"

11

On the same day that we got this enigmatic letter from Tony,
we got another communication, by telephone, which caused
us plenty of trouble. It was the last day of May and on this
date probate of the estate of the late May-Beth Codrington,
née Sleaford, relict of Earl Codrington, was finally completed. The sense of her will was clear and unchallenged.
Everything went to Edie, the house, the paintings, the family
property and business, full ownership of *Codrington Hard-
ware and Builders Supplies, Since 1867.* The retail business
had had to be carried on as a going concern while the estate
was in probate; there had never been any question of selling
it. It was Edie's, and we both wanted it to remain Edie's
property until such time as decisions had to be made about
passing it on to Anthony, Andrea, and John. All that was
plain enough, but it is not at all easy to administer the affairs
of a large and flourishing and expanding wholesale/retail
business when the authority at the top remains indefinite
because of a question of inheritance. We were very lucky to
have a man like Morley Cunningham to handle the administration and the continuing expansion program while the
property was passing through probate.

But administration and control of the family business were
minor matters compared to the difficulties of determining the
value and ownership of Mrs. Codrington's artistic legacy, her
dozen great paintings. I'd been spending far more of my own
time than I could afford in helping Mr. Fitzsimmons develop
an accurate legal account of the pictures for estate purposes.
This was not an arduous or demanding or almost impossible
undertaking. The courts, and the legal agents employed in
the settlement, and the funding bodies who helped to get the

Codrington Colony off the ground, and the art critics and evaluators and editors and committee members who cheerfully and freely offered their counsel about how this artistic legacy should be manned and mounted, were invariably immensely co-operative, helpful, interested, concerned to find the proper solution to our difficulties. It was considered unthinkable, by all concerned, that the pictures should be allowed to travel, that they should *at any time* be allowed outside the country, or that they should be sold. They might be disposed of by the legitimate owner to her heirs, but ought not to be made the object of a simple sale designed to render liquid a capital gain. There was a heap of stuff like that involved in settling the estate. I spent almost all my time on it, when I wasn't running back and forth to Montréal house-hunting. By the time probate was accomplished, I was starting to feel like I'd been hired permanently by the Codrington estate as some kind of infra-legal functionary. And I had no genuine authority in the whole affair. I was my wife's spouse and adviser, but I had no specific personal right or interest in the estate, though our children did and do. No. It was not easy.

But at least by the end of May 1965 matters were clarified by the settlement of all outstanding claims against the estate, all estate taxes, all the legal costs of administration to that date. We knew definitively, on that date, that Edie had all rights in the estate and the pictures. We knew what we could do and what we were responsible for, in preparing the pictures for public display. Edie had the last word in everything, and I had a purely consultative capacity. And all this time we had a lot of money coming in from the business, which is never matter for complaint. This was money that I managed, by and large. I'll say this for Edie, at no time in her life was she ever mean or penny-pinching. May-Beth and Edie arranged a regular allowance for me, a large one. I might not have been seen to be in the most dignified circumstances in the world. There have not been wanting unkind people to say things like, "Lucky old Matt Goderich, living on his wife's money." There are always people like that, ready to throw the first stone, and the second and third too. But given my position, I have no complaints. My income from the Codrington estate allowed me to do work, to write, and to accept various consultancies in my field that I would never otherwise have been able to do. I think the great Canadian public has had its full value out of me, for monies received.

When May-Beth died, and the project for the organization of the Codrington Colony for the Encouragement of Visionary Art was put on foot, it seemed natural to most observers that I should be appointed as project manager. That is where my salary came from for many years, and a very handsome salary it was, and let me tell you, I earned every cent. I supervised the design and reconstruction of the upper rooms in the Codrington house. I saw to it that the paintings were properly mounted and displayed. I nursemaided those paintings in a way that nobody else could possibly have done. It was to me, for example, that May-Beth first stated, "I want none of my pictures to leave this house." I was the witness.

When once you'd seen all twelve of them it was clear why she made this decision. They form a set like no other set of paintings that I know of, anywhere. Anywhere! Right from the wide view of Stoverville in *The Stoverville Annual Regatta*, through the twin portraits of Mayor Lawson robed as Herod and of Philip Horsbaugh, MP, presented as Judas "with spilled salt and traditional moneybag," to the extraordinary final triptych. Certainly those works cannot be separated, and I would never have allowed it, even if May-Beth hadn't given me specific instructions. I don't think that it's too much to claim that the preservation and conservation together of those twelve works has been the one great task of my life, at least until the present moment. Some new undertaking may lie before me, shrouded in futurity, but if it does, it hasn't yet revealed itself. I live in hopes. Back in 1965, in the uncomfortable position of Edie's consort, situated too in the office of project manager for the Codrington Colony, I often found myself walking a pace or two behind Edie with my hands clasped behind my coat-tails, much in the position of Prince Philip — and I do not mean Prince Philip Horsbaugh. I mean the real and original Prince Philip, the one who married the Queen. I think Prince Philip has managed to preserve a certain standard of dignity, and God knows I've tried to do likewise.

Once it got to be public knowledge that the whole Cod-rington estate after probate lay in Edie's possession, we started to get all kinds of solicitations on behalf of one or another public work. There were veiled invitations from all three political parties at the federal level. I even received a feeler from the local NDP association — consisting of eight people — wondering whether I might be interested in trying to join my father in the House. Yet *another* election was already on its way. My poor father was certainly going to find himself obliged to contest East Gwillimbury at least one more time, his seventh candidacy. He first ran successfully in a by-election in 1952, took the seat again in the Liberal victory of 1953, retained it through three Conservative triumphs in 1957, 1958, and 1962, won it again when the Liberals took office in 1963, and now looked able to retain his seat almost indefinitely. No serious candidate had ever emerged in East Gwillimbury to challenge my father's incumbency. It was the safest NDP seat known to man. But for anybody to suggest that I run for the NDP in Stoverville/Smith's Falls was lunacy.

I've always rather wondered whether rumours of a possible Goderich candidacy in Stoverville/Smith's Falls might have been the real reason George Robinson suddenly began to show such marked interest in Edie and me, and our children and family affairs, in the summer of 1965. The reason he gave for getting in touch with us in late June was so peculiar and extravagant that it didn't adequately explain his interest. I had known for more than a decade that he considered my father a dangerous man, but I'd invariably taken his declarations on the subject to be somehow ineffably comic, not really meant, not to be taken as effective in the practical arena of human interaction.

"A profoundly disturbing, alarming, manifestation of History's Will to REVOLUTION!"

The first time my father told me that George Robinson had said that about him, in open debate in the House, I laughed heartily and said that Robinson must have been reading some popular analysis of Marxian thought, which he had been unable to understand. George Robinson couldn't possibly have had any views on history, and history's will to

revolution. No Canadian politician of any party affiliation
ever held notions of that stripe, not even the most sincere
CCFer or NDPer. Politicians in Canada don't make use of such
terms; they prefer to talk about the tariff, language legislation, whose ox is being gored, the Crow Rate. In their hearts,
the leaders of the New Democratic Party do not entertain
philosophical speculations about whether history is the
Name of God working Himself out in time. They do not
conceptualize history as the incarnation of the absolute, nor
do they raise the question of the immanence of the dialectic.
What they like to think about is escaping third-party status,
or whether they'll ever get to form a national government.

When George Robinson telephoned us one sultry evening
in early summer and invited himself over to our place to
discuss the Horsbaugh portrait and its place in the forthcoming election campaign, we were thunderstruck. We knew
that May-Beth had shown him the picture just before she
died, and a hell of a picture it was. I can understand that
Robinson must have calculated perfectly legitimately that
May-Beth meant the picture, at least in part, as a commentary
on Horsbaugh's political morality. Earl Codrington had
never felt it proper to identify himself explicitly as a Liberal,
during his various terms of office as mayor of Stoverville, but
most observers in the region wrote him down readily enough
as a friend of George's and at the least a closet Liberal. What
I remember about Earl's politics was his statement to me that
no CCFer would ever be elected to the post of dog catcher in
Stoverville, let alone Member of Parliament. In that he was
one-hundred-per-cent right. I miss Earl. He was a nice nice
man.

Anyway George Robinson figured, I guess, that the long-
term friendship, plus the fact that the Judas portrait would
undeniably make marvellous political propaganda, and
furthermore that May-Beth had invited him into her home to
look at it — an unheard-of occurrence — gave him some sort
of proprietary right to make use of the work in his political
adventures. Naturally we wouldn't permit this. We couldn't
select one of the twelve pictures, divorce it from context, and
allow it to be reproduced as an attack on a sitting member of
the House. Unthinkable! An unforgivable proposal. What

can he have been thinking? And, do you know, he wouldn't accept a discreet refusal on the telephone? He came right over to the house and made a terrible stink about it. Well, I mean, I ask you!

12

If from the public way you turn your steps, taking the
Markham Road, Highway 48, north from the expressway,
you find yourself surrounded, as you draw away from the
urban sprawl, through Markham and up the back highway
towards Sutton, by the signs and artifacts of an earlier
civilization, the old Ontario of the last century; you are
approaching East Gwillimbury. About thirty miles north of
the city you come to a turn-off to the right announced by
faded and half-indecipherable billboards and clusters of
finger signs, tin Orange Crush advertisements screwed to
barns and garages, cylindrical open-ended orange reposi-
tories for *Globe and Mail* delivery. You are entering the first
ring of cottage country, for along the road to the right lies
Musselman Lake, smallest and nearest to the city of the
central Ontario summer resorts. As you approach, the odours
and the atmospheric effects of the nineteen-twenties and early
nineteen-thirties become almost overpowering, the tiny
rickety cottages crowded together in little groves, the worn
grass, the absurd lake, a stone's throw across, and then the
dance hall where, in your tender youth, you came from the
city in a carful of kids hugging to themselves their first cases
of beer, mickeys of rye, girls, on some forgotten Friday night
in 1937 or 1946.

Jump forward now to a soft October night in 1965 and
admire the glow of twilight illuminating the leaf-green-
painted wooden building that stands on low piers consisting
of three cement blocks each. The dance hall possesses no
cellar, and scanty underpinnings, and in the days of its youth
the floor used to sag ever so slightly when a halfways decent
band played its stock arrangements with some real musician-

ship, setting the children's feet to sliding and tapping on the smooth boards. Inside the hall one finds checkrooms, toilets, the refreshment booth, lines of folding chairs laid out in sufficient numbers to accommodate an eager and responsive crowd of voters, friends of Andrew Goderich, come here tonight to listen to an election address.

Though it is the first week in October, in fact the Friday night of Thanksgiving weekend with a holiday Monday impending, an auspicious date for an election appeal, the night is warm even as the twilight glow dies, the moon rises, the crowd comes into the hall. It is a peaceable prosperous crowd, no gaggle of dissidents and complainers, at the same time not exactly the sort of crowd you'd expect to assemble to hear an NDP speaker a scant thirty-five miles from the intersection of King and Yonge. For the peculiar thing about Andrew Goderich's riding is that despite its closeness to the city it remains fundamentally a farm constituency, no town of appreciable size being enclosed within its borders. The nearest towns are Aurora, Newmarket, Sutton to the north, and Markham down the road. The latter centre has of course been swallowed by suburbia, and North Yonge Street, a few miles westwards, has made of Aurora and Newmarket mere fringe bedroom towns. For various reasons, however, the very small villages on either side of Highway 48 have been left alone by the passage of time and the thrust of metropolitan development. Such a community as this, one supposes, might time and again return to Parliament some central Ontarian simulacrum of Leslie Frost of Lindsay (about fifty miles away at the other end of Lake Scugog), but strangely enough East Gwillimbury, rural and retired as it is, nevertheless remains the safest NDP seat in the federal House, the seat held by one of Canada's two Nobel Peace Prize winners, a man now invariably referred to in his party's propaganda as "the conscience of Canada." It is a phrase that Andrew Goderich has learned to detest. He didn't coin it, never sought to have it applied to himself, insisted that nobody speaking on his behalf ever employ it. "Imagine being in bed with the conscience of Canada," said Andrew Goderich one night.

Yet here came the disagreeable sobriquet one more time, in the mouth of the local man on the platform who is intro-

ducing tonight's speaker, as the last of the twilight disappears
in the west and the smooth darkness of early autumn sur-
rounds the brightly lit interior. On the bandstand at the lakeside end of the building are a table, a row of four hard maple
office chairs, a lectern with a microphone mounted on it, and
the apparatus of an excellent PA system. At Andrew Goderich's electoral meetings there is never any of the low comedy
associated with more amateurish goings-on of this sort. The
PA system works perfectly. Mr. Goderich himself never uses
it.

On this night the voice of the local man, a union official
who works in Oshawa and lives just north of Stouffville,
comes across in the hall as clear and well reproduced as if the
speaker stood beside his hearers and spoke to each of them in
a lowered and confidential tone. This quietness is the
recurring characteristic of any Goderich campaign. No
shouting, no hysteria, no promises, no bad-mouthing the
other candidates. Quiet peaceable straight talk.

There wouldn't be much point to bad-mouthing the other
candidates anyway, because by now neither the Liberals nor
the Conservatives bother to run a serious contender against
him. Their nominations go as a rule to young women who
are being dubiously rewarded for their hard slogging as party
workers at the lowest level, or to young men who may
perhaps in a later election contest another seat seriously, but
who are paying their dues to the party by this early hopeless
gallop, a species of early-morning workout to see if the colt
can go a distance.

"The conscience of Canada, folks," declares the union
official, "I don't need to tell you any more than that. You all
know him. You've all seen him on television more times than
you could count. Whenever there's a tough question or a
hard decision before the Canadian people, everybody knows
where to go for the answer, and here he is, your Member of
Parliament for East Gwillimbury, my very good friend Mr.
Andrew Goderich. Come on up here and take a bow, Andy."

The candidate, who had been standing at the refreshment
counter eating a really good, warm-in-the-hands, grilled
frankfurter, loaded with trimmings, now advanced down the
centre aisle of the hall, pausing once or twice to chew on the

last of his snack. He bit and swallowed casually, and waved a hand to this or that friend in the throng.

"Watch out," he said to an elderly woman sitting in an aisle seat. "I'll get relish all over you." A blob of mixed red and green fell on the lady's skirt. "Now look what I've done," said Andrew. He knelt beside the lady and took a handkerchief out of his pocket. "Let me get that for you." People in the crowd turned around and craned their necks.

"Would somebody get me a paper towel from the kitchen? Put some water on it, would you?" said Andrew. Several moments passed while the blob on the skirt was erased, the material wetted and rubbed clean.

"It's Mrs. Greenham from Cedar Valley, isn't it? How are you, Eleanor?" said Andrew. "And how's Deac? Have you brought him with you tonight? I don't see him."

"He's sitting on the platform with you, Andy," said Mrs. Greenham with a good deal of quiet pleasure.

"I thought that was him," said Andrew, rising to his feet. "If you can't get that stain out, be sure you send me a bill for the dry-cleaners or for a new skirt."

"Oh, go on," said Mrs. Greenham, "I never."

Andrew smiled at her warmly, then turned and mounted the bandstand, shaking hands with his organizers, the head of the riding association, the union official from Oshawa/Stouffville, and including in the group with his characteristic cordiality a columnist from the *Globe and Mail* who had made a practice of attending the Goderich meetings, perhaps to try to find out what the magic potion was. It was all done so unobtrusively, the chat with the woman in the audience, the easy conversational manner. Dropping a blob of relish on somebody's skirt, thought the columnist — a fearfully clever woman — that's a stroke of political genius. Nobody else in Canadian politics would risk such a gesture. Could it have been planted? Could it have been staged? She listened as Andrew moved into his address to the crowd with his customary low-key shift from chit-chat into serious and complex analysis.

He walked right to the edge of the platform and stood there, teetering slightly, facing the sizeable crowd, choosing to get out from behind the lectern and the microphone to a point where everybody could see him top to toe. And he could pitch his voice in such a way that no matter what the size of the hall — barring Maple Leaf Gardens — he could be heard in the farthest reaches of the balcony without any appearance of strain. This was a great gift, a remarkable asset for any political campaigner, one of the elements of Mr. Goderich's political persona that had been instrumental in gaining six successive victories for him, and would bring more.

"I've been thinking a lot about the Automotive Production Trade Agreement," he said to the electors of East Gwillimbury, "because I know that more and more of you have jobs linked to the auto industry, either in new-car production or in the parts business. And those of you who don't have anything to do with manufacturing cars will probably buy a new or used car sometime in the next two to three years. Or else you'll be looking for a rebuilt engine of original-equipment quality, or some other replacement part, a transmission or a differential. Everybody in Canada has an immediate interest in the automotive business because we're about the most car-oriented people in the world. We have to depend upon our personal transportation, especially in winter, as much or more than any people in the world. And we all know that we routinely pay twenty per cent more for automotive products than they do south of the border. If you buy a Canadian-built Pontiac — you all know this — and take it into the States for a vacation trip to Florida or the southwest, say, and you pull into a Pontiac dealership to have some minor service done, what's the first thing he's going to say to you?"

A voice from the audience: "He's going to tell you to take it down the street to the Chevy dealer." Applause, cries of "Hear, hear."

"Quite right," said Andrew, "or else he'll say, 'I see you've got one of them Canadian Pontiacs.' And then he'll have a good laugh over it. Now I'm not attacking Oshawa, and why? Because there are jobs in Oshawa, as you all know, an awful lot of jobs, which we're going to have to work very hard to protect over the next few years, because the APTA isn't primarily designed with the interests of the workers or the small consumer in mind, is it? We all realize that. Do you know who's going to benefit from the integration of the Canadian and American auto industries? Sure you do, and so do I. The large corporations will benefit, and control of the industry will be more and more gathered together into their hands, and that means the hands of a small number of US citizens, not Canadians. Who else will benefit? Parts manufacturers with low-labour-intensive plants, who can supply the whole integrated market without tariff barriers, making one or two small components and supplying the whole industry. Do you remember the old-time Eaton's catalogues, say from around 1920? Beside one item after another, bicycles, stoves, baseball gloves, it used to say 'Made in Canada.' It doesn't say that any more, does it?"

Voices from the floor: "Damn right!" "You can't buy a Canadian stove." "What about McClary?" "Well, maybe McClary." "How come the Swedes make their own cars?"

Andrew waited for silence. "I can hear what you're asking. I know all about these things, the same as you. The large appliance industry is completely Americanized. GE. Westinghouse. RCA. Nobody in Canada makes television sets. We can assemble them, all right, and the government can proclaim that it insists on 'Canadian value-added' elements in final assembly. But there's no Canadian automobile manufacturer like Volvo or Saab or Volkswagen, no Canadian stove and fridge manufacturer like GE or Westinghouse. And don't you ever think that there aren't monopolistic practices in those industries, because there are, and the consumer is always the victim. I don't want to cry wolf; you know that I've never been an alarmist, but I don't think anybody in Ottawa, and certainly not in the government, has the faintest idea what the structure of the international automotive industry really is. For one thing, it's enormous. For another, it doesn't just include the US and Canada, it takes in Volkswagen from West Germany and Volvo from Sweden, and I don't know whether you ever think about them, but there's a certain highly industrious people on the other side of the Pacific Rim who know just about as much about industrial research and development as our American cousins, and if they ever take it into their heads to move into the North American auto market, then the Automotive Production Trade Agreement won't protect your jobs from anybody, and the Canadian automobile market will be rocked by turbulence that none of us can begin to imagine. Nobody knows where the auto industry is headed. I don't know, and neither does Bud Drury. The difference between us is that I'm trying to find out."

The woman from the *Globe and Mail* devoted her column to this meeting in the Saturday edition. Her version of Andrew's views excited highly critical attention in Ottawa, even in Stoverville.

13

There was a certain red-brick dwelling on Lewis Street, a scant quarter of an hour from the House, where people used to meet and watch television together and make little wagers on political futures. Ottawa is a city in which the newspapers devote page two to which civil servant will seek which posted vacancy. Government is the major local industry, the largest employer in town, the big payroll. Here on Lewis Street, next to the pretty little park, persons of the rank of appointive commissioners or assistant-deputy-ministers used to come to the long, narrow, semi-detached, three-storey salon to get away from the vulgar, and exchange professional analyses of public opinion, its shifts and trends. Polling and pollsters had not acquired the ascendancy they possessed fifteen years later. Journalists were still esteemed as opinion-makers, folks with their ear, or ears, to the ground. It never seemed to strike anybody that to have your ears, both of them, to the ground, would be to have very long ears, possibly ass's ears.

On election night that November the gang in the house on Lewis Street had three television sets to watch, one in the rec room, one in the ground-floor library, which gave on the back garden, and a third in the hostess's bedroom, a pretty retreat done in tones of lemon and navy blue. There might have been thirty people in the house, including the host and hostess, and excluding their children, who had been sent to the movies with instructions to stay overnight with friends. By eight-thirty the laborious process of counting — over and over again — the seats in the "Liberal Victory" and "Conservative Victory" columns was well launched. What everybody in the room, and in the city, was dying to learn was whether a firm trend towards majority government and a return to a workable two-party system would declare itself tonight. There was no ideological or ethical agreement among these opinion-moulders about the effects for good or ill that might be produced by the clear ascendancy of either party. Some of the opinion-makers present were pretty exhausted, and hadn't made an opinion, or even half an opinion, for days or weeks. You can't expect opinion-makers to be always at work, slaving away over hot opinions, any more than you can expect movers and shakers to be always vibrating. Pundits too have their moments of fatigue and generalized wish to retire from the world and seek spiritual refreshment. On election night, 1965, the opinion-makers, the pundits, the movers and shakers who were gathered in the Lewis Street house all shared a characteristic stance and set of the shoulders. They looked tired, slumped, bored out of their tiny skulls, with the course of Canadian electoral politics. They wandered in and out of various rooms, peering at the television sets, making small side bets, exchanging pawky observations on the see-saw vote counts in individual ridings, the runaway leads quickly established by more fortunate candidates in other ridings. November 8, 1965, a night on which all these good folk: the magazine editor from Toronto, the columnist from Vancouver, the writer of one-liners for high cabinet officers, the token woman broadcaster, the depressed member of Ottawa City Council, the twice previously defeated Conservative candidate for Ottawa Centre, all these worthies in the Lewis Street house, and their fellows, all these good and kindly folk wished to see the tormenting burden of electoral indecision removed from the conscience of the Canadian voter for at least a political generation, say a couple of decades. Canadians were not a people who loved minority government; they never had been and they never would be. What Canadians liked was a strong one-party government masquerading as a two-party system, in which a single centrist party remained perpetually in office, as in Ontario, with few or no interruptions to its tenure. Elections were held at the constitutionally required intervals, but no Canadian hoped or wished for change.

When a political party in Canada had managed to establish itself in office, the federal Liberal party, the Union

Nationale in Québec, the Conservatives in Ontario, the NDP in Saskatchewan, such a party might be allowed to remain in power for around twenty years with a clear mandate to govern. Why change your shirt in the middle of a generation, or your horse in deep waters? This habit of the last few years, of trying to elect a majority and failing to succeed, was gradually demoralizing the voters. Their political wisdom as a group was betraying them. Canadians had wandered from the path. They had tarried too long in the courts of irresponsibility. They must be led back to the straight and narrow, and tonight's the night!

"I don't like the look of these figures from Nova Scotia," said the token woman broadcaster to the syndicated columnist from BC. "I can't see a trend."

"They've got to have a hundred seats in the win column before they're out of Ontario. Say a hundred and ten," replied the columnist. He didn't say who "they" were, but everybody in the room realized that he meant the Liberals, the only party with the hope of getting a majority. There was a striking agreement, more powerful because unspoken, among the guests, that the Liberals really had some sort of natural right to form the government, that on the whole it was as well that they should form the government at any given time. Conservative irruptions into power in Canada since the time of the First World War were occasional, eccentric, short-term, best forgotten. Meighen, Bennett, and Dief the Chief. Not much there for dynasts.

"I see that the three wise men are safe," observed a very young and somewhat naïve mover and shaker (more of a pusher and shover really) as he poured himself a ceremonial libation and raised a brimming glass. Nobody paid much attention to him. He had only been in Ottawa for a few months, having moved over from Montréal for the FP newspapers, in the wake of Marchand, Pelletier, and the other fellow, the funny-looking one.

"Oh yes? How's he doing, that friend of yours, the one who looks like he'd been scraped down with a carrot grater?" inquired the token woman broadcaster. She had private reasons for this rather unkind phrase.

"Do you mean Trudeau?"

"Bet your ass she does," said the magazine editor from
Toronto, a bulbous, peering man with an impressively
domed forehead. "She has a bit of a thing for the guy, haven't
you, sweetie?"

"It's his car I like."

"You'll be seeing plenty of that car, because he's just been
declared elected with a thirteen-thousand-vote majority."

"What about the other two? They're the important ones."

"They're both in, but they didn't get as many votes as he
did."

"It's the safest Liberal seat in Québec though," said the
magazine editor with easy assurance. "I was co-host on a
public-affairs show with Trudeau last year," he continued,
"and I have to admit I'd vote for the son of a bitch. I didn't like
him, but I'd vote for him."

"Why?"

"He reminded me of JFK. He's got style. He came into the
studio wearing a flowered silk neckerchief, you know, it
looked pretty goddamn faggy, and I thought to myself, wow,
this guy doesn't make it. It looked so affected, but you know,
he made it stick somehow. I'd have died with embarrassment
if somebody spotted me wearing a silk ascot, but he got away
with it. And then, he'll say anything, on air, off air, he says
what he thinks and he never, but never, takes anything back.
Of course you can't win elections acting like that."

"I don't know about that so much," said the Vancouverite.
"Look at Mike. Everybody loves him, nobody ever says a
word against him. He's above attack, but he can't seem to win
an election, even with his Nobel Prize."

"Speaking of Nobel Prizes, Andrew Goderich is in again,"
said a previously unheard voice from a cloud of cigar smoke.
Everybody laughed.

"I've got a girlfriend who follows his campaigns," said the
woman broadcaster, "and she says he might just as well
phone them in. He never even works up a sweat. How did he
do tonight?"

"First win conceded in Ontario."

"Poor old NDP, never going to form a federal government."

"It's true," said the magazine editor from Toronto, "not in
your lifetime or mine."

"Tell you who else is in. George Robinson is back."

"How did the old bastard do it this time?"

"By spreading ugly rumours about the incumbent, how else? Something about somebody calling him a Judas. Who knows? George Robinson is capable of any nonsense. Let's see, what have we got here? They're going to flash an estimate of the final standings. This should be pretty close."

". . . and Canadians have once again failed to furnish a clear mandate to either major party. As things stand at nine-fifteen, our computers are predicting yet another minority government, with the Liberals obtaining a hundred and thirty-one seats across the country, still short of their majority. The Conservatives, it seems as of this moment, will fall just short of a hundred seats, with the fate of the government in the hands of the other parties . . ."

"Poor old Mike."

"Yes, he really has to go now," said the woman broadcaster.

14

> The Government of the United States, during the session of the United States Congress commencing on January 4, 1965, shall seek enactment of legislation authorizing duty-free treatment of imports of the products of Canada described in Annex B. In seeking such legislation . . .

"Here's where the hard part begins," muttered George Robinson between his teeth. His lips moved jerkily as he spelled out the densely constructed following clauses.

> . . . the Government of the United States shall also seek authority permitting the implementation of such duty-free treatment retroactively to the earliest date administratively possible . . .

"The earliest date administratively possible," said George to himself, "now when would that have been?"

> . . . following the date upon which the Government of Canada has accorded duty-free treatment. Promptly after the entry into force of such legislation, the Government of the United States shall accord duty-free treatment to the products of Canada described in Annex B.

"I don't know; it seems to say the same thing twice over without any change in the wording. Maybe I missed something." He went back over the text yet again, and it was in this studious posture that Golmsdorfer found him, when he entered the music room. The cheerful bluish-grey-green sheen from the face of a rudimentary computer terminal was reflected on Uncle George's bent head, which in its turn was reflected, strangely distorted, on the terminal screen. What you saw on the screen was the ear, the hair, the bone of the skull, but it didn't quite come together as a recognizably human image.

"Stop worrying about that paragraph, George," said the good son-in-law. "We're absolutely and utterly in the clear on that one. We haven't a thing to worry about. I don't know what might satisfy you. Here you're back in the House with a substantial majority in your riding. The person Horsbaugh has been reduced to insignificance."

"But they wouldn't lend me the Judas picture," said George, frowning. "I'll get even with them for that."

"George, you sound like a child. You don't want to waste your time on such matters. Don't you realize that Lyndon Johnson has signed APTA into law? It has passed the Congress. Forget about the Congress; it has no investigative function except by committee, and there's no Congressional committee at all interested in us."

"Not yet," said George Robinson worriedly.

"And George, if Ford goes ahead with that assembly plant in Talbotville, do you realize what that will mean? That's only fifty miles along the 401. Virtually no shipping costs. we might as well own a huge block of Ford stock, acquired at a third of its true value. We've got ready access to the largest purchasers of our product in existence, in Ohio and Ontario, and the vehicles assembled in Ohio come in here duty-free, while the vehicles assembled in Ontario go into the US duty-free. Ontario is only Ohio with a few letters added. I don't see what more you can expect of life."

"Presents," said George, "I want presents every day."

"Nobody gets that."

"I'm very worried, Henry. I have a suspicion that their accountants will be after us about duties payable on either side of the border while enactment was pending. We made no such payments, as you know, and neither did our customers."

"Neither did any other manufacturer or purchaser."

"A period of more than eight months, a considerable saving to the industry of interest payable on working capital flow."

"Nobody's going to think of that, George. The legislation is too popular in both countries. It's highly cosmetic. In the

last two years in Canada fifty-three new parts plants were
built. The Department of Industry doesn't want any damned
accountant spoiling its public image. You can put your
mind at rest about accounting technicalities."

Something about the keyboard of the computer appeared
to fascinate George Robinson, who had never before put so
much as a finger on a typewriter key, thinking the act suitable
only to small young girls who otherwise fetched coffee for the
male multitudes who wandered in and out of his various
headquarters. Perhaps it was the up-to-the-minute angular
design of the finger pads atop the keys that beguiled him. It
seemed to derive from the pages of some trade journal of
industrial science, and was shaped in a subtle ellipse that
cradled the fingertip smoothly and efficiently. There was a
childlike and endearing element in the gaze he now fastened
upon the keyboard. He activated the terminal, and the screen
lit up with the unearthly gleam then unfamiliar to most of
us, suggestive of science-fiction colour film. His head was
more clearly than ever reflected in the screen. A soft hum now
became audible. He extended his hands, poising them as he
had done fifty years before when obliged to endure music
lessons in this room.

"Miss Holdship used to whack my knuckles with a ruler if
I didn't bend my fingers just so." He chuckled.

"What are you fishing for?" asked Golmsdorfer.

"This machine performs ultra-high-speed calculations."

"So . . ."

"So look at this." He handed Henry a wide sheet of paper
with holes along its margins. On the sheet were the details of
the calculation he had just coaxed from the machine, and at
the bottom of the series of operations a single figure appeared. Henry Golmsdorfer examined it, ran his eyes up and
down the operations sequence, performed some mental
arithmetic, and finally indicated agreement with the total.

Uncle George said, "You're verifying the machine's
reckonings?"

"It's a habit I find hard to break. When I get the result I
check it out in my head."

"Why bother with the computer then? Why not just do it
in your head?"

"Who would check me? There have to be two totals to compare."

"I'll never understand accountancy," said Robinson. "Do you accept the figure?"

"I do."

"But, my God, look at the size of it! That represents the sum uncollected in duties on both sides of the border between the time the agreement was signed and the time of its formal passage into law by the Congress, plus the interest payable on the sum at six per cent, cumulatively over the eight months of the retroactivity period, totalled daily with a monthly balance taken off. Look at the amount of money, and the interest, which the industry has in effect withheld from Treasury while the legislation was pending."

"Nine months isn't long enough for either department of revenue to undertake recovery."

"They might reconsider later on."

"They could but they won't."

"They won't?"

"No."

"How can you be so sure?"

"George, for goodness sake, you're being paranoiac."

"I never know exactly what that means."

"Do you think that you, newly returned to the House, in a key position to affect the choice of a leader to succeed Mr. Pearson, perhaps about to move closer to cabinet office yourself, do you think that anybody is going to look cross-eyed at you or me? I regard myself as strictly under your protection. As a member of the family, that is."

"Thank you for nothing."

Henry assumed an expression of pain, perhaps not wholly sincere.

"Henry, I'm sorry."

"It's nothing."

"No, seriously, I'm deeply sorry. I'll protect you, Henry. I'd go to bat for you in front of a Congressional sub-committee, if necessary."

"We'll hope that won't be necessary."

"But Henry, there's just this," said Robinson, taking up the printout and scanning it once more, "if any muckraker were to get hold of these figures and publicize them, he could embarrass us. Some Socialist. We would look bad."

"Those figures are spread over a nine-month period in the first year of the agreement, and they refer to the entire North American industry. For example, there's an engine plant in Mexico included in the data."

"Mexico?"

"Correct."

"I don't think we've much to worry about from Mexico, Henry, except possibly a whole lot of wet-back engine-blocks, ha, ha." George laughed a trifle coarsely, a laugh less perfectly sane than of old. "I can't believe these results, and we're only at the end of year one."

"It's going to go on getting better, George, I believe that with all my heart and soul."

"We'll have to go right ahead with Supernopainal."

Golmsdorfer averted his face hastily, to conceal his amusement. "Is that your name for it, George?"

"It's simply Nopainal at this moment, but when the acquisition is completed we're coming out with all-new Supernopainal with triple-strength salicylate additives for round-the-clock relief from headache distress."

"George, you're a genius."

"Pretty good, isn't it?"

"It's magnificent. Congratulations!"

A vigorous girl with masses of trailing black hair came into the music room, causing George Robinson to quiver with alarm as he spotted her. She approached and kissed him enthusiastically.

"How are you, Daddy? Is this your new toy?" She bent her head over the computer screen, examining the information on it. George Robinson casually switched the machine off.

"Nothing to interest you there, my dear," he said heartily. "I thought you were going to Montréal with Maura this weekend."

This was his daughter Angela, the mystery girl, now in her final year at Trinity College, at the University of Toronto, and already giving evidence of that radical predilection for the life of francophone Québec that afterwards made her for a time almost notorious in Montréal. She seized the printout, which lay forgotten on the keyboard, and read it through. A puzzled frown crossed her face: she examined it much more attentively. At length she looked up with a grin. "You realize," she said, "you realize you're all in violation of the General Agreement on Trade and Tariffs."

The two men recoiled in horrified amazement.

But on December 20, the GATT organization granted a waiver to the general agreement covering the case, and Angela's objection was mercifully overborne.

III

15

CongestoVape, holy and gracious trademark. When the present century was in its teens, the inspiriting chest rub that bore this memorable portmanteau word as its brand name burst out of Appalachia as one of the first nationally advertised brands, those marvellous creations of the first great wave of mass-media advertising campaigns. Nobody has charted this evolution, which lasted from the time of the Spanish-American War ("Remember the *Maine!*") to the week of the stock-market crash in 'twenty-nine. Those were the halcyon days of novel sales and promotion techniques, the era that first discovered poetry in the celebrated slogans. "I'd walk a mile for a Camel." "Be happy, go Lucky!" "They satisfy." "Good to the last drop." "The pause that refreshes." "Ask the man who owns one." "Time to re-tire." "Not a cough in a carload."

CongestoVape had begun life in a housewife's kitchen in the West Virginia hills around 1908. It was simply a compound of goose grease and a few aromatic substances, principally camphor, eucalyptus oil, and menthol, which mothers rubbed on their childrens' chests as a vain defence against diphtheria, and which made the skin feel agreeably warm and tingling. The presence of the penetrating scents of mint and camphor and eucalyptus may have helped to clear the nasal passages, though nobody ever pretended that chest rubs of this type had any medical value whatsoever. No miraculous cures were claimed for them; all they did was make you feel better. At the time of the First World War several of these nostrums were in circulation all over the northeastern United States and Canada under competing brand names, of which CongestoVape eventually became the

most celebrated, doubtless because of the relentless sales
campaign waged around the calendar by its owners and
promoters, the Bartlett clan of West Virginia.

The Bartletts were real down-home country people. It was
in Mam Bartlett's little kitchen that CongestoVape was
developed, and it was her son Elroy Bartlett who initially
fetched the occasional wagon-load of the precious substance
into Charleston, and later Wheeling. By 1916 the famous
poster of the CongestoVape girl had been painted by Leyendecker, and in 1917 the first of hundreds of thousands of
reproductions of the CongestoVape girl were manufactured
in the form of large crimped tin display signs, with holes for
screws in each corner. These signs were afterwards affixed by
travelling salesmen to every discoverable barn, crib, wagon-
shed or privy not more than a hundred yards from the
roadway throughout the northeast. The CongestoVape girl
was painted from life, of course. She was Emmy Bartlett,
Elroy's little sister, who later married a Princeton grad and
passed the twenties in Paris. She was never shown but in the
one posture, pale right hand at throat, left hand clutching the
economy-sized jar, slogan underneath in flowing script.
SLEEP FREE AND EASY.

Brilliant advertising!

The brand went national after the Armistice and the tin
signs became ubiquitous. Along ten thousand rural highways from Ontario to Texas, from Vermont to California,
swarms of eager drummers in Fords, back seats laden with the
signs, sought out general stores and exiguous pharmacies,
rejoicing when they located one that had not as yet been
visited by their promotional device. These enthusiastic
young men, fired with the generous commission arrangements of the Bartlett home office, would charge into grocery
or general store or soda fountain, brandishing the image of
little sister Emmy, shouting, "Just going to lay this blonde
on the counter for you, Mister Brown, Mister Kincaid, Mister
Willis." It didn't really matter what the proprietor's name
was. Then they would attack his cherished butternut show-
cases before he had time to object, laying the cheap sheet of
metal against them, whipping out a stout mechanical screw-
driver and fastening the advertising message irretrievably in

the most prominent display location in the store. Those
Bartlett salesmen were notorious. They would put up a sign
anywhere. Anywhere! Cemeteries abounded with them.
Churches were not exempt from their unsolicited presence.
The image of the fair Emmy became one of the two or three
best-remembered icons of the Roaring Twenties. Long after,
when the rickety, ancient crone who had been baby sister
Emmy was found dead in her exquisite apartment in the
seizeième, the newspapers didn't hesitate to reproduce the
dead woman's picture next to the image from Leyendecker's
rendering of 1916. But few persons cared to draw painful
moral inferences from the juxtaposition. Sleep free and easy,
Emmy!

Her nephews, Elroy Bartlett, Junior, and Joe Don Bartlett,
pushed Congesto Vape mercilessly, down through the period
of the Second World War and into the fifties; but then they
too reached an age when their product could not revive and
energize them. Both men predeceased their Auntie Emmy,
and the third generation of Bartletts, grown effete and
languid, living at a great distance from old Mam Bartlett's
country kitchen, began to look around for a purchaser for
their interests. These young folk now made one of the
historic errors in sales and merchandising strategy of the
century. If they had hung onto CongestoVape for just five
more years, they'd have found themselves in the middle of the
nostalgia wave of the nineteen-seventies, when those tin
images of their great-aunt became cult objects, collectables.
They sold CongestoVape to RobPharm in early 1966, and by
the beginning of the next decade the new owners had to set up
a small factory as an affiliate, just to produce new signs,
which were sold to antique dealers and interior designers in
great numbers, for use in period re-creations. The greasy
chest rub itself, clinically valueless, enjoyed soaring sales and
mass popularity throughout the sixties and seventies and for
long after, because of its mythical stature as holdover from a
more innocent time.

Many persons felt that they had been brought up on
CongestoVape, that their infant lives would not otherwise
have been worth a plugged nickel. I feel myself that I wouldn't
have survived without it, and when my throat grows scratchy

and my sniffle becomes obvious and uninviting, I still retire
to bed with a thick smelly coat of CongestoVape on my chest
and throat, the same unwashed old woollen sock that I've
used for years pinned carefully around my neck. In the
morning I invariably wake refreshed, feeling that I have done
everything that I could have done for myself. Deployed, as it
were, all the resources of modern science.

George Robinson had arrived at manhood under the same
persuasion. Born in the same year as the CongestoVape girl,
1902, he felt obscurely, as adolescence and young manhood
drew on, that he was close kin to sister Emmy Bartlett. He
once actually met her, in Paris, not long after V-E Day, when
he had the pleasure of passing part of an evening with her
and her friends. You could still just make out the pearly
beauty of the young blonde girl of the posters and tin signs,
in occasional flashes and gleams, as late as 1946. This
encounter with Emmy Bartlett became part of George's
permanent mental equipment. He had gotten blonde beauty,
and the solacing odour of camphor and menthol just under
one's nose and chin, permanently fused in his imagination.
He followed the progress of the sales of the chest rub from
afar somewhat the way Lancelot kept track of Guinevere;
when the foolish young Bartletts of the sixties began to give
indications that they wanted to liquidate their holdings,
George Robinson and Henry Golmsdorfer closed in on them
so fast they never knew what hit them. It was with the acquisition of CongestoVape and Nopainal (afterwards Supernopainal) that RobPharm began to transfer large capital
holdings to the State of Delaware. Soon after, RobPharm/
Delaware acquired Betahistazine-D, and the forward evolution was in full spate. Within two years RobPharm/Dela-
ware was accepted on Wall Street as a big-board listing that
fully merited the appellation "multinational," and at the end
of the decade *Fortune* included the organization in its list of
"Hundred Largest US Corporations," a dizzying eminence to
have been gained from trade in patent medicines and auto
parts.

Incorporation in the US carried with it a number of legal
benefits connected to the structure of Canadian subsidiaries.
For example, Automotive Lock and Latch, which issued an

annual balance sheet treating itself as a Canadian entity, was able to obtain duty-free entry to the growing Canadian market for its products, at the same time introducing them to the ten-times-larger American market free of all impost.

There were other benefits. At the time of the introduction of the Automotive Production Trade Agreement in 1965, there had been widespread alarm among Canadian parts manufacturers about prospective dislocations in the Canadian market. Predictions that wholly Canadian-owned parts manufacturers would be driven from the market were widespread. It is correct that prices for Canadian-built cars came down on the 1966 models, compared to 1965 models with comparable equipment, but fear in the industry of heavy retooling costs to accommodate new patterns of production more or less dictated government reaction, and an Adjustment Assistance Board was put in place, empowered to make low-interest capital loans to parts manufacturers not affiliated with vehicle producers.

Golmsdorfer and Robinson, never inclined to precipitate an ill-considered action, passed nine months in contemplation of this loans program. They observed the agreeably long-term repayment arrangements and the give-away interest rate. Why not use government money for plant investment and retooling, if it were available several percentage points below bank prime? It's an easy calculation. If you can borrow at six per cent, you can use your own capital for investment at eleven per cent, sometimes higher. If the sums involved are very large, the five- or six-per-cent difference will yield enormous increments. Six per cent of fifty million is invariably worth pocketing, especially if you don't have to do anything to earn it except to draw up the papers. It amounts to three million dollars worth of money for jam, for the whole period of the loan and its complementary investment. The Golmsdorfers of this world are never loath to realize opportunities of this kind. As a famous football coach observed in another context, the long gainers run to daylight.

16

I knew it was going to be one of those days when the mail turned up at breakfast and there were two letters from galleries for Edie, one from Toronto, one from Montréal. I never said a word. I sat there clutching my coffee cup and listening to the sounds of the distant workmen, still causing enormous disturbance to the Codrington house as they continued their work upstairs. The Codrington Colony for the Encouragement of Visionary Art was due to open in three weeks, on Thursday, June 23, and for the life of me I couldn't see any likelihood of its opening on time; the latest problem was the plate-glass sheets that had to be fitted into a system of slotted frames on the south wall, allowing contemplation at once of the river and the twelve paintings. The sheets of glass were too large to be moved through the house; there were too many corners on staircases around which they simply would not pass. Result: the hasty construction of a system of scaffolding directly outside the morning room where we ordinarily took breakfast. This did not sweeten Edie's temper. Like myself, she hated disturbance over breakfast, for us a meal not to be taken lightly or too early. From long habit we ate breakfast between nine-thirty and eleven in the morning, sometimes dragging it out through noon. I've never been a quick starter, something to do with blood-sugar levels, I suppose. Everything has to do with blood-sugar levels. When I get down to breakfast, say around ten, I feel mighty sluggish, and it takes that first fast shot of fruit sugar in the old orange juice to get my eyes open and my head ticking over. Edie is just as bad, if anything, worse. She is one slow riser and she doesn't like disturbances (sudden sharp ringings of the telephone, people at the door trying to sell her things, workmen trampling the flower beds and constructing scaffolding with loud celebratory hammerings) while she ingests the various life-giving fluids that accompany shards of toast, tops of soft-boiled eggs, hard reflections at the beginning of the day. She didn't like having Maura Boston in the house so much, not that Maura wasn't a good friend, for she was. But being a poet she was always surprising us with impromptu readings, sometimes at breakfast, which Edie considered an inadmissible tactic, certainly for that time of day.

Maura had moved into the curator's apartment, bedroom and bath, office and sitting-room, adjacent kitchenette, all crowded into the ground-floor corner of the house next to the main entrance, just a few weeks earlier. Now she was busy with the installation of the technical library across the hall from her quarters. The room available for Edie and me and the children was shrinking, though still amply sufficient for ordinary family life. What the changes amounted to was the loss of half the living space in the building: the curator's apartment, most of the ground-floor hall, the three bedrooms for resident students, the gallery at the top of the house. Fortunately for us the original design of the building had included two back staircases, well removed from the main public rooms in the building, which allowed easy and private access for us to our own quarters. And I must state for the record that Maura Boston never at any time intruded in our living quarters unless we invited her to join us. Her own small apartment was very quiet. When she shut her door of an evening, you wouldn't have guessed that she was in there writing poems. You might find out about them when you invited her over for breakfast, at which times she was apt to whip them out abruptly and commence a first public reading. Sometimes too she would make emendations on the basis of remarks offered by either or both of us, and once to my horror she actually made a change suggested by young Anthony, then aged eight. Such evidence of her pliable nature was clearly gravely unsettling to Edie, who accepted suggestions from nobody, not even God, and especially not from me.

Now she lifted her eyes from the first of her letters. I had to admire the dexterity with which she spooned away at the inside of her egg with the left hand while digesting the contents of her correspondence, successive sheets of which she clasped tightly in her right hand. Edie is just about ambidextrous, I believe, though she usually paints with her left hand. She can do very finely detailed and precise lettering with her right hand. I have once or twice seen her draw with the left hand and print with the right simultaneously, and her printing in this situation was clearer and more elegant than my lettering or handwriting done with focussed and concentrated care. I sometimes wonder about her two brain halves and their relative dominance.

She was looking downwards in a peculiar attitude of annoyance. I wondered which hand had faltered. It was in fact the left. She had tilted her spoon unthinkingly while reading her letter, and egg yolk had fallen on her skirt, at which she now wiped distractedly. I rose and sped into the kitchen, seizing several sheets of paper towelling, moistening them, then bringing them to the stricken woman.

"Damn it," she ground out, "I should never read letters from these assholes while trying to eat. Why won't I learn?"

My eye fell on the sheet of writing paper at her elbow, as she continued to dab at her skirt. Most of the viscous yellow substance had now been removed. I noticed the letterhead, Galerie Anéantie, and towards the bottom of the sheet the words, "returning your submission under separate cover." I guess she saw my eyes flicker as they roved across the page.

"Taking it all in, aren't you?"

"Is it a Montréal gallery?"

"Is it a Montréal gallery?" she repeated in irritated tones. "What did you suppose it was? You'd never use a name like that in Toronto or New York."

"I don't know about that so much," I said. "French names are pretty popular in Toronto and New York. Le Pavillon, La Chaumière. Arpège. Lanvin. Chanel. You might call a gallery by a French name in New York if you were handling school-of-Paris work, or wished to give that impression."

"It's Abraham Shumsky's gallery, as you know perfectly well. The best gallery in Montréal, the only one I'd want to be associated with. He's been here to look at mother's work, you know. You must remember that."

"I remember," I said. "He handles Alexander MacDonald."

"Do you know," she said discontentedly, "Alexander MacDonald has got to the point where he only does five or six things a year, and they're all sold in Europe before they ever go on show. He has to put it in his sales contracts that the pictures must be returned to Montréal for any show he cares to mount. A new MacDonald can cost up to seventy-five thousand dollars, and you can't get them, even at that price. I expect he charges pretty much what he likes. I don't think there have been more than two or three purchased in Canada since MacDonald had his first big show in New York, two or three years back. I thought that Shumsky might be looking for new talent since MacDonald has taken to working so slowly, but I suppose his place is full of French painters. That's where he does most of his Montréal business."

"Doesn't he have a Toronto gallery too?"

"Yes, he opened it as soon as MacDonald made a hit internationally. I was hoping that he might give me a show in both locations, a kind of small travelling show."

"I'm really surprised that he didn't take you on. He loved your mother's work." These were exactly the wrong words, but having said them I felt obliged — the way one does — to add some qualifying phrases, in this way entangling myself further. "I mean, I didn't think he'd take you on just for your mother's sake. Your work is as good as hers, in a totally different way. Better in some ways. You don't have to cope with all those mystical implications."

"Shut up, Matt!"

"I mean, I think your work has a more ready basis of popularity."

"Shut *up*, Matt!"

"Anyway you did right to start at the top."

"It was a bracketing shot," she said, "but I got the same reaction from these really unimportant people on Bloor Street. If you don't make it with Shumsky, and you don't make it with a third-rate outfit like Belair Gallery, where do you try next?"

Three men who were supposed to be erecting scaffolding were looking in at us through the morning-room windows; they seemed to be trying to follow the line of our discussion. Edie looked at them and stamped her foot. "Anybody can look in at us," she said bitterly. "Do you realize that mother was sitting right here looking out those windows the afternoon she died? It unsettles me. I can't cope with it, Matt. I really can't. All that newspaper and magazine coverage has buried me. They only ever mention me to imply a comparison. I'm a working professional but I don't paint remotely like my mother. Well of course I don't, I don't want to. I don't encounter the same pictorial problems and I don't imagine in the same way. I couldn't have painted *The Population of Stoverville, Ontario, Entering Into the New Jerusalem,* but there are lots of things I can do that she couldn't. I need some big major work to establish myself, something that's a real novelty, that nobody's done before."

"There's our book," I said insinuatingly. "That'll draw attention."

She gazed at me pityingly. "A portfolio of architectural drawings and paintings with a learned commentary. It's nice. It'll have permanent value. We can sell an edition, but it isn't what I need to move me. I have to get away from here, Matt, I really do. Would you mind terribly if I weren't here when you open the Colony? I honestly don't think I can face it. I'll take the kids and go out to the lake, and I promise you I'll work on our book while I'm there. I might go over and look at that house in Newboro before some lunatic tears it down. And I can do some renderings of old-time cottages on the islands in the lake. Some of them go back to before the first war. You can handle the speech-making and the formalities. I really will get started on our book, I give you my word. But if I don't get out of here I won't get anything done for the rest of the summer, I can feel it."

I was desperately disappointed but I couldn't let her see that. I have a certain amount of pride, and then I had her interests at heart. "You're taking the kids?" I said.

"Anthony has only one more week of school, and nobody minds if I take Andrea out of kindergarten — they don't have exams in sandpile or rhythm band. And Johnny won't be any trouble."

"If you're sure you'll be all right. . . ."

"And you'll have Maura to keep you company," she said.

"Maura's OK," I said, "but there are too many poets in this country."

She took Anthony, Andrea, and John with her and went out to the cottage at the start of the following week. I kept busy. I had to find billets for a dozen visionary painters, not the easiest assignment this side of Paradise.

17

When a child, Tony had read a couple of dozen of the highly engaging romantic adventure tales composed between 1895 and 1940 by the Scot John Buchan, who ended his life as the first Baron Tweedsmuir of Elsfield and Governor-General of Canada. In the way that attachment to his favourite books may lead an enthusiastic reader to try to locate himself in the scenes in which those books take place, Tony had come north for his holiday following a route very similar to that taken by Richard Hannay in *The Thirty-Nine Steps*.

Most people remember *The Thirty-Nine Steps* from its celebrated film version starring Robert Donat (one of the most agreeable screen actors of the thirties) and Madeleine Carroll, who first exemplified for film-goers the image of cool, aloof blonde beauty so often teased and trifled with by Alfred Hitchcock. What most of us — though not Tony Goderich — don't remember is that there is no coolly beautiful blonde woman in Buchan's story. She was inserted into the script by Hitchcock, whose attitude to women of this physical type, Grace Kelly, Tippi Hedren, is now well-known though perhaps imperfectly understood.

In Hitchcock's version of Buchan, the cool blonde is a terrible encumbrance to the hero. She finds herself handcuffed to him without any real opportunity for escape; she is dragged about, frightened to death, handled very roughly by the hero, until that singular night when she succeeds in freeing herself from the handcuffs, then decides that she cannot bring herself to desert the sleeping Richard Hannay, with whom she is by now falling in love. This is all Hitchcockian fantasy with a faint flavour of sadism running through it. The director meted out similar rough treatment to a series of heroines in later films.

That was distinctly not John Buchan's way with women. He had his little blind spots, to be sure, one of them much more than a little blind spot, his frequent show of mistrust and fear of Jewry. But he cannot be proved guilty of any degree of sadism towards women as represented in his written work. His characters worshipped women, not in that tricky way that is really disguised dismissal. The women in his narratives are never banished from the action; they take a vigorous and central part, but as it happens not in *The Thirty-Nine Steps.*

The great portrait of the heroine in Buchan is certainly that of Mary Lamington in *Mr. Standfast,* the best of the Richard Hannay books and Buchan's most fully realized work of art, a few of his excellent short stories apart. If you came north following Hannay's route in *The Thirty-Nine Steps,* which takes him through Edinburgh to the central Highlands, you would find that at some point in your imaginary reliving of the books you would be obliged to make a transit of the central Highlands, which would lead you towards the west, to Skye and at last the outer islands.

For Buchan, certainly for uncountable other visitors, Skye and the western islands form a focal point for the poetic imagination, mysterious in atmosphere, singularly beautiful, other-worldly, hard to come at, sinless. The great Cuillinn Hills are the poetic centre of *Mr. Standfast,* lying far to the southwest on Skye above a secret deep-water inlet, the best hiding place for an enemy submarine anywhere in Britain, in the opinion of Richard Hannay.

Buchan was a great walker among the hills who thought nothing of doing thirty to thirty-five miles on foot, tirelessly, over ridges and into corries and along the cliffs of the coast-line, ending the day with arduous rock ascents that recalled his long history of mountaineering. A character in *Mr. Standfast* may make his way through the whole of the western Highlands and the islands on foot, negotiating one difficult ascent after another, always with the image of a clean-run slender boyish fairy child with shining hair and eyes before him. Buchan's girls are sometimes distressingly boyish, though this is said without prejudice.

Tony was no walker, no mountaineer, and he differed from John Buchan as well in the image of women he had in view.

Not content with preserving the image in his mind, he had insisted on bringing the living creature along with him on his northern wanderings. So in early June, at the precise moment when his brother and his brother's wife were wrangling over Edie's proposed departure for the lake, not very long before the formal opening of the Codrington Colony, Tony and Linnet were making their way through the Highlands from east to west, terrain richly familiar to Richard Hannay; they might have been going to meet him. They didn't undertake this on foot. Instead they came north from Inverness to Dingwall one glittering morning on a slow train destined for Thurso and Wick. They got off at Dingwall and passed the middle parts of the day in wandering, which took them to the shores of Cromarty Firth, which opened out before them like the guardian of the Black Isle, not an island at all but a low peninsula of rich soil, bounteous crops, and splendid cattle. Returning to the Dingwall station in late afternoon, they saw rising in the northwest the enormous bulk of Ben Wyvis.

This was their introduction to the Highlands. They had paid very little attention to the scenic beauties on either side of the rail line from Edinburgh to Inverness. The novelty of their situation, alone with each other away from the tumultuous media world, had strictly controlled their attention. Neither was a pretentious person. It would never have occurred to either of them that first-class accommodation on the railway or travel by air might be preferable to the ordinary rail service. They enjoyed the plastic teacups, the cellophane-wrapped fruit-cake, the ham rolls, the tables between the seats across which they leaned looking into each others' eyes. Tony may now and then have invoked Buchan's favourite epithet for the women of whom he deeply approved, "clean-run," but he had no clear idea of what it implied, something to do with sailboats perhaps. The adjective evoked strong impulses in his heart. If ever anybody deserved to be described as "clean-run," Linnet Olcott was that person. At the same time, she didn't possess the boyishness of the Buchan girls. Slender, with swinging gait, hair the colour of those entrancing gleams of sunlight on the wide reaches of Cromarty Firth, she would at no time have been mistaken for a boy.

It grew windy as they waited for the early evening train for the west. It was Monday; the station was all but deserted by 6:00 PM, and the long Highland evening was just beginning to hint at shadows to come, when the tiny toy train appeared from the direction of Muir of Ord. There were few travellers that evening. Linnet and Tony had no plans and no fixed itinerary; they intended to leave the train whenever they pleased, seek whatever lodging offered itself, stay in one place for a day or two, do some short walks and climbs, then proceed some miles farther. They watched from the windows of the little train as it pulled out of Dingwall station, moving away up the valley on its way to Garve. On the south side of the railway a narrow lost road followed along beside the rails, sometimes circling behind a cluster of stone buildings and losing itself. Presently the railway began to mount towards higher ground. Ben Wyvis, hard to take in from its sprawl, bulk, and distance, seemed to move around behind them to their right. Loch Garve came in sight with long broad shadows spread over it; to the southwest were glinting suggestions of Loch Luichart. A heavenly place to fetch up on a sun-drenched blue and white night. Each carrying a small travelling bag, they wandered down from the station to the hotel, where they asked for a double room. Tony was intensely mindful of the comedy of *The Thirty-Nine Steps*, in the Hitchcock version, in which the innkeeper's wife instantly deduces, quite incorrectly, that the apprehensive young couple before her are a runaway pair of lovers on their first night together. Asked for a name for the register, Tony gave the crazy rejoinder, "Smith." The eyes of the innkeeper's wife wandered idly to Linnet's left hand, all innocent of ornament. There was some fleeting hesitation before she assigned them their quarters, which proved to be most handsome, with an enormous fireplace at one end of the room and a grand double bed of ludicrous, even suggestive, proportions at the other. They left their luggage in this room, made arrangements for a later meal with their hostess, then sallied into the blue shadows now unfolding down the hillsides.

The thing about Linnet, Tony reflected, was that she had all the marvellous qualities of the women of Buchan and

Hitchcock and none of their defects. She had the exquisite
beauty, the charm, the gentlewomanliness, of Hitchcock's
blonde stars, and the comradeliness, the readiness for adventure, the shining hair and loving eyes of Buchan's lasses. She
didn't look like a boy and she wasn't a frigid bitch, and you
couldn't speak any fairer than that. They strolled up a
narrow hillside road which, if they had pursued it, would
have taken them all the way to Ullapool and the far northwest. Away towards the heart of the interior rose Beinn
Dearg, massive, distant and immense, beginning to show
some of the purple that would shine from its shoulders in
another month. To their right, the protective slopes of Little
Wyvis seemed to lean very near; they thought they might
walk that way next morning. Behind the first slope there
came plainly in sight the vast cragged seamed ruggedness of
Ben Wyvis, still in early June bright with snow along its high
shoulders, the new heather changing tone below, from
spring brown-red to royal purple. Charmed with these
colours, intensely drawn to one another, they turned and
went back to the hotel to dine. As evening drew on, their hosts
persuaded them to try the traditional drink of the Highlands,
the Athole brose — whisky, oats, honey, and spices, indes-
cribably flavoured and unforgettable. A glass or two and they
retired hilarious to pass eight uninterrupted hours asleep side
by side.

   They passed the next three days in this place, then moved
along the rail line to Achnasheen, "the field of rain," tucked
under the bulky glacis of Fionn Bhein. Here they passed two
days in climbing along the road to Kinlochewe. They were
now precisely in the centre of the country, just at the height of
land, and as they gazed from the heights they could see below
them the slopes and widening floor of Glen Carron, through
which they would descend to the western shore at the Kyle.
The close of their first week in the Highlands found them
riding in the little train along the short stretch of line from
Achnasheen to Stromeferry. They passed along the rocky
shores of Loch Carron, which now and then strongly
suggested Canadian scenes. Not far west of Achnasheen the
road petered out in a wilderness of rocky barriers; in some
places evidence of road construction could be seen. As late as

1966 the road had not been cut through to the west, though assiduous workmen were evidently attacking the rock with explosives. It was several years before the last miles were opened. The little rail line was still the only easy means to passage here. So they came to Stromeferry and made their last stop before descending to the Kyle and the Inner Sound.

At Stromeferry they started to feel that they had worked themselves into that agreeable state of physical conditioning that would allow for longish walks, and on their first morning they set out on a Buchanesque ramble down to Plockton and back, a distance of about fourteen miles. They were out of the high country by now, strolling along the shore of Loch Carron where it merges into Loch Kishorn, insistently picturesque painter's country. That night they boarded the little train for the last time, arriving at Kyle of Lochalsh about eight-thirty in the evening.

As the train ran down the last two or three miles, they sat entranced, contemplating the splendour of the place with a stilled and tranquil calm. It was now almost Midsummer's Day. The sunlight would persist far into the night, last traces of light lingering in the western skies past midnight, the rays of dawn almost immediately succeeding.

They felt no hunger, only a passionate desire to sink into the remote loveliness before them. A brief appearance in the hotel, a choice of room, and they set out towards the nearest climb, the hill that lies above Railway Terrace, a vantage point that offers one of the greatest prospects in the world. As they climbed into the glorious light, they could see the whole sweeping width of the Inner Sound, Applecross, the Crowlins, with Rassay to the northwest. On their left hand, as it were at their feet, lay Kyleakin, the gateway to Skye.

Above Kyleakin, long miles removed in the gleaming southwest, shining high and far, the serrated peaks of the Cuillins were plainly visible.

"One of these days we'll go there," said Linnet in an undertone. "Very high up." They fell into their deepest embrace in the late night sunshine.

After that illuminated night it was one of their settled ambitions to come to Skye and venture far out along the coast, to Carbost or Dunvegan, maybe past Portree, and there

find a house and a bit of shore from which to contemplate the
western ocean, the Minch and the islands, Barra, Eriskay,
Uist, the very end of the ride.

But they had to be back in London the following week for
shooting, for rehearsals, for conversations with their agents
and Tony's publisher, himself a godly and a canny Scot.
They crossed to Kyleakin next morning, making their first
formal visit to Skye, and took the bus to Armadale along that
little road where the cars can't pass and narrow lay-bys are
found every mile or two, in which the most courteous drivers
in the world wait for the wandering buses to pass. Soon they
came into sheltered country overlooking the sound of Sleat,
and here Tony, seated on the right side of the bus, looking
inland at the half-hidden houses, happened to notice a small
child standing alone in a little grove at the roadside. Behind
her there seemed to be a tiny village but she was framed in a
foreground of utter solitariness. She paid no attention to the
bus as it went slowly by, fixing her regard closely on some
small stones at her feet, at which she kicked with precision as
she moved along. Tony took out his notebook and attempted
a poem, something he hadn't done for a decade.

> Skye girl young and solitary
> in blue pleated skirt and grey jumper
> in a world of nine people and an old pony
> seen once from the window of a bus
> and never forgotten
>
> Head bent gaze fixed on pebbles and shoes
> kick as quick and aimed as a fish's flip
> no thought of distances to cross
> only the love of home and the old pony
> whole world hiding in her head

18

David and Stephen and Ed and Stanley and Tommy and all
— the best minds in the party — found themselves lurking in
the wide hollow behind the Rosedale subway station, while
their host tried to point out a landmark on the other side of
the grassy stretch. Twilight had come on and these half-
dozen proponents of social good were overdue at a private
conference in the Goderiches' new apartment just along
Crescent Road. But Andrew, indefatigable explainer, held
them close behind the exit from the station while he tried to
locate the Studio Building in the gathering gloom.

"I think you can just spot it over there. It's a sort of loft
with big windows, see? They all lived there on and off,
Thompson, Jackson, Arthur Heming."

"Arthur Heming?" said David softly as he freed his coat
sleeve from Andrew's grasp.

"Doesn't anybody remember Arthur Heming? Pictures
with canoes and silver birches."

"Never heard of him," said the youngest theorist in the
group. "Shouldn't we move along, Andrew? Your poor wife
will be wondering where we are."

"Are we all here?" asked Andrew, peering around. "The
whole caucus?"

"A hanging jury," said somebody. It was an NDPer's private
joke and the little band made what they could of it as they
paced off the short distance towards the new midtown
residence of Andrew and Isabelle Goderich. Convenience of
location, spacious high-ceilinged rooms, wide lawn, made
their ground-floor flat the ideal residence for two people no
longer young, in Ishy's case no longer eager to walk long
distances in search of public transportation. It took the small

group three minutes to saunter up the slope east of Yonge
Street past Cluny Drive to where a broad veranda and a
prospect of shining windows welcomed them. It was just on
9:00 PM.

"Cluny," mumbled Stanley. "I wonder what the Cluniac
association is."

"I've wondered about that myself," admitted Andrew.
"Probably just a family name."

"Cluny, Cluny, Cluny," repeated another distinguished
public man; he continued this distracted mutter during most
of the later proceedings, "Cluny, Cluny." Andrew had
invited these leaders to his home on this grateful summer
night to lay before them some of the hard necessities of NDP
policy, as affected by the Automotive Production Trade
Agreement, a policy as yet inchoate in official statements of
party positions. No body of writing or corpus of systematic
thought had been promulgated by David or young Stephen
— from whom it might have been expected — nor from Ed,
the leader with the auto workers at his back, nor from the
strong element of western thought in the group. Andrew
wished to propose the foundations of a policy looking
towards North American industrial and resources integration together with a searching canvass of the implications
of any such policy for Canadian industrial labour in the
decades to come, the last of the sixties, the seventies, possibly
even the eighties. The question before them, he thought, was
the economic question laden with the most serious consequences for Canadians of all the questions that might be put.
For the automotive industry, love it or hate it, was the bell-
wether of industrialization everywhere in the world, and
nowhere more so than in North America, where production
techniques and labour settlements had for a long time
determined the course of social and economic history. The
privately owned passenger automobile had undone Marxian
socialism as it had driven out Marxian sociology. The
miracle of German recovery after V-E Day was precisely a
miracle of automotive production. The sad decline of British
industry could be read in the history of their exports of
automobiles, for a long time after World War Two flourishing, now in sharp decline. The French, as always true to

themselves and to no others, continued on their way with largely publicly owned automotive production and high import barriers, which EEC regulations never really succeeded in toppling. The gutsy independent Swedes in their Socialist paradise were somehow able to support the existence of two producers of worldwide reputation, Saab and Volvo, because of the special nature of their economy. The Italians went on their jovial way, making every kind of car from the great luxury and sports marques, Alfa-Romeo, Bugatti, down through the standard small five-passenger sedan, the Fiat 120S, which was to become in its various versions one of the four best-selling cars in automotive history. Only the Beetle, the Model-T, and the various incarnations of the Chevy Nova from 1967 to 1974 outwent the Fiat 120S in longevity, widespread distribution, and rabbit-like tendency to reproduce themselves. In the twenty years that followed this evening conference, the Fiat 120S reincarnated itself almost everywhere in the world under new names, Lada, Polska. You couldn't watch a news film from eastern Europe or from beyond the Urals or from Afghanistan without spotting legions of units derived from the miracle of Togliattigrad, the establishment in the deepest USSR of an enormous automotive plant that subsequently marketed its products across the highest import barriers, at the greatest distances, over peaks of ideological opposition. The Lada version of the 120S was in the best and truest sense of the word value for money, and it proved once and for all that the automotive industry was the greatest industrial instrument of political policy, diplomacy carried on by other means, as it were. In mid-July 1966 it was essential that Canada establish a sane and rational policy on automotive production.

"For there's no use," said Andrew to his companions, "in creating policy as you go, on an *ad hoc* basis. We require a consistent and articulated policy, and we have to decide whether we're nationalists or socialists on this point. Every Canadian auto worker wants wage parity with his pals in the UAW south of the border."

"Hear, hear," said Ed.

"Thank you, Ed. But can we make that our declared aim as a party? If we do, we're accepting the principle of what our friends in government call the 'rationalization' of the industry. And the first consequence to Canadians of that move is loss of control of our own industry. We have to recognize that production will be planned at the least cost; plants will be built as close as possible to the centre of the market, for ease and low cost of distribution. Our friends in Québec are at this moment demanding that the most popular GM products be assembled in Sainte-Thérèse, when the new plant there is ready to go into production. But Sainte-Thérèse is a very long way from the market for GM compacts. The thing that must strike us all is this: we have to abandon the principles of international socialism and act as Canadian nationalists in this affair. That means that we have to review the APTA constantly to insure maintenance of wage scales, new plant construction, Canadian right to produce popular models. We have to defend the national interest, making certain that a few clever investors and corporation lawyers don't use the so-called rationalization programme to enrich themselves by taking advantage of the free-trade provisions of APTA."

"Andrew," said Ed, "aren't you taking this a little too seriously?"

As he said this there came a little scream from the darkness of the dining room, then a loud crash. In bumping herself against some projecting serving table, Ishy had managed to drop an entire tea service.

"I've been having a little trouble with my eyes," she conceded sadly.

19

George and Valerie Essex found their way out to our place at the lake on Labour Day weekend, ostensibly to report on Stage Stoverville affairs, and the degree of acceptance by various concerned committee members of Edie's proposed mural on the back wall of the theatre. Edie had been occupied all that week with sketches of her conception on all kinds of paper, with charcoal, graphite stick, pen, pencil, Conté crayon, oil pastel. There might have been sixty sheets of drawing paper of various weights and sizes lying in heaps on the sun-deck. She uses such expensive paper that the fresh breezes of summer aren't strong enough to blow them away. It would require tempest, winds of hurricane velocity, to budge a pile of Edie's drawings. That summer I had the feeling they were like a compost heap, a weighty pile of rotting organic matter in which strange fires lurked. In this imagining I was all too correct.

When I got back from my morning stroll in the woods up behind our cottage, I spotted the Essex automobile at the roadside and the sight made me chortle. The car was not itself an Essex, that make of automobile having been absorbed into other corporate structures, then banished from the free market, thirty years before. The Essex was conceived and put on the market in the early twenties as an inexpensive baby brother of the very popular Hudson. In the fifteen years of the marque's history, successive versions of the Essex enjoyed considerable popularity, the Essex Challenger, nimble straight six of the late twenties, later on the Essex Terraplane — about my favourite name for a line of cars. Terraplane! A nice stroke of copy-writing, suggesting rapid, quasi-aerial flight on land. The Terraplane disappeared as

the automobile industry consolidated itself and refined its
marketing techniques in the years just before the Second
World War. The parent car, the Hudson, remained an
immensely popular and successful make until well into the
nineteen-fifties, when it too was absorbed in a merger, finally
disappearing from the North American market not too long
before our cottage conference in the late summer of 1966.

Staring through the brush at George and Val's smartly
conservative automobile, dark blue, eminently suited to the
comings and goings of an Anglican priest and his young
spouse, I was reminded of Jimmy Durante's remark in a radio
sketch heard once many years before and never allowed to
lapse from memory.

> Durante: I am Lord Essex, and a man of many parts (pause)
> and you know how hard it is to get parts for an
> Essex these days.

Thoughts like these reminded me of the enormous place
held in our social mythologies by automobiles. Jack Benny's
Maxwell, for example. Jack thinks at one point in his career
that his Maxwell has at last become obsolete. He sallies forth
with Rochester beside him in the front seat in search of a high
trade-in allowance, and at once confronts a used-car salesman. Benny asks the salesman his name.

> Salesman: just call me Bill (laughter). Just plain Bill.

For the rest of the sketch Jack refers to the salesman as "Plain
Bill." This is a richly complex joke, having in it many of the
aspects of the higher poetry: ambiguity of reference, metrical
organization, comic irony. North American advertising
copy, especially that composed on behalf of automobiles and
those few other products utterly central to our lives, has
increasingly possessed this nervous strength of rhythm, this
wealth of ambiguity and cross reference. When the salesman
invites Jack to call him Just Plain Bill, we are being told that
his used cars will not yield carefree operation. We get as well
a cross-reference to a hugely popular soap opera of the
thirties, now totally forgotten but in its heyday as a mid-
afternoon radio serial listened to by a daily audience of
several millions, including legions of children just home

from school. Lord Essex, a man of many parts. Just Plain
Bill. From the misadventures awheel of Chaplin and Keaton
and Harold Lloyd and Laurel and Hardy and Ford Sterling,
from the magnificent "Roadhog" sequence featuring Bill
Fields and Alison Skipworth in *If I Had a Million,* to
*American Graffiti, Bonnie and Clyde, Drive, He Said,
Gumball Rally,* and the folk-tales of television, *My Mother
the Car, Route 66, Car 54, Where Are You?* and countless
others, the car has been treated as our great object of desire, of
love, truly our mechanical bride.

So George and Val were Essexes in name only; their
current car was a neat, sizeable, prosperous-looking dark-
blue Buick with Kleenex boxes in the well beneath the rear
window, flashlight and collection of road maps in the glove
compartment. Royl-Cord Bounceaway Superlastic original
equipment stock encircled and adorned their wheels. I found
these persistent and courageous motorists standing with
Edie on the sun-deck amid piles of drawing paper. As I came
around the side of the building and mounted the steps to the
deck, Valerie gestured widely at our cherished prospect of the
lake. "Hello handsome," she said, or maybe just, "Hello.
(Pause.) Handsome!"

"Very European," I said.

George Essex said, "European? With all those evergreens?"

"A wide and happy prospect," I said pedantically. "That's
what 'Europe' means, or so I've been told. It's what various
barbarians are supposed to have thought when they arrived at
the Hellespont and gazed across. Imagine your first sight of
Europe after having traversed the Anatolian highlands."

Edie made a series of faces at me, indicative of several
modes of displeasure. She didn't like it when I teased George.
"They've found out why Uncle George hates me," she said in
a small voice, which a less well-instructed observer than
myself would have taken to be doleful.

"Oh now, Edie, we never said he hates you. He's very keen
on the mural and he loved your folks. If he hates anybody it's
Matt and his father, but I can't see Uncle George actually
hating anybody."

"Certainly not," said George, speaking as a man of God.
"He has expressed great interest in the Drama Festival; he's

backing it to the hilt. He's making certain that the prime minister sticks to his commitment. He's Mr. Pearson's parliamentary secretary now, you know. He has his ear."

Who wants a prime minister's ear? Not me! "I suppose the other parliamentary secretary has the other ear," I said waspishly, "the fellow in Montréal."

George Essex said, "He won't make any trouble. He has no power base."

"I expect not," I said, "so come on, tell us, why does Uncle George hate me? I've never done anything to him."

"He sees you as the power behind the Codrington Colony."

This made me laugh. The idea of my being any sort of power behind anything is deeply comic. If there is one thing I don't have, it's influence. "I have my hands on all the ropes," I said to Valerie. Edie scowled at me again, from her concealed vantage point.

"And he's still on a low boil about some favour you refused him, something about a picture of Mr. Horsbaugh. He keeps babbling something about Judas, but he doesn't mean you. Would that be your dad?"

"Golly Moses, Valerie," I said with severity, "have you really checked out May-Beth's pictures since they were put on public display?"

"Weeellll . . ."

"We've been so busy with the theatre," offered George by way of exculpation, natural in a Christian minister.

"Make an effort to get over there sometime," I said drily. "The picture you're talking about is the potentially libellous one — that's between ourselves, you understand. I've never taken advice of counsel. It's the picture May-Beth showed me when she said she didn't want any of her work to leave the house. That's what gave us the idea for the Codrington Colony."

Edie said, "If it hadn't been for that we'd have had the house to ourselves."

"Forget about that," I said, a trifle brusquely. "I was told by your mother to keep the works together and I've done exactly what she asked. Uncle George wanted to borrow the painting of Phil Horsbaugh to have it reproduced in campaign literature and in newspaper photographs. I wouldn't be surprised to hear he was using it as a dartboard at Liberal headquarters. It's a damning portrait, but as long as it doesn't get out of the house, then it can't be introduced as evidence in a libel suit. I don't believe it's libellous anyway, but I wasn't about to have my opinion solicited by the courts."

Dim light began to illuminate the Essex faces. "I think I recall the picture you're talking about," said George. "It's the Judas picture. Sure. I get it. I thought it was a pretty fine rendering of the Judas suggested by the Gospels, a bewildered fearful man, weak, very human, greedy, vain. Fond of his rôle and his authority as treasurer. A university registrar, in fact. I remember it vividly. *The Honourable Philip Horsbaugh, Member of Parliament for Stoverville/Smith's Falls Represented as Judas, with Spilled Salt and Traditional Moneybag.* I was so struck by that picture, the first time I saw it, that I preached a sermon on the subject the next Sunday at Saint Saviour's, and I'll tell you something else, George Robinson heard that sermon. He was sitting right down in front of me in the family pew. That was just before the last election. The election of the Just."

"Well there you are," I said, "that's probably what made him think of the idea. He came to us and demanded to be allowed to make use of the picture in order to discredit his opponent. He said that we owed that much to him. He said that May-Beth had given him instructions, which amounted to her deathbed wishes, which is utter nonsense. I knew May-Beth as well as anybody alive except Edie and I know she didn't want her work used in any such way. Not but what it wouldn't make a sensational political poster." I thought this over and started to laugh. "Can't you just see it, Edie?" I said. "Why that old monster! He'd have demolished Horsbaugh with that poster. With your mother's signature in plain sight at the bottom it would have represented an endorsement from beyond the grave. Why the scheming old bugger!"

"I must go and see it again," said Valerie defensively. "Not that I haven't seen it already. You took me over the gallery yourself before it opened."

"Well maybe I didn't make enough of a point about the Judas picture. Although it's very well hung. It's the first thing you see as you come in. Then you see the one of Mayor

Lawson treated as Herod and then you're right into the room and you see the triptych across the space in front of you."

Valerie's mind wandered off. "He hates your dad too. *Really* hates him," she said faintly.

20

"It's unheard of. At least I never heard of such a thing," said Charlie Pope to George Robinson. He lay far back in his deep leather swivel chair, one of those old-time expensive genuine-leather office chairs from Grand and Toy or Stainton and Evis, rich ox-blood cowhide studded with heavy brass nailheads, old gleaming wood frame, no squeaks, not so much as a noisy sticky castor to disturb the meditations of the Undersecretary for External Affairs. The room was shaded, sequestered, guarded. A framed signed photograph of Andrew Goderich hung in a deeply recessed embrasure looking towards the light. Similar photographs of other notables, not too many, were distributed about the room in situations of quasi-monastic modesty: Mackenzie King of course, Hume Wrong, Norman Robertson, Agnes McPhail. There were one or two of more recent date. Paul-Edouard Martin. V.K. Menon. Sitting in an only slightly less comfortable armchair, across from the Undersecretary's calm form and massive desk, George Robinson sensed obscurely that this meeting might more prudently have been conducted on neutral ground, better yet in his own office, but that would have been truly unheard of. In the tables of precedence that bedevil the nation's capital to the present day, Parliamentary secretaries, even those of the prime minister of the day, though arguably of junior cabinet rank, do not wisely or correctly issue invitations to the permanent Undersecretary for External Affairs. He doesn't come to see them; they go to see him. Quite a lot of this formal jockeying for precedence and position still goes on in Ottawa and will forever, human nature and governments being what they are. Our citizenry might be greatly surprised if they understood how time-wasting and ineffective these rubrics are.

George had to back and fill and take his turn, but being what he was, a man of extreme tenacity and concentrated purpose, he had at last won through to these secluded quarters. An occasional typist's bell, the subdued clatter of keys, hushed womanly voices, these were the only sounds that penetrated the shadowy room.

"Do you record your visitors' conversation?" he asked Charlie Pope suddenly, hoping to place him off guard.

"It depends on the visitor," said Pope simply. He placed his lean pale hands palms downward on the desk blotter before him. He wore a small silver signet ring on his right little finger. His hands could not have been made cleaner, smoother, whiter than they were. One blotchy liver spot showed on the back of the left hand, otherwise the skin was unblemished. Neither hand betrayed the smallest hint of nervous tremor. In other ways Charlie Pope's appearance was equally intimidating. He wore a very dark three-piece blue suit with the faintest trace of pin-stripe — traditional mandarin costume — and an almost black tie with a small red figure stitched into it. His linen was of overstated whiteness, his hair clipped close and still in places rather silver than pure white. He had a small neat closely trimmed moustache, and the most persuasive voice in the public service. "Is this visit official in nature? Do you wish to place material on the record for the files, ours and yours?"

"No to both questions."

"Then I see no reason to record our chat," said Charlie. He moved his left hand an inch or two along the underside of the edge of his desk, turning the recording apparatus on. As the various bugs in the room were sophisticated in the last degree, George Robinson's observations and proposals — some of them almost indiscreet — were placed permanently on record with complete, almost hallucinatory accuracy. You could hear the rubbing together of his trouser legs as he crossed them. Once he suppressed a tiny burp.

"As you know," he began slowly, "there is a working division of responsibilities between my opposite number and myself, a division that originated with the PM and has been endorsed by him."

Charlie Pope inclined his head gravely.

"Has the PMO communicated this to you officially?"

Pope was silent for a moment, seeming to consider whether the question was improper.

"I could give you an informal clarification," said George Robinson.

"I think I can state that I have been in unofficial communication with the office you mention. But I have nothing on paper," said Charlie.

"Very wise, very judicious. Well then, the working division of duties boils down roughly to this, that Pierre replies to questions of a broad theoretical nature concerned with the philosophy of this administration, questions that might bear on constitutional proposals, for example, or inter-governmental relations within Canada. Issues annexed to the problems of bilingualism. You see the sort of thing I mean." He seemed to suggest by his tone that affairs of this general cast cut very little ice with him, indeed with any man possessing a demonstrated capacity to grapple with "the real world." "My responsibilities are of a different nature, as you can well imagine. Nuts and bolts of administration, day-to-day review of trade policy, occasionally of fiscal policy, aid to industry. I'm right down there in the arena where the horse trading goes on. I've swapped a few horses down there in my time."

You surely have, thought the Undersecretary, staring peaceably across his heavy desk. A rich, powerful man, he decided, examining the member for Stoverville/Smith's Falls carefully. A rich, powerful man with legions of powerful friends at home and abroad. Sixty-four years old, just a couple of years younger than me, still spoken of as a coming man. He clips his eyebrows, thought the Undersecretary, and he tweezes the hairs out of his nose, or somebody does. No critic on the floor of the House had ever reproached George Robinson for his barbering. The neatly trimmed, almost shaven eyebrows, the still abundant hair carefully cut and brushed, the minutely razored cheeks in whose folds no traces of unhandily applied talcum appeared. The cosmetic arts had been lavished on George Robinson in his later years. No longer the small-town companies director with qualifiedly great possessions — say a paltry twenty million — he had become in these latter years the associate of persons so highly

placed in the organization of continental patterns of industrial development, and the movement of investment capital,
that at sixty-four great opportunities, expanding horizons,
lay in front of him. Charlie Pope could well remember when
— as recently as the beginning of the decade — there had been
a tendency in the press gallery and on the Hill generally, to
write Robinson off as a sport of nature, a powerful man
without any brains, somebody who had risen as high (and
perhaps a rung or two higher) on the ladder of advancement
as his native gifts would reasonably allow. A few years into
the sixties most veteran government-watchers would have
been prepared to consign him to well-merited obscurity, at
length decent retirement and a few years' enjoyment of his
possessions until the shades should be drawn in the windows
of storied Robinson Court, notoriously the most opulent and
distinguished place of residence of any man in public life in
the country. But new patterns of industry and investment had
somehow excited new vigour, new convictions, in Robinson's
heart. He had regained his seat in the last election when
nobody had expected him to, and had become the most
stalwart exponent and defender in the House of official
policy on matters connected with industry, trade and commerce, apart from the personnel of that ministry. Hence his
appointment as parliamentary secretary to the PM, an
appointment that in the normal course of events would never
have been given to a man of his years.

    And there he stood at question time in the House from one
week to the next, giving answers on behalf of the prime
minister to questions on all sorts of things of the greatest
import — programmes and policies that he was pleased to
describe as nuts-and-bolts, horse trading, in fact the true
business of government. Nobody could have predicted his
sudden emergence into real power and influence as recently
as eighteen months ago. Yet there he stood, making statements — statements — in the House, and fending off television news reporters towards 11:00 PM two or three nights a
week. This development was bizarre. Could there lurk in the
breast of Robinson, so Charlie put it to himself, subtleties of
reflection, powers of mind, at no time previously revealed in
the course of a long and wholly undistinguished public
career?

Mr. Pope knew that such transformations of character were exceedingly rare, almost never found in human history, the case of Saul of Tarsus being almost the only one on record. What weight of light had fallen upon George Robinson in these last years? Why not change his name, if he was so altered *à l'intérieure*? Perhaps he contemplated some such change of name and identity privately. Maybe he had in mind a change of state and place even more magical. Who could tell?

"A complete transformation of the order of precedence among our trading partners," said George, as Charlie Pope shook himself mentally and began to listen to what his visitor was saying. "A whole new identity for Canada abroad. So you do see, there is a kind of overlap between Pierre's ideas and mine. Pierre has been to China, they tell me. He went with a friend and they wrote a book about it, am I right?"

"*Deux innocents en Chine rouge,*" said Charlie.

"I beg your pardon?"

"*Two Innocents in China.*"

"Right, right, I remember now, one of my girls was reading it recently I believe, my daughter Angela who lives in Montréal."

Charlie almost said, "The one who's so close to Roger Talbot," but decided to withhold the observation.

"So Pierre is interested in China too, genuinely interested. I sometimes see him chatting with Andrew Goderich in the lobby, and I guess that's what they have in common."

"Andrew Goderich? I don't quite see. . . ."

"Andrew Goderich speaks Chinese," exclaimed Robinson, as if this bit of information had just occurred to him. "Of course, the very man."

"The very man for what?"

"The very man to head a Chinese olive-branch. It has to come, sooner or later. That's why I've come to clear this discussion with you, because strictly speaking our relations with a foreign power, with whom we do not exchange diplomatic missions, are none of my business."

"My dear George," said the Undersecretary in his friendliest tones, "by no stretch of the imagination could our stance towards the régime on the mainland be thought your business. It couldn't be any of my business. It's nobody's business. Diplomatically speaking it doesn't begin to exist. It is comprised of pure non-being."

"Sure it is," said Robinson, grinning a grin that Pope found almost insufferable. That this boor and bounder should venture to take a hand in matters of which he knew nothing and less than nothing! Incredible. Unacceptable!

"What exactly do you have in mind?" asked Charlie in his most honied voice.

"If we don't get in first, somebody else will."

"Somebody else will what?"

"We have to examine these conflicts in the light of global power relationships," said George. Having delivered himself of this pronouncement he began to act like a hen who has produced an outsized egg. At no time prior to this had he been rated as a parliamentarian capable of evolving such views. Mr. Pope, who tended to conceive of foreign affairs as pretty much a hedged preserve — the occupational failing of diplomats — felt increasingly offended by the intervention of this tyro in what he took to be his own guarded sphere of expertness. He had an idea by now of what the man was driving at, though the prospects invoked in the discussion were so vast as not to yield immediate meaning.

"What power relationships do you have in mind?" he inquired.

"We have to ask ourselves what the potential successors of Mao think of Ho."

"Who?"

"Ho. Ho Chi-Minh."

Charlie had to resist the temptation to carry on this musical exchange by remarking, "Aha, Ho," or perhaps, "Oho, Ho." Instead he simply observed that he found his colleague's reasonings too swift and subtle to follow. "Could you make the connection a little clearer?"

"Everything depends on the degree of American involvement in Southeast Asia, don't you see? There must be plenty of people in the coming generation of Chinese leaders who aren't friendly to the Viet Cong."

This was so palpably just an observation that the Undersecretary was taken aback. Where can he have got these notions, said Mr. Pope to himself. He never hit upon Henry

Golmsdorfer and Angela (Marie-Ange) Robinson as their source, because he realized only vaguely that these folk existed.

"The time is drawing near," said George Robinson weightily, "for a North American rapprochement with the People's Republic of China."

This was exactly — exactly — what Charlie Pope thought.

"And there are certainly plenty of people in China who will work actively to that end, especially among the forces who are opposed to the military adventures of the VC. When an end comes to the conflict in Vietnam, we will certainly see a readjustment of Sino-American relations."

Where's he getting this, thought Pope again.

"We can't yet begin to suspect who will be at the head of American diplomacy after the 1968 election, but it will most likely be the Republican nominee. As I read the situation, President Johnson grows more unpopular every day, with a wide stripe of American opinion. I would not be surprised if he failed to obtain the Democratic nomination. I believe therefore that the next president will seek to extract the US from its entanglement in Southeast Asia, and that a movement towards normalization of Chinese-American relations will follow."

"That may be."

"Well, but don't you understand me, Mr. Undersecretary? China will prove to be an enormous market. Already our annual balance of payments is functionally related to our Chinese grain sales, an element in the Canadian economy of great political importance. We have to sell our wheat."

"I see, yes."

"Now suppose we were to move towards an exchange of diplomatic ties with China in the next year or so, before the Americans manage to get themselves out of Saigon. Suppose that."

"I am supposing it. Go on."

"We'd have been first in the field. Think of the opportunity to cement our economic ties with the heirs of Mao. We'd be in a position to sell Canadian manufactured goods to China anywhere from two to five years ahead of the Americans. I propose a Canadian economic and fact-finding mission to China and, as you suggested, who better to head such a mission than our Nobel Peace Prize winner? Admittedly not a recent award, but all the same. . . ."

"There is much in what you put forward," said Mr. Pope. "But now, I'm afraid, I must ask you to excuse me for the time. I have another appointment and we've gone on a little longer than we'd planned. We must get together on this again, very soon."

George rose and smilingly bowed himself out, whereupon Mr. Pope buzzed frantically for his head-of-secretarial-staff.

"Mrs. Melhuish," he said, as she came into the room, "I want the tape of the conversation I've just had reproduced in four copies, which you are to hand to me. The master tape is to be retained in the file under the usual security provisions. And I want you — you personally, if you see what I mean — I want you to transcribe what's on the tape in four typed copies, which you are also to hand to me. Four and only four copies, Mrs. Melhuish. Do I make myself perfectly clear?"

Certainly, sir. I wonder . . . would the Undersecretary like me to type up the transcripts right here in your room? That way they would be absolutely leak-proof."

Mr. Pope thought this an excellent notion, and he praised Mrs. Melhuish lavishly.

21

Not very long ago somebody had remodelled all the bedrooms, six of them if you counted the sleeping porch. There was another room on the ground floor that might be used as a guest bedroom or as a study, and then there was some space in the cellar, where there was a finished recreation room. A big house, though it was only two storeys. For some obscure reason I'd had my heart set on a house with attic rooms. Just one more flight of stairs to climb and trouble with your cleaning woman and her vacuum cleaner, and this and that.

There was a little conservatory on the ground floor off the dining-room on the south side of the building, with that greenish glass curving up to a recessed roof line, and terracotta tiled flooring. There was even a little drain in the floor, suggesting serious potting and planting. I liked that. It made me think of Forest Hill. There was a large kitchen and pantry, and a back staircase leading from the side entry to the kitchen and then to the two small bedrooms at the back of the second floor where there was a small but perfectly serviceable bathroom. The house was designed to accommodate a family of five and a live-in couple. Imagine that! We never hired a live-in couple at any time, not even when the children were very young, though we did from time to time have a maid or an au-pair girl in the house for longer or shorter periods.

I'd have thought that young Anthony was a little too old to take much interest in a back staircase, but it charmed him. He imagined it at once as a secret passageway. While we were inspecting the building he kept racing up and down the back stairs, or hiding in between the upstairs and downstairs with both doors closed. The younger kids liked this feature of the house too. They were more impressed by the row of hooks and hangers inside the door to the back stairs than they were with the way the bedrooms had been tarted up.

We imagined that the boys would share a room, with Andrea in a room to herself, and Edie and me in the master bedroom with bath en suite. There was a smaller bathroom between the childrens' bedrooms, and another in the "servants' quarters." And there was a powder room just inside the front door, so we would be pretty well off for bathrooms. There was even a remote and secret toilet somewhere in the recesses of the cellar, in a smelly cubicle next to the oil tank. Some toilet-bowl salesman with a gift for the gab must have caught the builder on a good day.

The boys' room had built-in beds along the walls, gotten up to look like berths in a stateroom aboard ship. The wallpaper carried out this motif; there were portholes pictured on the paper. There were actually a couple of framed charts hanging on the walls, "Approaches to Spithead" was one of them, as I recall. I thought that these suggestions of life afloat might have triggered some reaction from Anthony. No such luck. He never mentioned them once, and John was too young to take any notice. He was still only three and a half, and his older brother might have been expected to rebel at the prospect of sharing a room with baby brother. But he never did. He was very good about it. The boys seemed to enjoy being in there together. They poked around in the built-in lockers. John found two marbles left behind by some former resident. When he displayed them to Andrea, she began at once to weep and beg that we try to restore them to their rightful owner; there could be no question of our keeping them. She kept asking me about the fate of those marbles for years until she finally forgot about them when nearly in her teens. I sometimes wonder whether she's ever forgiven me for not taking the trouble to hunt down their "rightful owner." That girl's too tender-hearted to live. She cries at card tricks.

Now it's true that there had been another bomb incident in Westmount not two blocks from the house, just a couple of weeks before. A sergeant-major in charge of a bomb-disposal squad, who was trying to extract a small explosive charge from the corner mailbox, had been maimed for life when the thing went off in his arms. But we were very keen on the house and its location on Belmont Avenue, just south of Westmount Avenue. We liked the layout and the excellent condition of the building, and were ready to treat the bombing as an isolated incident.

When we got around to talking price, however, I had to call a halt. Forty-nine thousand and a twenty-year mortgage, renewable every five years starting at eight and a half. Well, my God, eight and a half was bad enough, but every five years the trust company gets the chance to shove the rate up, and don't ever think they won't, even to a most-favoured client. We were now in early December. Edie was very much on edge, largely because of her work on the theatre mural; we wanted the place as a Christmas present for ourselves and the children. But I couldn't hold still for the price.

"House prices must be inflated out of all proportion around here," I told Edie when the realtor, a bulky woman with a talent for closing deals, had left us alone. "I imagine it's because of Expo."

"Matt, the house is a bargain at that price and you're just too goddamn dumb to see it. If you try to get smart about it, we'll lose the chance of a lifetime."

I couldn't see it her way. "This house will still be on the market next fall, when Expo is over and the hoopla has died down, and prices will fall to a reasonable level. We'll get it for thirty-nine thousand."

"OK, kids," said Edie, "back to Stoverville!"

"Awwwww, Mom!"

IV

22

The promotional piece had taken much time to develop, had probably not been shipped to customers and suppliers quite in time for the holiday, but would likely come into offices and boardrooms across the continent early in Centennial Year. This reflection comforted George Robinson as he played with the stunning toy, sitting at one end of the games room in Robinson Court. He had the piece set up as if for display on the billiard table, where the clear Lucite (polymerized methyl methacrylate) moulding that enclosed the working parts shone softly, taking on a greenish-yellowish tone from the green-shaded lamps that hung low over the table, no doubt also from the green of the table covering. The rest of the long room was in semi-darkness. The night before there had been a formal party in celebration of Philippa's sixtieth birthday, and a scent of face powder, champagne dregs, expensive cigars, the sugary tang of birthday cake, lingered in the games-room air. This evening all was silence; the lamps over the table hung still, their wide shades forming rings of light suggestive of an old-time pool parlour, a subtle accent intentional and effective in the interior design.

The Lucite moulding was almost as perfectly transparent as fine crystal or plate glass, but not quite; there was the faintest suggestion of steam or mist in the panels, not unpleasing to the inspecting eye. They couldn't have used crystal or glass anyway, because the whole point of this model display piece was that you could swing it open and shut it with plenty of oomph. When you closed it, the miniature door was meant to fasten shut with a satisfying thunk like that of an expensive new car. The product design staff at Automotive Lock and Latch had been made to study and had finally solved the problem of reproducing in miniature the authentic new-car-door-thunk in order to encourage production execs to play with the piece. The idea was to send several hundred fully assembled mini-kits around the industry at Christmas with a little instruction booklet entitled AN OPEN AND SHUT CASE: THE A.L.L. STORY. Once the unsuspecting executive had been persuaded to open and shut the little toy door (and not so little neither, the whole installation standing twenty-six inches high on a teak base) he might find the feel of the heavy little door in his hands so satisfying, so evocative of what everybody in the industry was always trying to produce (solidity at a price) as to keep the gift on his desk or at least somewhere on display in his office.

Some nervous and anxiety-ridden vice-presidents and board chairmen might even acquire dependence on the gadget, a nervous habit of swinging the door open and shut, punctuating their addresses to superiors, associates, inferiors, whole meetings of them, with the repeated thunks of the A.L.L. model door. Golmsdorfer, whose idea this had been, imagined an industry-wide rhythmic percussive chorus of door closings and openings, clickings of latches, clunkings as the door swung back on its perfectly machined hinges, thunks as door and frame met in perfect alignment. On the two-inch-thick teak base, in the precise centre just below the door-frame, there was a shining brass plate set flush with the wood, bearing the promotional announcement:

> Door-handle, thumb press-release, inner door release,
> Connecting arms, latch-tongue, matching door-frame
> receptor,
> Lock with on-off activator, assembly kit for GM Nova
> Series 1967 —
> By Automotive Lock and Latch of Woodstock, Ontario,
> A wholly owned subsidiary of RobPharm Delaware.
> Christmas 1966

The parts of the assembly were all in plain view, set into the protective and revealing Lucite panels. You could readily study the elegance and complexity of the apparently simple A.L.L. solution to the ancient automotive-industry bugaboo, the rattling loose-fitting door, the noise it created, the poor impression it gave of plant quality control. All over the world when auto salesmen tried to impress potential customers with the high production standards at the factory, the simple richness of the product, the second thing they did was open and slam the right front door. The first thing they did was kick the right front tire. They would insinuate to the buyer that once he got this unit out on the bumpy pot-hole-ridden roads of his native region, whether it be Paraguay or Pennsylvania, no door rattles would be encountered from this assembly for at least the length of the warranty. Nothing ages a car faster in the eyes and ears of the road tester than rattling doors, trunk lids, hoods, glove-compartment doors that flop open.

A cynical analysis of marketing practices might suggest that auto makers designed their equipment in such a way as to cause the doors, trunk lids, hoods to start to rattle halfway through the fourth year of vehicle operation, at approximately the thirty-five-thousand-mile mark. But nobody has ever been able to pin this on the auto-parts industry, and certainly the door-handle-and-lock kit embedded in the clear Lucite of George and Henry's fantastic Christmas present to the industry worked an articulated door and frame as a single, tightly fitted unit in a manner that met the highest standards of production quality control. You might open and shut the model door a hundred thousand times, and the rich baritone sound of the closing door would be as impressive at the hundred thousand and first slam as at the first. All the parts of the assemblage had been chromed and buffed to a high permanent shine, providing industry executives with an almost surreal insight into the obscure workings of the guts of an ordinary automobile door. Hardly anybody realizes what goes on inside a car door when you open it to climb inside, swing it shut behind you, depress the on-off lock activator, roll the window up or down. In fact Automotive Lock and Latch never got into window assemblies; that's a whole different world. Locks and latches were enough for them. If you count in every little screw, the total number of parts in a Nova front-door assembly, as produced for the 1967 models and the later production run, exceeded a hundred and fifty. And that's just for the right front door. And every one of those tiny parts had to be available in massive quantities at all times during the long production run of the vehicle in its various incarnations from 1967 to 1974, and for the life of the surviving vehicles after production ceased. This particular assembly kit was but one of more than four hundred types of equipment produced by the RobPharm subsidiary from the mid-sixties to the present. Control of inventory, continual modification of design and production schedules, sponsorship of research in alloys and plastics, redesign of handles, switches, buttons, repeated attempts to simplify the solution to the problem of how to open and shut a door — and keep it safely shut during operation at constantly changing speeds on bad roads — all these undertakings had to be scheduled, monitored, sometimes abandoned, sometimes speeded up and intensified. It is a curious fact that the basic principles of the door lock and latch were understood, the fundamental design worked out, before the invention of the internal combustion engine. When you pulled shut the door on your wagonette, brougham, landaulet, barouche landau in the 1860s, the door handles worked pretty much the same way they do now. There have been minor advances in design, and the metallurgy of the operation is more sophisticated, but the lock and latch mechanisms remain classical in design and no modification of the classical layout is looked for in the industry. It was much to the credit of the Woodstock plant that they had succeeded in establishing themselves as one of only three major suppliers of lock and latch components to the North American industry, standing in relation to the market somewhat as Delco-Remy, Bendix, Continental, and a very few other major subcontractors did in their areas of specialization: electrical equipment, brake shoes and linings, six-cylinder engines. The RobPharm subsidiary stood almost alone in its field, the other major suppliers being based in Texas and California, with distracting specialization in equipment designed for the aerospace industry.

"Concentration," muttered George Robinson, squinting in the green light at the door-frame of his toy. "Division of labour, specialization." Philippa entered the other end of the room, standing for a moment in the shadows to look anx-

iously at her husband. She listened hard, hearing only
inconsecutive and confusing mumblings. George poked at
the inner door-frame, pushing at something with his forefinger. Then he drew the little door full open and inclined his
head, to stare closely at the inner upright of the door-frame.
With his right hand he jiggled a small piece that protruded
from the frame, the grooved receptor bed into which the tiny
tongue of the latch was designed to fit.

"Loose," he complained. His wife felt a chilling shiver
traverse her spine. The games room was always cold at this
time of year. She glanced at the sliding glass panels that
secured the room from the moving winds of January, sound-
ing outside like a demonic voice. Centennial Year, thought
Philippa. A hundred years of this. The frozen river waited for
them outside in the dark. She shivered again and decided not
to address George. She realized that she missed her son Gus
dreadfully.

Like a sensible wife she forbore to trifle with a man's
concentration on his purposes. Instead she went rapidly to
the distant suite of rooms inhabited by Esther and Henry,
where she spoke urgently to her son-in-law. What she said
alarmed him and he descended the stairs, a back staircase very
remote from the public areas lying towards the entry hall of
the great house. He traversed long, ill-lit passages, and at
length found himself standing behind a barely opened door
around which he could peep into the games room, so close to
George that he could almost touch him. He could easily hear
and understand his father-in-law's breathless exclamations.

"It's hanging loose; it won't fit." The distracted Solon
swung the little door shut with ferocious energy, then flung
it back violently on its hinges and let it rebound from the full
open position until it stood halfway shut. He slammed it
again, and the sound it made was not a thunk. It was more of
a thunk-clatter-rattle.

"It's rattling," said George in the accents of deep pain.

He opened the door wide and performed a desperate
action. Taking a small gold penknife and cigar cutter from
his vest pocket, he bent and brought his head as close to the
door-frame as possible. He started to tighten and loosen the
four infinitesimal screws that held the shiny receptor compo-

nent firmly in place in the cast Lucite frame. All of a sudden
the tiny piece fell abruptly to one side. Robinson gave a
perplexed grunt. He then tried to shut the door. Now it
wouldn't close, the tongue failing to fall into its groove. It
was a question of readjusting the receptor plate in precisely
— precisely — the correct position to receive the moving part.

This is an adjustment of fiendish subtlety, to be accomplished by hand only by the most experienced of servicemen.
George Robinson's faculties were not equal to the delicacy of
perception required for the task. Once he almost succeeded in
finding the proper angle, but at the last second the piece slid
off abruptly at a bad angle, just as he tried to tighten the third
screw of four. In desperation he held the deeply grooved little
piece, about the size and weight of a square of hard rubber,
tightly in his left hand, while rotating the screws feverishly
with the point of the small blade in his penknife. Henry
gazed breathlessly at him — the strained bent back and
tensely working elbows. There were mumbled curses and
sudden expulsions of breath, gasps that were almost sobs of
frustration. The four tiny screws were tightened to the point
where they would be next to impossible to displace, the small
part forever affixed to the door-frame. George stepped away
from his handiwork, then turned swiftly and slammed the
little door. Thunk!

He gazed at it with profound satisfaction.

Then came a second sound as the tongue slipped in the
misaligned groove. The door was locked shut all right, but it
rattled, hanging off true in the frame. Robinson felt around
the top of the frame with his long arm, unlocked the door,
bent forward again and attacked with his knife an almost
invisible freely rotating toothed wheel that caused the
moving tongue to alter its angle as it moved, something like a
worm gear or a differential. He inserted the tip of the blade
into the notched piece that held the cog in place. It immediately came away from its position and the cog fell to the
floor, bouncing once and rolling away under the billiard
table.

Golmsdorfer stepped into the room now, deeply annoyed.
"Now you've really gone and done it good."

White-faced, trembling, the older man breathed at him, "I

deny it. I don't in the least know what you mean." A hand scrabbled behind him on the piled carpet, feeling blindly for the escaped part.

"You will never get it back together." Voice of doom!

23

Linnet examined the tops of her thighs, which lay open to inspection, study, assessment, before her as she sat on a wobbly chair in the alcove at the rear of the Trattoria Alpina. The proprietors, Domenico Varetto, his wife, and their small son Angelo, would have died rather than expose her to any unwelcome public gaze. They always seated her and Tony in this place behind the staircase and the bar, where no more than four could dine at any time, at the two narrow tables in the small recess. Angelo, five years old, approached them with a wide flat bowl of steaming minestrone, which he lifted with every precaution and set before Tony, motioning silently at a shaker of cheese that stood at the other end of the table. Tall for his age, with pale skin, deeply hollowed cheeks, a long head and a serious, loving expression, the child reminded Linnet forcibly of the central angel in Giovanni Bellini's *Dead Christ with Child Angels* at Rimini. There was the same purity of concentration in the child's regard, the same tender innocence and pity in the unmoving eyes, as in Bellini's touching study of pure spirits contemplating without comprehending the passionate dead Christ.

Proportion, thought Linnet, proportion. He's only a child in a restaurant carrying a bowl of hot soup. But the resemblance was inescapable, the faint colour in the pallor of the tilted cheek, the fall of the hair identical.

"*Angelino mio,*" she said, and the child giggled.

"*Carissima Donnalinetta,*" he said in reply.

The boy's father brought Linnet an enormous pile of greens. "I have dressed it myself and you will like, you will like." He laughed exuberantly. The scent of the dressing was mouth-watering; she ate copiously.

Tony said, "You eat like a cock sparrow."

"Have you ever watched a cock sparrow eat?"

"Yes."

"They're at it all the time."

"But they don't get any bigger."

"I'm getting bigger," said Linnet, looking down at her exposed thighs. They seemed needlessly plump to her but would not have seemed so to anybody else. "I tell you what it is, I'm bored to death with these ridiculous skirts. I want some decent covering for my legs and I'm tired of being stared at. I'm going to get myself some ankle-length tweeds."

"And very nice too," said Tony placatingly as Domenico arrived with their veal, huge succulent portions festooned with tomato and strips of melted cheese. Linnet looked at her portion almost adoringly. She chased a last cucumber slice around her salad bowl for a moment, caught it in her fingers, licked the pungent oil and vinegar from it and swallowed, crunching the slice briskly between small teeth. Tony appreciated this action: he enjoyed watching the woman eat and eat and never grow any bigger or change at all except to grow more blonde, more wide-eyed, more lovely. He thought, she has the most perfect temples known to me.

"So Sadie and Adam are packing it up," said Linnet, bending her head over her plate and inhaling with satisfaction. She took up a fork and poked with authority at a layer of cheese, which she peeled away from the veal in a single strip. A look of extreme pleasure stole across her face.

"I expect they will sooner or later but nobody knows where or when."

"Why ever not?" said Linnet around a mouthful. "I could give a shrewd guess. I don't believe Sadie will join Adam in . . . what's the name of that place where your brother lives?"

"Stoverville."

"That's it. Stoverville. It sounds like something from the American writing of the eighteen-eighties. It makes me think of *Tom Sawyer.*"

"When did you ever read *Tom Sawyer?*"

"Every well-brought-up young English girl reads masses of American books that were popular at the end of the last century. *Helen's Babies. What Katy Did. The Story of a Bad Boy. Little Men. Little Women,* for the matter of that."

"Now I never knew that. What else did you read?"

"*Huckleberry Finn. The House of the Seven Gables.* And the one about the white whale."

"As though the American classics were books for children. There's something to be said for that view."

"I don't think it was for that reason exactly. I remember loving Rip Van Winkle and Ichabod Crane."

"Isn't that funny," said Tony, "and yet, I can see it. I read all kinds of English books when I was a child in Toronto."

"Stoverville, on the river," said Linnet dreamily. She had gotten through her plate of veal and now looked hungrily at Tony's.

"Shall I order you another serving?"

She considered this, then sighed. "No." She looked at her lower half again with misgivings. "It's odd. When you overeat you expect to see the weight appear on your frame at once, long before you've assimilated the meal." She pinched herself. "Bugger miniskirts," she said. "Tweed for mine."

"What do you think Sadie will do?"

"Oh she'll jettison poor Adam at any moment. I simply can't imagine Sadie in Stoverville. Ah, Stoverville, quiet river village of the nineteenth century. Punts. Scullers."

"Sadie has been in places like Stoverville often enough."

"No doubt. But has she remained there?"

This was an unanswerable objection.

"I never thought it would last this long. What is it, three years?"

"They were married in December of 1964, that's two and a half years. Not quite two and a half years."

"And what's been the trouble?"

"Darling Tony. I should think that what poor Sadie needs most of all at this moment is a guiltless fuck."

"But would Sadie ever feel guilty about anything?"

"Tony, Tony, she's raddled with guilt, just as we all are." Linnet eyed her companion over the rim of her outsize wineglass. She rinsed a mouthful of wine around her teeth, enjoying its rough flavour, then swallowing.

"What are you guilty of, Linn?"

"You don't have to be guilty to feel guilty."

"It certainly helps though."

Linnet giggled. "That's a line straight from *Dirty Duck*."

"*Down Off a Dirty Duck?*" said Tony. "Is it really? I can't place it."

"It isn't really but it might be."

"What are you getting at?"

"There's Sadie, ensconced — if that's the word I'm looking for — in fabled Bel Air, filming with Moses, imagine that! Still making pots of money from *Out by Midnight,* with the ball at her feet, the ring on her finger."

"The rope round her neck, the wolf at the door."

"Boo-hoo-hoo," said Linnet. "I want another good part, Tony. Since you require me to spit it out, I want a part in a play that becomes a film, and not a *succès d'estime* either. A success with everyone."

"That's what we'd all like, isn't it?"

"I expect so, but you and I could manage it between us. Tony, I want to play Linda Mountjoy."

"What, Linda Mountjoy in *Down Off a Dirty Duck?*"

"Oh yes, yes."

"I'd never allow it. Why . . . she's more or less a grown-up Zazie. Or Lolita."

"Yes yes yes," said Linnet delightedly.

"It isn't at all your part. The name itself is a rather dirty joke."

"More shame to you then. I want to do it."

"Oh God, I'd have to write another *play*! The nonsense, the horror, and, my dear, the *people*!"

Linnet fixed Tony with a piercing gleam; he felt himself begin to melt. "Oh Linnet," he said, "is that all you want from me?"

"Not quite all."

24

"Not quite right."

"Not right at all, far from being right. Wrong in fact."

"Can you come up, Mrs. Goderich?"

Why do I hate being referred to as "Mrs. Goderich," thought Edie. Is it because there can only be one Mrs. Goderich, the lady in the apartment in Toronto, poor old thing? Is she going to lose that eye? Is she? Ishy. She had never liked to think of her mother-in-law as "Ishy." The name had seemed over-sweet, immature, almost baby talk, and yet Andrew used it. Is she going to be lucky with that eye?

"Mrs. Goderich?" The workman's voice was lifted inquiringly in a hail, which blew away down the river. She would have to mount the scaffold.

"I'm coming up," she screamed into the March wind, just as Linnet Olcott, thirty-five hundred miles away, finished Tony's plate of veal. It was mid-afternoon in Stoverville, the unveiling of the huge mural only four weeks off, with much remaining to be done. The last coat had been applied to the upper third of the enormous painting, but about forty feet down from the roof line the painters had struck a patch of the brickwork that had suffered water damage at some time. The surface was soft, crumbly, permanently wet through as it seemed. Much time had been expended on an attempt to resurface this area with an artificial sealant, in the previous month when the chill of the last weeks of winter frustrated all attempts to glue or bond new surfaces to old. Various quick-drying cements and poly-fillers had been applied to the damaged surface, with mixed results. For a time the problem would seem resolved; then after a weekend or a wet night the surface would blister, grow porous, turn to wet dust. Unluckily the damage lay just at a crucial point in the narrative organization of the picture, where the figure of the Ideal Counterpart of Dramatic Art stood in her strong upstage-left position, about to receive the hand of Dramatic Representation from the Genius of Politics. The face of the Ideal Counterpart (Miranda, Sadie) and her flowing tresses, and much of her diaphanous drapery too, so suggestive of the figure of the beautiful Dale Arden (Flash Gordon's little pal), had been given in the painting with careful refinement, but dampness and rot kept on breaking through to obscure the delicacy of the rendering.

Up on the scaffolding near the decaying courses of painted brick stood Gregory Diachun, while his partner, Ted Buzinski, stood beside Edie at ground level, his face turned anxiously towards the bad place. These men, proprietors of the largest building-maintenance shop in the twin counties, had made time out of old friendship to supervise the execution of the mural; they had subcontracted out the actual application of the paint, but preparation of the surface, erection of the scaffolding, and concealment of the actual development of the picture under tarpaulins of the largest size, all this had been their responsibility. Most of the back wall of the theatre had proved sound and substantial and dry, but this one place, about thirty square feet in extent, baffled even Greg and Ted, like nothing else in their experience.

Careful measurements and a close structural examination of the interior wall, high up in the recesses of the fly galleries in the theatre, had not revealed the source of the continual damp decay. Was there maybe a concealed drain-pipe buried in the middle of the old brick courses and their plaster cladding? Examination of the roof revealed nothing. A body buried in the walls? Probes and electronic echo-soundings showed that the material of the wall at the suspect point contained only bricks, no human clay. Ambrose Small had managed the building in its earliest years but his body wasn't hidden in the walls, sixty feet above ground level. There must be some perfectly simple explanation — a fissure in the brickwork, a natural deficiency in the original building materials. Perhaps these bricks had been defective in the very kiln, uncommon clay. Whatever the cause, a remedy must be found before the end of the month.

"Greg, I'm coming up," shouted Edie. She walked with

Ted Buzinski to the open elevator platform, which was
operated by a highly informal arrangement of pulleys
powered from the four-wheel-drive take-off of a Land Rover.
There was a small wheelbarrow full of brick on the platform,
the only thing to sit on in the cramped space. Edie plunked
herself down on the bricks, which were piled unevenly in the
barrow, and watched edgily as Ted went over to his Land
Rover and threw a lever. Belts slapped on their drives. The
cables attached to the corners of the platform tautened, then
the platform rose from the ground, swinging cheerily in the
half-gale, and Edie rose, not too fast and not too steadily past
the rusted frames of the lower uprights. Ted seemed to grow
smaller beneath her as she ascended. She felt like some
princess in an Arabian Night seated on an improbably
enchanted rug. Where were all the camels and elephants?
Thump, bump, wobble. She came to the sixty-foot level and
walked with what composure she could muster onto the
walkway of plank laid over the frames. There was a safety rail
of sorts on the outward side of the scaffolding, but it was a
means of protection in which she could lodge small faith.
Her knees felt weak. She had been up two or three times
before, to see how the prepared surface took the paint. Now
she felt as though she could never have tackled the Sistine
assignment, even supposing it had been pressed on her.

"It'll all have to come out; we'll do it as soon as you go
down. Look, we'll knock it out from here, blue sky, that bit of
cloud, this bunch of the lady's hair, and the head and the neck
and the, uh, bust, all the way over to here, where the topless
towers are sticking up. The sky over the towers is all right and
that seagull or whatever it is, but the head and the neck and
the stuff that frames them, all that has to come out."

"You should have been a dentist, Greg."

"Talk about fillings, eh? We'll put you in a filling here
that'll last longer than the rest of the wall. Then we'll match
up the primer and the new paint job to the rest of it so that
you'll never be able to spot the repair, but we've got to work
fast. We can clean out the hole in the tooth and prepare the
filling in under an hour. I'll do it myself with Ted. Here,
look."

He showed her a wrecker's bar. One of those heavy steel

tools curved at both ends, with a chisel edge at one end and a split hook or probe at the other, just the thing for a mammoth dentist to use on mastodon tusks. Grinning with anticipation, he started to rip out the soggy bricks two or three at a time. In moments he had made a gaping hole in the wall.

"Easiest thing in the world," said Greg Diachun with deep satisfaction. "We'll work across till we're satisfied the old stuff is solid. Then we'll re-lay the courses. Why aren't you wearing a hard hat? Then we'll prime the new brick on Saturday and you'll be able to apply three coats before the unveiling. Here," he said, flourishing his mighty hook, "want to give it a go?"

"Why not?" said Edie. She took the wrecker's bar between her hands in the overlapping grip and swung the barbed end at the face of the Ideal Counterpart. This gave her considerable enjoyment. Face and neck were at once defaced, then caused to disappear entirely as a clotted group of sandy bricks came away from the wall in a rush. She felt the keen delight of the artist engaged in wholesale revision of a cherished work. The gap in the wall widened.

"Hey, this is great," she said. Puffs and clouds of brick dust and powdery mortar floated around her; she resembled some demonic agency discharging itself against the very idea of the drama, a mythic notion of great force.

"I wish I had a picture of this," said Greg. They could hear hard-hatted Buzinski hollering rapturously from below as bricks rained down upon him.

"You're looking real good in there, Edie," said Greg.

She was starting to puff. She had succeeded in dislodging elements of ten courses of brick, perhaps seven or eight square feet of the area to be reconstructed. She felt over-excited and slightly ashamed of the fervour with which she had attacked a design that was, after all, entirely her own conception. She had no personal feelings that she was aware of about the Ideal Representation of Dramatic Art nor about Shakespeare's Miranda nor certainly about Sadie MacNamara. Why had destructive energy so mastered her, lent such an expressive thrust to her assault on the wall? She turned away from the broken and cracking surface to hand her tool to Greg, and all at once she realized how high up she was. She took a step towards her companion and felt herself choking on a great cloud of swirling dust; it was very windy here. Particles gritted in her eyes, making them burn. She put her hand to her eyes and blinked rapidly, executing a swift half-turn as she passed the heavy metal bar to Greg. The planks lurched under her feet and her turn to her right towards the guard rail became swifter, more precipitate. As she opened her eyes she became aware of the vertiginous breadth of the prospect before and below her. She was looking out towards the river, still sheeted with late-winter ice. Yesterday and this morning a Department of Transport ice-breaker had been moving up and down river, just below the last of the islands, occasionally disappearing behind some point of land, then reappearing slowly, the throb of her powerful engines audible for miles, a very low steady all-pervading pulse. Edie admired the elegant execution of the red maple leaf on the vessel's stack. She could see for miles down river; the ice-breaker swam in her vision as dizziness overcame her. For several years she had felt increasing uneasiness whenever obliged to contemplate a long view in wide focus, some muscular adjustment of the eyes perhaps functioning incorrectly. Now she felt as if her eyes were struggling to take in too much. Her knees buckled and she grabbed at the inadequate safety railing. Greg Diachun, noticing her discomfort immediately, moved close and steadied her with his arm.

"Send 'er up again," he shouted to his partner. The cranky banging noise of the returning elevator was almost lost in the rush of the wind. Edie felt that she very much wanted to be someplace else. I've got to get down from here, she thought. Greg tightened his hold on her. Where's Matt this afternoon? Probably watching some damned rehearsal. I've had just about enough of this. She made her way to the elevator and was assisted to the ground.

"We'll rebrick it on the weekend, prime it Monday, see how she dries, then we can get the first coat on the middle of the week. It'll be fine," said Ted, helping her off the platform. "You'll see."

But Edie went away unpersuaded; she felt about ready to give up on the whole stupid undertaking.

25

If I'd had any idea, when the whole stupid business was getting started, of the unconscionable amount of trouble it was going to cause everybody, I think I'd have quashed it at the start, at the very first moment I heard news of it, when Valerie caught me on a public thoroughfare and boasted of her assurance that "the star from Stratford" would eagerly come to Stoverville accompanied by his renowned consort, to adjudicate the Dominion Drama Festival in Centennial Year. Surely I ought to have grasped at once that the whole business was misguided, likely to implode upon itself from excessive mass. How could I have been so stupid, so led astray by misconceptions and false hopes — and by my own malicious sense of humour — as to encourage Valerie in this folly? What in the name of God impelled me to lead Edie on the path of error towards the execution of the mural that now shone on the back of the theatre, destined to excite mirth from passers-by for the rest of the century, perhaps well into the next millennium? You never know what deplorable effects may flow from innocent compliments. A banal reflection, and it is no comfort to reflect that most reflections are, if not banal, at least reflections other people have entertained before. There is nothing new under the sun. I will spare myself further reference to Ecclesiastes, of all Biblical personages the most irritating in tone, the monarch of the I-told-you-sos. I seem to have had a hand in fucking up — to use no stronger term — the innocent pleasures of thousands, to have assisted at the destruction of a perfectly decent man who can have had no idea of what he was getting into when he agreed to adjudicate the Festival. When Valerie mooted the possibility that dangerous day, the day before I had my vision of the princesses (was it a vision or just a day-dream?) I ought to have scotched it, nipped it in the bud, told her that Adam Sinclair would not function in Stoverville as an ordinary human being, that alien elements would repel one another. How can I put this? When she told me that he would be coming in the spring of 1967 — almost a year away — I could have put a stop to it. I struggled nervously to conceal an impulse to hysterical laughter. How much better it would have been if I'd laughed in Valerie's face, told her and George that their proposal was absurd! But I allowed myself to believe that it might work out. I let it creep ahead, on all fours, with the development of the Codrington Colony for the Encouragement of Visionary Art. Were both projects founded on fissured and trembling premisses? Was the very existence of Adam Sinclair, even for so short a time as the inside of a week, so contrary to nature as the encouragement of visionary art in Stoverville, Ontario? Many reflections seem banal because they have long ago been found to be true. You can't have it both ways. There is nothing new under the sun. Innocent undertakings may issue in destruction. I wish I knew why antinomies perplex ethics and morals so insistently in a time when philosophy has turned itself into analysis of the meanings of sentences. You'd think at least that the ordinary language philosophers could teach us to say only what we mean, neither more nor less. No ironies, please! Gollies, how I hate irony! If I had laughed in Valerie's face and told her that Adam was leading a desperate and infinitely sad personal life, that we shouldn't bother him, that we should leave him alone, that he could not mesh with the ethics of Stoverville — never mind the morals — I'd have been saying what I thought, no more, no less. I'll have to work on that. I don't mind seeming dull and stupid and out of things. That's the moral postulate or *point de départ* of all Canadian men and women who see things as they are. It's a complex fate to be a Canadian, and a big hello to you, Henry James. Damn it, there I go again. I've reached the time in my life when I've got to stop fooling around and teasing other people out of thought by refusing to say exactly what I'm getting at.

"Valerie," I should have exclaimed loudly, "Adam will be a most unsuitable adjudicator."

But then I'd have had to explain myself to her, and any remarks I might have made would have lain widely open to charges of self-interest or malice or worse. I didn't know anything for certain about Adam or Sadie. I didn't even know what Tony thought about Adam. You can only discover these things by going ahead in the dark and accepting the consequences of your decisions.

I used to think, very naïvely, that the only grave problem to be met with in an analysis of the phenomena associated with our notions of time, of pure temporality, of succession, was the problem of the varying values of events. We are told by physicists that the universe began from nothing in an almost infinitely small interval of time and that universal history was forever plotted in that interval. Why, I wondered, do certain portions of experienced time seem more intense, more valuable to consciousness and memory (especially to memory) than other portions of equal duration? On that assumption, sequences composed of valuable moments may seem to unfold at different speeds than sequences composed of less pressure-filled moments. I remember observing that time somehow dictates its own dismemberment into parts, the years, the milliseconds. There is nothing either novel or subtle in this simple-minded observation. But at the time when I first put it to myself I had not had sufficient experience of the way in which time appears to fold back in upon itself as our memories grow longer, our length of time lived longer, like a carpet stretching out behind us, red, deep-piled, as we approach the place of enthronement. (Why red, why deep-piled, why clutter the argument with metaphor?)

As we age, it becomes evident that our meditations will often skew the values of previous events and their shapes when we revisit them either in memory or in later acted-out events that are connected to them. Valerie's decision to name Adam adjudicator was inextricably linked to my failure to advise her not to do this thing, linked too to Adam's collapse on the public platform last night. On close inspection later events reveal their linkage with earlier, and the earlier *grow in meaning and value,* change their shape, become tragic or comic or neither in reinterpretation, in light of later happenings. Time dictates a continual and polyvalent rereading of itself, such that everything that happens — absolutely everything — is continually being reinterpreted.

> Time present and time past
> Are both perhaps present in time future,
> And time future contained in time past.

Lines that I had read to me during my second week of university studies. I had no idea what they meant at that period and felt convinced that they were mere gibberish, a consequence of the then well-advertised "obscurity of modern poetry." "That's not poetry," I declared roundly to the man who read me the lines. Looking back on them now, I see that far from lapsing, as much of the poetry of that time does, into incoherent puerility, the quoted lines gain in significance with the passage of time. They have the peculiar feature of being an example of the metaphysical condition they assert.

We should never forget that new events, things that are happening now, are pregnant with heavy meanings as yet undelivered. The future is in the present and the past events. Our presence is futurity to what we were in the past. Adam's ruined torment — and who knows what Adam may survive to perform in the future — was future to Valerie's invitation of last year and has just started to become the past. I don't doubt that I shall have to revisit that horrid event many times yet, folding back over last night's disaster accretions of new meaning that may alter the intensity — the value as a coloured experience — of the event in inconceivable ways. I remember thinking at various times that the temporal process is involved with value in some way. Meaning and value are the fruit of which time is the seed. No. That's too poetic. Say simply that both meaning and value are involved (weak word) with time in some necessary way. You cannot understand, or segment, what is happening to you as it is happening. You can't see it straight; it just comes at you and over you, raw and hard. You shake your head and exclaim, what does that mean? What's that? And then, what *was* that? Later you ask, what did that mean?

Long afterwards you begin to see what was implied, to understand what happened and to compare what happened with other events; you become capable of valuation. Time passes: meaning emerges: values clarify. These are points I ought to have raised with my father as soon as I began to be conscious of the guilt I felt after Adam's adventures in Stoverville. This process should have begun the moment I took his phone call. The telephone rang in the Essexes' front hall as we dragged out a mournful Sunday brunch — on my birthday, as it happened — on the day after Adam's ignominious exhibition.

"Judge not," I said, "lest ye be judged." The phone rang in the hall and George took the call.

"He's right here," I heard him exclaim. He put his head around the door and spoke to me. "A call for you from Ottawa, redirected from your house."

Besides fatigue and terror I now felt mystification. "I'll take it," I said unwillingly, but I cheered up at once when I heard my dad's voice.

"I'm glad I got hold of you," he said. "I wanted to tell you about this, so that you don't see it first in tomorrow's paper."

I thought, what's he up to now?

"They're sending me to Peking," he said laconically. Only a veteran Goderich-watcher would have sensed how pleased and excited he was.

"You can't go to China," I said. "We have no diplomatic representation there, none to speak of anyway."

"I'm it," he said gleefully.

"An embassy?"

"Not precisely. Chairmanship of an exploratory committee with an accreditation to seek out ways and means of establishing trade relations, perhaps diplomatic relations in three or four years."

I said doubtfully, "Is your health up to it?"

"You know that I've always wanted to go there."

"I'm coming out to Ottawa," I said, "and we can ventilate the whole question of your health. I'm not letting you go junketting halfway around the world without a medical clearance."

"Come on up," he said with great vivacity, "you can go into the whole question with your friend Marianne. I'll probably be taking her along as principal secretary."

"Marianne?"

"Surely you remember my *chef de cabinet,* Marianne Keogh."

"Oh her," I said, "why should I consult her?"

"She has all my health records. She can put your mind at rest."

"I'd sooner discuss it with you," I said. For some reason I never feel really comfortable with Marianne Keogh.

26

You know how you can go for years without taking a really close look at somebody you know very well? That's how it was between me and Andrew. Me and my father. I never called him by his first name, and I shouldn't pretend that I did. Everybody else called him Andrew but I never did. Edie called him that, and there was always genuine affection in her use of the first name. I can hear her now.

"When are you coming in from Ottawa to see us? We never see you, Andrew."

It was Andrew this, and Edie that, between them. I used to sit and listen, on the rare occasions when the three of us met, with that peculiar sense of guilt mixed with exclusion and resentment that you have when a close relative, mother or father, discusses matters of interest to all three of you with your spouse. They always seem leagued against you, nodding in your direction now and then with seemingly indulgent chuckles. You feel left out and you don't like it one bit.

"We never see you, Andrew."

When Edie spoke to him in that familiar tone, which was perfectly well mannered — there was absolutely no reason she shouldn't address him by his Christian name — I was always made to understand that no matter how old I might grow I would always stand towards this man in a special relation that would not allow of perfect ease and familiarity. I've dozens of friends and acquaintances who are as old as my father, whom I address routinely by their first names. Past forty nobody is really any older or more experienced than anybody else, so I speak perfectly politely to Sam or Leo as though we were all the same age, though they are as old as dad. At certain times in one's life these generational distinctions should disappear into mere neatness of alignment.

One's parents, and especially one's father, are exempt from this graceful reconciliation. What usually happens, if they live long enough, is that we revenge ourselves upon them for their special ascendancy over us, by refusing them, when they grow old, any more than the status of our own wilful, irresponsible, rather naughty children. How often do we hear (as we ourselves age) the prideful and malicious explanation.

"I'm putting them into an apartment. My goodness they have no need to stay in that big house."

"I put her into a nursing home. There was nothing else I could do really."

I'm prepared to guess that in a hundred per cent of such cases the child who has reached the age to be in authority — as he thinks — over his aged parents, is taking a mean revenge upon them. What difference need it make to him if they want to stay on in the house in which they brought up their family? Maybe they like having the extra space. Maybe they're glad to be rid of the crowding and the noise and the mess, once their children are blessedly absent and the dog is dead. We children are perhaps uneasily conscious of how convenient it is for our parents to have us finally and definitively out of the way, when once we quit the nest, so that they can use our bedrooms for libraries, TV-watching rooms, music rooms, all those nooks and niches and special places that they've always wanted for themselves. A couple of adults in their seventies can very readily use ten or twelve rooms if they're lucky enough to have the space available and aren't in want — as so many are.

Think of the luxurious feeling of being able to wander quietly around the old house from room to room without the rushing bodies of the young thrusting against you. "We made them go into an apartment. My goodness, they didn't need all that space!"

Ten times out of ten this is said to explain an action that has a simple economic base. Why spend all that money on taxes, insurance, maintenance, paint, paper, simply to maintain two old people in luxurious spaciousness? The expenditure comes out of the potential estate. If they're allowed to spend ten thousand a year on an old house in an unfashionable neighbourhood (although it is never wise to write off an old neighbourhood too soon) that ten thousand is money thrown away that would be better invested in guaranteed-investment certificates or tax-exempt municipals or in growth securities or in. . . .

Honour thy father and thy mother.

At no time in my life would I ever have been able to say of Andrew and Isabelle (there, I said it) that I'd made them go into an apartment, or put them into a nursing home.

Isabelle ended up in a nursing home but I didn't want to put her there.

These matters never occur to you, not until you close in on deepest middle age, and where does that begin? Some people are middle-aged at thirty, some not until they die, and after they're dead nobody thinks of them as middle-aged, but as eternally young. To me, Bing Crosby will always be a college boy.

When Andrew called me from Ottawa to announce his mission to Peking, or Bei-jing as he shortly began to call the place, I'd never thought of him as any of those polite synonyms for old. Getting on. A bit long in the tooth. A little frail. There are people whose careers are vested in frailty and obvious mild suffering. They come out of the bedroom in the morning, saying nothing about how they passed the night, brave little smiles on their drawn faces, cold-water compresses at the temples. They don't want to have any special attention paid to them. If they just sit here for a minute it'll be all right.

The only way to fight this is with your hat. Grab it and run!

My father never descended to these stratagems. His ploy was to look exactly the same forever. When he was in his thirties and we were infants he used to sing nonsense songs of his own devising while wandering apparently aimlessly around the house.

> Don't use your niblick on the Kniblocks.
> Use your niblick on the Kniblocks' lawn.

That was his golf song. He and I knew what it meant but nobody else ever did, not even my mother. I admired deeply the exquisite poetic control of the inner rhyme of "niblick"

and "Kniblock" and the alliterative turn to the concluding
line of the couplet, "Kniblocks' lawn." My dad had many
nonsense refrains of this kind, peopled by improbable beings
with names that could have been invented by nobody else.
Nonsense which I can associate specifically with different
periods in our lives. He never abandoned this habit of
singing to himself in a loud, well-produced tone and an
exquisitely definite diction. The persistence of this annoying
habit into the later phases of his life was one of the things that
in my eyes kept him eternally young. He never showed
fatigue, frailty, impoverishment of ideas, lessening of motive
power. He was always the same.

When I told him that I'd come up to Ottawa that summer,
while he was assembling the staff members who would
accompany him to Peking (Bei-jing), mentioning that I
knew his health would be a factor in the undertaking, I was
simply entering the routine protest that one does when he
knows that somebody of sixty-seven intends to assume heavy
new responsibilities. I meant the remark as a formal acknow-
ledgement of a responsibility I'd never felt before.

"Is your health up to it?" I'd never have dreamed of putting
such an invasive and impudent question to my father at any
previous time. His health was his own responsibility. Neither
he nor my mother had ever indicated that he had misgivings
about his physical powers. I wasn't seeing enough of them to
have any proper sense of how they felt. When I heard the
impudent question pop unprompted from my mouth, I
realized as I uttered it that I was simply voicing my own
uncertainties. How can a man of sixty-seven propose a
voyage to the other side of the world, I asked myself, when I'm
afraid of a move from Stoverville to Montréal? I'd never gone
anywhere special. It is true that I was thinking about taking
a trip to Italy for purely personal reasons; there were paintings I hoped to see before the impulse to travel faded forever
from my thoughts. I never went anywhere outside Canada,
however, until I was well past my fortieth birthday. And here
was my father, who hadn't been out of Canada for more than
a few days since he came back from Stockholm in 1950,
suddenly declaring his intention to proceed to China, or
about as far away as possible. How long would he be gone
this time? When he went to Europe in 1941 he was gone for

seven years — just the time of a good solid well-worked fairyland spell — like Tiresias or True Thomas or Tom Thumb or some other figure from myth or folklore. Now that he was bound for the Northern Court, would seven years once again prove the term of disappearance? If so, he would be seventy-four upon his return, and I would be in my mid-forties.

I went up to Ottawa the next morning. I had an appoint-ment with him in that little suite he used to maintain in the Lord Elgin. I parked the car near the hotel and went into the news-stand to pick up the *Globe and Mail,* the *Gazette,* and *Le Devoir.* I went into Murray's for coffee; it was about ten-thirty and I had time to spare before I went upstairs — my appointment was for eleven. I looked quickly through the three newspapers; there was no official announcement of any projected mission to Peking. I thought back to our conver-sation of the previous day, Sunday. He must have spoken to me before the public announcement, which would probably come this afternoon if it were to come at all. It wasn't meant to be a secret mission and it wasn't any kind of formal diplomatic move. It remained to be seen, therefore, precisely what sort of gesture was implied.

There had been regular exchanges of purely commercial representatives between ourselves and Peking prior to this date, almost all of them connected to the shipment of grain from our west-coast ports to their mainland, or with the banking arrangements necessary for the transfer of credits that paid for these shipments. There had been occasional furtive private visits, possible soundings of opinion about closer contacts. Fred Nossal was in place on behalf of the *Globe* from the last days of the nineteen-fifties. Naturally Canadian policy towards the regime would always hew closely to the lines laid down by the US, in and out of the United Nations and in private exchanges between Ottawa and Washington. Nobody in the Canadian government in the mid-sixties cared to appear as the Trojan horse or the stalking-horse, or any other kind of horse belonging to the US. Our grain sales had been achieved in free and open competition with producers in the United States. We had not tailored our grain-sales policies to suit our neighbours.

There were sound international reasons for Canada's

entering into preliminary discussions with those in power in
Peking. The first generation of Maoist leaders was now
entering old age. At some time towards the end of the decade
or the beginning of the seventies there must come the begin-
nings of a transfer of power to younger men, whose management of affairs might proceed on quite different lines to those
already laid down. There was the vexed question of Chinese
atomic research; there was the proposal invariably put up by
the occasional Chinese official who found his way to Ottawa
of a relaxation of tariffs on the entry of foreign cottons. Entry
of low-cost Chinese textiles in quantity would reduce the
Canadian textile producers to the status of clients of the
federal government, a development that would deeply
antagonize the province of Québec. But the Chinese could
supply low-cost fabrics in uncut pieces or in the form of
cheap trousers, shirts, blouses, an endless list of items, in
quantities and in selections of colours, and weights of fabric,
that would simply drive Canadian producers out of the
industry. This would be a boon to Canadian consumers but a
great hardship to Canadian textile workers.

There were multitudes of matters like this to be thought
over and discussed informally before any rapprochement
could be mooted between Canada and the People's Republic.
At the same time, Peking must sooner or later be brought
into the international community, if the policies of the great
powers were ever to achieve any stability. The US could not
maintain a stance of unrelenting hostility to both China and
the USSR. Washington must eventually befriend one of the
two Socialist powers, if not both. Which was it to be? Wea-
pons diplomacy would most likely force that decision upon
whichever American president moved towards an understanding with China or Russia.

China, after all, possessed a common border with the
Soviet Union that extended from Vladivostok along the
boundaries of Manchuria, Mongolia and Sinkiang as far as
the eastern panhandle of Afghanistan, almost to Kabul, a
border that extended halfway across Asia. Any Soviet move to
strengthen an already powerful influence in Afghanistan
would be regarded with profound mistrust by Peking. Outer
Mongolia ranked as a most sensitive area in the estimation of
both powers.

US moves towards some sort of understanding with Peking obviously could not be postponed much longer. Could Canadians, by luck or by sound quiet diplomacy, become the front runners in the courtship of China's leaders? Would not great benefits accrue to Canada if this were to prove a possibility? I scanned the three newspapers with care; there was nowhere any indication of a move towards such an undertaking. Was my father's mission to be purely informal and private, lacking the endorsement of the government? Time might tell.

I discarded the papers, which told me nothing, and went upstairs. As I came along the shadowy corridor towards my father's small suite, I was not wholly surprised to observe two blocky solid obvious RCMP types chastely patrolling the area outside the suite. They made no move to intercept me as I stepped briskly forward and knocked on the door. But they made me uneasy. They looked me over with dismaying care. After all, I've nothing to hide.

Marianne Keogh let me into the sitting-room. I remembered the Norval Morisseau lithograph on the wall facing the divan, from my only previous visit to these quarters. I hadn't liked it then and I didn't like it any better now.

"He's in the bathroom freshening up," said Marianne, not paying much attention to me. She bent over the coffee table, straightening up the bulky files and dossiers that lay there. I could hear Andrew chanting nonsense syllables to himself as he washed his face. "Don't use your niblick on the Kniblocks," he sang cheerily, "use your niblick on the Kniblocks' lawn."

This bright refrain helped to banish my forebodings. He came out of the bathroom looking astonishingly fit, thin, as sandy-haired and trimly barbered as I remembered from long ago.

"You remember Miss Keogh?" he said. "You see, I'm in good hands."

"I guess so," I conceded. I never really liked her.

27

When the letters started to arrive from China at the end of the summer — fit contributions to my enjoyment of Centennial Year — they weren't entrusted to ordinary postal service. They came in the bag, of course, as far as Ottawa, routed through from Seoul, and I had to go up to Ottawa and receive them by hand from a foreign-service officer, in the event almost invariably Mr. Pope, a person who had figured in my early adolescence as the big bogyman from Ottawa who had snatched my dad away on some mysterious errand. Now fast approaching retirement age, beginning to show the weight of years, smaller than I am, he seemed much less a terror out of the night than he did in 1942. All through Centennial summer Ottawa was a city swirling with unsubstantiated rumours. That Charlie Pope had overstayed his welcome at External. That Mike would retire as soon as the great Centennial observances were behind us. That the major contenders to succeed him would be: Paul Martin, Paul Hellyer, Mitchell Sharp, and Robert Winters. That John Turner might be everybody's second or third choice in a series of leadership ballots. I don't know how they can stand to live in that atmosphere in Ottawa. Rumours are begotten from lies and misrepresentations and only beget further lies. Brrr!

I used to be ushered into Mr. Pope's office precisely at the appointed hour; he never kept me waiting. He seemed to feel some obligation towards me. I believe that he knew that Amanda Louise lived with Tommy in New York and that Tony lived in London. Anyway the letters were always addressed to me, with instructions that I should communicate their contents to my mother who at that date could only have read them with extreme difficulty. I always read them to her, sometimes over the phone, sometimes face to face in the darkened apartment on Crescent Road. My mother never came to terms with the harsh grinding dictates of necessity. She minded my father's prolonged absence very much. It was the second time in their married life that he had gone away and left her alone and much in need of help. He had been lost to her from 1941 to 1948, when they were both still comparatively young people. My mother was only thirty-seven when Andrew Goderich went in search of Georg Mandel, very deep in the deadly shadows of Dachau. She had until then retained much of her girlish beauty and carefree manner. I think of her as she was in those days, as eternally young, vivacious, able to carry off her hard lot with dignity and energy. She had the hard consolation that tens of millions of young women all over the world had given up their husbands to the wars.

In Centennial Year, a quarter of a century down the road, no longer a young woman, she found it much harder to accept another long separation from her great love. Nobody knew in the summer of 1967 how long Andrew Goderich might be gone. Not very many people knew or cared that he was out of the country. The media coverage had certainly been stifled by the administration: there were scanty paragraphs in the *Journal* and the *Citizen* and the *Globe and Mail* — nothing whatsoever in *La Presse* or *Le Devoir* — which intimated that a well-known NDP member of the House had taken a little trip entirely on his own initiative to a place where most people could not freely go. He had been permitted to enter mainland China, so the stories suggested, because of his world-wide reputation as a man of peace, the Nobel Prize winner, enemy of all forms of prejudice. His official identity as an MP elected under approximately Socialist colours gave a modicum of credibility to these tales. It is highly instructive to learn how much can be enacted, of a highly confidential nature, right out in the open, if it seems slightly comic and boring, especially if the newspapers and television networks can be persuaded to ignore the venture as a cold story. The best way to get them to lay off is to be, or to seem to be, open, truthful, and dull. By this time of day most of the people in the media had become utterly bored by my

father and his doings. He hungered and thirsted after justice,
and everybody knows what the media think of that. High-
mindedness and truthfulness are the qualities that repel
newspapermen most of all, the professional qualifications
for their profession, and that of the television "journalist,"
being those of the pathological liar, the man who prefers lies
to truth. When my father simply went to the Far East with a
small staff, they wrote him off as somebody who had had his
time, who might be able to get himself elected in East
Gwillimbury any time he wanted but who would never
exercise real power or influence. They ignored him.

This was to his entire satisfaction, naturally, and to the
perfect satisfaction of Charlie Pope, who would receive me
with overstated cordiality, taking me by the hand and steer-
ing me to a comfortable armchair. Once or twice I noticed
that his hand betrayed a very faint tremor and perhaps a low
fever. He would hand me a sealed envelope that had so
obviously been opened at least twice before that it was
mutually embarrassing. Given the amount of time available
for this meeting, I might perhaps read over a few key passages
from the letter, more from courtesy than anything else, as if to
suggest that the contents weren't already perfectly familiar to
Mr. Pope. I read this particular letter to him in its entirety.

The *tze-kin ch'êng*. September 1st, 1967.

This is a much more northerly city than I'd ever imagined.
Imagine Philadelphia, but with many more hills, and houses
of lighter construction, and with tramways. The two cities
resemble one another in the way that Montréal always
reminds me of Hamburg. We have what appears to be
complete freedom to come and go, no Intourist surveillance.
Of course this freedom is somewhat hemmed in by our
linguistic incompetence, although I can tell you that I have
received many comments on my Chinese, which is said to be a
deplorable mixture of northern and southern dialects. I can
understand a lot of what is said to me, but my own expression
is limited. We will have to use interpreters for some time to
come. There is always that point at which you start to
anticipate what the interpreter is going to tell you, and then
you can get ready to dispense with his services. We may come

to that yet. Miss Keogh speaks no Chinese and appears to regard my humble efforts as wonderful, unheard of. She is very quick to read correctly other people's expressions and gestures, though she seems to grasp little of what is being said. I find her an invaluable sounding-board. We go over what we have been told every night, and we make a confidential résumé of all proceedings. I think that we may be invited to remain some time. . . .

You probably know that we came by way of Seoul, which greatly surprised me. I had automatically assumed that we would fly to Tokyo, then traverse both seas on a last leg to Peking. I found Seoul alarming. I don't think any of my colleagues in Ottawa will consider this an insecure or injudicious remark. It *is* alarming. It's a crossroads of the world to a much greater degree than Cairo ever was, full of brooding and throbbing unseen presences — you feel them in the air — of the USSR, the US, Japan of course, China, the four greatest powers on earth, in a situation which I might describe as explosive if I were a man who employed that diction. Seoul made me acutely uncomfortable; it's a little like Sarajevo, a city of no importance in itself for its geography or population but of acute, terrifying importance strategically. It's not that far from Nagasaki either.

I may have more to say about Seoul later on. They really sneaked us in and out most unobtrusively. I suppose the US intelligence services were aware that we passed through but I'm inclined to think that they weren't very interested in us. All to the good. The way to handle this mission is to routinise it as much as possible, wrap it, muffle it, in statistical reports. I suppose there's a banality of good as well as evil. I've disguised myself as a middle-grade civil servant and the disguise works admirably.

Peking. Peiping. Pékin. Nobody knows how to spell the name for certain. The orthography we use in the West is a bastard combination of French and English spellings arrived at a hundred and fifty years ago, perhaps longer, when almost nobody in the West could understand the tongue, or even hear its sounds. They have an orthography here based on something called the Pinyin alphabet, in which Peking becomes Bei-jing, which is supposed to be much closer than anything else to the true sound of the name. I can't hear the phonemic differentia myself. The main man I've been talking to here spells his name, in Pinyin, quite differently than I'd expected. I'd heard of him beforehand as T'eng Chiao Pin, and now it appears that he's really Deng Xiao-ping. I'm probably mispronouncing the name. He's no middle-level civil servant though. In the next evolution he'll emerge close to the top, I shouldn't wonder. This man has offered me a tour of Sinkiang and the Mongolian border, and has had much to say about the cultural parallels shared by very large countries. Guess which countries he considers the most important! You might be surprised. He's a man perhaps five years younger than I am, and looks about forty; you know how they are.

My best love to all of you:

28

I hadn't seen a garden swing in that conformation for thirty years, but I felt that as I was setting up a household of my own for the first time in my life, with a wife and children to care for and the customary parental responsibilities in hand, I ought to try to provide the same set of family icons as I'd cherished when an infant. They still make those red-and-white garden swings in Québec and I had no trouble laying hands on one for our back yard, where it immediately became the favourite vehicle of my son John. We'd done it, you see.

We'd signed ourselves into bondage for twenty years to the mortgage and trust company. We bought the house at 620 Belmont Avenue, corner Westmount, in which we intended to live the rest of our lives together. We completed the purchase in the middle of a killing transit strike in October, and moved in at the end of that month. Saturday, October 28, coincidentally the last day of Expo 67. I remember that because Edie persuaded me to take the kids to Expo, while she told the movers where to put things. I found this a tricky assignment. I spent six hours taking John to the bathroom or looking around in a parent's agony, trying to spot Anthony and Andrea. Once I instructed them to stay on a specific bench while I wrestled with John's many buttons in the lavatory. When I emerged with him, they'd vanished. Next thing I knew I was standing open-mouthed on the ground as they soared past sixty feet in the air on the Minirail hollering as they went.

"We're going all the way around. Wait there for us."

And with that they disappeared into Bucky Fuller's geodesic dome, the glamorous American Pavilion, receding in the distance while John tugged at my hand and demanded

impatiently that we follow their car. Nothing would please
him but a ride on those aerial cars, as he called them. I don't
have any idea where he found the words. Could he read?

John Sleaford Goderich had at that date a voice that I can
only describe as furry. A furry, textured sort of little voice,
which he could make amazingly emphatic from time to time.
He never screamed or cried; he simply grew more and more
precise in enunciation.

"Daddy, I want to go on those beautiful aerial cars."

I have invariably been charmed and persuaded by accurately delimited demands.

"Wait till they get back, and I'll take you all around
again."

"But then they'll have had two rides and I'll only have had
one."

I thought his use of the complex verb-structure "only have
had" quite remarkable in a four-year-old. He always talks
like that.

"Then we'll ask them to stay here, once we've all gone
round together, and you can come with me. That'll even
things up."

"You won't give them extra money for snacks?"

"I won't give them anything that you don't get too. Mind
you, they're older."

"Well, since they *are* older, you might allow them an extra
hot dog while we're gone."

Trying to balance out the total number of Minirail rides
became a group preoccupation as the day wore on. In the end,
all four of us got to inspect every corner of the grounds from
the vantage-point of those beautiful aerial cars at least three
times. I'm not wildly keen about riding on more or less
exposed seats high in the air. But I was willing to exchange a
certain amount of vertigo for the chance to keep the three of
them close under my eye. Tony was nine that year, and very
little bother. He would make reasoned proposals, very
seldom disobey, and if disobedient could always produce
persuasive excuses.

Andrea was something else. She was seven when Expo
ended, and she was a handful. On that visit she was the shit-
disturber. Never a noisy or crudely intransigent person,

neither obstinate nor stubborn, she was very hard to lead in the direction in which you hoped she might move. She always ended by going where she wanted to go, unless coercive force were brought to bear. It was Andrea who quitted the assigned spot when I took John to the bathroom, causing her older brother to follow her with, as he stated, the object of keeping her in sight. I can see them now, Andrea standing there with her little air of sweetly reasonable evasion, Tony very responsible and unable to clarify his sister's motives, John concentrating on various buttons and zippers in the region of his pants, as the thinning crowd swirled around us. The great and storied World's Fair breathed its last.

They'd been there before, at least two or three times. We all loved Expo 67. I think it might have been the single greatest element in our decision to move to Montréal. It made me see that house property in Montréal was going to continue to inflate in price. I'd predicted that house prices in the city would fall after Expo was over, but they didn't. Prices continued steady and rising, and they have continued to do so ever since, with modest readjustments occurring during periods of political unrest. It seems clear to me now, looking back on it with heightened insight, that the previous owners of our house had set a price for themselves and stuck to it, Expo or no Expo. We couldn't talk them down at all, and in the end we paid a substantially higher price than we'd expected.

I'd outsmarted myself. That wasn't the first time I'd done it, and I don't suppose it will be the last. I was none too bright about our mortgage arrangements either. Edie kept insisting that there was no need for a mortgage, that we could take a capital sum out of the estate holdings. But no, I was too smart for that. I had no idea that drastic inflation, rising in the end to double digits, was to become a constant element in Canadian life — in the life of the entire world — over the next fifteen years. I thought that prices would reach a plateau, then perhaps decline. We accepted one of those twenty-year mortgages that have to be renewed by both parties every five years. I had declined an interest rate of eight and a half per cent the previous year. We had to agree to nine and a quarter when we made the purchase. Renewable in 1972, 1977, and 1982, and at no time did the rate decline in the renewal years. It fluctuated once in a while but every time we signed up again the rates were on their way to new peaks. I never try to give the impression that I'm always right, about everything under the sun. To be right all the time, never to make a mistake, would be an intolerable condition for a human being and boring besides. I'd sooner be wrong than be president.

We took on the mortgage, and my goodness, what a huge sum of money we threw away on interest payments! There is just this one further point to make. Edie never reproached me for that, not once. I cost her and the Codrington estate plenty, but we both realized that we'd been caught in an economic change that was world-wide. I guess that Edie didn't feel inclined to blame me for something that was happening to people everywhere. At least we didn't carry that mortgage right through the twenty-year period. Over the full twenty years we'd have paid more than the face value of the loan in interest. Me and my investment strategies. Huh!

We could have moved into the house long before October 28, if it hadn't been for an occurrence that seemed unheard of and unique at that date, later on revealing itself as the first or second link in an endless hideous chain of inconveniences to the public. I'm referring to the transit strike of October 1967, which buggered up Montréal life for most of the month. There is nothing like a transit strike to bring out the best and the worst in a city's population. At first it seems almost exhilarating. Young women bicycle along the crowded thoroughfares on their way to the office, showing their legs and getting their pictures in the papers. Skirts were very high that year; visible elements of leg were extensive. People hitch rides and other people pick them up quite cheerfully, carrying on detailed and intimate conversations they would never undertake otherwise. Some few lasting relationships are inaugurated in this way. Friendships, flirtations, court-ships, intrigues flourish under these artificially induced conditions of strain, and the opening ten days of the strike retain a tone — progressively attenuated — of nervous vivacity. But when this first glamour has dissipated itself in the miasma of inconvenience and anxiety caused by ten thousand minor traffic accidents, by fist fights excited by crumpled fenders and ripped-off chrome strips, when ten times ten thousand evening meals have been spoiled by reheating, then the climate shifts and the attention of the citizenry directs itself first towards the strikers and afterwards to both parties indifferently, in the classical "plague on both your houses" attitude.

Finally, three weeks or thereabouts into the strike, mass indignation boils over; there are alarming incidents with pickets and transit users exchanging flurries of blows. A carton of human excrement is delivered in the mails to the chief of the management-negotiation team. The public camaraderie of the first ten days is now forgotten as hitch-hikers begin to launch exceedingly rude gestures in the direction of unco-operative motorists. The various liaisons begun from day one to day ten now begin to unravel. A very ugly palpable unrest shows itself on the streets, and a settle-ment ensues. Then that essentially Québecois activity begins, the negotiation of the back-to-work agreement, in which the malcontents and the instigators (to use the words of the managers) are allowed to return to their jobs instead of being got rid of.

The strike organizers have neither been proscribed nor blackmailed, which seems pretty civilized to me.

The Montréal transit strike of 1967 wasn't too discom-forting, as these things go, and would by now have been forgotten by everybody who lived through it, if it weren't for two circumstances. Primo: it was broken by bitterly reac-tionary legislation that defined the attitudes of all subsequent governments in the province to such strikes. Secundo: it was only the second of a series of interruptions of bus and Métro service that finally became annual events. By the end of the nineteen-seventies, the phrase "bus strike" or alternatively *"grève de transport commun"* would produce foaming incoherence in the mouths of Montréalers of all races, creeds, politics.

All the same, the weather was marvellous that last week of October, the mildest Hallowe'en of my time in the city.

V

29

The lady pundit of Lewis Street awoke one winter morn in her lemon and blue boudoir to find her pleasant counterpane overspread with the five morning newspapers she and her hubby took in: *Le Devoir, Journal, Globe and Mail, Free Press, Gazette*. No wonder she had felt so warm in bed. All the news that's fit to print, she thought drowsily, and plenty that isn't. She asked herself why her husband, Mr. Public Opinion, had so bestrewn her. She could hear him chuckling in the bathroom. She sat up and seized the first newspaper that came to hand, the *Globe and Mail*. Headlines glared at her.

PEARSON DECIDES TO STEP DOWN
PM ENDS SPECULATION, DECLARES RACE OPEN

Le Devoir was as explicit, and more elegant.

LE PREMIER MINISTRE PEARSON RENONCE
LA COURSE COMMENCE DES AUJOURDHUI
ON NE PEUT PLUS MACHER SES MOTS: MARCHAND
PELLETIER CANDIDAT AU LEADERSHIP DU PARTI LIBERAL?

The *Free Press* spoke in unaccustomedly parochial accents.

PEARSON RESIGNS, SAYS RACE WIDE OPEN
WESTERN LEADERSHIP HOPES SLIM

The *Journal* spoke largely of capital concerns, preoccupations of social engineers, hopes for a revitalized civil service.

PEARSON RESIGNATION TO END ERA OF UNCERTAINTY
RETURN TO TWO-PARTY SYSTEM INDICATED

The *Gazette* professed ignorance.

LIBERAL SUCCESSION UP FOR GRABS
PIERRE ELLIOTT TRUDEAU QUEBEC STALKING HORSE?

It was the morning of Friday, December 15. Madame Pundit called out briskly to her husband, who was apparently shaving. There came a sound of rapid rushing waters, then a sequence of sharp slapping sounds as he patted on his after-shave, an odoriferous compound that she could smell in the bedroom, redolent of the piney woods, yet with a terrifying after-scent of some deadly metallic mixture of evil chemicals.

Her husband appeared in the doorway, grinning at her with annoying complacency.

"Told you not to go to bed before the news."

"But darling, I was exhausted. Did you know about this, you little old inside-dopester?"

"I knew it was coming but I wasn't sure when."

"We all did, we all did. But did you suspect that it would be last night?" She scrutinized her husband narrowly; they were not exactly in competition with one another, but insofar as any marriage partakes of the nature of open warfare — continual pitched battle — sempiternal struggle for the upper hand — prior certitude regarding this momentous event would place her husband securely on a higher rung of the movers-and-shakers' ladder than her own precarious position somewhere about the middle height. He might have been discussing this over lunch yesterday, *before she had heard anything about it.* The reflection was gall to her, bitterly irritating.

"He's given the back-room boys a Christmas present such as comes once in a lifetime, if it comes at all. They'll grow fat on this."

"That's Mike for you, ever mindful of others," said her spouse. "The man whose charm can't be captured in print or on the air. It's such an elusive charm that it's imperceptible, invisible. It's like the emperor's clothes. Maybe it isn't there at all."

"But haven't you always told me that you admired him?"

"That was while he was prime minister. Actually I dis-approve of him, a diplomat of international stature who doesn't know any French. It seems a fundamental limitation, an acceptance of crippling gaps in the necessary equipment, like a concert pianist without a right hand."

"Ravel wrote a concerto for that man."

"So he did, but how many others are there? And what about an entire recital assembled from music composed for the left hand, would you want to sit through it?"

"Most likely not."

"Take my word for it, you wouldn't. I've listened to that repertory out of curiosity and there simply isn't much of it that's any good. The chess-playing dog. He won't win many games, but it's wonderful that he plays at all. Pearson lacked the essential qualities of a successful prime minister under the Canadian parliamentary system. He was not a compelling figure in the House. He had no overpowering appeal to the electorate. He never won a majority. He perpetuated the sequence of drawn elections. What we need now — really desperately — is somebody who can settle in and give us a decade of continuity by winning a couple of elections in a row."

"Do you think Bob Stanfield can do it? The man who invented the trapdoor in the rear of the union suit?"

"Now sweet, now sweet, you know very well that he didn't invent the trapdoor union suit."

"But he looks like he did."

"There is that, of course."

The choice of Robert Stanfield as Conservative leader in the previous September had seemed to inject an important new element into the electoral stand-off that had persisted in Ottawa for a decade. A leader cast in the traditional Canadian mould: upright, honest, candid, not terribly good-looking, not very quick on the uptake, a mould the Canadian people — at least the English-speaking group — believed to be that from which their greatest leaders had been cast.

In fact none of the greatest Canadian leaders had possessed all or even very many of these characteristics. None was particularly upright or honest or candid; none of the greatest was at all slow on the uptake (King, MacDonald, Laurier). Perhaps the absence of striking good looks or photogenic appeal was the only prime-ministerial characteristic believed by Canadians to be typical of their leaders that was so in fact (and Laurier at least had been remarkably good-looking). The brief reign of the lamented John Kennedy might change all that. Canadians are terrible copy-cats. They often make

178 HUGH HOOD

choices — in all aspects of their social behaviour, and their private behaviour too — that reflect several years afterwards aspects of behaviour and choices originating among their southern neighbours. If some candidate for the Liberal leadership were now to demonstrate those very unusual characteristics among Canadian politicians, real photogenic appeal and memorable looks, he would have to be found among the potential successors of Mr. Pearson who had not yet declared themselves. For no declared candidate, as Centennial Year ended and 1968 drew on, possessed any physical charm whatsoever.

"What about John Turner?" demanded Madame Pundit.
"No gleam of intelligence behind those big round eyes."
"He might grow out of that."
"There isn't time."
"No, I guess not."

The Liberal leadership convention was rushing towards the nation at horrible speed. It would take place in the Ottawa Civic Centre from Thursday, April fourth, to Saturday night, April sixth, at which time Mr. Pearson's successor would be known. By New Year's Day, 1968, eight serious possibles had appeared: two men who could wear tailored suits with some conviction, one old, one young; four party wheel horses, two talented, two untalented; two oddball also-rans. Winters, Turner, MacEachen, Sharp, Martin, Kierans, Hellyer, Greene, in the order named previously. An impressively varied yet not a persuasive gang of eight.

Winters: too obviously manufactured and too slow-witted.
Turner: too young.
MacEachen: too non-committal, no power base of any size.
Sharp: doesn't have the looks.
Martin: wants it too much and Mike dislikes him.
Kierans: simply an impossible choice.
Hellyer: mistrusted by the Establishment.
Joe Greene: Joe Greene???

Not a convincing speaker of the French tongue amongst them. What would become of *l'alternance*? What was wanted — this began to become agonizingly clear as the weeks passed and the gang of eight went around the country with all

sixteen feet in their mouths, without a single TV turn-on in
the crowd — was somebody who could wear tailored suits
convincingly and sports clothes with flair, somebody who
had legitimate Québec connections and a mastery of both
languages, who was evidently honest (or anyway fairly
honest), smart, favoured by Mike, not Minister of Agriculture
or anything like that, young but out of his thirties. There
must be somebody in Canada somewhere who fits that
description, somebody who can win elections and majorities,
somebody who can lead us out of this nightmarish succession
of appeals to the voice of the people.

A few ingenious professors at a francophone Québec
university made a series of *sondages* at the end of January, in
which they discovered to their amazement and pleasure that
the Minister of Justice, who was not an avowed candidate for
the leadership, was nevertheless getting more than a quarter
of all the press coverage devoted to the race — more than five
of the other candidates combined. What were the personal
attractions possessed by this reluctant débutant that seemed
to be forcing him, almost against his stated will, into a try for
the leadership, and the consequent term, however brief it
might be, as PM?

He could certainly wear a well-tailored suit convincingly,
without showing the resemblance to a stuffed dummy that
grossly impaired public acceptance of two other candidates.
Stuffed shirt, the public told itself, and the public won't buy
the stuffed shirt anymore. The two stuffed shirts stayed in the
race to the end and lost to the man with the good tailor, out of
whose shirt front straw didn't seem to be sticking.

He had legitimate Québec connections and an assured
mastery of both tongues. He was apparently honest. He was
Minister of Justice, wasn't he? Nobody gets to be Minister of
Justice in Canada who isn't honest, that's a well-known fact.
Smart. And maybe Mike didn't like him any too well, but he
was Mike's favourite all the same. He certainly was not and
had never been Minister of Agriculture (he possessed an as-
yet-unstated reluctance to sell wheat) and he was provably
young within the meaning of the act, though there seemed to
be some mystery about his precise age. He might be a year or

two older than he claimed to be, like a prudent actress who wishes to prolong her best years.

And he could win elections, sure he could. He'd caught on like the Beatles and Beatlemania. You might even, if you wished, speak of Trudeaumania, yeah, yeah, yeah.

30

Saturday night at the Civic Centre with the hockey game coming on at eight, the crucial last weekend of the schedule in the first expansion season, 1967–68. Everybody in Canada felt that the balloting for the Liberal leadership intruded upon a fated occasion in the nation's history. In the fall of the previous year, six completely new teams had commenced life as full-fledged members of the NHL, doubling the league's membership in a single stroke: Kings, North Stars, Blues, Flyers, Penguins . . . Penguins?

Waddle, Penguins, waddle! Get in there and flap!

Seals. San Francisco Seals to start with, the Oakland Seals, California Seals, California Golden Seals, then a lot of other things and a final lapse into the blankness of things absolutely past.

In the spring of 1968, four of these fledglings — on this very weekend — made it to the NHL play-offs and attracted huge fan interest in their home cities plus a modicum of interest from old established cities of fifty years' standing in the league. The expansion clubs would battle through two play-off rounds among themselves, producing a divisional champion that would play off for the Stanley Cup against the best of the established teams. No well-informed hockey fan could hold out much hope for the expansion division's title-ist in the final series, but such a series might provide a bench-mark for later competition. If the expansion champion could make a few of the games fairly close, then the league could maintain that its doubling in size and the watering-down of its product was justifiable, that the expansion had been successful. Now the end of the regular season was at hand, and here were the bloody Liberals all over the TV screen to the exclusion of all normal red-blooded programming. The only thing to be done about it was to treat the leadership contest as an heroic struggle, a spectacle for the fans. In Canada all issues of national significance are discussed and evaluated, their place in the national culture fixed, so far as they remind the citizenry of the Stanley Cup play-offs. If the balloting, on that last desperate Saturday night, were to run too far into hockey TV time, the accident could do grave harm to the party's courtship of the electorate. In the event, the fourth ballot was concluded and the result announced just in time for you and me to get down to the Forum, to get comfortable in front of the set. How one remembers waiting for that result!

The second ballot shook out the vacant and the vain and made hard decisions press uncomfortably upon power brokers and delegates alike. Some of the power brokers were delegates themselves, and, I am afraid, all of the delegates thought that they were power brokers, which was not so. George Robinson was both; there could be no question about that. A parliamentary secretary, very close to the PM, prominently mentioned for the Cabinet, closely identified by those in the know with international investment and finance, locked into the North American industrial organization in its most important and most vulnerable undertakings. A very very rich man. Oh yes, George Robinson was a bit of a power broker; he controlled the votes of the riding association. He even allowed, out of his great magnanimity, his defeated rival for the riding nomination, Anne Woolsey, to come along for the ride as an official member of the delegation. Mind you, he had her bound pretty tightly to his chariot wheels, always an uncomfortable position. She was pledged to vote as he dictated, although for her there could only be one choice.

"What? That television idol?" exclaimed Robinson when she mentioned her preference. "Why he tried to keep Mike Pearson away from the drama festival in Stoverville, only last spring."

"Are we certain of that?"

"Certain of that? Of course we're certain of it. We were both parliamentary secretaries to the PM. We had constant contact. What the hell is all that racket? I wish they'd put a stop to that

horrible shouting. I can't hear myself think. Am I sure that he
kept Mike from turning up for the drama festival? Well he
tried, but he didn't stop him. I distinctly recall that he was
there on the last night, when some lunatic actor had a public
breakdown and made an ass of himself. I remember what
Mike did afterwards."

Anne Woolsey could scarcely distinguish the old paladin's
words, the noise around them was so great. The results of the
second ballot had just been announced, and their immediate
effect was to eliminate all but four candidates: Winters,
Hellyer, Turner, and Trudeau. Left to wage a struggle that
might keep people away from the hockey game and create an
impression of irredeemable internecine struggle were exactly
the candidates whom an informed political analyst might
have picked out: three guys who looked good on TV and a
maverick who didn't look too bad. Two with Toronto
connections, two with Montréal connections. No woman, no
westerner, no ugly, slow-on-the-uptake, craggy-featured,
simply honest man. That corner of the field was to be left to
Bob Stanfield.

George Robinson found himself facing the third ballot, on
the floor of the tumultuous, stinking, dreadfully hot and
smoky crazily lighted Civic Centre, with his little delegation
looking to him most anxiously for a lead. He felt pressure
under his temples. Was he too old for these exercises? Sixty-
six, with a limp. George couldn't take in or accept the fact
that he was sixty-six. He felt the same as he'd always felt,
except that he seemed to get tired quickly nowadays, and he
wasn't sleeping too well. The huge amphitheatre seemed to
divide into several scenes. He swayed, and somebody took
him by the arm, a delegate from Cornwall. Everybody was
looking at him for their cue. If only it weren't so noisy. He
had come to the convention on Wednesday night at the head
of the local delegation from his own riding, responsible for
their voices and his own, and those alone, a tiny number. But
there were no other sitting Liberal members in eastern
Ontario, and the delegates from all the riding associations
that surrounded his own, people from Cornwall and Prescott
and Gananoque and Kingston, from as far away as Perth, five
or six circumambient ridings, were treating him as their

natural chief, the voice of that perennially dissatisfied region, eastern Ontario. He now found himself — and this was the most pressing responsibility ever visited upon poor George — at the head of a considerable bloc. Thirty-four delegates had assured him that they would vote as he directed, relying on him to protect the region's interests when he should accede (as he certainly would if he made the smart choice) to a Cabinet post under the new leader.

Great billows of cigarette smoke — he hoped it was nothing more than cigarette smoke — it had a funny odour — burnt his eyes and sank into the weave of his suit, leaving it unpleasantly scented. People plucked at his clothes. A face he knew appeared in front of him, a floor man for CBC-TV.

"We're going to go now to George Robinson; we've got him right here. This is George Robinson, one of the party's major power brokers, leader of the influential eastern-Ontario bloc."

He realized with terror that he was about to speak on national TV. He thought he might now have his fatal stroke, but it didn't come.

"Mr. Robinson, George, you were very close to Mr. Pearson. And you're at the head of a very sizeable delegation. Did you fulfill your commitment to Mr. Sharp in the early balloting?"

"Yes, why yes, Peter, we went with Mr. Sharp as long as he stayed in contention. We're sorry to see him out of the race, he's a great Canadian."

"Can you give us any indication of where eastern Ontario may go on this next ballot?"

"It's a tough choice, Peter. I'll have to poll my associates."

"Can you give us a hint of your own preference?"

Oh God, what to say? APTA had to be protected. Goderich must stay in China. Got to think about a Cabinet appointment. What portfolio could he hope for under Winters, Turner (no, Turner couldn't win it), Hellyer. He teetered.

"I'm going to keep my mouth shut for one more ballot, Peter."

"There you have it, Canada. It looks like this Liberal leadership struggle is going to remain a horse race right down to the wire, and now, back to Leadership Central."

The Hellyer people were over there. The Winters people were on the other side of the floor. He could see John Turner not thirty yards off, with his sleek head shining black and his wife Geills beside him. George wondered idly, like a condemned man studying the texture of the hemp, why Turner's wife spelled her name that way. How was it pronounced. He never knew.

"What are we to do, George? Who should we go for? Oh George, everybody will know where we go. They'll figure it out. We have to be right. Do we move to stop Trudeau? Can Hellyer win it? Can Bob Winters get over the top on the fourth ballot? Suppose Turner drops out after the next ballot and his votes go to Hellyer, to Winters? Help us, George. Help!"

Then he saw what to do. There was no use holding off through the third ballot to declare himself at the very last moment. After the third ballot the choice would be down to two, Winters or Trudeau. Young Turner would remain in the race and hold his strength solidly until that point. It was obligatory to move now, to retain credibility with the winner. He passed a trembling hand over his forehead, took out a handkerchief and wiped the sweat and the tears from his eyes. He tried to clean his glasses but they only smeared. They were getting ready to hold the third ballot. Everything pointed to Winters. A businessman with a strong internationalist background, South American interests, close ties to London finance.

Something inside George Robinson turned over heavily. He felt as if his heart had suddenly grown too big for his chest. He could feel it, about the size of a football, under his ribs. The taste of bile lay bitter on his tongue. He looked and looked around the wide smoky field of combat. Then he saw what he was looking for, and he squared his old shoulders and set off through the throng. He started with his thirty-four eastern-Ontario delegates trailing along behind him, but there were more than forty in the little band when they came to the river and crossed.

"Tru-deau!" croaked George Robinson. "Tru-deau!"

Eastern Ontario took up the cry, "Tru-deau, Tru-deau, Tru-deau, Tru-deau, Tru-deau." Watchers up in the Leader-

ship Central booth spotted the swirl of motion as the little
band crossed the floor. The cameras zoomed in on George
Robinson as he accepted a big round Trudeau button from a
cheering, weeping young woman in an orange jacket,
pinning it to his lapel. He reached over her shoulder and
extended his hand upwards to the Minister of Justice, who
never forgot the gesture, and the third ballot began.

31

When I was a little boy in Toronto, the nuns who directed
Our Lady of Perpetual Help Parish School used to spend
more time instructing us in the details of the vestments worn
by the priest during the celebration of Mass, and in the exact
description of the sacred vessels used in the liturgy (chalice
ciborium monstrance paten pyx), than they did in canvassing
the mediocre necessities of geography. I can still recite the
exact order in which the celebrant vests himself prior to
mounting the altar steps. I can recall the materials of which
each article of attire was composed. But I can't tell you the
names of the townships of York County, though I learned
them in geography class in third grade. How recover them?
Why? I'm coming to that.

The counties of Ontario — most of them — come reasonably readily to mind. I'm not going to list them, but I will
just note here that my native county, York, is bordered on the
east by Ontario County, and on the west and northwest by the
counties of Peel and Simcoe. I even recollect some of the civil
and legal functions of the counties of Ontario. Most of them
seem to be annexed to the preservation of records connected
with transactions in real estate, with the maintenance of
roads, and with the administration of justice at the level of the
county court. The counties, in short, bulk pretty large in the
complex system of provincial government. They have a real
function that has continued to the present. I was taught all
this out of a little red book called *Civics*, published for the
Ontario Department of Education by some Toronto book
manufacturer and vended to pupils for little or nothing.

Townships on the other hand seem less significant, less
effectively functioning administrative units than the larger

entities of which they form part. I feel annoyed with myself that I passed the time when I ought to have been memorizing the names and the functions of York County townships either contemplating the symbolism of the liturgical colours or the shine, the lustre, of Eleanor Nugent's back hair. She sat directly in front of me, in the third row from the window, in grade three, and she had long soft silky light-brown hair, brushed shiningly away from a white, white parting.

Eleanor Nugent's hair is probably the reason I can't remember anything about the townships of York County or any other county, and I feel that I should know about them because at least two of them have the word "Gwillimbury" in them. Maybe three. I'm pretty sure that there's a North Gwillimbury. There may be a South Gwillimbury.

Now as it happens, my father's parliamentary constituency, the one he first contested in 1952 and held forever, was called East Gwillimbury, as everybody knows. But I'm not sure that it bore the name of a real township. As a rule, a constituency is larger than a township. Stoverville/Smith's Falls, for example, George Robinson's constituency, contains all or part of at least five townships, and I believe that my father's East Gwillimbury did so as well. And what I want to know, and believe that I should know, is the whole truth about this word "Gwillimbury," its whence and whither. The names of the townships often conceal pleasant surprises. There is a Bastard Twp. in the back parts of Leeds, for quite good and sufficient reasons. But I worry about "Gwillimbury." I really do. "Gwillim" is simply William, Guillaume, Guglielmo, the Welsh "Gwilm," and bury" is Scandinavian *byrig*, Scottish *burh* or *borough*. Gwillimbury therefore is just another Williamsburg or Williamstown. What the dickens is the name doing in the middle and western parts of York County, twenty miles and more north of Yonge and St. Clair, the safest NDP seat in Canada? The names of places are our first poetry. What are Newmarket, Sharon, Cedar Valley, Ballantrae, Holt, and Vandorf doing in East Gwillimbury, and why did their citizens love my father so? I wish I knew.

I wish I knew.

For, you see, he had coaxed those decent, God-fearing, sensible people into such a commitment to him, such a love-affair, that he no longer even had to show up for an election. They just voted for him when they saw his name on a ballot. This had long since ceased to be a party allegiance or endorsement. If he'd been running for the Rhinoceros Party — and perhaps he should have been one of their candidates — the electors of East Gwillimbury would have returned him to office with perfect assurance that he was the right man for them, and so he was.

In the first Trudeau election of June 25, 1968, the Liberals were headed for that clear-cut, decisive ascendancy with the voters that neither party had enjoyed for a decade. The aftermath of the contest for the leadership was a public-relations triumph such as no previous public figure in Canada had enjoyed. Every accidental circumstance, every chance, every scrap and atom of press coverage, pundit pomposity, public-opinion poll, told in favour of the new Liberal leader. He couldn't put so much as a single pink toe astray. There were quite profound reasons for this, reasons that students of the game are still combing through. I don't think I can give them, but I'm quite certain that they reach deep down into the rich mulch of Canadian political consensus; they were roots that held tight for sixteen years.

On the night before the election, Pierre Elliott Trudeau, the new darling of federal politics, found himself sitting on a reviewing stand in downtown Montréal, watching the Saint-Jean-Baptiste Day parade. It had taken courage and decision for him to come there at that moment. There were plenty of young men and women in the province and in Montréal that night who despised Trudeau for the course he had followed.

They considered him a sell-out (*un vendu*) to Ottawa, no true Québecer, a turncoat and worse. It enraged them to see him seated on that platform, clearly on the verge of a great political triumph that might dam up their aspirations for a decade. They thought him a house nigger. They started to throw things at him and the other people on the reviewing stand, almost all of whom scuttled at once for safety, personal physical courage forming no part, as they thought, of the equipment of the leader. The TV cameras were getting all this, good stuff, look great on *The National*.

Trudeau didn't budge, except to move forward to the
railings before him. His companion, the only other person
who stayed on the stand, Montréal's Mayor Jean Drapeau,
showed some slight apprehension at this turn of events.
Trudeau leaned way forward, looked downward, and
exhibited a challenging anger. I'm not sure he gave the rioters
the finger, but I like to think he did; the gesture would have
been wholly in character. His foolish enemies could not have
chosen a more effective way to advertise his personal bravery,
and the rest of the nation bought it in quantity, next day in
the polling booths. With that kind of publicity he might have
carried every seat in the country, and in fact he got one hundred and fifty-five seats, a solid workable majority based on
forty-five per cent of the popular vote.

These publicity breaks made not the slightest difference to
the men and women in East Gwillimbury who loved Andrew
Goderich. In a sea of Liberal victories in the ring around
Metropolitan Toronto, East Gwillimbury stood out, giving
their favourite an extraordinary seventy per cent of their
votes. The Liberal candidate — in the first Trudeau election
— finished so far up the track as to be invisible. "If you've got
Gwillimbury behind you, you're home free." An axiom of
Canadian politics in which "Gwillimbury" is roughly the
equivalent of hog heaven. And what I'll never understand,
and find suspicious, is why my father was allowed to contest
the election virtually unopposed. Everybody knew that a
Trudeau sweep was on its way. There was a clear, sharp
inclination among voters towards the renascent Liberal
party, and an obvious wish to get back to stable government
and four-year terms of office.

Why then was Andrew Goderich more or less handed East
Gwillimbury on a platter? The Conservatives had no chance
whatsoever to win the seat, which hadn't returned a Conservative in the present century. But given the circumstances
of the Trudeau wave, the Liberals had a solid shot at it, and
my father *didn't return to Canada to contest the seat*. He
allowed himself to be nominated, and I think he may have
expected to lose a close contest. He won overwhelmingly,
because the Liberals nominated a complete nonentity and
made no attempt to gain the seat for him.

No Cabinet minister made so much as a fleeting passage through the riding on a motorcade headed towards the Kawarthas. No back-room boy, no searcher after clumps of disadvantaged-minority votes, no wheeler and dealer and mover and shaker from Toronto headquarters, made so much as a mild pass at the electors of East Gwillimbury. I know this, because I was on the spot throughout the campaign. Without even being a paid-up member of the NDP, which I have never been and never will be — not being in any sense a party man — I managed what little there was of my father's campaign. I met with local workers in a hall next door to an old leather factory in Newmarket, which stank horribly. There we doled out the green lawn signs with dad's picture on them, and such a picture! God only knows from what primeval period that picture dated. I think he was wearing a stiff collar in the picture, as featured in those formal portraits of notabilities of the nineteen-twenties like Frederick Philip Grove and J.S. Woodsworth. I suspect that collar was meant as a joke; it gave my father a marked resemblance to an up-the-country Methodist minister, an appearance he may have wished to cultivate for dubious, comic reasons of his own. I don't mean to attribute to him a wish to satirize, to poke irreverent fun at any segment of the Protestant clergy. My father often remarked that the most intelligent and best-educated men in any Canadian town or small city were invariably the clergy, and in English-speaking Canada more particularly the Protestant clergy, and more particularly still for some reason the Presbyterians. I am not sure why he singled out the Presbyterians; he was always able to give multitudinous reasons for dicta of this kind. He probably had his own private and very good reasons for using a campaign picture that seemed to date from very long ago, which gave him the look of a Methodist clergyman right down to the hard collar . . . or perhaps that of a high-school principal. He resembled that picture in no way. When he was in his fifties and sixties my father adopted an extremely relaxed and almost modish style of dress. Late in life his bearing and his personal style much resembled that of the popular TV idol Perry Como. They had in common the expensive cardigans, the golf slacks, the carefully barbered head and ears, the slow-moving casual physical manner. It used to make me chuckle as I motored around East Gwillimbury to remember how unlike his campaign pictures my dad really was. There was certainly an element of joking in his choice of the photograph that served as his emblem, set in the middle of the ugly lettering and the bilious prevailing green of NDP campaign materials.

I would find myself parked on the well-formed shoulder of some lost section of an apparently unnumbered highway somwhere north of Buttonville and south of Gormley, in what still appeared to be relatively open country. This was in 1968, remember! Dusk would be settling down in the soft late-May air, and I'd yank one of my dozens of lawn signs free from the pile in the back seat, compare my location with a list of names I'd been given next door to the leather factory, then march up the drive onto the veranda. I would knock at the door and three dogs would start to bark. Presently an ageing woman would haul open the heavy golden door and smile at me. They always smiled at me as soon as they saw the sign, then peered into my face.

"You must be Andy's boy!"

I can't tell you how many times I heard that sentence, delivered in the homey accent of this township (South Gwillimbury?) around eight-forty-five. The organizers warned me that early evening was the best time to make a call. Never visit a farmhouse in the morning or the mid-afternoon.

"You look just like your father."

"I'd have known you anywhere."

"Come right in, Mr. Goderich, while I look for the hammer."

When they'd found the hammer, or some light mallet, they would come down the sloping lawn with me right to the road, looking for the best spot to hammer in the sign.

"You can't see her from behind these trees here. Just walk down the road a few hundred feet, would you Mr. Goderich, and see if you can spot her from a distance." And I'd saunter off in the twilight, then holler back to them, "Just shift her another few feet this way, eh?"

Afterwards they would offer me whisky and mixed nuts, commenting further on various aspects of family resemblance.

32

So I remember that summer as oddly shaded, dark, warm, and filled with intimations of coming change. I had only once or twice before visited the "new" flat or apartment on Crescent Road, a part of Toronto so charged with memories that it hardly requires revisitation. I did not then and cannot now imagine any apartment on Crescent Road as possessing in the smallest degree the character of novelty. Crescent Road, and all that it implies, is so layered over for me with perceptions of the infinitely various and infinitely subtly connected modes of social reality that the place makes me shiver only to think of it. It has become impossible for me to see Crescent Road as it is in itself without any superadded impression of what it has been rolling through the whole imaginative structure. The same is true of St. George Street between Harbord and Davenport Road. Those enormous brick houses and the self-assured men and women who lived in them. I don't ask myself Thurber's classic question, model of so much journalistic nostalgia, "Where are they now?" I know where they are. I've found out. They're in Mount Pleasant Cemetery of course, and their great-great-grand-children are yuppying around with computer software somewhere in the bowels of the University of Toronto, if the University of Toronto can indeed be said to have bowels.

As you came up the front steps of the house on Crescent Road in which the "new" apartment was located, you espied a pair of those large cement spheres, one on either side of the steps, atop low brick columns. I always used to examine those big balls, wondering how they were made. They seemed to be composed of some sort of coarse cement mixture with a lot of sand in it. There were funny wandering cracks in their surfaces, like the traceries on maps of the great rivers of the globe. And there was discoloration, growth of lichen, water stains, occasional spots where the exterior of the massy ball had been bruised and broken. Those ornaments might have been eighty years old; they seemed older than God. They fixed themselves in my mind as suggesting more than they stated, just a pair of big cement orbs about two feet across. I never understood how they were attached to their supporting columns. You couldn't roll them about; they may have been sited on metal reinforcing spikes of some kind. I began to think of them in the terms of an obscure body of symbolism, as soon as I began to visit the apartment regularly. This was in that darkening summer of 1968, in the classical year of the decade of twaddle and bullshit, which began sometime around 1964. It was the summer of the first Trudeau election, but also of the return to political activity of Richard M. Nixon. How well I recall sitting beside my mother in the study, the vacant study never used by my father, on Crescent Road, watching the TV as Nixon accepted the nomination.

I said to my mother, "Maybe the office will ennoble him."

"Not a chance in hell," she said.

By no means the last of the astute judgements I had been accustomed to receive from her lips, but among the most strikingly prescient of them. She could not admire or approve Mr. Nixon; she had a long memory, and the image of his celebrated "Checkers" speech rested vividly in her imagination. She often quoted it during the run of the Republican National Convention of '68, when the two of us sat waiting for my father's promised return from Peking.

"My wife has a simple cloth coat," she would recite, biting her lips in disgust, "and my kiddies have a pet, a little doggie given to them by somebody who agrees with what we're trying to do in the Republican Party. And no matter what anybody accuses me of, I do not intend to ask my little girls to give up their pet, Checkers."

She had her Cassandra look on her still unwrinkled face. She did not as yet show her advancing age, as she was shortly to do. My mother seemed to look much the same as she had since Dad got back from Europe; that is, she appeared to be in hale middle age. I'd acquired the habit of thinking of both my parents as being in their mid-forties, with the excellent health and high level of vitality customarily enjoyed in that decade. You can persist in believing that the sand is hanging at the same level in the glass; all of a sudden it combs and climbs to a fall. A swirling sinking depression swims around the centre of the surface. Then you begin to see the changes coming down.

When my parents moved into their new apartment, I was in my late thirties, and I was never a speedy developer. I continued very immature well into my middle years. This isn't an agreeable confession: when I was thirty-eight, the year my father made his flying visit home from Peking, I still instinctively thought of myself as my parents' child. This retardation in my development — to put it in neutral terms — did me a great deal of harm, and did some of the people around me perhaps even more harm.

I don't mean that I carried on like a baby. I discharged my private and public duties. I could get the job done, as they say in professional sport. I could play the position. I think that I convinced our three kids that I was at least an adequately authoritative parent. I was a considerate and deferential husband. If I'd been more fully developed emotionally, I wouldn't have been so deferential. The truth is, I was always a little afraid of Edie, and more or less in thrall to her. That's my problem, when it comes to the question of women and how to handle them. I don't handle them. They handle me, or they did for a long time. I don't think I really grew up until I was in my mid-forties. I often wonder how many people find themselves locked into the same situation emotionally. Until about 1975 I always looked to somebody else to certify my decisions. My father was the big certifying authority in my life. I applied to him for counsel, for leadership and understanding, say simply for wisdom, all my life, and he never once failed me.

A day or two after Mr. Nixon accepted the Republican nomination, my father got back from Peking for the first of a series of proposed visits. There appeared to be some covert agreement in Ottawa, and especially at the highest levels of the new administration, that he was to remain at his post in Peking until some meaningful new development in Sino-Canadian relations appeared as a result of the exploratory talks that were going ahead. One of the reasons my mother so distrusted Richard Nixon was that she sensed — I don't know how — that this evil man would try to cut the ground from under my father's feet by hastily and unthinkingly moving towards a rapprochement with China, thereby blighting and maybe destroying the possibility of a special relationship between Peking and Ottawa. One of the recurring dreams of people like my mother and father is that of the emergence of Canada, finally and decisively, from the tutelage of Britain and the United States. From the earliest times in their marriage, she and my father, without the explicit profession of a formal political philosophy, had hoped to see a new kind of politics evolve at world level that would break down and finally drive out the traditional conception of "the great powers."

They both felt that leadership in political affairs shouldn't come out of the barrel of a gun. Nor should it be a function of a nation's wealth and population. Why should "the great powers" be those that were the richest, the most populous, the most wholly committed to the authority of big guns and big armies? A state's political wisdom was not the expression of its strength and wealth. That was *realpolitik* and *realpolitik* was the invention of people like Hilter and Stalin. God, in their view, was securely encamped behind the lines of the power with the biggest battalions.

Canada had tiny battalions, was always being criticized, precisely for the size of its battalions, in NATO, as well as for the general Canadian disinclination to staff and equip large military forces. From the time of the first Trudeau election forward, a debate was always raging in Canadian society, not always with the fully conscious awareness of the whole citizenry, about the status of arms in our society. What is the point of Canada's maintaining an army? Surely a Canadian army is a natural contradiction in terms, much like the notion of Jewish police.

The only use of a Canadian army is a purely imaginative or poetic one, as an expression of our goodwill towards our ideological allies. When my parents dreamt of the abolition of the distinction between the greater or lesser powers, they were looking towards the abandonment of brute force in the political arena. They hoped to make Canada a leader among the powers by reason of her wisdom, moderation, the beauty and openness of Canadian life and liberty. I can't condemn their hopes as foolish, but they certainly haven't been realized. The Nixons are coming on as strong as ever, maybe stronger. How well I remember greeting my dad as he sauntered up the walk towards the Crescent Road veranda. He put his hand on one of the big cement spheres as he gained the top step, and stood immobile for a moment. My mother had to grope for him in the twilight. Then we got him inside. I saw suddenly how much older he looked.

33

We had him to ourselves for the weekend; he had to get back to Ottawa early on Monday for a series of high-level policy conferences. They were overworking him. I know for a fact that when he was in Peking he had a staff or four, not more, and a tremendous amount of consultative activity to get through, and much travel. He was taken repeatedly to the farthest recesses of central Asia, shown sights that no other westerner was to see for a decade. Once, I recollect, they brought him to the northern shoulder of a little green glen that widened to a ravine farther down a watercourse. From where they stood they could look across into Nepal. His escort told him that the border was heavily guarded for security reasons, but he couldn't see any guards. He said that the glen seemed much like similar sights in the Canadian Rockies. He spotted a lot of small animals such as you'd expect to find in such a place, squirrels and a creature that looked much like a porcupine. From what he said I got the impression that they were somewhere southeast of Lhasa, but I can't be sure. He had travelled so much, and in such a hurry, that it was like listening to Marco Polo. He had been to Sinkiang, to border points not more than a few hundred miles — an hour's flight — from Samarkand. He had been conducted on tours of the great port cities and the manufacturing centres. He looked exhausted, in my opinion, and he had certainly been receiving medical treatment, which he refused to discuss, except to say that he had tried the resources of traditional Chinese medicine and found them very effective as palliatives, though not as remedies. He was referring to the method of insertion of needles into the bundles of muscle fibres adjacent to the major ganglia, later much discussed in North America as acupuncture.

"One resembles a hedgehog," he said.

"A hedgehog?" I couldn't visualize this.

"Or a porcupine. Perhaps I'm thinking of a porcupine. Anyway something with quills. Here, they took some pictures for me." He handed my mother and me a number of small coloured photographs, which showed him sitting in a heavy wooden chair under bright lights, surrounded by impassive medical practitioners in pale-green tunics. He was smiling at the camera. He was stripped to the waist — and he looked very thin to me — with some sort of towelling draped around his head and neck. Behind this towelling you could see the spines of four long thin needles, exactly like knitting needles, three on his right shoulder, one on the left. They were sticking into him. This sight made me feel quite sick to my stomach, and I expect my sensations showed in my face.

"It's a most peculiar sensation, but perfectly painless. It feels like — well let me see, I've never put it into words — it feels like a ribbon being pulled through your shoulder. There's no feeling. There's pressure at the point of entry, no more, and then this peculiar sliding sensation. I'm glad I tried it."

"What's this treatment for?"

"Relief of arthritic discomfort. I'd been having a lot of trouble with my neck, and the muscles at the top of the shoulders. I though it might be bursitis, but apparently not. Anyway the needles would give me distinct relief for about ten days. I don't think they profess to cure anybody of anything."

"You'd have been just as well off," I said disapprovingly, "with a good layer of CongestoVape and an old sock around your neck." My mother nodded with approval.

"I'm sure I would," he said. "Medical treatment is much the same everywhere, a means of inducing a healthful state of mind in the person under treatment."

"And how is your state of mind now?" quavered my mother.

"Excellent. A little perplexed but on the whole sound."

I persuaded him to take me along when he returned to Ottawa for talks at External, Trade and Commerce, and the PMO. He couldn't get me into the talks as an observer, but he asked me to stay with him in the Lord Elgin. That suite had too many tables in it. Everywhere you turned there were tables. There was a coffee table and a largish conference table in the sitting room, as well as a sofa, some bookcases, and about eight chairs. There was a small writing table in a corner, which Miss Keogh used to use for correspondence. There were the customary hideous lithographic prints on the walls. I believe that Miss Keogh passed her days in the Lord Elgin suite rather than in my father's parliamentary office, across Wellington Street. There was also the riding office in Newmarket, which had to be staffed by temporary and volunteer personnel, at least some of the time between elections. Marianne Keogh must have had to follow a triangular route among these three locations at great expense of travel time. She too felt fatigued and uncertain of the prospect before us, during those few days towards the end of the summer. I think that the time I spent in Ottawa with my father extended past Labour Day, but I'm not certain about that. It was one of those fearfully hot, steamy Ottawa summers, now just drawing down towards slightly cooler evening weather, which always make me remember that the country roundabout is largely low-lying swampland. Driving in from Stoverville, you traverse long stretches of low brush and marsh, extending right up to the outskirts of the city. I used to sleep in the same bedroom as Dad, the single bedroom in the suite. Sometimes when he seemed more than usually run down by the continual conferences, I'd open out the sofa in the conference room and sleep there. I could flop it open or shut in a minute or so. I used to enjoy a private awareness that this was my bedroom, when various distinguished people gathered around the conference table to talk about Nixon. That's what they were up to, of course, trying to guess what Nixon would do about the war in Vietnam. If he were to be elected (and they all expected that he would be) then some move to cut losses and get out of Southeast Asia could be expected from the Americans, in which case, once a withdrawal were effected, moves towards rapprochement with China must surely come.

When they came, according to External and the PMO, the Americans must find us first on the ground. I understand now what the dignitaries and the technocrats were urging on my father. They were talking him into taking on another year to eighteen months of service in Peking with a slightly expanded staff and — I'm convinced of this — the secret assurance that if an election were to come, which wasn't an immediate likelihood, he would find himself once again virtually unopposed in East Gwillimbury. It was during those brainstorming sessions that I finally understood why my father had had no effective opposition at the polls in the previous June. The incoming administration wanted him to continue in the House as an absentee member, more or less on permanent assignment to Peking for the good of the country. During the election campaign one voter after another had asked me if Andy would be speaking at any of the election meetings. I had always felt vaguely guilty about having to pretend that I didn't know, I couldn't be sure. And that was when they would say to me, "Well you've got quite a look of him yourself. Anybody could spot you for one of Andy's boys."

And do you know, that was the earliest point in my life at which a resemblance to my father showed in my face. I'd never observed it before. I knew what they were referring to, flatness above the cheek bones, a certain spareness of flesh over the skull, abundant hair neatly trimmed. I never wore my hair long in the sixties or seventies. My father never wore long hair or a beard. He once went so far as to culitvate a smallish moustache; this was when we were still children. My mother complained repeatedly that it tickled her during kisses, and in due course the appendage vanished, never to reappear.

My father and I were about the same colour, pale pink. Neither of us ever displayed pallor or that pasty look that we find in men in public life who have passed long hours under television lighting. Even though serving eternally in the House, or in committee, Dad made it a point to get out into the fresh air as often as he could. For one reason or another I've passed much of my life out of doors. The result of this has been that by the time I drew near forty our resemblance peaked, and I started to find my father looking out of my shaving mirror. I began to hear myself speaking in his tones with much of his phrasing, and I remembered how often I'd mistaken my uncle Philip's voice for Dad's, or for that of my grandfather, the Squire, when they were around our house in early days in Toronto.

It began to seem clear to me that just as performance traditions can be transmitted over many generations by musicians or actors, so family characteristics can be preserved in the accents of successive parents and children almost in perpetuity. I've arrived at the stage where casual telephone callers mistake my speech for that of my older son. And soon enough the younger boy will sound like me, when his voice completes the evolution from treble to baritone. The resemblance is close enough that I have now and then amused myself rather cruelly by allowing a very young woman to pour out her feelings to me under the impression that she was addressing my son Anthony Earl. The consequences of this ill-advised action have been disastrous; he once refused to speak to me for ten days after an incident of this kind, and the next time I saw the girl who had taken me for my son she burst into flustered and hysterical weeping at the thought of what she had confided to me. Her revelations had however been of the most innocent kind; all the same they were better addressed to a boy-friend than to the boy-friend's father. Procession of the Son from the Father.

And of the Holy Spirit from the Son.

The homoousion controversy.

I don't know how much is remembered — except by specialists — of this interminable technical debate in theology, which persisted under varying forms through long ages of the history of the Christian Church. Were the Second and Third Persons of the Blessed Trinity "one in substance with the Father" or not? And if They were "one in substance" or "one in Being," as the term is now sometimes translated, how could this be? How could the Three Divine Persons be One in substance or in Being?

A sterile theological discussion, you say, unworthy of the attention of the most superficial mind. And in saying that, you would be wrong, because the matter preoccupied the shrewdest and most gifted intellectual analysts in Europe and the Near East for about a thousand years. The choosing up of sides in the controversy divided Eastern Europe from the

West, broke the unity of Christendom and visited the most dire consequences upon the world, all because of a supposedly arid and technical point of theology. But nothing entails more pressing consequences than theological analysis. We are still employing the tools of analysis, the intellectual capital, bequeathed to us by the Jews, the Greeks, and the primitive Christian Church, and our intellectual dilemmas are the immediate consequences of theirs, our political and social dilemmas too. In this matter of the procession of the Son from the Father, and of the Holy Spirit from both, I can make common cause with James Joyce, who made this theological problem (it is really a mystery, not a problem, one of the chief mysteries of existence) his most pressing concern, the thing he wanted most of all to embody in his art.

For what is at issue is the general question of how one being can reside actively in another, uniting itself to it, whether in or out of time. History is the great example of the residence of earlier things in later things. Understand me, I am not proposing heretically that God the Father came first in a sequential development. But He is the First Person in some nice theological sense, which I am not competent to unfold. The Father is in the Son and in the Holy Spirit. And They are in Him.

My father is in me, not in the way that the Father is in the Son, but in an analogous way. It would not be possible for my father to be in me, as an agent, in any way, unless we had the example of the Triune before us as a model.

If God does not supply the model of Being according to which the world moves, then our lives are greatly changed. Succession, sequence, the before-after relationship that makes history possible and meaningful and liveable, the curious fact that we always grow older, that things always wear out and die, all this is of God and from God. It is His Reason and His Will that the world is as it is. Nothing ever wears in. I came after my father and he is in my face and my voice and my mind, and now he begins to declare himself overtly. My grandfather is there too, and his father. Time will forever yield new being, all new being will retain and possess its inheritance from the old. I remember reading about some orchestral players in Vienna who had set before them in the

1960s the score of a symphony by Joseph Haydn that had not been performed since the death of the composer a hundred and fifty years before. When the players came to rehearse the third movement, before recording it, they all took a casual look at the score, noticed without even being aware of it how the notes lay on the stave. They took the downbeat from the conductor as one man, launched into the music, and what came out was perfectly a Viennese waltz in the style of Lanner and the elder Strauss. There was no indication in the score, apart from the tempo, that the characteristic hesitating lilt of the Strauss waltz should be given to the third movement of Haydn's Symphony 57.

They just knew how it should go, and out it came.

That's why I sound like Dad on the phone, and my son sounds like me, so that I can play cruel jokes on his girl-friend, jokes that I would not repeat. Procession of the Son from the Father and the Spirit from the Father and the Son.

34

I tried to get him to come down to Montréal and spend some time with us but he couldn't work it in. My mother was alone in Toronto. Amanda Louise was with her husband, Tommy Underwood, in New York and sometimes in Washington. Tony was in the UK. It seems a very long time since we were all together. I think that our wedding in June, 1953, might have been the last time that my parents and Amanda and Tony and Edie and I were united. The great family festivals, weddings, christenings, funerals, seem to be the chief occasions for reunion, but as time advances members begin to be absent from them. Tony wasn't at Amanda's wedding in the mid-fifties, and neither was my wife. It took place in Toronto at the old church we knew as children. Attendance was sparse, the occasion one of tempered merriment. Amanda was getting on towards her thirties, and for quite a long time we'd given up imagining a possible mate for her, not that she was a difficult or intractable woman, far from it; it was her mild, sweet, well-adjusted tractability that seemed to us to reduce her opportunities to marry. She was too nice, too uncompetitive, to insist upon male attention.

She ran into Tommy Underwood on some public occasion. He was the Toronto bureau chief for *Time* at that epoch. He used to write most of the four pages of *Time's* Canadian section, with help from stringers in Ottawa and Montréal. Tommy was marking time until the opportunity he was waiting for opened up in New York. I think he and Amanda had gone to a Diefenbaker press conference in Toronto, some time before the Old Chief won his first victory at the polls. Dief was reaching the height of his career; attendance at this conference was obligatory for media folk. Amanda Louise

was free-lancing in the arts-journalism world of Toronto.
She used to take contract jobs at CBC Radio, doing a bit of
writing or interviewing, sometimes voicing her findings
on-air. She was like a favourite daughter to the mandarins of
the CBC. She sounded very pleasant, very agreeable, very
well informed, in an amateur and rather hit-or-miss way. She
never applied herself very diligently to the art of radio
broadcasting, but she was something of a hit, on a series of
morning network shows on AM.

Sometimes she would do a stint as PR girl for a small
publisher, or she might pop up at *Maclean's* for a season, or
the *Star Weekly*. She was living at home, keeping an eye on
household matters for my mother, giving every sign of
lapsing into a comfortable spinsterhood. There was a series
of male friends, but no passionate commitment on either
side.

Then one afternoon she went to Convocation Hall at the
university to listen to John George Diefenbaker at the
summit of his forensic and rhetorical powers, a sign, as I say,
of a grand climacteric in Canadian life, not to be missed.
There was some official academic function going on. I never
knew what it was, but in the press of journalists penned
together near the dais or platform upon which Mr. Diefenbaker was holding forth, Amanda Louise found herself next
to a formidably agreeable young man whom she had seen
around town and knew to be *Time's* bureau chief. They
exchanged grins. They began at once to wriggle free from the
crowd and at length, just as the speaker was rising towards
his peroration, they fled through a side door and found
themselves on King's College Road looking north across the
campus.

"Can I buy you a drink?" said Tommy Underwood, that
old charmer . They went at once to that little bar on the top
floor of the Park Plaza and had a lot of drinks together, going
on to dinner and at last to a jazz club on Queen Street. They
were married three months afterwards, the minimal time
necessary to arrange a wedding in a Catholic parish, for all
kinds of practical reasons. It wasn't till some time after the
marriage that my parents found out about Tommy's extensive acquaintance with Chinese affairs, expertise that soon

brought him the appointment in New York for which he had
been standing in line. It had been a question of waiting out
the last days and hours of an old Yalie, almost a classmate of
Henry Luce's, then moving into the highest councils of the
Luce empire as a confirmed Sinologist. Tommy and Amanda moved permanently to New York at the beginning of the
sixties, and I'm ashamed to say that I didn't see them for
most of that decade.

I started to get regular letters from Amanda Lousie after
Dad went to China for the first time. Apparently neither she
nor Tommy had had any expectation that Dad would take on
this tour of duty. Neither of them was any too pleased about
it, although Amanda, charming and agreeable as always,
gave me no reason to suspect how deep her feelings went in
the matter. When Dad came back in the late summer of 1968,
however, it was a different story. I started to get phone calls
from New York at almost any hour of the day or night,
requiring me to inform them about his activities. I knew no
more about them than they did. I think we all felt a certain
touchiness on the subject. Amanda had not long before
undergone a surprising pregnancy rather late in life. I don't
know that she and Tommy had expected to have any children, but all of a sudden, after twelve years of married life,
Amanda found herself pregnant, and experienced some
anxiety, and even some danger, during the course of the
pregnancy. She carried the baby to term, thank goodness;
their daughter Emily was born a year or a little less before my
father signed on for his China expedition. Emily, an exceedingly pretty child, was born on her mother's birthday, just the
sort of birthday present one always hopes for, seldom re-
ceives. Tommy and Amanda were utterly bowled over by the
unlooked-for arrival of this lovely child; they named her for
Tommy's mother and gave her our mother's name as well.
Emily Isabelle Underwood: welcome to the club.

My father never got to meet her. This rankled a bit with the
Underwoods. When Emily was born, Dad was already in
process of being drawn into the great vortex of contemporary
history, the puzzle, the mystery, the enigma of China and her
allegiances. Maybe Tommy felt that my father might have
deferred somewhat to his own grasp of Chinese affairs.

Perhaps my father suspected that any request for assistance or information he put to Tommy would at once be transmitted to the State Department. This might have been an injustice to Tommy. God knows, the Luce empire has always been ready enough to try to influence foreign policy at home and abroad. Tommy was astounded by Dad's first flight to Peking. He sternly resisted the idea that Dad should go back. Hence the round-the-clock phone calls to Montréal.

"Talk him out of it, can't you? He's too old and too much honoured to be made a cat's-paw."

"Tommy, Tommy," I said, "if you knew him better you'd know that he isn't anybody's cat's-paw."

I could hear Amanda Louise's voice raised beseechingly in the background. When Tommy had had his say she came on and told me what she thought of me. "Stand up to him, Matt! You're such a baby. Tell him not to do it."

Such good advice, just what I needed. He flew back to Peking in October.

35

I once encountered a character-assessment test that was regularly administered to candidates for junior-executive positions in the head office of one of the multinationals. I didn't take it myself. I saw copies of it on somebody's desk. A certain number of questions were put to the candidate, in a section of the test called "Family-Situation Encountering," of a type that seemed tendentious to me. Questions like these:

a) Was your mother a strict disciplinarian?
b) Would you describe the exercise of authority by your parents as: 1; rigorous, 2; relaxed, 3; excessively permissive, 4; growth-enhancing, 5; none of these?
c) As a child of eight or nine, what were your feelings about your mother and father?

There were right and wrong answers to each of these questions; there may even have been a neutral response. Anyway when the occupant of the room came back unexpectedly and caught me studying this part of the test, he gave me the right and wrong answers to these three leading questions. To c) for example, the absolutely perfect thing to say in the context was, "I loved my parents dearly, but father just a little bit more."

Father had to come first, no matter what your own sex was. Boys and girls alike, apparently, were to cleave to the masculine-authority principle, the absentee lawgiver — not the cuddler and soother — no matter what inclinations and prejudices their own sex might urge upon them. This seems a fundamental defect in the design of such tests, yet at that period and for long after they continued in use by personnel departments, often had practical consequences in the lives of many. Now your veteran test-taker very soon figured out what responses were the approved ones. Not the right and wrong ones. There is nothing wrong about placing your mother first in your affections; it's done all the time. There can be nothing surprising or unnatural in preferring your mother to your father, if once the act of preferring is admitted to the category of true acts. I think we have to challenge the assumption that father always has to come first.

If one section of the test, "Family-Situation Encountering," could be so fallacious, so open to criticism of its assumptions, very likely other sections were full of holes too. There was a multiple-choice, general-information section to this same test, I remember, in which one of the questions was: " 'The Emperor' is the name of: a) a symphony, b) a concerto, c) a string quartet, d) a cello sonata, e) none of these."

The supposedly correct answer was "b) a concerto." Such a stipulation penalizes the student with a superior knowledge of music history, and tells us something about the general level of culture of the composers of the test. For of course there is a celebrated string quartet known as "The Emperor" from which an even more celebrated anthem is taken. I would certainly say that to anyone of real musical culture Haydn's quartet is at least as celebrated as Beethoven's concerto. But the tester doesn't know this, and what's more, in his terms it doesn't matter. What he's looking for, he supposes, is the average level of knowledge to be expected from an aspiring junior executive, about whom he has many other unexpressed assumptions, and from whom he requires much that goes unspoken. Whoever takes this test must be male, white, religious, but not too religious, with a knowledge of music and the sister arts that is adequate for the purposes of, say, an office party, but not oppressively expert. He will be the kind of person who, at eight or nine, loved his parents deeply and his father just a little bit more.

It is clear how strong a drive towards conformism, more than that, towards the imposition of a mindless, uncritical, and emotionally frozen conformism, is nearly overt and unashamed in the notions of the people who compose and administer such absurd personality assessments. For surely everybody knows that his feelings towards his parents are in such a constantly shifting, self-adjusting, many-sided state that they cannot even be described as feelings; they have no determinate singleness.

In Proust's great work, the mother is close to the centre, the father at its edge. The Narrator is fully and with greatly poetic comprehension aware (and unaware too in certain aspects of his situation) of how significant this ordering of his familial encountering has been in his life. "Filial Sentiments of a Matricide." This is the title given by Proust himself to the extraordinary article he supplied to *Le Figaro* at the request of his friend Gaston Calmette, concerning the shocking case of Henri van Blarenbergh. This young man, a casual acquaintance of the author, on the twenty-fourth of January, 1907, violently attacked and killed his mother, then retired to his bedroom where he stabbed himself repeatedly, then shot himself through the mouth, blowing away the left side of his face. He survived only long enough for the police inspector to shout an unanswerable question in his ear, then closed his remaining eye forever.

Proust had actually been in correspondence with the young matricide some months before this dismal affair, had in fact addressed a letter of condolence to young Henri van Blarenbergh, writing on behalf of his own dead mother, on the death of van Blarenbergh's father. Young Henri had been gravely distressed emotionally at his father's death, had passed many months of 1906 in travelling, trying to forget his terrible grief. His father, wrote van Blarenbergh in reply to Proust's graceful letter of condolence, had been the "centre of his life, the source of all his happiness." A few months afterward, the desperately grieving son murdered his mother, then turned his weapon upon himself.

Which of his parents, think you, was loved more by Henri van Blarenbergh? Which of his parents was loved more by Marcel Proust, or by his Narrator? It is a commonplace, even vulgar, observation about Proust that upon reading of the horrible circumstances of his acquaintance's death, he at once judged *himself* to be a matricide. He had killed his mother by his shameful conduct, his failure to amend his life, his excessive demands upon her love. He was himself, this

analysis runs, another van Blarenbergh. Proust ended his
article for *Le Figaro* with a paragraph considered in questionable taste by the editors, and eliminated from the published version . . . an emendation that greatly offended
Proust. In that final paragraph he attained the superb insight
that coloured all his perceptions and his understanding of
himself in the years that remained to him. He spoke of the
special, profound religious veneration paid by the ancient
Greeks to "the tomb of Oedipus at Colonus and of Orestes at
Sparta — that Orestes whom the Furies had pursued to the
very feet of Apollo and Athena, crying: 'We chase from all
altars sons who slew their mothers'."

I loved my father and my mother dearly but my father just a
little bit more. Nobody can know at any time in his life, never
mind at eight or nine, whether such a statement be true or no.
The statement itself cannot even be made. We act at all times
in our lives under the pressure of our perception of the relation of our two parents to ourselves. The raw act of out-
living a parent brings guilty feelings . . . perceptions . . .
judgements . . . what are we to call them . . . in its wake. But
we cannot all predecease our parents, no matter how little we
may wish to survive them. A people whose children die
before their parents would be in a parlous state indeed. How
do parents feel about their children's deaths?

For the rest of his life Proust harboured dreadful feelings of
guilt and responsibility for the death of his mother, feelings
and reflections that indisputably went to give form to the
great work of his life. He allows the father of the Narrator a
brief eminence in the opening pages of the work, then places
him at the periphery of the action. A search for a new father
— perhaps Swann — now preoccupies the Narrator, until
Swann too is banished from the story. Grave perplexities
about sexual identity, the entanglement with Charlus, and
the destructive effects of Time Lost now supervene, controlling the work until that supreme moment after the war when
the past is found to be ideally enshrined and fully recoverable
in art.

I give Proust's experience and its consequences for his art
as an instance of the miraculously full delivery of the possibilities of family relations as a subject — *the* subject — for
art. Proust, more than any other writer of our age, with the

possible exception of James Joyce, has made the question of how we are to feel about Father and Mother — how we are to think about them as well — the source of the finest art. Everybody wants to know what he or she should feel and think about Mom and Dad. Orestes. Oedipus. Iphigenia. Electra. Hamlet. Bloom. Dedalus. The Narrator. It is the great question of our lives as the children of those parents, the only ones we have. How are we to free ourselves from them, at the same time exercising the greatest of the secular virtues, filial piety?

I can see that I'm never going to get my father and mother out of my life, and what's more I don't want to banish them from the action, any more than Proust wished to dismiss his "real-life" parents from the fecund teeming womb of recall, from which the great work of his life was generated. What else have I got to go on with but my experience of my parents? Piety, *pietas*, strange and awful word. You seldom hear it spoken today, and yet it is the name of an absolutely indispensable virtue. *Pietas*: "that form of commutative justice which consists in the child giving what is due to the parent." Honour thy father and thy mother.

I got a letter from Tony just at Christmas that year that consisted largely of admonitions and reproaches about Dad's second Chinese junket. He insisted, over and over: "You shouldn't have encouraged him to take it on." This was so false a judgement about my own place in my father's choices and decisions, that I was completely disarmed by it. I never discouraged my father from doing anything, either this or that. Who am I to tell my parents what to do? According to Wordsworth, the child is father to the man. I wish I understood that observation. Maybe it only means that little boys grow up to be fathers themselves. Is that all it means? After all, I've got children of my own.

In his Christmas letter, Tony went on and on in a rather self-pitying tone about his difficulties with Linnet. Either he had something she desired and wouldn't give it to her, or she wouldn't agree to comply with some urgent wish of his. Some question about marriage seemed to lie at the root of the debate. Tony is no chicken. By this time he was in his mid-thirties, quite time enough to marry. God knows he could afford it.

VI

36

In the sixties, I thought, looking around me as I sat in Mr.
Pope's anteroom, but not, thank God, of the sixties, neither
Charlie Pope, nor his personal and private head-of-secretarial-staff, Mrs. Melhuish, who sat near me at her outsized desk,
nor I myself. The sixties! When the decade began, I thought,
waiting to go into Mr. Pope's office, Flora MacLean was still
living. Mrs. Codrington wasn't yet quite a recluse. Edie and I
were still living in Stoverville. Kennedy was president and
Diefenbaker was his *bête noire*. Nobody had ever heard of the
Beatles, the drug culture, black power, the miniskirt, Pierre
Elliott Trudeau.

As the closing year of the decade drew on I found myself
searching in every corner for signs of imminent change. I
wanted nothing more than to be freed from the toils of
nonsense and folly that had suddenly been cast about us
sometime around 1965. What the hell had happened? Everything had seemed to be going along smoothly, just the way it
always had. All at once madness had flooded us. Was it the
series of political assassinations and attempted assassinations
in the US that had opened the floodgates to the forces of utter
irrationalism, the sudden disappearance of John Kennedy,
Robert Kennedy, Martin Luther King? I remembered where
I'd been when I heard of the assassination of JFK. I'd been
sitting in a cab with Edie, on a street in Montréal, deciding
suddenly not to buy a house in that beleaguered city. And
now, by God, I was living there, not very far from where I'd
heard the news of the president's death. Early in his administration Kennedy had committed the US to the space race,
promising that the nation would place a man on the moon
before the end of the decade. The sixties had another eleven

months to run and the Americans had met this deadline. I
laughed unwillingly as I remembered the racist joke about
the black-power space program: a coon on the moon by June.
We could put men on the surface of the moon but we couldn't
do it without the racist joke. It is not true that the more things
change, the more they stay the same. Space technology had
changed: racism had not. There is no point in reciting
cynical formulae about the movement of history. Somewhere
in the nineteen-sixties the world of values that I'd inhabited
up to that time had been sapped at its roots, withered, died,
been torn up. Everywhere around me, and around the rest of
humanity, in the late nineteen-sixties, indications of terrible
coming changes grew tall and flourished like dreadful
mutant sunflowers in the soil of some planet revolving
around an unimaginably distant sun.

In Mr. Pope's office the signs of coming mutation were all
present but unaccounted for, perhaps not even manifest in
the consciousness of the younger people who came and went
in the office of the Undersecretary. The age and deportment
of the charming Mrs. Melhuish, for example, were in
themselves ample indication that Mr. Pope's departure from
the hollowly echoing corridors of power could not long be
deferred. Mrs. Melhuish must by now, I concluded, be in her
early sixties, perhaps a bit older. She was the same size and
shape as she had been, ever since I'd started paying occasional
visits to this office with my father, fifteen years before. She
always wore tailored grey wool-jersey two-piece outfits,
neither quite a suit nor yet a dress, usually with a narrow belt
of some dark hue, black, deep blue. She wore sensible pumps
with two-inch heels. Her skin, finely wrinkled now but still
fresh and not at all dry, retained a youthfully pink tone that
may have owed something to the cosmetic arts. She had
prominent cheek bones and the characteristically poor
dentition of Englishwomen of a certain age. There were
vague reminiscences of Mabelle Buttermere, probably the
first Englishwoman I'd ever seen, when I was a baby. The
crowded front teeth and the pursed lips that imperfectly
concealed their slight protrusion. I liked Mrs. Melhuish
(pronounced "Mellish") but I never even knew her first
name. She was a remarkable example of the person in an

apparently unimportant and powerless position in the ranks of a bureaucracy, who could and did exercise great power, sometimes deputizing for a chief, sometimes simply exercising options left to her by tacit agreement among her associates and their masters. I know that my father's senior assistant, Miss Keogh, invariably spoke of Mrs. Melhuish with respect, with more than respect, with awe and admiration. Miss Keogh was some dozen or so years younger than Mrs. Melhuish, and in certain propitious circumstances might herself hope to rise to a similar tacitly conceded power.

That would depend on my father's subsequent activities. He and Charlie Pope were about the same age. I think that Mr. Pope was perhaps few months older. I remember my father once mentioning to me that Charlie was one of the survivors of the nineteenth century, almost the last to function at a very senior level of the Canadian government. If that were so, Mr. Pope must now be approaching seventy. I wondered how it was, as I sat there waiting to be admitted to his room, that he had continued active at this level of affairs so long after the normally prescribed age of retirement. He must have been specially selected as one of the central members — perhaps the absolutely central member — of the Trudeau team of transition, of which much had been made in the newspapers for the last six months or so. Surely, I thought, the transition has now been accomplished. Surely Mr. Pope must now be preparing to lay down the heavy burden of executive and administrative responsibility, which he had borne for twenty years and more. His ascendancy in government dated from a time not long after my father's return from Europe. Their subsequent careers had in some mysterious way been connected, bound and wound around each other like the strands of a vessel's mooring lines. Membership in the NDP had effectively excluded my father from office, and naturally Mr. Pope's appointments precluded any adoption of party affiliation. This only meant, in those days, that he was a Liberal without making a noise about it. Everybody at any level of seniority in the bureaucracy had been appointed by Liberal administrations since the nineteen-thirties. One of the recurrent criticisms of the

Diefenbaker government, by friend and foe alike, was that no
concerted effort had been made by the Chief to break the
Liberal stranglehold on the senior civil service, the diplomatic service, the judiciary. The country might now and then
be given an opportunity to vote the Liberals out of office, but
it never had any chance at all to vote the bureaucracy out of
place. The senior officers of the establishment remained at
their desks, as Charlie Pope had done, for generations.

Judging from the wave of hysterical approbation that had
greeted the new prime minister upon his election, it now
seemed likely that none but a Liberal government would
have the chance to restaff a civil service that had grown old in
the service of Liberal governments. The men now functioning at the level of deputy minister, undersecretary, had been
carrying out the policies of Canadian Liberalism since about
1935, and it looked as if this might continue to be the case for
the foreseeable future, for as long as the love-affair between
Pierre Elliott Trudeau and the people of Canada continued.
That might be a long time.

All the same, the undersecretaries, the deputy ministers,
were ageing. It suddenly crossed my mind that Mr. Pope
might have asked me to see him this afternoon with the covert
intention of offering me some extraordinary middle-level
appointment in the department. Like my dad at about the
same time of life, I had no real job, and such an appointment
might in other circumstances have been extremely welcome.

What could I have done in the office of the Undersecretary
for External Affairs? I haven't the faintest idea, but stranger
appointments than that have been made in various governments at different times of day. I watched people go in and
out of Mr. Pope's room, eyeing me as they passed, and I
wondered when my turn would come. I had been sitting on a
very comfortable divan in Mrs. Melhuish's room for more
than two hours. As a rule, when called to Ottawa to receive
some communication from Peking (Bei-jing) I was ushered
into Mr. Pope's presence at once. This afternoon there
seemed to be some sort of hold up, or planned delay. I have
the impression, looking back on the incident — which besides I remember with perfect clarity — that everybody on the
staff above the rank of messenger knew who I was and why I
was there.

There's no mystery about this. Everybody in the office must have understood that I wanted my father brought back from what amounted to protracted exile. He was receiving no press coverage; no reference was ever made in or out of the House to his Chinese mission. It had an entirely informal, even amateur, character. No budget existed in any department to cover the mission's extraordinary expenses. What was up? I doubt that you would find more than fleeting references to "the Goderich initiative" in any recent surveys of contemporary Canadian history, those that appeared from five to ten years after our relations with the People's Republic were normalized. What my father did in China in 1968 and 1969 seems to have been expunged from the pages of history, and it seems to me high time that his adventures be recorded, even publicized. The difficulty is that I'm not certain what he did. I vividly remember talking to a senior government officer who had served in External for twenty years before being seconded to other spheres of duty. This was nearly two decades after the wrap-up on "the Goderich mission." And he said to me, "I don't remember any of that. I remember that Nixon had his people in there at the beginning of the seventies, but I didn't think we'd gotten there first."

I had to refresh his memory about the whole business. (He may have been teasing me at that. Or pumping me. Could that be?) Because, you see, there's not a bit of good in being first on the ground if nobody remembers it. The Scotch Common Sense school of philosophy in some respects anticipated the thought of Immanuel Kant, but who remembers them?

I intend to see justice done.

Somebody spoke my name, and I looked up. It was Mrs. Melhuish.

"You can go in now, Matthew," she said, looking at me with the eyes of a loving auntie. Matthew?

37

Charlie Pope stood up behind his desk and extended his hand
to me; he was invariably most welcoming. I really believed
that he liked me, but the impression may have been produced
by his exercise of long-established professional habit. Who
can say? We shook hands and I examined him, as I thought,
covertly. He certainly looked his age. Beautifully clad as
always in one of those diplomatic blue pin-stripes. Where do
they get them? Bud Drury used to feature them. The best type
of Canadian, my mother used to say, perhaps with a hint of
irony in her tone. I hadn't known Mr. Pope as long as my
father had; their acquaintance dated back almost fifty years,
to the times just after the first war when my father was
courting my mother and beginning his university teaching
career. All that I know about that period, everything about it
that went into my own formation and my own character, I
have put down elsewhere. Let it suffice that what went on in
Toronto between my father and mother, with ancillary
characters like Mr. Pope circulating in the background in the
nineteen-twenties, was what made me the confused, vacil-
lating, oscillating creature that I am, an unstable mixture of
my parents' qualities, with their shared lives in the decade
before I was born issuing in my mental inheritance almost
from the womb. I know, I *know* what the obvious defects in
my character are. I'm too passive, I'm stuffy, I'm emotionally
unventuresome, colourless. The less obvious defects are
perhaps more interesting: enormous — volcanic — repressed
rage, terror, poorly compensated-for resentment. Where did
they come from and how soon were they there? What happened around the reservoir and down the ravine may proffer
some explanation of this inheritance. Mr. Pope was in at the
beginning of all this, and I may have had him and his pals to

blame for my laughable blandness and my night sweats, emotionally induced inability to handle money, and consequent fear of poverty and debt, for my status as the archetypal play-it-safe Canadian nice-Nelly.

I don't know how many times people have told me to my face, "Matt Goderich, you're the typical Canadian," meaning no compliment by it. How, I ask myself, did my mother's grace, sweetness, beauty, and charm, and my father's high gifts of energy and will and intellect, combine in me to produce what I feel? Did I get none of their best qualities and all of their worst? Did I inherit my father's confirmed tendency always to be somewhere else, always to be at a safe removal from the exercise of command? Did I receive whatever it was in my mother that led to the odd circumstance that despite their great love for one another my father took two very extended vacations from the marriage? He was away at one point for seven years, at another for three. This is not the behaviour of a lover of home and hearth.

I now found myself in the position of being unable to trust Charlie Pope or believe a word of what he told me. I realized as I advanced into his room and put out my hand to his that the Popean role in our family folklore, particularly his famous remark about Manitoba, Québec, and the Holy Land, might be seen long after the original declaration as an example of the smarmy high-mindedness — concealing depths of concentrated dedication to one's own interests — that characterized Canadian Liberalism from the beginning of King's first prime ministership to the end of Pearson's. The internationalism, the commitment to supra-national assemblies and judiciaries, the renunciation of effective defence policies, all choices made by the soft-voiced men who did well out of the war.

All the same I seized Charlie's hand and shook it and listened to his apologies for having kept me waiting.

"We thought we might have something new for you, just coming over the wire, but there's nothing in today."

I indicated complete acquiescence in this statement.

All the same I had my doubts about it. When once you begin to see duplicity everywhere, the ground seems to open under your feet.

"I've been wanting to have a chat with you, Matthew," said

Mr. Pope in the accents of extreme gravity. The phrase made
me recall a whole troop of high-school teachers whom I'd
detested. "I think we ought to furnish you with a bit of a
backgrounder on your dad's doings."

"The main thing I'd like to know," I said, "is whose idea
this was in the first place. Did he originate it? Did he bring it
to you or did somebody else put him — or you — up to it?
Why aren't the papers giving it any coverage? It's a matter of
public record and yet I never hear one word about it from any
of the commentators. This has the uneasy air of some sort of
conspiracy to ignore, an agreed-upon silence. Who could
possibly want to ignore my father or put him down? What's
going on?"

I guess the tone of these questions alarmed Mr. Pope. He
looked deeply pained. Plain speech is of course indigestible
fodder for diplomats, an observation so banal that I shouldn't
record it. All the same I was struck by how evidently these
plain inquiries troubled our old family friend.

"Don't try any of your 'These are high matters of state' on
me," I begged. "Because none of it is matter-of-state at all.
The whole damn mission doesn't really exist, does it? It has
no formal status, and what's more, it's depriving the electors
of East Gwillimbury of their right of representation in the
federal House. How do you explain that? I'm getting a lot of
puzzled inquiries from people in the riding. What am I
supposed to say to them? And my mother is deeply upset. She
isn't in the best of health. I'm taking flak from my brother
and sister about this; my wife is complaining that I don't pay
enough attention to her and the children because I'm worried
about my dad all the time. She says it's immature. I think I'm
entitled to an explanation."

"And so you are, and so you are, and you shall have one,"
said Mr. Pope in those smooth tones that had sounded in my
ears for decades with reassurance and calm, and now seemed
merely evasive and placatory. He spoke into the intercom on
his desk. "Mrs. Melhuish, would you bring in the files on the
Goderich mission, please?"

The door behind me opened and she came briskly in,
loaded with documentation, nodding at me smilingly as she
set the materials down in front of the Undersecretary. The

whole operation had an uncomfortable, rehearsed air, as though they intended to try to impose on my credulity which, as is well known, is immense. I'll believe anything. Anything that I want to believe.

"Now Matthew," said Mr. Pope, letting his voice drop into easy confidentiality, "I'm about to make a number of remarks that are probably covered under the Official Secrets Act, and I must ask you to treat them as absolutely confidential. I will make no record of any kind of this conversation and I intend to treat it as though it is not in fact taking place. Do you follow me?"

"I do," I said, "but I don't want to. I don't want to be liable to prosecution under that act or any other act. Perhaps we shouldn't have such a conversation." After all the halls were lined with RCMP, or if not RCMP, persons who resembled them in every particular.

"I can trust you to respect these confidences then?" said Charlie Pope. I hadn't said that, but he hadn't listened to me and it seemed that I would be taken as having committed myself. In for a penny, in for a dollar, I thought. What's one high matter of state more or less?

"Matthew, we're locked into what amounts to a race between ourselves and the Americans to close agreements with the Chinese leading to the establishment of diplomatic relations with them. The Nixon inaugural is only days away now, and we're on the point of losing our lead over the Americans. Whatever you may think of Nixon — and I despise him — he is a great pragmatist. Mark my words, Matthew, Richard Nixon will be parading along the Great Wall conducting his campaign for re-election four years from now. This is the man whose supporters consider him the arch-opponent of Socialist collectivism. He's nothing of the sort; he's the contemporary power-monger, the new Machiavelli who will do whatever is necessary to maintain himself at the head of affairs. Already the American romance with Japan is drawing to a close. Japanese industry and technology are on the point of surpassing those of the US. In automotive production, in computer science, the Japanese have made important breakthroughs, and we must never forget that they enjoy an almost unrestricted access to the enormously rich American market, access the administration can't yet attempt to control. Sooner or later — and probably sooner than later — the Americans will be forced to seek a new Asiatic partner to counterbalance their unwelcome tie to Tokyo, never their preferred far-Eastern ally. We have to remember that the Chinese were America's allies against the Japanese between 1930 and 1946, and that the Americans dropped no nuclear device on the Chinese. The Americans will move directly after Nixon's inaugural towards an understanding with China, and Chinese policy will rank high on any Presidential list of priorities for decades to come."

"That's all correct, I suppose," I said, "but what's it to us? We can never match the Americans as potential allies for China. We simply aren't rich enough or powerful enough."

"But we're big," said Charlie Pope quietly, "we're very big."

I was starting to get interested and I guess he could read it in my face.

"It's true that Canada isn't a great power in the old sense, the nineteenth- and twentieth-century sense that you meet in conventional history books. But to the Chinese leaders Canada is infinitely more a great power than Italy or Spain or France, because Canada is so like China in her geography. The Chinese think nothing of France or Italy, tiny European principalities; they don't even think that much of Germany, and have retained a guarded respect for Britain. But they can read a map, and they know that our country is even bigger than theirs; Canada is the second-biggest country in the world and to the Chinese leaders this means almost everything. They don't have our conventional notions of what constitutes a middle power or a great power. They are used to dealing with the same social problems as we are, consequent upon geography. And to them, Matthew, and you should never forget this, to China's leaders our scanty population, far from being a handicap, far from reducing our status to that of a middle power, is an immense, an unparalleled advantage. They envy us our tiny population and our enormous possessions. Put yourself in the position of Mao and Chou and their juniors, faced with the problem of dealing with a population of one billion that is increasing in geometric proportions, and able to contemplate in Canada a state larger even than the almost infinite spaces of China, with a population of twenty-four million! To the Chinese leaders, the Canadians are the most specially privileged people on earth. We have already met with inquiries from them, channeled to us by your father, about our policies of fresh-water management, vis-a-vis the United States, and I'll tell you something you must never repeat. In any show-down between Canada and the US over possession of North American fresh-water resources, China would be on our side. How do you like that?"

38

I liked it. I liked it fine. I could see, mind you, that he was
very cunningly restating positions that my father and mother
had proposed to me all my life. Perhaps, to do him justice,
Mr. Pope's notion that size of population no longer determined a nation's power was shared between him and Dad. It
makes perfect sense at the end of the twentieth century, an age
when possession of even one itty-bitty nuclear device puts
you in the big leagues, or at least the high minors. On the face
of it, given Canada's enormous size and small population,
and access to nuclear secrets of the most consequential design
— rockets, missiles, jet aircraft — there is no reason she
should not accede to the status of a leading political force in
the world community. Some such appearance in the foreground of world affairs had always been my father's dream.
"Canada, the first modern society, the pacific country." The
words with which he concluded his Nobel Prize address. Lots
of people have sneered at them, written them off as impossibly Utopian, idly idealistic, but they continue to describe
Canada's legitimate political ambitions. What Canada aims
at is the role of a great power that is at the same time not
"power" in any traditional political or military sense, but
rather the abdication of coercive power as between states, in
the interests of world peace. The pacific country. It seems
clear that no Canadian, French- or English-speaking, would
fight a sanguinary civil war to settle the differences of
national identity, language, religion, and culture that
separate the two great Canadian communities. A country in
which civil war is an impossibility is already a country that
has taken a mighty leap forward towards the possibility of
moral, even ethical statecraft.

Mr. Pope lost no time in pointing this out to me.

"You can't have any conception," he told me in soft diplomatic accents, "of the egotism and vanity and megalomania of the Chinese leaders. We think of the People's Republic as the true Socialist community realized in history. This is a joke. Present-day China comes as close to a Socialist heaven on earth as Israel does to Zion, or as the Papal States came to the heavenly city of Saint Augustine. The Chinese leaders are ruthless cunning imperialistic power-mongers who pursue the ancient Chinese policy of expansionism at every point along their borders at which it is strategically convenient, on the borders of Afghanistan and Nepal, in Mongolia and Korea. The rulers of the Middle Kingdom continue to see their power as the leading element in human culture. That is why we were obliged to send the most distinguished living Canadian to treat with them."

I gasped.

"No, Matthew, you can take my word for it. Certainly I consider your father the most distinguished living Canadian, the author of *Sin Quantified, Property and Value, The Place of Conceptual Thought in Ethical Judgements,* what a trio of books! The Nobel Prize winner. We couldn't have sent Mr. Pearson; he was a lame-duck prime minister when the overtures were begun and his power base was severely eroded; the Chinese leaders knew this. You'd be surprised at how much they know about Canadian affairs, internal and external. And there was no question of sending Mr. Trudeau. He hadn't been elected, for one thing, and once he was elected the problems of his first year in office were so challenging that he couldn't possibly have taken the time out for the Chinese venture, much as he might have wanted to. Your father sits in the House as a member of the only party in Canada with any sort of Socialist identification. Peking is perfectly aware that the Canadian Communist Party is a dead letter electorally. The name of Andrew Goderich meant a great deal to them. He was our only possible choice, and I think I can tell you, again in the strictest confidence, that his mission may bear unexpected and most valuable fruit, not simply in the form of agreements concerning wheat sales or other economic accords, but in an early and lasting rapprochement between our two countries. Who else among senior Canadian public figures has taken the trouble to learn Chinese? What inspired your father to take that step?"

"He's been babbling on about China since I was a kid," I said. "He used to talk to me about Manchuria, only I remember that it wasn't called Manchuria then. It had another name, something similar. What was it?"

"Manchukuo," said Mr. Pope. "You've put your finger on the real hot spot in Chinese affairs. Do you know why it was called Manchukuo when you were a child?"

"I don't, and I don't suppose anybody else does either, except an occasional diplomat or spy."

"You must remember that your father was very much a League of Nations man in the twenties and thirties, at least until the Ethiopian crisis."

"Wasn't that when the league refused to take effective action against Mussolini?"

"It was indeed. That was when your father, and Anthony Eden, and perhaps Winston and a few others in the English-speaking world, realized that the league was finished as an effective instrument for world peace. But a decade earlier, when Chang Tso-lin was rampaging around Manchuria to the great dismay of the major powers in the region, the league was able to avert a very grave confrontation that might have led to war between Japan and Russia, a renewal of the struggle of 1905, this time with much more competent and single-minded leaders in the saddle in Russia. You have only to glance at the map to see why Manchuria is such a trouble spot, as much as Korea. For Manchuria lies immediately between Russia, China, and Japan. Its vast wealth of un-developed natural resources in 1925 seemed far too rich a prize for any of these powers to let it drop into the hands of any other. The league was able to put in place an inter-nationalization of Manchuria, with its own observers on the ground; this was in 1926. But this settlement proved only a temporary resolution of the Manchurian question."

Mr. Pope was now well into his old-time lecturing stride, familiar to half a generation of students in the history department of the University of Toronto.

"By 1931 Japan was ready to initiate covert, and finally

overt military movements inside Manchuria itself, and within eighteen months the Japanese had made themselves masters of most of the province, with the exception of a small border strip in northern Manchuria where they dared not proceed too openly. Thenceforward, according to Japanese decrees, the province was to be known as Manchukuo, its Japanese name. In fact the maps of the 1930s use that name. It was because of these Japanese movements in the old kingdom of the Manchu that the Sino-Japanese war began. This brought American policies and sympathies strongly in line with Chinese aims and contributed directly to the outbreak of the war in the Pacific in 1941. For when Japan saw Britain and the US leagued with Russia in war against the Axis powers, an Axis to which she belonged, she felt herself encircled by her most powerful enemies, Russia and China by land, the US in the Pacific. A strike against American naval installations now became mandatory, and the attack on Pearl Harbor could readily have been predicted by any informed analyst of naval intelligence. There is in fact — as of course you are aware — a school of historians that holds that American intelligence was in full possession of Japanese naval plans because they had succeeded in breaking the most-used Japanese codes and ciphers, that while the Americans were entertaining the mission of Nomura and Kurusu, appearing to believe their every word, preparations were being made to foil the purposes of the sneak attack on Pearl Harbor by sending the three American aircraft carriers to sea, leaving only the seven obsolete battleships in harbour to serve as bait for the striking force. The 'day of infamy' on this view was allowed and even covertly encouraged, so that the Japanese would be forced to accept all the guilt for having attacked the Americans and begun hostilities without a formal declaration. The American nation would rally behind Roosevelt's call on Congress for an immediate declaration of war."

"Do you believe the revisionist theory?" I asked the veteran diplomat.

"I never believe revisionist theories; they invariably have some all too visible axe to grind. The attack on Pearl Harbor was without question a sneak attack, which caused the deaths of large numbers of American servicemen, and the putting out of action of the entire line of battle of the Pacific fleet for as much as eighteen months. The *Arizona* and the *Utah* never returned to service. I mention the Pearl Harbor raid as an instance of an incident that provably took place, around which several distinct narratives have taken form, any one of which can offer a more or less credible account of the event. We can't yet fairly assess how far the Japanese felt themselves hemmed in and threatened by America, China, Russia. This may have been a case of mass neurosis like that of the Ugeti people, faced with the presence of their neighbours the Pineals, in the unfortunate state of Leofrica, upon whose successful continuance I would not bet money. Like the suspicions of the Ugeti, those of the Japanese were intense enough to cause them to embark on a unwinnable war by means of an action that consigned them and their leaders to obloquy in Western opinion. The West doubtless accepted some revisions of the 'day of infamy' story in the decades following the war, but the odium attaching to the Pearl Harbor incident largely justified in American eyes the use of the first atomic bombs against the hated Japs — those squinty-eyed little yellow bastards — a description widely current in North America in 1945. It is worth remembering that of all the great and famous leaders of the Second World War, only the Emperor Hirohito remains in place, his position uneroded by time or circumstance. I often ask myself how this has come about."

"American guilt feelings about the destruction of Hiroshima and Nagasaki, do you think?"

"Oh undoubtedly. It was Pearl Harbor that excused Hiroshima and Nagasaki in Western eyes in 1945. But a reaction set in almost immediately afterwards, and was intensified by what was seen as the defection of China. When once the Chinese were seen to be on the side of 'history's will to revolution' (as some people call it), the Americans turned in their frustration and disappointment to the Japanese, making little gods of them and allowing them commercial privileges never accorded to China. All the disdain and hatred that had been poured out on those squinty-eyed little yellow bastards was now turned inside out and the Japanese were enthroned as the best ally of the West in the Far East — in my opinion an utterly ridiculous view. The Far Eastern power that must be conciliated and encouraged to take a central place on the world stage is certainly China. This is obvious. It's the reason your father remains in Peking, or Bei-jing. Like the Maoist movement he has himself been qualified as an embodiment of the 'world historical will to revolution.'"

"Oh sure," I said, "but never by anybody who could be taken at all seriously."

"My dear young man," said Charlie Pope, eyeing me disdainfully, "you will really have to learn that because you yourself consider an opinion absurd that doesn't mean that other people may not find it perfectly reasonable and acceptable. Quite a large body of thought in the major political parties of Canada considers your father an expression of an historical tendency that must be fought against even unto death."

I said, "I thought it was only old George Robinson."

Mr. Pope sat back and stared at me. "*Old* George Robinson?" he said. I saw that I had offended him. "Do you know how old he is?"

"Not for certain," I said weakly.

"He's a good three years younger than I am, and he's a very shrewd man, and don't you ever forget it. He's the only Canadian leader who has been effective politically and at the same time wielded immense economic force. Do you realize that George Robinson stands at the head of RobPharm? He is unquestionably one of the two richest men in the country, and he will probably receive the next Cabinet vacancy. Oh dear, I shouldn't be telling you these things, but I'll tell you just one or two more because I owe you something. When the consequences of Japanese industrial strategy become clear to Mr. Robinson he's going to wish he had your father as an ally, instead of which . . ."

"What? What?"

"Of course he was in favour of your father's mission. I have to concede that," said Charlie Pope. "George Robinson has gone a long way by allowing people to think him stupid."

I said, "But he is stupid, isn't he?"

39

"The beautiful Bellett," said Duncan McCallum, "from Isuzu."

"Nowadays I never know what you're talking about," said his young wife of two years, the beauteous Angela, née Robinson.

Her husband stood in front of a superb full-length mirror, recently installed in the bedroom of their suite at Robinson Court. They had returned to Ontario directly after Centennial Year, had been married from Robinson Court, then done a month-long tour of Japan on their honeymoon. Angela remembered the temple of a thousand Buddhas best. Duncan had been very impressed by his guided tours of certain Mitsubishi and Nissan plants.

"I can't recall who owns Isuzu," he said.

"What are you talking about?" said Angela. She sat in front of her dressing table quite naked, brushing her long black hair, which now, uncut for four years, reached below her waist. She could sit on it but she wasn't sitting on it now. She had her left arm wound around her back, supporting the lower strands, which she stroked in a series of awkward but effective gestures with the right hand. The hairbrush she manipulated so dexterously was backed by thick metal whose dull shine proclaimed it gold. The other instruments and vessels of the sacred rites of pride, from hand mirror to nail scissors, were likewise gold. It was nice to be home, and they were preparing for a little RobPharm family dinner.

"The Bellett was the first Japanese passenger car to be allowed into Canada in any quantity," said Duncan. "I should have called it a failure. The body styling was unpleasing to North American eyes; the car had the look of a shrunken and distorted 1955 Plymouth. In other respects it reminded you of a Skoda or Panhard. Those Panhards that came in just after the war, the most underpowered automobile ever introduced by an importer to the North American market. You had the feeling that the car was powered by two mice on a treadmill, not a confidence-inducing sensation. And then there was the Fiat Topolino, a sort of enclosed motorcycle with a 500cc engine and space — if you worked at it — for four passengers. You used to see those poor little cars hauling four fat Italian pasta-produced bottoms up hill and down around central Italy, reminding you of the little mules they still use in the hill towns."

"A sorority sister of mine in Toronto had one of those," said Angela reminiscently, "and the Nu Sigs hid it in one of the girls' toilets at Varsity Stadium on a football weekend. They had to blast to remove it. Another time they put it on the roof of Saint Hilda's."

Duncan gave a last twist to his black tie. He liked the look of himself in his dinner jacket, flat stomach preserved by summer gallops up and down the touch-football fields of adolescence and early maturity. Hair trimmed extremely short in defiance of the prevailing mode. Duncan would never wear a beard or sideburns, nor would he permit himself to go more than ten days without consultation with his hair stylist.

"You look divine," said Angela, setting herself to dress. One of the intense pleasures of their first years of marriage had been a shared delight in her clothes, particularly her underclothes. Duncan loved to watch her getting dressed; she knew this, and was able to exert considerable coercive force over her otherwise intractable husband by the subtle manipulation of his admiration for the look of the tops of her legs when sheathed in something sheer. She often asked him to help her select pantihose or briefs, then persuaded him afterwards to fall in with her domestic or public intentions by turning his burners up or down depending on what time was available. He watched her slide a pair of steel-grey tights onto her legs with enthusiastic admiration and some love. She got up and turned her back to him, ducking her head and slipping her arms through shoulder straps in a characteristic and exceedingly female motion.

"Do up the clip, will you?" she asked, and he complied

eagerly. There were a few more liturgical observances to be
carried out. Then they left their bedroom, passed through the
spacious sitting room that belonged to the suite, and along
the long corridor towards the stairs. As they descended they
saw the rest of the family idling in the hall; the gong had not
sounded though it was close on eight o'clock, doubtless
because of special instructions from Mr. Robinson. A family
party; there were only Esther, Henry, and Mrs. Robinson,
Philippa, in the hall. They gave an impression of lost
loneliness as they paced and jittered in the wide thickly
carpeted shining luxurious space. Duncan and Angela
hesitated as they came to the last step; then Mr. Robinson
appeared from the direction of the music room. He stepped
briskly past them around the corner and in under the staircase where the gong was. A sonorous thrilling echoing
boom, that of some enormous and exquisite cymbal, rose in
the air around them.

"Bring your drinks along," said George Robinson in high
good humour.

They dined in state, six of them, in a room meant for state
banquets of anything up to a hundred. The great table was
dressed in stiff and immaculate linen, with fifty unused
covers extending away from them into an indistinct glitter of
flashing mirrored illumination from five crystal chandeliers.
At that time in Ontario only one other dining-room approached in magnificence the interior of the dining-room in
Robinson Court, the grand public dining-room of the King
Edward Hotel in Toronto. In that place, though, there were
dozens of small tables, instead of a single grand T-shaped
oaken object, which vividly evoked the salons of the legendary Atlantic greyhounds, the *Aquitania* or *Normandie*; to
dine in state at Robinson Court was to imagine oneself far at
sea on an endless winter cruise of the North Atlantic, moun-
tainous seas rising outside, the table steady and unmoved as
the floor of heaven within, the ladies' gowns strange evoca-
tions of art-déco elegance. Lalique, Lanvin, half-forgotten
names for luxuries unsuspected in other parts of Stoverville,
passed current here. They sat along the crossbar of the great T
and gazed the length of the room past the clustered blossoms
and the mirrors, beneath the creamy arcaded pilasters and the

ringing chandeliers, inspecting their hazed images in distant glass. The six watched themselves as they moved in novel pairings. Philippa took Duncan for her partner, with Esther on his other side.

Henry sat on his mother-in-law's left with Angela between him and George Robinson. The conversation was general and they were placed closely enough together that Esther on the far right could listen easily to what her father was saying to Angela or Henry.

"New import quotas," said her father.

"What was that Duncan was saying before dinner?" asked Angela of the table in general. "Duncan," — across Henry and her mother — "Duncan, tell Daddy what you were saying about the beautiful Bellett."

George turned reddened eyes upon his younger daughter with some of the misgivings he always felt about her more opaque utterances. He had always — more than ever since her extended sojourn in Québec — treated the younger girl as some species of prophetess, a Sybil, perhaps a Cassandra.

"Bellett?" inquired George Robinson. "Some handsome young woman, eh Duncan? One of your old lady friends from Montréal, is that it?"

"No sir, a Japanese import," said Duncan. His remark had the effect of simultaneously discomposing his father-in-law and brother-in-law, a remarkable cannon shot.

"How did you guess?" said both Henry and George, almost at once.

"Guess what?" asked Duncan, really mystified. He speared a third section of smoked salmon and chewed it with relish.

"I was saving this for coffee and brandy," said George. "They've offered me Trade and Commerce or Energy, whichever I want."

There was a silence.

"Oh Georgie," said Philippa, "I'm so proud. It's what you've always wanted. Oh Georgie!" She rose from her place, stepped lightly along behind Angela and Henry. Esther did likewise. They flung their arms around the empurpled, grasping George, and there was a brief, touching scene of praise and compliment. Angela remained seated until her mother and sister sat down, then she embraced her father. "Of course you won't accept," she said as she straightened up. Philippa and Esther gasped.

"Quite right, my dear," said her father. He passed a stout forefinger around the rim of his starched high collar. "I shan't accept."

"But why, why?" Forlorn mewings from the less percipient ladies.

"My age. I'm sixty-eight, my dears, after all, too late to begin a life at Cabinet level. I would have to divest myself of certain of my holdings, which are too valuable to be sloughed off lightly. And I don't think I'm the man to deal with the challenges of the next decade. I might know what to do about Japanese imports but then I might not. And the question of energy supply is becoming a riddle indeed. I have had briefings at Cabinet level and what I hear isn't reassuring. The sheikhs" — he pronounced the word as "sheeks" — "are learning how to combine. The dogs bark; the caravan moves on."

40

John Sleaford Goderich, aged six, did not enjoy his new school, had not relished two years' attendance at *maternelle*. I have retained photos of him among his French-speaking classmates at nursery school, and I can see that he must have felt quite lost when called upon, at the age of four, to adjust his linguistic expectations to those of people completely unknown to him, largely disagreeable to him, making unintelligible noises, wearing garments in which no Stoverville boy would wish to be seen, the knee socks, the little satchels, the neat jackets. Perhaps we did wrong by John in shoving him off the dock. In later life he has shown only occasional wish to use the excellent French instilled into him by those years of French-language nursery-school play and instruction. How many times after all does a young man speak of nap time, ring toss, rhythm band, baby bunnies? I can't recall the French for nap time but I'm sure John does. However he seldom or never mentions it.

When he got to be six in the last year of the nineteen-sixties, Edie and I suffered the usual *crise de conscience* of enthusiastic parents who wish to do right by their kids' education. Should John continue into a French primary school? Anthony was doing reasonably well in an excellent French-language institution, Andrea less well, possibly because of the two years' difference in their ages. We'd been eager to get our children into French schools when we moved to Montréal and it had not been easy to accomplish at that date, indeed for some time afterwards, the better French schools of the day being inclined to reject children knowing no French and older than, say, four or five. Anthony had been nine when he was switched to French. At first he hated it because he was totally unprepared for it. He knew no French whatsoever, and Edie and I had counted on his native adaptability to allow him to function in the novel situation. He made the adjustment but at considerable cost, as we discovered a long time afterwards.

Andrea just fought the whole idea from the beginning. She was prepared to use certain French words in her conversation, but she simply never believed that people could live their whole lives in any tongue but English. I really believe that the gestures, attitudes, sound patterns, of persons speaking French do not seem perfectly human to Andrea. It is an aspect of her personality that we had not encountered in Stoverville.

About John we were unable to make clear judgements for a long time after he began to grapple with his second language. He survived the two years of *maternelle,* hanging on grimly to his self-possession and managing almost never to shed tears of anguish or frustration. He may have shed tears of pleasure once or twice.

By the end of October 1969 I was starting to think that we might have to switch him to an English primary school, which would mean that of our three children, one had coped with the exotic experience of second-language learning in late childhood; one had resisted it and refused to consider the possibility; and one had survived the years of early childhood, then turned away from the experience at an early opportunity. I suspect that this strikes a national average, and not simply an average for the behaviour of children. As for myself and Edie, there were no grave problems; we both could function acceptably in spoken French, could read it without trouble and had the usual difficulty in writing the language. I can compose a letter to a friend or a business asscociate in French, always with a grammar and a French-English dictionary to hand, and a prayerful attitude mingled with hesitation.

But I still find long conversations at cocktail parties or in the lobbies of theatres or at *vernissages* vexing and exhausting, and I don't readily understand spoken French on the telephone where the facial expressions of the speaker aren't available. But yes, I can live in French, and in the late nineteen-sixties I used the language in my personal and professional life with competence. It's really a question of how much you're using it. If you don't mind making occasional mistakes, and being uncertain for a long time about how much of the conversation you're missing, you can use your second language without too much extra stress.

You have to learn not to mind seeming pretty stupid. There are plenty of nuances and implications that I can get into my English speech that I just give up on in French. I can live with that, and what's missing lessens from month to month as one goes on, but an element of minor misunderstanding always remains, except perhaps in the case of people with a natural gift for languages, polyglot from the womb, who really can speak several languages almost indiscriminately. And I always wonder whether they don't perhaps miss the most important five per cent of what's being said to them. Who knows? I don't.

I think our family's adjustment to the second language was pretty typical. The only thing I've had second thoughts about is the notion of obliging one's children to dive into the new situation without any choice. I don't think I'd do it that way again; fortunately I won't be obliged to. That particular situation isn't going to recur in my life, at least I hope and trust that it isn't.

Of the five of us, Edie had the most difficult time in getting settled in Montréal — and it was she, after all, who had instigated the move. I think that she had expected to cut right across the linguistic and (I hate to use this word) cultural barriers, moving without hindrance and with relaxed ease into the French-language artistic milieux of Montréal. It's too bad that her path never intersected that of Angela Robinson, who moved back to Stoverville with her new husband, Duncan McCallum, at the same time as we were moving to Montréal. Angela could have told us, I guess, that 620 Belmont Avenue in Westmount isn't the best address from which to operate if you want to immerse yourself in Québec life. Angela had passed for a Québecoise for quite a while in the middle sixties. Then for whatever reason — a love-affair gone wrong, professional disappointments, the feeling of being up against a stone wall in her work, any or all of these

causes — she'd married a man who could not have been less a
Québecois, bringing him back with her to Stoverville where,
we heard, they were entirely happy, busy, successful in their
marriage and their personal lives. I hadn't met Duncan
McCallum at that time, but while we were in process of
uprooting ourselves we heard plenty about him from various
folks in Stoverville, Sallee Lennox for one, Dougie Crum for
another. He was said to be a young man of strong character
and high vitality, just right for Angela Mary Robinson,
herself no shrinking violet. Of course Duncan and Angela,
archetypal young marrieds, were half a generation younger
than us and we might have been slow to ask their advice
about moving to Montréal for that reason. Duncan is maybe
fifteen years younger than I am, just the right age for Angela.

We might even have been moving east just as they were
moving west, possibly passing each other at some point on
that stretch of trackage between Cornwall and Stoverville
where swampy brush closes in on the rails, suggestive of
dengue fever, malaria, low mists rising in jungle nights,
constant barrier, from the days of the Fathers of Confedera-
tion until now, to easy passage in either direction. I can see
our quartet, Edie and I, Duncan and Angela, treading warily
on the watch for deadly water moccasins, natives with
blowpipes, listening in the brumous hush to the whispers of
unknown birds.

"The galleries of Montréal are dung!" said Edie to me one
October morning after we'd finished talking about the kids'
schools.

This observation about the Montréal apparatus for the
dissemination of new art came roundly across our mutual
disappointment at Andrea's resolute monolingualism, John's
clear and pressing discomfort at beginning primary school
in his second language; he had so plainly been hoping for a
reduced sentence.

"Dung. Excrement." She fished around for the correct
French expression. *"De la marde! Ordure!"*

I was silent, knowing better than to offer counsel or
encouragement at this point. It wasn't as though we hadn't
had this conversation before, in the course of the two years
we'd been in the city.

"The French galleries won't look at you. Simply won't

hear of you. I've been right the way across town and there isn't a gallery east of Peel that'll look at an English artist."

The neologism "anglophone" had not become current at the time of which I write. A few years later, say by 1977, Edie would routinely have referred to herself as an anglophone artist, and I would not have considered it anything other than an acceptable English word in the Montréal context.

"What about the gallery in the bookstore on Mansfield?"

She spooned a chunk of grapefruit neatly out of the half in which it was seated, snapping at it with voracious jaws and allowing pale juice to escape at the corners of her lips. Then she wiped her mouth — not at all daintily — and grinned at me. "That gallery in the bookstore is a well-understood phenomenon," she said, "like the display of one's work in a newly opened restaurant or theatre or small-city public library. It isn't a really professional setting. The really professional setting is the commercial gallery. I don't like that. I suspect that the gallery system is on its last legs, but artists are always saying that. It's like the theatre, which is always on its last legs too, but unfortunately never expires. I believe that the goddamn gallery system will outlast my time and yours. Do you know, I've been into fifteen French-language galleries and not one person in any of them — not one — had ever heard of Mother. Unbelievable! In several of them I spotted back numbers of *artscanada* in which her work was written up extensively. I even saw copies of the special issue that was *all about her.* When I pointed it out to them they all — all — professed ignorance of the special issue, had never heard of it, didn't know that it had appeared or what it was on about. I don't think they read any of the English material in *artscanada* at any time. Can you beat it?"

"I'm not too surprised," I said.

"But worse than that," she said, swallowing another chunk of grapefruit and spooning up the juice, "worse than that. *None of the English-language galleries had ever heard of her either.* May-Beth Codrington, for God sake! Never heard of her. Never heard of the Codrington Colony, even though the curator's a Montréal girl."

"Actually she's a Stoverville girl who used to live in Montréal."

"But Matthew, she worked here for years and years. She did

CBC programming here. She functioned in the media. Her books were reviewed in the *Star* and the *Gazette*. She's often referred to in magazines and on the CBC as 'Montréal poet Maura Boston,' like Layton or Cohen."

I said sadly, "I'm beginning to suspect that you can live here most of your life and never be accepted as a Montréaler, either French or English, because you weren't born here." I thought this over. I remembered that I'd only lived in the city for two years. "I'm not going to quit on Montréal," I said with determination. "They've got major-league ball here."

She gazed at me with unreadable intensity. "Not only have the English galleries never heard of Mother, they've never heard of me. They've never heard of the great big stink at the drama festival. They've never heard of my mural, for God's sake! Can you absorb that? If I've done one piece that was newsworthy, that got *coverage*, if it's coverage you're looking for, if I've managed to draw attention to my work with one thing, it has to be the mural. It caused a scandal. It offended the prime minister of the day. It made the present prime minister bust a gut with laughter. It made all the networks. These idiots have never heard about it. It happened a hundred and twenty-five miles from Montréal, and they've never heard about it."

"English-speaking Montréal is a small community," I said. "You have to think of it as a city of a couple of hundred thousand souls, bigger than Kingston or Windsor, but not as big as Hamilton or Ottawa. Think of it as roughly the size of Hamilton, without another bigger city forty miles off. Hamilton doesn't have to defend itself against anything."

She was quiet for a bit; then she said, "What about taking the kids up to Stoverville for Christmas? They'd love it. Be a nice thing to do for them."

41

"Silver bells, silver bells," sang my son Anthony. "It's Christmas time and it's shitty."

I didn't reveal my presence in the next room.

"Ding-a-ling, hear them ring," he continued melodiously, "soon it will be Christmas time."

We exercise too great an influence on our kids. I'd been singing those words to that song for Anthony's entire lifetime. I don't think he realized that there *were* any other words, words possibly more in keeping with the Yuletide spirit than mine.

He switched to another seasonal favourite. "Rudolph with your nose so bright, won't you bugger bugger bugger in the mellow moonlight?"

"Those aren't the right words," I sang out.

There was a silence.

"Anthony?"

"Sorry, Dad."

"Don't be sorry, but we mustn't be too cynical about Christmas. It's one of the things we've got to hang on to." I got up and joined him in the little antechamber off the morning room in the Codrington house. The picture gallery upstairs and the public rooms were closed over the holidays and wouldn't reopen until the Tuesday after New Year's. We were for once pretty much left alone in the house. I had had two phone calls on Christmas Eve from art students on holiday, begging to be allowed into the building on Boxing Day as a special favour. I had felt a cruel pleasure in turning them down. People ought to have more consideration. And thesis writers and their directors are the last straw, let me tell you, I who have committed a thesis myself. Status as a serious student seems to suspend the customs of ordinary civility. As I lie dying the phone calls will be coming in asking for appointments about graduate theses on Mrs. Codrington or Edie, and when they come to lower my rough pine box into the hole, an enthusiastic student will lean over the edge and — trying to pierce the splintering lid with a researcher's X-ray vision — will utter the territorial call of the species: "If you'd just take a minute to look over these pages."

Anthony had been setting up an electric-auto-racing track of complex layout and impressive proportions on the carpet of this antechamber. His brother John had twice been forcibly restrained from assisting him, and could now be heard at a distance enunciating Yuletide protests, avowals of a precocious interest in his sibling's sensational new toy.

Playthings, like the food in unfamiliar refrigerators, like lovers, seem more interesting when others' property. Thoughts of grass, green at a distance, percolated in my brain. I wondered idly if Montréal would seem any more attractive to the children now that they were removed from it temporarily, than it had during enforced residence. I was growing to enjoy living in *la métropole* myself, now that the silliest of the political aberrations seemed to be a year or two behind us; the seventies would surely see a more pacific Québec fully restored to the bosom of the Canadian community. I thought of putting a question about Montréal life to Anthony, then reconsidered it. Why spoil Christmas, I thought, no time for sociological inquiry. Anthony stood up beside me and I noticed how tall he was growing. Not yet in his teens, eleven in fact, he was considerably taller than five feet. Another year or so would find us on a level; it looked as if he might eventually go over the six-foot mark, the first person on my side of the family to rise to that austere height. He's a nice person, Anthony.

"Do you want to be the first to race with me?" he asked, and I felt enormously pleased and flattered. At the back of the second floor, John seemed somehow to sense that auto racing was about to begin. His wails redoubled in fervour and penetration. I studied the pair of racing cars with attention. They were modelled in stout, virtually indestructible plastic, and have lasted for years. I could put my hand on them at this

moment if I were in the right city. The yellow one was a
detailed small version of a Thunderbird, the red one naturally a Corvette. They were the same size, doubtless closely
matched in other respects. I wondered as I examined them
whether the great auto manufacturers were paid a royalty for
use of their designs in minature form. George Robinson,
who had been taking a great interest in automotive affairs,
might know. I certainly didn't. Maybe I should ask him
sometime.

"These are very realistic models," I said to Anthony.
"They're just as detailed as the Dinky Toys I used to race,
down behind our school."

He gave the slight grimace, which meant that he had heard
that story before.

"Of course in those days our toy cars had no power," I
said. "We relied on gravity. We used to weight them by
pouring wax in at the bottom and they really held the
curves."

Anthony shuffled his feet on the carpet; he was dying to
start.

"Are you sure you want me?" Silly old fogey, I thought.
I'm not the right playmate for a kid with a new toy on
Christmas afternoon. "How about your sister? Isn't she
available?"

"She's in the library reading through her new Tintin
books," said Anthony with impatience.

Here now was a paradox. In every other aspect of life
totally and unalterably opposed to, and even contemptuous
of things French or francophone, Andrea worshipped the
work of the great Belgian Georges Rémi, *Hergé*, with un-
dying passion. She would examine with fascination the
text and drawings of any of his works in either language and
with a deft and accurate grasp of the subtlest nuances of her
second language. Whether she knew by some strange secret
process that Hergé was not French but Belgian, I can't say,
but there it is. She had the texts of all the Tintin books by
heart and could expound their intricacies and connections
with scholarly nicety, a remarkable anticipation of her adult
career. She could give the literal meaning and the symbolic
suggestions of those peculiar curses with which le Capitaine

Haddock punctuated his discourse. *"Mille sabords." "Moule
à gaufres."* Exotic expletives.

This Christmas we had given her another six of the books,
four in English, two in French. We didn't buy the French
ones to persuade her to study the language. That would have
been a shoddy, even a disgusting way to profit from making a
gift to a loved child. We gave her the French versions because
English editions of the two books in question had not been
available in the stores in Montréal and she was dying to read
them. The French ones were *Coke en Stock* and *On a voyagé
sur la lune.* I recall that very well because she read them first
and explained their complexities to us over Christmas
dinner. The other four were *King Ottokar's Sceptre, The
Castafiore Emerald, Red Rackham's Treasure,* and *The
Seven Crystal Balls.*

I don't know where Andrea's Tintin books are now. I wish
I did.

Certainly she spoke largely of *The Castafiore Emerald,* at
that date a work of recent appearance, over Christmas turkey.
For most of the meal the Tintin *épopée* was the central
subject of the conversation. At last, with strained politeness,
Andrea said to Anthony and me, "And how did you boys
manage with your racing?" Edie grinned at me as this was
spoken.

There was general laughter at the inquiry.

"Dad couldn't keep on the track," said Anthony. "I won
every race by default. But the star of the afternoon was John."

This was perfectly true. Around three-thirty we had had to
let John play. It was either that or be driven mad by the
sounds of his anguish and desire. He had proved singularly
adept at the controls, damn the little bugger, taking his red
car — he insisted on the red one — into the curves at just the
right speeds, slowing subtly as he entered the curve, then
accelerating out of it with remarkable dexterity.

"If my son John turns out to be a racing driver," said Edie
to Anthony and me, "I'm going to hold the two of you
personally responsible."

We all laughed and joked about it, and the huge meal went
on to sighs of replete contentment. "Isn't it awful," said

Andrea at last, "isn't it awful! We have to go back to stinky old Frogland next week."

"Now Andrea," I said, with what I'm afraid was recognizable as mock severity, "I've asked you not to speak like that. You know your mother and I don't like it."

"But I heard about Frogland from Mom," declared Andrea triumphantly, and knowing her I could be certain that this was so. Frogland, I thought, my God, what's next?

42

Last day of 1969. End of the sixties, seventeen years to the day since we saw the ghost ship under the ice, no such mysterious portent in view on this drizzling slushy afternoon on King William Street, excepting the fact that this year unlike the other ended a decade. The birds and the beasts reckon by the seasons, not by numbers. Doubtless they have their rudimentary intuitions of time passing, but they don't introduce artificial points of demarcation into the flow. For them the nineteen-sixties did not take place in our human and historical sense. One spring-summer-fall-winter sequence succeeded another without name or number. 1967, 1968, 1969.

But are such numbers purely fictitious? Isn't the universe getting older according to schematic formulae like the geological ages or the rings around trees? You can certainly calculate the age of the tree by counting the rings, one ring to a year as I understand it, or is it two? I never can remember and that's weird because chronology begins in memory. How many times has winter come around since we saw the boat in the ice? Some seventeen, my darling.

I think that the formal years, the decades, the centuries, are real and found in nature. The twentieth century is still the nineteenth in almost every respect, but we have grown deeply accustomed to our conviction that something ended around 1900, that something else will end, something vastly more significant, the next time the zeroes (three of them this time) turn up on the calendar. The end of the second millennium since the birth of Christ.

The lunar month, the solar year, exist in the natural world. It takes almost exactly what we call one year for the sun to give us our four seasons — if we happen to live in a temperate zone — and four weeks for the moon to wax and wane. Moon lovers instinctively understand that there ought to be thirteen months in the calendar instead of twelve: our unhappy suspicions of the number thirteen no doubt originate in this mystery of the missing month, the sun's year being inconveniently out of phase with the movements of speedy Miss Moon. Certainly the end of a year, decade, century, a millennium, is a true event. Real seasons and years have come and gone.

I always try to do something special to mark the end of an important chronological phase, make some significant change in my own regimen, resolve to do better, in some circumstances resolve to do worse. One can't always insist upon improving oneself. I should sin more. I'd be a better man. In Stoverville on the last day of a decade I could find no special line of demarcation showing itself as the hour of leaving the sixties approached. And yet the papers were full of consequential remarks about the dying decade and that which threatened to be born. The seventies, they all said, would be different than the sixties. As different from the sixties as the sixties had been from the fifties.

At this point, the writers of semi-humorous think pieces on op-ed pages would deviate into congratulatory comment on the sixties, which had given us the drug culture, the ongoing student revolution, late rock and roll, political assassination as a habit as comfortable as an old shoe, black power, the women's movement and all that it implied, Vatican II, Vietnam (of course the sixties didn't "give us" Vietnam), the miniskirt, all these novel modes of action and experience. The sixties had been great, and they really formed a unit. On January first, 1960, some strange power had supervened globally in human culture, and its rule had altered human possibility out of all recognition. This was true. Could this be true? Does this happen? In supposing that it does we are doing something that an age like ours should forbid itself to do. We are attributing a soul or a spiritual self-consciousness to a unit of time. The sixties, certainly, were governed by a particular spirit, and no vapid, goody-goody angelic spirit either, but a demonic pulsing driving all-possessing fatuous intelligence. Sure the sixties were self-aware. They were dominated by the whim of an indwelling Daffy Demon!

What might be the spirit of the decade to come? Surely not the twin of his or her predecessor; there couldn't be two nutty decades in a row. I pondered the identities of decades and centuries as I strolled along King William Street, heading slowly eastwards in the lowering drizzle and gloom. It was about three-fifteen and already almost dark, a mixture of Scotch mist, spitting rain, occasional blips of sleet hanging in the air. My face kept getting wet by some unfamiliar process of condensation. I'd wipe it clean and dry with my woolly mitts, in seconds my cheeks would be sweating a cool dampness, then dripping as though I had shed tears.

I didn't feel weepy. I felt on top of my form. I always feel great when something like this comes to an end, the end of a time, a year, a century. Managed to make it, I tell myself, hung on right to the end. Now what's going to happen? I had no notion what the seventies would bring, although like every other recorder of temporality I know now what the seventies implied. The angel of the seventies turned out not to be the twin of his or her dizzy predecessor. Angels have no sex: either personal pronoun will serve. The angel of the seventies wasn't, then, the twin or even the sister of her predecessor. The sixties had been a perfect bitch. Oh wow!

I'd come out by myself, putting behind me the wails of "Why do we have to go home so soon?" and the phone calls from homing visionary artists revving up for work after the holidays and deeply desirous of conferring with me about the indwelling structures of artistic insight. As I slumped along in the gathering gloom I was half-afraid that one of the visionary artists now residing in the Codrington Colony might accost me, ply me with reflections on the symbolic meaning of this dark eve. I did not want to hold any such discussion. I quickened my pace as a hesitant shape appeared at some distance on the sidewalk, moving towards me. But it was nobody I knew although it seemed the right age for a questing artist, some unidentifiably young person, male from the cut of his foul-weather gear. We passed one another silently. Keen glances were exchanged but no words.

Maura Boston had claimed, intemperately as I thought, that the activities of the Codrington Colony had already in just more than two years uncovered two genuinely talented new artists, one a painter and lithographic printer, the other a sculptor, from among the couple of dozen aspirants who had worked there. I could form no opinion. What I wanted, now that we'd moved out of the building for all intents and purposes, was to allow the programs of the colony to unfold without myself being called upon to take part in them. I am not a visionary artist, though I pay continual honour and homage to all who are (El Greco, Blake, Samuel Palmer, Bosch, Ensor, Mrs. Codrington), and I wouldn't really know what to say to a visionary artist if I fell over one. I'd never for example been sure what I ought to say to Mrs. Codrington; whenever we met she did the talking.

Edie more and more rejects the visionary element in the visual arts. I suppose that was why she was so keen to get out of the house and out of Stoverville. Nonetheless I had the feeling that she might at some point be drawn back to her birthplace, on the premise that you know you can't go home again, but you can give it a good try.

Stoverville wasn't my birthplace but even I, an exotic outlander, felt patterns of recurrence pressing hard on my imagination whenever I came back. This afternoon I found my footsteps directing themselves without conscious volition eastwards along King William Street past one after another of the big houses in whose fancy rooms my wife and her girl chums had first elaborated their destinies. Leaving the Codrington Colony, wondering how sculptors might embody vision in stone, always a tricky problem, I passed the old MacLean place, fallen almost into ruins after the lapse of a dirty dying decade. In 1960 the MacLean place had been in the same shape as in 1900. Now it showed indications of imminent collapse, instant archaeology. In another decade people might come and dig on the site.

Other houses along the street were still inhabited but the financial strain of keeping up an enormous show-place in an inflationary period, when costs of maintenance and repair were grotesquely magnified, showed wherever you looked. The Sherbourne house exhibited only a few lights. The Christmas display on the front lawns was attentuated, hard to interpret in the gathering gloom, composed mostly of flickering ice-blue lights. Further along — all these mansions

are on the south side of King William Street bordering the
river — the Invergordon house glittered with illumination.
Somebody was giving a New Year's Eve shindig but it
wouldn't be Bert. He had died a few months ago, to the end
preoccupied with the search for the definitive blonde.
Perhaps his heirs had decided to show the old home one last
round of gaiety before packing up and moving into a tract
house in Loyalist Park.

Largest of all, standing well away from the others "in its
own grounds," amid shrubberies and hedges in close to ten
acres, an enormous park and garden for an Ontario house in
the middle of a city or town, Robinson Court loomed in the
dark, grey, impressively bulky. I passed through the tall iron
gates, sparing no investigative glance for the long unin-
habited gatehouse. Once a family of five had lived there, their
only duties those of lodge keepers. Now nobody seemed to
care who went in and out. I came into the truly park-like
expanse before the front elevation. In this light the form of
the main mass of building, turretted, castellated, high and
broad and long, seemed that of some prehistoric monster, a
brontosaurus or diplodocus.

It was almost night at four o'clock. No light emerged from
the building, no automobile stood on the drive. Perhaps the
cars were parked around by the old stables. I approached the
front of the house, searching for a light. I had wanted to
inquire about automobile production and the licensing of
body designs, and a few other things like that. It seemed
unlikely that George Robinson would meet me on these
matters. Not tonight anyway.

I began to retreat, backing away from the *porte-cochère,* a
vague awe creeping up between my shoulders at the intimations of time passing and passing and passing away that
assailed me. For a moment I believed that I saw a light at a
second-floor window but all the panes appeared to be
shuttered over. The light came again and for a brief instant I
saw the face of Angela Mary Robinson McCallum peering
down on me. She's come back to stay, I thought. She couldn't
stick it out in Montréal. I don't call that the true bicultural-
ism. I'll bet I last longer in Québec than she did. The face at
the window faded into total darkness. Tomorrow the
seventies would start.

VII

43

Then right after the first of the year this arrived in the mail:

Linnet and I have packed it in and I don't really know why. It
was her decision; she just hit me with it on Christmas night.
You can readily intuit my feelings about Christmas. They
were never really jolly and now they're suicidal. You cannot
imagine anything more dreary and deserted than Swiss
Cottage on Christmas night. The Underground deserted —
Bakerloo line, noisy and dirty and empty and you can't hear
what your companion is saying. We'd gone down to Charlotte Street to dine. We've never lived together, not even when
she was living upstairs over the toy museum. It's been an
indecisive and noncommital and Platonic relationship.
How I hate that word. It suggests all the half-baked hatred
of women and reluctant homosexuality of the English
educational system which stinks of Plato, but not a Plato any
of his contemporaries would have recognized. A supposedly
fastidious dualist along the lines of John Addington Sy-
monds, not the tough mean bastard, the potential SS man,
whom I feel certain Plato must have been. I don't know why
I'm going on about that, I was talking about breaking up
with Linnet. As I say, it was her idea, although we'd both
been pressing for a resolution of the situation for close to a
year. We'd been together for six years off and on, mostly on.
The worst thing about this breakup is that she did it because
she figured I could no longer advance her career. She hasn't
become a film star, which is what she's had in mind ever since
the MacNamara bitch made it to Hollywood. Actually I don't
dislike Sadie and I don't blame her for anything that's
happened. She took on Adam for more praiseworthy reasons
than Linnet did me. Sadie supposed that she could stick life

with Adam and that she would be a credible cover for Adam's queerdom — with the great public, that is. Nothing could conceal Adam's fey ways from anybody who saw him up close. Sadie thought she could do herself a spot of good by taking on Adam and do him a goodish spot of good incidentally and by the way. I may have her priorities ass-backwards. I've fallen into a bad habit lately of assigning motives and invariably placing the lower motive above the higher, a cheap cynicism. It might be — it's conceivable — that Sadie, in some peculiar mode known only to her, genuinely loved Adam. It isn't utterly unthinkable. Just because there was something in it for her doesn't necessarily mean that her motives were entirely selfish. All motives are mixed motives. I believe that Sadie married Adam because she could see that he was going to be a big star. When she suddenly found after a couple of years that she'd surpassed him, as far as the big public reputation goes, she began to feel that she might have done better for herself. So far she hasn't done so. It might be the case that Sadie is incapable for some obscure reason of genuine feeling for anybody else, just keen on herself. That could be. But I don't think so. Very few people manage to survive into adulthood with complete selfishness as their mainspring. I think life winnows out those types in childhood and adolescence. Most likely Sadie hooked up with Adam intending to be true to him indefinitely, or as long as he was more famous than she was. I don't suppose she ever put it to herself in exactly those terms, but that's the sum of it. All at once she finds that she's world-famous and Adam, talented as he is, is never going to be a success like she's a success. She starts to feel superior to him and from that moment their marriage is finished. It wasn't sexual inadequacy or confusion that did poor old Adam in with Sadie. It was a shift in their power relationship. What an old-fashioned analysis, positively Adlerian.

Nobody mentions Adler these days; he's a spent force. Yet I would not be surprised to learn that if Adam were ever to have a great international hit with a big movie coming out of it or a huge TV series, Sadie might reappear and suggest that they give it another try. I don't think Miss MacNamara cares much about bed. What she likes is being seen; this assures her of her own existence. God, it's impossible to make any sense of such matters. Who knows about Sadie but Sadie? I've spent time in her company that I enjoyed hugely. She's got a really marvellous chest, you know, sculpted, firm, deep, and she's no spring chicken. She must have been well into her twenties when you knew her at Stratford and that's what, getting on for twenty years now? She must be around forty and she looks absolutely wonderful. Chest apart, she's very slender and small and she's got those slanty eyes. She can give you a very agreeable evening without ever a thought of bed on either side. If I were not a cautious old bugger I'd admit that there have been times when I quite liked Sadie. Adam of course was simply scared shitless of her, didn't know what to do with her. Whatever else you might say about yon wee Scotch farrrrttt, nobody would ever accuse him of bisexualism, the old Thespian.

Where was I? I'd gotten us on the tube coming back from Charlotte Street and really, you know, I think that's where she decided to make the break, because there's no really convenient tube route from Fitzrovia to Swiss Cottage. They're too close together, don't you see? You could take a cab but the drivers aren't any too keen about that run either. It takes them haring off on a trip that doesn't amount to a significant fare but removes them from a place where they might find a serious passenger. I've never had a London cabbie actually refuse to take me on a short run, but I don't like to inconvenience them, and I've reached that condition of affluence where I'm getting very mean. I can't see paying money for cab rides when there's the tube. If you're on Charlotte Street, you've got a choice of three stations, Warren Street or Goodge Street, which amounts to the same thing, Tottenham Court Road, Great Portland Street. Warren Street is on the wrong line. Great Portland Street is halfway there and you might as well walk the rest of the way. And to choose Tottenham Court Road is to walk in the opposite direction from that in which you wish to travel, something which is for me a psychological impossibility.

I mention these matters only to show how momentous decisions can rise from trivial occasions. I was

standing on the pavement outside the restaurant, counting
my change and telling myself that I'd left an adequate tip. I'd
noticed Linnet eyeing the money I'd left on the plate. I
suspected she thought it wasn't enough. The thing is, Matt,
I'm just as scarred by having been brought up in the nineteen-
thirties as you are; we express this in closely similar ways.
Now that I've got lots of money you'd think I'd be lavish,
throw it around, even waste some. "Only the wasteful virtues
earn the sun." Who said that, Yeats? He seems to have said
such a lot. I hope he was wrong about that. I simply can't
bring myself to leave too large a tip or to take the cab ride
when my destination is just outside of walking distance. It
was not a Canadian-style winter's night. It was almost balmy
by your frigid standards, and there I stood, counting out my
coins and asking Linnet to tell me which tube station we
ought to select.

Finally she said, very snappishly, "I don't want to
walk home, Tony, so please don't suggest it."

This required brisk response. "Nobody's asking you
to walk anywhere. Shall I find you a cab?"

As soon as I said this I realized that it amounted to a
veiled threat, because "get you a cab, find you a cab"
implies that the speaker isn't coming along for the ride. I
think that she suspected that I wanted to walk round the
corner to my own cozy little home, leaving her to
conclude that evening's entertainment on her own. So
far as I can judge, this was not a conscious motivation on
my part; it might have been at the back of my mind.
About that I am not competent to speak. I merely admit
the possibility.

"Won't you come home with me?" said she.

And we were launched on a quarrel. We know each other
much too well; she knew perfectly well that my apartment
was within half a minute's walk of where we stood. She's
been there ten thousand times since we've been . . . lovers. I
hate that expression.

I'll tell you what it is, Matt, we should have gotten married,
just the way you did. We should have thrown in our lot
together. We couldn't just cohabit. Linnet's father is a
parson, one of the ones who take it seriously. Linnet doesn't

want to scandalize her father and his parishioners. If that sounds odd to you — and knowing you I'm certain it doesn't — then we'll just have to put up with it. There you are, you see? She wants to be a film star, and she's a famous actress on the stage and the telly. She's been in five films. I think a couple of them have gone into North American distribution, but she isn't yet a world-class star. She can feel the dread approach of the thirties. She's twenty-eight or nine, I think. She thinks that playing Charmian Windrush hurt her chances. I tell her that nobody in the US or the European market thinks of her as Charmian Windrush, but it is true that a lot of people in the UK identify her with the character. People come up to her in the street asking for autographs, and it's always that part they remember. A couple of years ago she was after me to write a play based on *Down Off a Dirty Duck*, which I did. I wrote the part of Linda Mountjoy especially for her.

Now Matt you're a literary bloke to a certain degree, same as what I am, and you'll see at once what the name "Linda Mountjoy" suggests. "Linda" is Spanish for "lovely, beautiful," and "Mountjoy" suggests one thing and one thing only to the sort of chap who reads novels like *Down Off a Dirty Duck* as a regular thing. It's a literary joke. I'm not sure that it can be transferred to the stage. She's meant to be a blend of Marilyn Monroe and Odette de Crécy, but Odette in her Miss Sacripant period, very very sexy and very very tricky. It's a charming conception, though I say it myself, and I could see perfectly why Linnet saw herself as Linda Mountjoy. I sometimes wonder whether that was why she took up with me from the start, not consciously but almost. She wasn't trying to use me, any more than Sadie was trying to use Adam. All the same, it was clear enough when we were developing the script for *Down Off a Dirty Duck* that she had a big emotional investment in the property. The woman can write, you know. She was a big help to me on *Cross Now*.

We worked like smoke on the playscript of *Dirty Duck*, and I think we may have something. But the conception of Linda Mountjoy to which Linnet can relate . . . that we have not got. She blames me. She thinks that I'm holding back on her. I don't know that I can explain this, but I'll give it a go. Linnet

sees herself making a huge success with the character of
Linda Mountjoy, and all the more so because she's absolutely
the reverse of Charmian Windrush. Do you follow me?
"Charmian Windrush" is a farcical name. "Windrush" was
selected, I make no doubt, by the original authors of *Bed
Sitters* because of its faintly indecent suggestions, familiar in
British humour. Charmian had a big rump and huge tits and
a giggle and a blondined head of hair right out of the
bottle and the breathy voice and the monosyllabic dia-
logue. But the thing was, everybody thought she was
terrific. People loved her. Linda Mountjoy on the other
hand is thin, in the last degree upper-class, with a voice
like Maggie Drabble's and a double first in Greats.
Smashing looking but without a tit to bless herself with,
and no giggle. You can't squeeze laughter out of Linda
Mountjoy while she's devouring you, and the thing is —
God knows why — everybody who reads *Down Off a
Dirty Duck* falls in love with her. She resembles Charmian Windrush in only one respect. She's fatally attractive, the only woman in any room. I could see why
Linnet hoped to make a second success with her. She
could not be more unlike the average play-goer's notion
of Charmian Windrush, but she's the same person.

I'll tell you what it reminds me of, Olivier playing Heathcliff and then, right afterwards, Mr. Darcy, two characters
who could not on the surface be more unlike, yet the same
actor can manage both. What we have here is the Jungian
notion that every person contains his opposite in himself. We
can't picture Heathcliff in the world of *Pride and Predudice*,
and we won't bump into Mr. Darcy anywhere near *Wuther-
ing Heights*, but Olivier suited both roles. That's the kind of
tour de force that Linnet has in mind. And I believe that she
thinks I'm deliberately withholding this triumph, but I'm
not. My original idea of Linda Mountjoy had nothing to do
with Linnet. She was a caricature in an intellectual farce, like
one of the young women in Peacock or Stoppard or perhaps
Nabokov, not intended for stage representation except as a
tease. Linnet blames me for making the character too likeable
when I try to dramatize her but I can't help it. Putting her on
the stage warps the schema of the character, and because of

this we've arrived at an impasse. I've seen this coming. Naturally I'll try to talk to her again, but I don't think it'll do much good. We enjoyed six pretty good years together and that's something.

Have you heard from Uncle Phil lately? I write to him once in a way, and I haven't had a reply for ages. I do get the diplomatic messages from Dad, same as you. I have to go down to Canada House and there's always an awful lot of balls about confidentiality. One idiot tried to insist that I read the letters in his presence, then have them burned. I told him what to do with himself, I can tell you.

Tony.

What I was meant to make of all this I can't imagine. It was the most incoherent letter I'd ever had from my brother; perhaps he lives an incoherent life. He's made a remarkable success by uprooting himself. He'll never be able to live in Canada again, not with the full understanding of the place that a writer requires. He couldn't write a play or novel about this country and he wouldn't want to. If you can succeed as a writer in London, he'd say, what would be the point of trying to make it in Montréal or Toronto?

His reference to Uncle Philip puzzled me. As far as I knew they had no special relationship. I was ashamed to realize that I hadn't thought of Uncle Philip in a very long time; he'd faded right out of my sight. We saw him once a year. He'd come to Montréal over a long weekend, usually in the fall, Labour Day or Thanksgiving. Always a favourite with the children, Andrea in particular. He used to bring them expensive presents, often more than I thought he could readily afford. He was hanging on to his little job and saving his money, he said.

"I guess I've a right to give a present to somebody I like," he said, "I very seldom have the chance." It's not easy being a brother, or a nephew, come to that. Tony and Uncle Phil. Nothing in common, I thought, no discoverable link.

44

And then there's Gilmour Street, corridor of power. Gilmour, Lewis, Elgin. Ottawa is such a strange town. The joke in the diplomatic corps is that it's a number-three hardship posting, not because of the climate nor because of the grotesquerie of the public buildings, which are almost uniformily architectural disasters, nor yet because of the absence of commerce or industry or nearby cities and towns, but mostly for the peculiar bifurcation in the town's sense of itself. It is two totally distinct places, neither of which ever seems to achieve any communion with the other.

Don't make any mistake about it. Ottawa is now a world capital. Very large sums of money are collected and sent every year to Ottawa. Not quite the budget of Washington or Paris or Tokyo, but a very large amount. The direction and control of the federal budget attracts great numbers of detemined and highly intelligent people into its administration and spending. Therefore we find in Ottawa a considerable colony of exceedingly bright persons from the best schools and universities on the continent. I don't like them. I wouldn't want to be one of them, or resemble them in any particular, but I haven't given up on the democratic process and the possibility of a freely formed responsible government under the rule of law. Silly me! And if there's going to be some such animal it has to be attended to by competent people. That's the argument for the Ottawa men and women — as they call themselves — the people who, under Norman Robertson and Skelton, "formed the best civil service in the world," as they claimed. I'm not joking and I'm not lampooning this idea. I think of the arguments of Saint Anselm in the *Proslogion* for the existence of God, and I see that they may be applied equally to the question of the existence of "the best civil service in the world."

We observe that some civil services exist. This is directly intuited from the sensuous manifold and is unquestionable. But if some civil services exist there will be differences of virtue and excellence among them, a visible series of perfections and imperfections, since no two beings are perfectly alike. But this implies a scale from worst civil service to best civil service. All this is unquestionable and irrefutable. Now in the concept we form of "best civil service" we must necessarily include existence, since existence is a perfection and some civil services can be seen to exist. The best civil service must exist.

I'd have thought that the claims of the French and British civil services, and those of the old Indian civil, would at any time have overridden those of the Canadian. I don't say this out of colonial-mindedness but from observation and careful reflection. Was the Canadian civil service in the time of Robertson, Skelton, Charlie Pope, Hume Wrong, John Deutsch, arguably the best in the world? I don't think so, but some persons would disagree with me. It's a thinkable thought, and the fact that various people have thought at different times that Ottawa housed the best civil service in the world bears out my argument. Ottawa is a place where some exceedingly civilized, humane, judicious, responsible, and able public servants have dwelt. We have to concede that. They have never made up the whole population of the city, however, and they do not at this time. I should guess that the numbers of this gifted and fortunate administrative body have never exceeded say fifteen per cent of the population, at most twenty-five per cent.

The other seventy-five per cent of the citizenry of Ottawa are either support staff for the senior civil service or those same solid hard-working people of Scottish or Irish stock found up and down the Ottawa Valley from Pembroke and Arnprior to the Québec border, or, finally, people whose first language is French but who are often stigmatized by Québecers as mere franco-Ontarians, second-class French Canadians because resident outside the borders of home. These French-speaking citizens of Ottawa and Perth, Carleton Place,

Smith's Falls, Alexandria and Hawkesbury live in a state of
mixed and conflicting allegiance, which reflects very well the
confused state of all the people in Ottawa who don't hold
senior posts in the government service. Your Ottawan is a
voting citizen of Ontario, therefore votes in the provincial
elections and sends members to Toronto where the provincial legislature, a rich and powerful body, sits in state in
Queen's Park. But Toronto remains a distant and second-
level capital when compared to the immense and present
sway of the federal government.

And there is always the municipal administration to be
reckoned with, its elected officers often highly vocal and
insistent on their legitimate rights. Being mayor of Ottawa
must be a complex fate, to which only the strongest and most
persistent women are called.

So your Ottawans find themselves perplexed by the claims
of three governments representative of three totally distinct
loyalties, which represent in distilled, concentrated form the
stresses on all Canadians. There are the French, the Scots, the
Irish, the English, the other minorities, crowded together in a
smallish eastern-Ontario city, with a super-class of well-paid
functionaries sitting on them. No wonder fairly acute
schizoid confusion seems characteristic of your poor silent
Ottawan who holds no government post.

It's simply a government town. There's no other industrial
or entrepreneurial base. There used to be the lumber barons
but they are all gone into the world of light, leaving not a
dollar behind. It turned out that they *could* take it with them.
My father used to joke about Ottawa that none of its citizenry
ever paid his or her bills because he or she had no money and
his — or her — salary could not be garnisheed. This happy
circumstance no longer conditions Ottawa life. Civil servant
or no, your salary can be attached if your creditor succeeds in
getting a judgement. The decent oldsters who live in the
ageing red-brick houses on Lisgar or Gilmour seethe quietly
in resentment and desperation; now and then one of them
sells off his house and goes to live with relatives in Pembroke
or Smith's Falls, and a functionary moves in and "gentrifies"
the structure.

Marianne Keogh would not have cared at any time in her
career to have been described as a functionary. For one thing

it's a French term (*fonctionnaire*) inexactly adapted to the needs of the English half of the public service. She never would allow herself the status of the mere functionary. She preferred that of mysterious presence, neither secretary nor *chef de cabinet*, another term she refused to accept as definitive. I never knew, for instance, what her civil-service grade was, couldn't tell you that now. You could not think of Marianne Keogh, able, discreet, single, trim, and invariably handsomely dressed, nevertheless without specifically sexual attraction, a closet Liberal in my opinion, you could not consider her, I say as thinkably somebody's secretary. And yet, what was she? She had been with my father off and on for more than thirty years, at first as a casual employee in my parents' ill-starred restaurant business before the war, then again from late 1939 through 1941 as their helper in the management of the Lakeview Hotel on Centre Island. This was just before my father disappeared into the European theatre in 1941.

When he came back to Canada in 1948 he located Marianne Keogh and employed her as his assistant during the reprintings and successive editions of *Sin Quantified*. By then she had her B.A. and was finishing an M.A. in history at the U. of T. She might even have finished the M.A. by then. She never went on to a Ph.D but her M.A. work at Baldwin House had put her in touch with many people who then and for long after counted for much in Canadian public life: Underhill of course and Careless and Creighton and for a while James Eayrs. She knew all about Mr. Pope's connection with the Toronto history department, may even have exploited it successfully now and then during her years as my father's *éminence*, well, not precisely *grise*. She was no Richelieu nor was she a Mazarin partly because my father, to — as I now think — her secret and lasting chagrin, never could bring himself to be co-opted into the ranks of the Liberal Party. I know now on unimpeachable and direct evidence that he could have held high office as a member of successive Liberal governments. He knew this too. I've got the letters and other documents to prove this and one of these days I'm going to publish them. I'd publish them right now if I had an executive assistant as able as Marianne Keogh.

As soon as he accepted the CCF nomination in East Gwillimbury his destiny was fixed; he would never hold the office to which his gifts might have been thought to entitle him. Marianne Keogh had imagined that he might become prime minister or at the very least Secretary for External Affairs. Her ambitions for him were directed into quite a different channel when he ran for the the CCF in East Gwillimbury and proceeded to turn the riding into the safest CCF and NDP seat in Canada. That happened specifically because Andrew Goderich was the member. I'll say this for Marianne Keogh. When she understood that this was to be her master's fate, a fate he had deliberately embraced, when she finally grasped that he didn't want to become PM or Secretary for External Affairs, she followed him devotedly into a position of purely moral influence. He never held cabinet office, never would have, never could have. He wasn't made of that kind of clay.

Marianne was thrust into the position of a connoisseur of power, a student, almost at first hand, of the power-broking of the inner ring of the Liberal Party. Of all her associates in Ottawa, my father apart, the person of whom she most approved was Jack Pickersgill, whose instinct for the management of power amounted to genius. I say this without the smallest ironic intention. Pickersgill was unquestionably a great man in his way, which is how we put it when we don't want to admit that he was a great man subject to no qualification. Nobody says of Andrew Goderich that he was "a great man in his way." He was a great man. But Jack Pickersgill rose high, went far, got to be a great man with but a single qualification.

Certainly Marianne was a Liberal in her heart, who wished for decades that my father had run for the govening party. But she followed him into the wilderness and was absolutely and utterly loyal to him forever after. Whatever her title might have been, whether *chef de cabinet* or executive assistant (I don't think it ever rose to that), she was my father's right hand. And then, she loved him.

He sent her back from Peking in late May of 1970 and I met her in Ottawa a week later, when she cross-questioned me severely about Canadian public reaction to Dad's journey.

"Nobody seems to know anything about what he's accomplishing," she said angrily.

"You're dead right. I can't figure it out. He might as well be dead or in prison somewhere. Hardly a word in the press; no reaction from the Americans."

"And yet," she said thoughtfully, "the mission is bearing fruit, you know."

"Is it?"

"It could be that all the silence is simply an appropriate diplomatic silence. It may be that the negotiation has had to be soft-pedalled. When I left, it looked as though matters were coming to a head. And my goodness, won't the Americans be annoyed!"

We were sitting on the sun porch at the back of her little house on Gilmour Street on an early June afternoon. She never seemed to go near Dad's Parliamentary office, and I'd been occupying the suite in the Lord Elgin and I knew she wasn't working there. I found out long afterwards that all the correspondence and memoranda that documented Dad's political career were in her possession, filed neatly away in the attics of this house. Letters from Mackenzie King dated 1947, which had gone to Switzerland and Paris, letters from the same source a year later directed to Toronto. It looked very much from those letters as if my father could have had the Liberal leadership for the asking in 1948, at the time of King's pending retirement, and again in 1957 after the pipeline débâcle, if he had not by then committed himself to a career as a third-party MP. In 1948 Dad would have been forty-eight years old; his chief opposition for the Liberal leadership would have been Louis St.-Laurent, who became prime minister as everybody knows. King would have preferred Andrew Goderich as his successor, but my father would have none of it. Miss Keogh had the King letters and my father's replies, and exchanges with Mr. St.-Laurent and others, all preserved at Dad's direction for me to examine and do with as I thought best. I didn't get my hands on them for a long time but they were upstairs in the Gilmour Street house on that pleasant end-of-spring afternoon. Miss Keogh knew what was in them.

She sat there fanning herself with a folded newspaper, composed and handsome, her hair with scarcely a thread of grey in it, her figure full and mature but far from undisciplined. I suspected the presence somewhere of an admirable foundation garment.

"He sent me back," she murmured disconnectedly. Grave dissatisfaction was imperfectly concealed in her slow speech. All at once she began to talk in a less diplomatic fashion, saying things that she'd felt obliged to conceal from everybody else.

"The RobPharm interests are keeping him there," she said bitterly. "They're scared shitless of his remarks on the auto-parts agreement. If they only knew what I know. George Robinson and his gang, they think they're so damn clever. I tell you, Matthew, they're about to get a swift kick in the . . . teeth. They think that because they've locked themselves and everybody else in Canada into a trading agreement with the States that enriches them, and them alone, because of their manipulation of the entry regulations, that the automobile industry in North America has the status of Holy Writ. Well it doesn't. I've been to Japan and I've been to Korea and I know what I know. They've wiped out the British and American motorcycle industry. Nobody in Britain or the States bothers to manufacture motor-bikes any more; the Japanese big four have engrossed the whole of the market. Now they've turned their attention to passenger cars. Watch and see, by the late seventies even General Motors and Ford will be in terrible shape because of Japanese competition, and eventually Korean competition. The auto-parts agreement is a broken reed and they've exiled Andrew Goderich simply to keep it from coming under criticism."

"Miss Keogh, Miss Keogh," I said, my mouth falling open.

"Why can't you call me Marianne?"

Powerful, intimidating, snugged up tight and rigged for foul weather, she leaned towards me, tapping the inside of a bare arm with the folded newspaper.

I said, "I couldn't be that familiar. I don't know why."

45

I went back to the Lord Elgin, agitated by that peculiar feeling, common in highly nervous states, of struggling to bring to mind some important reflection that would explain much. I knew that an important realization that had up until now eluded me was almost at the surface of consciousness. It was in some way connected with Miss Keogh and my father, but I couldn't quite get a handle on it. I had a solitary meal at a restaurant on Elgin Street a block from the hotel, then went to my father's suite intending to watch television for an hour or two, then give Edie a ring in Montréal. She would be at the house instead of her studio, I felt certain, putting the children's clothes in order for a summer at the cottage; we meant to spend ten to twelve weeks there this summer to give ourselves a rest from Québec news, which had more and more taken on an obsessive, ritualized and inflamed character. Ten weeks without any mention of the leading actors in the provincial drama would be like a refreshing year-long voyage around the world.

There was nothing special on mid-week television. My father's suite was stuffy, not well ventilated, overcrowded with furniture. I wandered around the suite, moving small objects around on table tops, then anxiously setting them straight. On that coffee table there, I recalled, my father had spread out relief maps of the Peking district and environs, explaining the terrain to me. We had briefly discussed Manchurian politics. At that clumsy conference table there, much too big for the room, various Sinologists had explained to Dad the defects of the Chinese railway system, the fascination of the Chinese leaders with Canadian rail services over long distances in difficult country. More than two years had passed, but I could still recollect vividly their hopes for a Chinese-Canadian understanding and a formal diplomatic accord. I could bring very vividly to mind my father's thin face, his intense gaze, the level tone of his remarks. Miss Keogh had been present, and Arthur Menzies. I began to feel a grateful anticipation of bedtime more common in states of emotional fatigue than physical. I rang the house in Montréal about ten-fifteen but got no answer. I suspected that Edie had taken the children to the Dairy Queen for refreshments. I'd place the call tomorrow, perhaps at breakfast time.

The bedroom was the most agreeable room in that suite. It had larger windows than the sitting-room because of the form of the front elevation of the hotel, which looked across Elgin Street towards the canal. Immediately below, across the street, work was continuing on the new National Arts Centre. These buildings, gloomy enough in prospect at ground level with their confusing layout and prison-like walls, were far more successful when viewed from above, their disposition on the ground distinctly attractive as a geometrical pattern spread out between the surrounding streets and the canal. I've never seen a postcard that gives this view of the Arts Centre and it seems a pity because the view from eight storeys up is an artistically impressive one. I stood looking out at the darkened city, trying to form some theoretical estimate of the converging lines of power and influence that came together in places just at my feet. In the eyes of many a mingy one-industry town, a hardship posting, a fever-ridden swamp in June and in December an icy steppe. All true enough and yet something about the city pleased me. I felt glad that my father had discovered how to find the best of Ottawa, the place at the exact centre of our continuing national struggle to survive without the soul-corroding burden of power and responsibility. Suppose indeed that he were to become the architect of a Canadian-Chinese special relationship. Wouldn't that be a great personal triumph for the author of the visionary idea of "the new state, the first modern country?" More fitting even than authorship of *Sin Quantified,* and his unwilling witness of the dreadful events that had inspired that work. I felt happy when I thought of all this.

When I retired towards midnight I fell asleep at once. I was sleeping in my father's bed, the one closer to the window. Maybe the rather cool night breeze that began to blow an hour or so later inspired the dreams that ensued. Or it might have been something I had eaten too hastily without taking time to chew.

I dreamt I was naked in the other bed, the unused one, and of all people in the world whom I might have dreamt of as partner an unimaginable one was there. Miss Keogh. Only I wasn't thinking of her as Miss Keogh but as Marianne. I kept moaning to her, "Marianne, Marianne," and I realized increasingly that what lay under her trim daylight attire was not as firmly resistant as its exterior suggested. She was smooth and soft and despite her forty-nine years as sexually exciting as when I first saw her, when she was a young woman of eighteen and I was a small boy of nine. We were entwined in the most intimate of embraces, my head at her feet. I grew aware of desperate passion and stimulation. She was doing something to my legs and then my buttocks which was in the last degree pleasurable. I felt as if I were about to burst apart, when she began to climb up on me, forcing me into a posture of submission that was ridiculous and degrading, and at the same time made me faint with delight. I ejaculated violently and woke sobbing, "Mummy, Mummy."

46

CARACAS, July 14th. (Reuters) At the conclusion today of the semi-annual pricing conference of oil-producing and exporting countries (OPEC), new measures were announced on price supports, gradual movement upwards of ppb. (price per barrel) levels on the spot market, and resistance to countermeasures towards price control proposed on world markets by the so-called Seven Sisters, the major international petroleum marketing and processing corporations, European and American, Shell, British Petroleum, Petrofina, Standard Oil, Texas Company, Gulf Oil, and Atlantic-Richfield.

OPEC spokesmen foresee a continuing trend through the early 1970s towards well-head control of production, moving to a prime crude ppb. of $18.75 US, by the end of 1973. In-the-ground reserves especially in the near and middle East continue to expand under steady research and development studies. In Saudi fields during the last eighteen-month period exploration has revealed more exploitable reserves than the entire commercial production of Saudi Arabia so far in its history.

Other Arab nations reported similar reserve development to OPEC. Ongoing discoveries in the region had had the effect of cutbacks in production in North America and elsewhere, with the effect that Arabian fossil fuels have throughout their history been purchased at low or "threshold" prices, with smaller North American and European reserves being held off the market for later exploitation at correspondingly higher prices, with marketing cartels the ultimate beneficiaries.

OPEC energy ministers have unanimously resolved to overthrow marketers' stranglehold on petroleum sales and consumption. Mr. (Sheikh) Hassan b'n Ibrim, spokesman for the assembled energy ministers, has announced specific measures to place control of production and vending in the hands of the producing states. These measures will include constant review of price structures and the state of day-to-day marketing situations by an OPEC board, close monitoring of production relative to new finds, a consistent oil-in-the-ground conservation program, finally an informal agreement among members to permit most-favoured-nation status to known friends of OPEC. Political action and new diplomatic initiatives in the near and middle East and elsewhere seem indicated by this language.

Most western energy ministers today reserved comment on novel OPEC proposals.

I looked this over and thought, boyoboy here's trouble for somebody. I wasn't sure who. But if you think it over you can see that in 1970 the whole world was either going on foot, painfully, in the dust, or buzzing around on wheels powered by cheap gas. My God, I remember the Sunday drives we took when the kids were small, when I used to make a bet with them that they couldn't find a gas station with a price lower than a given amount. Say thirty-six-point-nine-cents per gallon.

"Save Daddy some money," I'd say, "and we'll invest the savings in prizes and ice-cream cones."

That always put them on the alert. This was in the mid-sixties when you could always buy gas around forty cents a gallon in southern Ontario. A tankful cost, typically, a little under five bucks. Throw in the price of a quart of oil and something for normal wear-and-tear on your car and you're still getting the cheapest transportation in the history of human culture.

I remember once when Edie and I were touring around southern New England in the first years after we were married; we drove from Hartford, Connecticut, down to the oceanside along little back highways where a gas war was in progress, with gasoline advertised in successive stations as low as eleven-point-nine cents a gallon. That's the lowest price for gas that I can recall. We were driving around on the backs of Arabs.

The price at the well-head for a barrel of Middle Eastern

oil at that time was around seventy-five cents. Even at twelve cents a gallon retail, the Seven Sisters could carry a barrel of oil to North America, refine it, distribute it, promote it, and make a profit on the gallonage. This went on for a long time, ever since the large-scale exploitation of near and middle Eastern reserves began after the First World War, when corporation names like Anglo-Iranian Oil (later BP) began to figure in the financial columns of the world's press. Dylan Thomas composed a publicity brochure for Anglo-Iranian, I recall, to publicize the putting into service of a new catalytic cracker or "cat cracker."

"I'd crack a lot of cats for that," quoth Dylan cheerily. It seems that they paid him well.

I've forgotten how many gallons there are in a barrel of oil, but the figure seventy-five occurs to me and I think it may be right. If you sell at retail seventy-five gallons of petroleum products at about eleven cents a gallon, your retail gross is $8.25 for a commodity that cost you seventy-five cents at the well-head, that is, eleven times what you paid for it. Now I do see that there is some shrinkage in the refining and distributing process, but not more than fifty per cent. You could very well retail your barrel of oil for five and a half times what you paid for it, after all expenses for marketing. This is what the Seven Sisters always intended to do, and they did it successfully for decades, earning absurd profits. Mind you, if they were able to avoid price wars and keep the price at more than twenty cents a gallon in the US, they were making profits that rose far beyond absurdity into the empyrean of thievery, at prices that seemed quite satisfactory to American and Canadian motorists. Load the family sedan with the wife and kiddies and all their luggage; throw in Bowser for make-weight, and drive five hundred miles for five dollars. Makes you think! And the whole damned North American culture was built on the premise that this state of affairs was going to continue forever. Highway systems were built to designs that allowed folks from the Texas Panhandle to drive to Norman, Oklahoma, to see Bud Wilkinson's great varsity squads of the fifties, returning to Texas the same night, a journey of five hundred miles. You pointed the nose of your gas-guzzler north along the Interstate and floored her.

In Kuwait, Oman, Bahrein, Iraq, Iran, Saudi Arabia, the petroleum just kept on welling up out of the sand, the Biblical naphtha or "rock-oil," and we were shuttling back and forth between Montréal and Stoverville with never a thought of the price of oil at the well-head or the pump.

Then in the early nineteen-sixties the oil-producing and exporting countries took it into their heads to defy the Western marketing agencies, the folks who brought us *Hockey Night in Canada* and the Saturday-afternoon opera broadcasts live from the Met. Standard Oil and the Texas Company. It took the Arabs, the Nigerians, the Venezuelans, the better part of a decade to organize their production policies on a common schedule. Once they had managed this the revolution in energy supply could not long be deferred. The producing nations wanted their fair share of the thievery, and the marketers wanted to go on thieving. If profit margins were to decline, the oil companies declared genially, there would be less money for exploration in search of new oil reserves in the West. There could be no question of reduction in the level of profit! And the riggers and drillers would leave Alberta. Canada would be dependent on the whims of dark-skinned buggers in burnooses.

There existed at this time a lively petrochemical industry in the east end of Montréal. Judging from the stink around the huge refineries somebody was cracking a lot of cats in there. All the majors were represented, Texaco, BP, Shell. We used to go for Sunday drives along the extremity of the island to try to get a sight of the river where it flows away to the east. This was impracticable; there were too many refinery installations in the way. All you could see were enormous shiny silver bubbles with fragile staircases spiralling around them to the platform at the top, the kind of platform on which Jimmy Cagney hollered, "Made it, Ma. Top of the world!" as refined gasoline burst into flames around him in *White Heat*. Those spiralling delicate staircases were surprisingly graceful and pleasing in design.

It never crossed my mind to wonder in those days where all that oil and gas came from. I assumed naïvely that it had been produced in Canada for the benefit of Canadian motorists at prices well below those obtaining in less fortunate nations like Britain, which possessed no known petroleum reserves. North Sea oil was unheard of at that period. I don't think I ever paused to wonder how oil got to Montréal. There was no pipeline from Alberta that I'd ever heard of. There were no bulk shipments of oil in seagoing tankers from the Canadian west to Montréal; that seemed an impossibly costly way to transport it. How did gasoline get into those pumps all over Québec cheaply enough to be marketed in the early sixties at less than forty cents a gallon? I never knew, did you?

That Reuters despatch from Caracas was the first shivery small intimation to me — perhaps to hundreds of millions — that all was not well with the cheap energy supply and the Sunday drive in the big car, that the days of the cheap round trip, Montréal-Stoverville, were numbered. I began to see the acronym OPEC (OPEP in *La Presse*) more and more often in my reading of the press. And a first tang of rot, corruption, price manipulation, conspiracy on an unimaginably large scale, the stinking whiff of death, began to drift into my nose.

At the beginning of that summer Robert Bourassa and the Liberal Party were voted into office in Québec with an overwhelming majority; the opposition party obtained only six seats, and was in effect silenced. Mr. Bourassa promised jobs for everyone. He was chiefly preoccupied as first minister with employment, the development of industry in Québec, the preservation and development of a cheap energy supply, consequently the bringing onstream of hydroelectric capacity from northern Québec. He said that he'd provide a good job and a swell boss for all Québecers, and the lid was tightly on the bottle in which, according to the opposition leader (not himself seated in the national assembly) a pair of scorpions were locked in stinging, perhaps fatal, combat.

47

Maybe scorpions were thrashing around inside the Québec bottle but once you crossed the Ontario border and settled into a summer vacation at the lake, you could just as well have been twelve thousand miles away from the arena of combat. Ten miles across the border, in Lancaster or Williamstown, the struggle for self-definition of the *indépendantiste* Québecer became a non-issue. This was restful. We used to pass our winters listening to sharp differences of opinion among our friends. We had many friends in the francophone community, whom we owed to Edie's professional activities in the arts.

I doubt that there's a collection of people anywhere else, certainly not in Belgium or Switzerland, which employs two great languages with ease and competence so readily as the Montréal world of *vernissages,* book launchings, chamber-music concerts, film premières, university lecture series, the small change of group intellectual life. The defect of this world is its limited size. We always used to see the same cordial and jovial folks leaning over each others' wrists, kissing hands and exchanging bilingual forms of greeting, wearing closely similar clothes whose accessories alone betrayed difference in linguistic or group allegiance — the placement of a handkerchief, the colour of an over-the-shoulder bag. The English-speaking men were just as well turned out as the French, though with marginally shorter and less well cared-for hair. The English women — I speak of this small group alone — closely resembled in *coiffure, maquillage, chic,* their French sisters. One glimpsed these folk at the Elysée, the concerts of the Ladies Morning Musical Society, at the Double Hook bookstore for launchings, at the

MMFA or at the Salle Wilfrid Pelletier, perpetually greeting one another with perfectly genuine goodwill.

These people, to whom Edie introduced me, formed but a tiny segment of Québec life, and their characteristic and rather chilling *bonne-ententisme* was by no means the common possession of Québec society. There were great forces in the life of the province that were distinctly un-cordial, unforthcoming, on either side of the major socio-logical and political issues of the day. We met few or no unemployed people, few members of trades unions, few people from the country or the small towns, almost no people who could speak only French. So we didn't know anything like enough about enough people to make sound judgements. Though we read the French press with attention and respect, we often could form no true idea of what was being discussed so interminably and with such obvious rancour. Arguments continued among the French citizens of Québec of whose inner content we had no conception. They never stopped. They seemed in essence interminable. Finally these discussions might grow boring to the point of distrac-tion. Sometimes after years or decades of apparently aimless debate some issue could very suddenly boil over into sharply divisive political action, as in the matter of the use of French in air-traffic control, an issue at the outset purely professional in scope and content, afterwards turning into an ugly con-frontation of linguistic groups with clear elements of totally irrational prejudice, which finally determined the outcome of a pivotal election campaign. Yet nobody we ever met cared two pins about the language of air-traffic control in the Québec skies so long as she or he got back on the ground in one piece after a flight.

Debates of this kind, about whether Québec paid more in taxes to Ottawa than it obtained in return in services and subventions (a debate to which there could be no end because the question was unanswerable), or about the right of Québec to maintain a quasi-independent foreign policy including diplomatic representation abroad, used to smoulder away in the communications media like brush fires, which might at any change in the wind be fanned into immense and raging sheets of orange and red with accompanying suffocating smoke and terrible noise. The worst aspect of these unending arguments was precisely their inconclusive quality. After many years of considering them you felt that you might grow desperate, run mad, from the special and unique, eye-glazing, mind-numbing, tormenting form of boredom to which they gave rise. That despairing certitude that you might go to your lakeside cottage at the end of June, as I did that summer, and come back in September (or after twenty years like a new Van Winkle) to find the same matters being turned over and over in the press of both language groups, none of them so much as a step closer to resolution. Stark unreasoning stupefaction might now supervene.

That paralysed indecisive hovering mode of experience required a special kind of poise, a testing acceptance of irresolution. I'm a man of a somewhat obsessive character. I admit it. It would be impossible to deny. I used to find that damned *hovering* over decisions and solutions almost impossible to live with. I really hated it. I'm not saying that I yearned for an immediate and decisive civil war, but I would now and then have liked a sudden sharp end to one or another of these disputes. None ever came nor, as it seems, ever will.

I went to the cottage as soon as I could get away that summer, directly after the first Bourassa election, feeling that the snake had been, if not precisely crushed, at least scotched. I hoped for the next ten weeks or so to hear nothing about the present discontents of Québec. I made use of a high-quality AM-FM radio all the time, naturally, the kids, especially Andrea, now having reached the time of life when music must be continuous. What Andrea liked at that stage was top-forty pop. The summer's hits. I could gauge Andrea's approach to maturity by making a catalogue of her favourite recordings from successive summers. The White Album was on the air a lot that summer but it wasn't Andrea's pick of the pops, she being ten years old at the time. A song about leaving a cake out in the rain floats to the surface of remembrance. "I don't think that I can take it 'cause it took so long to bake it." Might that have been the big hit of summertime '70 in the great southeast?

"The great southeast" was the local name for that bit of

Ontario extending from, say, Deseronto and Napanee and Tweed to the Québec border, with Kingston as its acknowledged capital, a piece-of-pie-shaped region with a culture and speech of its own, intensely conservative and self-preoccupied in its politics, just as Québec was, but far less able to articulate its discontents. "The great southeast" never seemed to be getting its fair share of whatever sweets and goodies were being distributed by governments. It was the business of the AM broadcasters of Stoverville, Cornwall, but especially Kingston to proclaim these discontents. Open-line talk shows and top-forty pop were what I heard all that summer. The consequences of Edie's venture into mural painting, the sad defensive outbursts of an Adam Sinclair, fading into the recesses of memory. It was a good summer, prolonged, peaceful, and best of all without news from Québec. I used to lie for hours on the dock, sunning myself all over except for those parts concealed by an exiguous bathing suit. The weather continued very fair, at times burning hot, down through Labour Day.

There's always a lot of routine preparation for school during the first week in September, and Labour Day came late that year, on September seventh. School started the next day, so Edie took the children down to Montréal before the holiday weekend started. I know that I had the whole of a long weekend to myself, to put away the life-jackets and the deck-chairs and the boating impedimenta. We usually do these things as a family but everybody else had gone home. I might have got through most of what remained to be done in a single morning but I was idly attracted by the notion of a final holiday weekend to myself. I lingered over the stowage. Oars and paddles in the rafters. Canoe under the cottage; row-boat likewise. Drain the outboard motor. Fetch up the deck-chairs. Saturday and Sunday went serenely by and Monday was wet. A misty drizzle began about daybreak and continued till evening, when the radio announced that tomorrow would be very fair. I decided to hang on for one last day, Tuesday morning and afternoon lying in the sun if there was going to be sun. Then I'd tote up the last of the recliners, stow it in a back bedroom, and drive to Montréal that night.

I didn't have a steady job at the time and there was no special assignment waiting for me in Montréal. I had had some talks with the CBC about a series of broadcasts about Montréal domestic architecture but it looked like the project wouldn't go through. The trouble with any discussion of architecture on the radio is obvious; the listener can't see what you're talking about. And television production of a series devoted to the domestic architecture of one of our major cities is naturally unthinkable. Cost.

I was mulling over the potential beauties of a television series in colour with appropriate music showing some of the most remarkable streets and houses of Montréal or Toronto or Halifax or Saint John, the last-named a city with many beautiful wooden houses. I lay stretched out, enjoying the late sunshine. There was nothing more to be done around the cottage. I amused myself now and then by studying the antics of our neighbour, whose cottage is screened from ours by a considerable stand of evergreens, but whose dock-side activities are wonderful, and easy to behold. He and his wife had been trying to build a kit boat that summer; they had not had very good luck with the attempt. I believe neither Bronson himself nor his wife possesses any native skill with boat-builder's tools. Bronson is quite a decent bloke, and I shouldn't make fun of him. He waves his arms around in an unending series of distracted gestures, and he swims like somebody endowed with a profound mistrust of all things marine. I squinted at him and noticed that he was winding and unwinding his arms at me in what seemed to be some sort of warning or beckoning gesture. I stood up and looked straight at him through intervening pine branches and caught the words "news broadcast . . . radio." I felt obscurely frightened. I climbed up to the sun-deck of our summer place and turned on the FM band, which was tuned to the CBC, and I listened.

"And now once again tonight's news headlines," said the news reader. "The veteran NDP Member of Parliament for the suburban Toronto riding of East Gwillimbury, Mr. Andrew Goderich, collapsed and died suddenly today near Peking while on a hiking tour of the Great Wall. Mr. Goderich, who had recently celebrated his seventieth birthday, was participating in exploratory talks between Canada and the Chinese Republic. He will be remembered as Canada's first Nobel Peace Prize winner in 1950." And that's how I heard that my father was dead.

48

They all came. Trudeau came. Stanfield came. Diefenbaker didn't come but George Robinson was there and Charlie Pope, looking very frail now. Mr. Pearson came, and he too seemed close to the end of his tether. Tommy Douglas and Stanley Knowles. Marianne Keogh looking raddled with grief. Air Marshal Ferrier came, but not in uniform, long since retired to private life. Georgie-Balls Bannon came, although he had to take a day away from the Leafs' training camp with the exhibition season in full swing. The Leafs had an exhibition game in Boston that night and Georgie-Balls wasn't behind the bench, the only time in his coaching career so far that he's missed a date. Romola Kechechemaun came from the reserve with her husband, also named Kecheche-maun. Emil Fackenheim attended a Catholic observance, rather a remarkable thing for him to do. David and Stephen were there of course, and a whole host of constituents from the Musselman Lake district. Arthur Menzies. Some people from UN headquarters in New York flew up for the day. Many Chinese with obscure and fudged credentials. I saw folks who used to live at Centre Island in the old days, whom I'd never expected to see again this side Jordan. Ramona Trousdell, now a successful, much-admired painter, was there with her husband, a shrewd-looking man, her dealer. A major contingent came as official representatives of the University of Toronto, the president, the chairman of the board of governors, the principal of University College, the chairmen of the history and philosophy departments. I didn't get to chat with any of them. Dougie Crum was very helpful. I like old Dougie. I believe that I saw Sallee Lennox and Dougie's sister Faunce somewhere in the throng. Faunce doesn't look

well. One of the Forbes boys came and I would never have
recognized him. I wasn't sure whether it was Jerry or Jakie.
Bankers. Why bankers? He was no lover of the banks, God
knows. All the same they were there, treading with heavy
purposeful steps along the neat curving roadways. And there
were ancient folks from along Summerhill Avenue and Saint
Andrew's Gardens. Old Mrs. Millen came and some of the
Silcoxes, recognizable still by their corn-coloured hair, if, that
is, they had any hair left. Mabelle Buttermere looking a
thousand years old, still gushingly kind and eager to be of
use. Mildred and Marigold Smith, both married with
husbands in tow whose surnames never clicked with me. Bea
Skaithe, still unmarried, was helped to come by a niece. Poor
Bea. An old lady came up to me and introduced herself as
Mrs. Harry Angstrom, and I recognized in her the elegant
pretty young housewife who used to take the *Saturday
Evening Post* and the *Ladies' Home Journal* from me,
paying for them with agreeable promptitude when I delivered them to her door on Saint Andrew's Gardens more
than thirty years before. I could trace the blonde, vaguely
Norse loveliness that had stirred my childish affections in the
wrinkled powdered face and the silky grey hair. She seemed
older than her years. Perhaps she'd been older in the thirties
than I realized. She pressed my hand and smiled with the
direct engaging regard of somebody who has been a beauty
all her life, and I felt a sudden awful awareness of how little
time we have and how fast it goes. I didn't want to ask after
her husband. I don't know that I ever laid eyes on Mr.
Angstrom though my mother would now and then refer to
him, always in a context of steadily mounting success. I have
an idea that Mr. Angstrom did not survive his fifties. There
were many members of Parliament in the gathering, from all
parties, a surprising number from Québec. Some party
functionary had perhaps passed the word along that attendance at the ceremony would be good PR for the Liberals. I
may be assigning wrong motives to those harmless back-
benchers; no doubt many of them admired him. I can never
fit individual faces to the names of Liberal back-benchers
from Québec, but I suppose somebody knows who they are
because their votes are always scrupulously recorded. There

must have been two dozen of them in the assembly. Perhaps they came because it was a Catholic ceremony at which they could feel at home, black vestments, Requiem High Mass. My mother wore a heavy veil, and as she couldn't see very well at the best of times she was in some danger of tripping on the uneven ground. I had asked Tony and Uncle Philip to see to her. I had the whole thing to organize and I couldn't be with her at the church and the cemetery as much as I'd have liked. But there was a problem with the order of precedence. I had to make certain that the right dignitaries were placed together in the limousines. It would not have done to place Mr. Stanfield and Mr. Trudeau next to one another whether in limousine or before the open grave. There were hordes of photographers there, you see, and certainly the two leaders would not have relished appearance in the same picture on a wholly amicable footing. Death is the great leveller but there is such a thing, one imagines them feeling, as levelling too far and too fast. Time enough to reconcile differences with opponents at their own obsequies, at which nothing ill would be spoken of them.

Uncle Phil and Tony led my mother to the open space beside the grave, behind the coffin expertly held and moved by professional pallbearers, with eight honorary pallbearers, four on either side: Tommy Underwood, Air Marshal Ferrier, Charlie Pope, Robert N'debele from UNESCO, Onésime Archambault, a cousin of my mother's, Paul Ryan from my father's constituency office, Emmet Fitzgerald of the Lord Elgin Hotel in Ottawa who — I was surprised and moved to find — had been an idolatrous admirer of Dad's for nearly twenty years. I was the eighth pallbearer. There was some question from the undertaker about the propriety of a son acting as a pallbearer, some question of protocol or perhaps only funeral directors' convention. I wasn't going to let them deny me this final contact. I think we eight were a representative choice.

Tommy and Amanda Louise came in from New York as soon as we got the news. Tony arrived from London the following afternoon. It seemed that Dad had formed a habit of taking long walks along the parts of the wall lying fairly close to Bei-jing. They told us that he sometimes did twenty-

five to thirty miles in a day; it was almost his only recreation.
On the day of his death he had shown no signs of exhaustion
or discomfort. He had simply bounded up the steps inside
one of the towers, which are placed along the wall at short
intervals. At the top of the stone steps he had paused, looking
towards the west. He put his right hand to his side quite
suddenly and spoke a few words, which none of his hearers
understood. He took a few steps away from the tower in the
direction of the afternoon sun and fell dead.

That was on Tuesday, September eighth. Because of
certain formalities connected with registering the death of a
foreign national on Chinese soil, and problems about
transport, it took another two days to arrange the flight
home. They brought his body back on a Canadian Forces
aircraft on Friday and it was prepared for the state funeral on
that weekend. The actual burial service took place at Mount
Hope Cemetery in Toronto on Monday, September four-
teenth. He is buried beside the Squire, who had acquired a
family plot at the time of his wife's death, and a lucky thing
too. There's no more space in Mount Hope and as Dad
would have remarked, they're stacking them in there three
deep. He always found funerals peculiarly comic and so do I.
So do the Chinese, they tell me.

Behind my mother, Uncle Philip, and Tony were Amanda
Louise and my older boy Anthony. They seem as Anthony
grows older to be achieving some sort of special relationship,
of which I may come in the end to feel jealous. I felt a pang of
envy when I saw how solicitous for his aunt my son was.
Nobody feels like that about me. After them came Edie with
our other children, Andrea very subdued — an exceedingly
rare circumstance — and young John, simply uncompre-
hending at seven years old. I tried to remember how often
he'd seen Dad, and couldn't recall any close contact. They
might have met half a dozen times. I wondered idly how
much John would remember of his grandfather and decided
that he'd have to discover him in the pages of the history
books.

Mount Hope Cemetery has been very cleverly laid out to
give an impression of long perspectives and boundless space,
though it isn't a really extensive parcel of land. As you enter

by the main gates the usual funeral procession curls around
to the right and up a slight rise on the typical one-way narrow
drive found in such places. There are many connecting drives
and turn-offs, which loop around to the left, and between
these linked driveways are knolls on which stand the impressive monuments of an earlier day, dedicated to the hard-
working faithful Toronto Catholic community that created
this "new" cemetery after old Saint Michael's on Yonge
Street below Saint Clair was full. I guess that was in the mid-
twenties. I know we thought of it as the "new" cemetery in
the thirties when our great uncles and grandparents were
being laid to rest. Two generations have since come and
gone, but those big old angels and saints in limestone or
granite are still to be seen and studied there, creased and
stained by rain and lichen, darker in hue than at first, but
lasting.

It might still have been high summer. It was hot and the
trees were still green and fully leaved, the sun high, the crowd
beginning to perspire. They wanted to break away and go
home and it would take them quite a while to escape from the
throng. There were dozens, perhaps hundreds of cars, and
television trucks and the usual gang of people shooting the
scene with news cameras or hand-held TV equipment. I kept
scanning the scene to make sure that all the decencies were
preserved, that nobody who looked about to collapse from
the heat or from excess of sorrow should be ignored. There
was a team there from the Saint John's Ambulance Corps,
which I don't remember arranging. Possibly they turn out at
all major funerals without waiting to be invited. If so, good
luck and a hearty thank-you to them. They gave emergency
treatment to at least three people who felt unwell in the crush.
There were moments when I didn't feel too steady on my pins
myself; the ground was very uneven and I couldn't seem to see
it too well. I kept looking up at the tops of the trees, then at
the snake-like line of Cadillacs following the slow hearse of
Lindsay and Estcourt, Funeral Directors.

Once or twice I saw Tony and Uncle Philip sort of hike my
mother up and swing her over a lump of turf or a curb. I don't
suppose she saw a darn thing the whole time. She could only
see out of one eye by then. How much sight she retained for

the future would depend on what could be done for the good
eye, itself threatened with cataract. I know she still had
accurate colour vision in the good eye at that time because
she made some remark after the funeral about how many
shades of black there are, an observation I found strangely
encouraging.

I had ridden to the cemetery in the hearse with Marshall
Estcourt from the funeral director's office. I was amazed to
recognize in him one of my grade-eight classmates from Our
Lady of Perpetual Help. We greeted one another with
restrained warmth and he begged me — this was at the
funeral parlour — to accompany him in the hearse to keep
careful track of the many high officers of state and the
security personnel and television crews, first-aid staff, police,
traffic controllers. It was no ordinary funeral in Marshall
Estcourt's specialized terms. We sat in the back of his vehicle
on little *strapontins* next to the coffin, and all the way up
Mount Pleasant Road Marshall conversed with outriders and
security people on his walkie-talkie, which kept squawking
and buzzing like the radio in a cab or a patrol car while I was
trying to compose my mind towards a state of prayerful
recollection of my father's life. The dolly on which the coffin
was lying rode on tracking, which was bolted to the floor of
the hearse. From time to time the dolly moved slightly,
backwards and forwards, longitudinally with the motion of
the hearse. This gave me an eerie feeling as if some unexpected resurrection were about to take place. The radio
whistled and sputtered. We had arrived and the rear doors
were flung open, the professional pallbearers standing ready
to receive the heavy weight. Marshall Estcourt released a
retaining clip and the dolly rolled smoothly down to the rear
of the hearse. In a few moments the eight men moved off
towards the burial site. I climbed out of the hearse and
surveyed the ground. My place was at the graveside with the
other seven but I was delayed unexpectedly by an unlooked-
for apparition, the figure of a large old man much reduced,
almost shrunken, certainly bent by grief. He hobbled in my
direction over narrow roadway, curbing, thick grassy turf,
moving carefully, with a marked limp. He wore what used to
be called "morning clothes," striped grey trousers, black

tailed coat, formal starched wing collar. He held a silk hat
unsteadily against his thigh as he stood before me. He seemed
immeasurably ancient, a figure from a time much removed
from the present. This was Uncle George Robinson, utterly
transformed by either grief or guilt, perhaps both. He lifted
a swollen reddened face and stared at me fixedly. He didn't
seem entirely in control of himself and I realized with a start
that his face was tear-stained. He struggled for speech. I was
afraid that he might erupt into an hysterical denunciation of
my father's political principles and acts. I was thunderstruck
when he seized my hand and clasped it warmly between his
own two hands. They seemed feverish and moist.

"We never should have encouraged him to go," he said
thickly, "we had a wrong man. The wrong man. I knew that
Andrew, my old friend, my old friend. I knew that he wasn't
strong. I thought the assignment might kill him, and so it
has." He clutched my hand as though he were wringing his
own, swinging his arms gently back and forth between us.
"He was on our side all the time, if only we'd known. He saw
further than any of us. Oh Matthew, you are Matthew, aren't
you? I mean it isn't the other boy I'm talking to?"

I nodded towards my brother who was leading my mother
slowly up the little hill.

"That's Tony over there with my mother," I said. "I'm
Edie's husband."

"I was sure, I was sure," said George Robinson. "I'd do
anything to bring your father back, Matthew. Anything! If
there's anything I can do for the family I want you to call on
me at any time." A younger person, his son-in-law Duncan
McCallum, appeared behind Uncle George, put an arm
around his quaking shoulders, and began to lead him away.

"He's very upset," said McCallum grimly.

"I see that," I mumbled apologetically. "I'm so sorry."

Lindsay and Estcourt had set up one of those systems for
lowering a coffin into the hole, a complex device of metal
tubing, little catches and releases, and several bands of stout
webbing that serve to hold the coffin in place over the open
grave while the burial service goes ahead. My position as the
last of the honorary pallbearers brought me right to the
corner of the open hole and the coffin, and I found myself

casually examining this lowering device, wondering how it worked and how the slings were recovered from underneath when the heavy load had been lowered into the prepared space. I wasn't paying much attention to the priest's readings, which seemed strangely distorted in their unfolding, sometimes seeming to pass in a rapid gabble, sometimes seeming intolerably drawled out and nonsensical. Then there came a halt. A man from the undertakers stepped unobtrusively forward and manipulated a release switch. The coffin started to descend slowly and evenly into the ground, with an intensely characteristic rapid click-click-clicking that I have never heard in any other situation.

All at once there came a hitch. The further end of the coffin continued to sink, but the end nearest me stopped. A tilting motion became evident. The webbing had lodged in the lowering wheels and was jammed there. Marshall Estcourt, his face distorted with alarm and excitement, now leaped forward, went to his knees and started to yank anxiously at the snarled and taut webbing. He began to curse frantically in lowered tones; his words were perfectly understandable. I stepped out of my place and went to my knees beside him, realizing mechanically that I had placed the knees of my very best suit squarely on oozing mud. I put a hand on Marshall's anxiously working shoulders. I guess he was enduring frightful visions of the coffin's being upended and dumped downwards-end first. This could result in a sudden terrible exposure of the body. The single most prestigious funeral in his career and *this* has to happen.

I spoke to him reassuringly. "Marshall," I said, "let's take our time. Relax! It's going to be all right." He turned to me and let go of the webbing, which snapped taut. We hadn't seen each other since 1942.

"It's perfect," I said. "Let me do it." I put both hands in under the metal tubing and worked away at the thick material. I hoped I wouldn't crush my fingers in the little cog wheels, which I could see biting into the belting or webbing. I pressed on the cogs as hard as I could with my thumbs, forcing them back to release the caught stuff. The click-clicking started. The coffin levelled off. In moments it was at rest. I never did notice how they recovered the slings from the grave.

A few handfuls of earth landed on the lid of the box. That's a sound you remember. Soon the empty space was packed close and he was gone.

49

"I'm almost fifty years old," said Miss Keogh distractedly, "and I could never have imagined anything like this." We were being inspected by an armed security guard at the entrance to the Parliamentary office suites. I had to produce a number of documents *ad hoc* before I chanced to locate one in my wallet that bore my photograph, an old clipping from the Stoverville *Intelligencer*, a surprisingly good likeness.

"That's you all right," conceded the guard, eyeing me glumly. He had accepted Miss Keogh at sight, having seen her in the building during the previous week, the famous or notorious week of "apprehended insurrection" when political kidnapping and bargaining with terrorists seemed about to become standard modes of Canadian life. On Monday, October fifth, exactly a week ago, a British consular official had been taken by force of arms from his residence in Montréal. Now in consequence Ottawa swarmed with serious-faced young soldiers bearing side-arms and looking determined to crush whatever resistance might be offered them. Montréal was simply odious then, a nightmare town in the following days. As I had much business to transact with Miss Keogh I had come up to Ottawa at the end of the week. I was staying with her on Gilmour Street. This morning we intended to begin the sober work of examining all the files and deciding which records and correspondence were private property that should be passed to me, which the property and responsibility of the federal government, which again might be deposited with the offices of the NDP. I foresaw long weeks of discussion ahead as one file or secret document after another was held to the light and studied to determine its ownership. I had no wish to take over my father's archival material; eventually most or all of it would find its way into the Public Archives or some other institutional repository. A few letters, one or two memorabilia, photographs of friends and family, might be retained for personal veneration.

I'd gotten it quite clear in my mind that I would at no time attempt to write a book about my father, whether informal memoir or formal scholarly biography, and I knew that Tony had made the same decision, he and Amanda readily conceding ownership of these materials to me. I stood in the empty office and gazed in confusion at the exposed piles and piles of records. Then I heard strangled sobbing and to my embarrassed surprise Marianne Keogh threw her arms around me and put her head on my shoulder, giving way completely to grief. Her face was scarlet and very hot, and her tears fell on my neck and shoulder. I held her tight as she wept.

"Oh God," she cried, "oh God, what am I going to do with the rest of my life?"

That was on Monday. I passed that day trying to console Marianne; by nightfall I felt closer to her than to any other woman I could think of except my mother and of course Edie.

On the next day the governments of Canada and China exchanged formal documents of recognition. Later the same week the prime minister invoked the provisions of the War Measures Act against the kidnappers of Pierre Laporte and Jasper Cross.

DATE DUE

	261-2500		Printed in USA